THE RED CROCODILE

END
GAME

STRUBEN CLINTON

3

Text © Struben Clinton
Illustrations © Jemima Catlin
Designed and printed by Ditto Press
Typeset in Caslon

First edition 2015
Published by Archaeopteryx Imprint
www.archaeopteryx-imprint.co.uk
ISBN 978-0993174780

TABLE OF CONTENT

New Renaissance Woman

By the time Gus came to Castello Giugno for his Christmas break I had a new mattress there for him to sleep in comfort. My husband would be the first to share it with me. When Gino brought it and we had man-oeuvred it around the bend in the staircase we found that its standard size made it longer and narrower than the ancient bedstead, so we had to push and squash it to fit between foot and headboards. Waiting on a chair was a neatly folded stack of laundered bedclothes and I was too pleased with its air-dried freshness to have it sullied by Gino, who was only too eager to strip off his shirt and pants, damp with sweat. The shabby old mattress lying on the floor for taking away seemed a more appropriate ground for his exertions.

"Let's give this disgusting old thing a final fling before we throw him out," I said and knelt down, knees touching the floor through the thin kapok padding.

I felt as if it were Gino himself I was getting ready to throw out with the mattress and so, not to look him in the face, with my cheek on the worn ticking, forcing him to force me. When he had finally poured out his soul, crying for mercy, together we lifted the soiled thing and chucked it down over the gallery onto the flagstones below where he would pick it up on his way out and dispose of as he saw fit. I thought, even if he lazily tumbles it down the ravine it will quietly decompose and return its fibres to enrich the soil. I closed the bedroom door behind us as we left, determined he would not come there any more. I would sleep alone until Gus came.

I thought: this vow of celibacy is more Nick's sobering influence than

Gus's. By squandering the first money Nick gave me and not using it to make my escape when that was still possible, I had accepted him into my bed, so now by not throwing his wedding ring out the window I realised I had accepted that too, as Toby advised me. Just as now I felt wedded to Gus — a word that represented a feeling I didn't know existed until I recognised it in myself — Nick had achieved the same effect, in his devious way, in a shop in Bond Street and a Mayfair fish restaurant with oysters and champagne, with Toby as his best man. I still didn't know if they had been playing games with me. I longed to see Gus, the one fixed star in my firmament.

I drove the Alfa to the airport to collect Gus like a proper wife and he arrived like a proper husband in his city suit and his leather case and we kissed like children playing at being grown-up.

"My God, Wee, are you still growing? Look at the size of you!"

"It's the testosterone surge I get every time I think of you."

"Have you kept Dr Tsang's lecture on promiscuity in mind?" I asked as I drove him home.

Gus groaned. "I wish I'd had the chance to test it," he said. "I've been slaving away, but next term I should get promotion and more pay. Then I'll be able to splash out on whores, drink and drugs if I want to. As it happens I don't want to, but that is incidental. No, I'm afraid I can't excite you with tales of debauchery, I had nothing more than Evita for light relief, and she doesn't even swallow with relish like you do, but spits politely into a carefully ironed and folded white linen handkerchief. I'm sure the nuns who taught her to do drawn thread work would approve. But it's better than nothing. At least I don't have to rely totally on self-abuse to stay sane. The curse of being twenty years old with a gorgeous wife 1000 miles away!"

He did not ask what I had been doing. The reason for my visit to Nick was probably already known to him, but the sublimely sustained killer fucking with which Nick and Toby had blown my resistance sky high wasn't mentioned.

"I keep Adam company now and then. Have you brought your camera? He wants some new pictures."

"I won't have you fucking for the camera," Gus objected.

"No, Adam has rather taken a fancy to the edifice of the castle. He wants me to pose in the chapel, every time he walks across my living room floor and feels it sway under his feet he imagines the destruction below if it collapses."

"With structural nudes in the rubble, no doubt."

"His mind is running on ruins at the moment, he keeps talking about deconstruction and the attraction of scrap metal such as the skeletons of antique farm machinery scattered around the estate, graveyards probably going all the way back to Leonardo."

"A new angle on glossy car advertisements," said Gus, "naked sirens on rusting tractors luring men to their deaths. I'll enjoy that, especially if the man is Nick Deathridge."

"Nick is far too quick for me," I said, "it's Gino I'm busy luring to destruction at the moment."

"Watch out Gino doesn't destroy you, you dozy cunt," said Gus, an unusually pejorative remark from him.

"Is Nick still pursuing May?" I asked.

"He thinks he's winning," said Gus, "but..."

Our drive along the Chiantigiana was interrupted by a brief but blindingly torrential downpour which made progress impossible, so we pulled off the carriageway to shelter under a bridge. We sat holding hands across the gearbox to wait out the storm, simply happy: no inappropriate behaviour on the highway with Gus even when cut off from the world by a curtain of rain. Inopportunely I remembered the time Nick gripped my hand to hold me off from trying to kiss him, in spite of the anonymity of a taxi. I thanked God and all my lucky stars and the forces of Nature that my future was securely fixed on Gus Wittersworth.

When Gus and I went into the dining room where Clare was orchestrating her guests for her pre-Christmas dinner we found Adam and Tomàs waiting for us at our table, and to my chagrin Gino and Giulietta too.

I could blithely acknowledge to Gus my glory in Nick's cult of Sibyl worship; that was something Gus could comprehend. I'd have to convince him that my Harpy-like pursuit of Gino was merely the reverse, the dark side of the Moon Goddess.

When I saw Tomàs take his place at our table I understood he was placing himself as a buffer between Gino, Gus and Adam, maintaining his customary non-committal tolerance towards me. Clearly Gino's amorous extravagances did not trouble him unduly, neither did he takes sides between us. Clare was not so tolerant and though admitting that as Augusta's possible father Gino couldn't quite be dismissed as irrelevant, she avoided the embarrassment we caused her, on this occasion by keeping herself busy attending to a lively party of Germans on a gastronomic tour.

Adam said: "as long as they don't burst into song! If we get any O Tannenbaum-ing I'll have to leave the room. Christmas is enough of an excuse for sentimental nonsense without having to suffer Germans in close harmony."

Tomàs laughed at him. "I'm surprised you came creeping out of your den at all, you old Scrooge."

"I wouldn't miss a good dinner and the company of my best friends for all the baby Jesuses in the world," said Adam.

I wondered if the Furzys were enjoying Christmas with Nick and his baby Jesuses. Their quarrel might be getting acrimonious but I couldn't see Nick allowing himself be excluded from the feast and the opportunities it would offer him for discord by day and midnight mayhem.

"We mustn't go home too late," said Giulietta. "To-morrow Gino and I will be at my grandparents with the rest of my family. They've invited him to sing for them."

With her calmly possessive air beside her fiancé she seemed quite unconscious of the penetrating lustful gaze I was meeting across the table. She caused me a moment of confusion though when she said, "That's a really beautiful ring you're wearing. I didn't notice it before."

"It's new," I said. "It's an eternity ring; it is supposed to mean undying love."

Then for the benefit of the others I added, "it can't mean fidelity because it was that utter infidel Nick who gave it to me. He just felt like spending money."

"It still means undying love," said Adam, disapproving that I was disparaging Nick in front of his friends.

"We know you are worth something very special to him." Clare agreed with Adam, looking more closely now Giulietta had drawn attention to it.

"Worth a good fuck," Gino muttered, not too loudly. The presence of Adam intimidated him.

Only Gus said nothing, so it was to him I answered.

"Yes, I suppose all those things are true, but really it is because of you adopting May. This is how Nick says no."

"The usual exaggerated Deathridge way of saying it," said Gus, untroubled by the comments. "He tried to get a rise out of me when he told me about the successful outcome of your visit — and his other exploits. What pleased him most was that apparently you flattered him into buying a horse. The vanity of the man! All you have to do is say the horse looks good under him and he buys it as if it were a new suit. It doesn't matter to him if he pays £2000 for a suit or £20,000 for a horse, it's all the same."

"Why not?" I said. "He looks on top of the world in his suits and he is genuinely good with animals. Don't forget he also fell in love with a goat."

"His attachment to the goat may have been more than sentimental."

"You've been listening to Paul," I said, highly amused that even Gus was being provoked into malicious gossip by Nick's extravagance.

"A horse is a different proposition. He'll go riding once in six months but leave his friend to all the work and worry, months of training so when Nick comes his horse is at the peak of fitness for a cavalry charge across the downs. It's the same with May; what he wants is a certificate of ownership, stamped with the Queen's head on it, just as getting you to wear his wedding ring is equivalent to putting his seal on you."

"With his death's head signet ring," I said, laughing.

"Outsmarting the Wittersworths is one of his great amusements," said Gus. "But don't forget, the Wittersworths now includes you. It may be a long war but I'll win."

I was reassured that Gus was so confident. It made me feel less guilty that I had let myself be charmed, caressed and beguiled into acquiescence, even to my shame postponing my return to Willie by a day, giving in to Nick's desire to show off in pukka riding britches, flying with him down to Frank's, an exciting trip in a Cessna that skimmed along not much above the trees and church spires which Toby identified for me with a road map on his knee, a practical lesson in geography. Nick of course sat beside the pilot taking a keen interest in everything he did, even advising him how to approach the grassy gallop for landing.

Characteristic of Nick, I remarked to Toby, he thinks he could do it better than the professional...

"... He probably can too," said Toby dismissively.

This should have prepared me for being sneaked in under the radar and dropped off on a remote runway at Heathrow — where in later years the fifth terminal would be built — where Nick left me to find my own way to Alitalia. Apart from his ring I'd acquired no surplus luggage so with my cabin bag I set off briskly across the tarmac until rescued by a baggage handler on a buggy, a somewhat alarming experience. I had to take it as a compliment that Nick trusted me to look after myself while he made good his getaway.

Gus's equanimity allowed me feel less guilty that Nick's ring meant too much to me not to wear it in tandem with my genuine wedding-ring.

"I haven't told you about my visit to Gianni's nightclub," said Gus. "Not much joy there, I was lucky to get out with my life."

Dramatic though that sounded, Gus was smiling when he said it so I wasn't too alarmed, though Gino looked nervous. This might be something he'd prefer Giulietta not to hear.

"I thought I'd pass by one evening and have a word with him to clear up our position regarding Augusta."

"Augusta is the happy outcome," I said to Giulietta, "of Gianni and Gino's competitive fucking, love against lust, man against beast... they gave me a hard time but the baby I got out of them is utterly adorable."

Tomàs and Adam simultaneously put down their forks. They had been enjoying their Christmas dinner. Giulietta looked blank.

"Paul insisted on coming with me," Gus persisted in amiable dinner-table conversational tones, "in case Gianni got rough over the kidnapping. Besides, Paul knows much better what such places are like so he advised me how to dress. He said wearing a hand-me-down Wittersworth DJ with a deconstructed, ironic air would be all right — my grandfather has about forty laid out on tables in his dressing room and Amanda always manages to scrounge something for me when she goes to see him — she's the only one he'll talk to, he thinks she's his sister — with his straw thatch Paul doesn't have to do anything really, a black jersey and clean jeans is all he needs to look cool. Anyway, I presented my card to the doorman and asked for Gianni. You know the scene: lots of boozy people; jazzy music; fancy lighting; girls in shimmer wafting around — if we hadn't been seeing Gianni we wouldn't have escaped the girls, a predatory lot, but they seemed pretty much in awe of him. It was a scene from a mafia movie with Uncle Joe — Giuseppe — sitting at a table looking malevolently inconspicuous watching everyone, cigar, half empty glass, Gianni apparently drifting around, but I could see he was taking orders from Uncle and passing them on to the staff."

"Uncle Joe sees himself as head of the family," said Gino, "but I have nothing to do with him."

"I didn't get time to study him properly because Gianni whisked us into his back office to talk. Well, I had taken those photos of you and Gianni naked so I know pretty well how perfect he is, but strangely enough, there in that louche ambience, it was even more striking how superb he is, rising above all that noise and vulgarity with a kind of purity, a classical Greek look."

"You're right, Gus," I said. "That is the difference between him and Gino. You captured it beautifully in that photo of us three: Gianni's penis modestly present and correct; Gino's dubiously out of sight."

"Mine's as good as his," Gino protested.

"That's not the point," I said. "It's its moral attitude. His stands up for itself; yours is shifty."

"There's nothing bloody wrong with my..." Gino pulled himself up with an eye on Giulietta.

"He was dangerously polite to us," Gus went on. "The suggestion that it might be better for Augusta to be brought up by her mother's husband in a legitimate, stable family didn't go down at all well since that is what he aims to provide for you and I am the spoiler."

"Did he know you kidnapped her?"

"Obviously, obliquely, though we didn't discuss it in any vulgar detail. I went to the club so he wouldn't think I am afraid to confront him in person but Paul and I felt we were lucky to reach the exit again without getting a knife between the ribs."

"In spite of the mafia-like atmosphere Uncle Joe creates, Gianni is far too decent and good-natured," I said.

"Gianni's big mistake," said Gus, "was that he thought you would go back to Nick, so what really hurts him is that you married me. This is an outcome he hadn't anticipated. He really doesn't know what to make of me, but after all, he has nothing to complain about. He had you for over a year, if he couldn't get you to marry him it was because it was always certain you were going to marry me."

"That wasn't so obvious to anyone but you, darling Wee."

"And Nick. Nick did his best to stop me."

"You see," I said to Gino, "You aren't the only one Gus gets the better of."

"No one gets the better of Nick," said Adam, speaking up on his son's behalf. "except you, Sibylla — it's you who provokes him into the suicidally high-risk ventures he goes off in pursuit of... and you he returns to when he survives."

"So he can hump and howl away his anxieties," I said, knowing Adam wouldn't say it though Tomàs was nodding in agreement: The White Goddess at work.

In the days when I watched Mr Deathridge leaving the house every morning at 7.45, the unvarying ebb and flow of his days seemed as fixed as the cycles of the moon. But then the red crocodile made its appearance on the scene. That should have alerted me to other Nicks: the masquerade of the baptism and the Halloween party as I imagined it, Nick, taking up a dominant position amongst his colleagues, holding his fire until there was a challenge to engage his wit — I had Witters to thank that I could see that what passed for humour amongst men like Nick would be low-key exchanges based on implicit understandings, no laughing out loud.

"His death-devoted heart," said Gus, pleased with the insight Adam's observation gave him. "Sibylla brings him back from flight into the eternal night of his suffering self."

"How is the battle with Dr Tsang over the Jesuses going?" I asked, anxious to avoid being burdened with responsibility for Nick's salvation.

"Badly," said Gus, not unduly concerned. "Nick turns up at inconvenient moments to annoy Father William so they can do a bit of mutual blackmailing — Father actually likes Nick. They get on fine. Nick invited him to join him at the chess club; Father said no, thanks, he gets enough aggravation in his day job."

"That's a pity," I said. "Nick sees Father William as his most serious rival. They could fight it out over the chess board."

"Father is too busy for such tomfoolery but all the better for me, he pays me to act as his go-between. In the business with Tsang, the more time they waste the higher our fee. Nick offered to pay Gianni's legal fees if he wanted to challenge me over the baby-snatching but Gianni obviously couldn't accept however much he would have liked to, his own position is far too shaky. If only he had agreed I'd have a lovely time demolishing both of them in court and we could have stung Deathridge for colossal costs. I might even have made enough out of him to rescue my wife out of his clutches."

"You two need a home of your own," remarked Tomàs.

"I'm working on it," said Gus, "I started at the bottom but I'm rapidly climbing to the top of the heap in the Wittersworth pecking order. Besides, Sib and Willie are better off here at the moment; it's total chaos in London, rats everywhere. Nick is teaching his juvenile delinquents to use air guns so they can be his pest control squad. He uses them himself for target practice, blasting them to minced meat — the rats, not the boys."

Tomàs went to change places with Clare for the second course and she came and sat beside Gus, sighing. She still found it quite a strain to hold conversations in German. Her Scottish accent was more pronounced in German as she took to rolling her rrr's. I thought, it's really Gus's voice she likes; surrounded as she is by foreigners it's a pleasure for her to listen to beautifully articulated English English. She trapped him into her favourite game of finding out what mutual acquaintances they might have, at first not very fruitful until she realised the link was the Hon. Henrietta.

"How surprising!" said Clare, finding it hard to reconcile Gus with the intimidating lady who had handed out badges at some Girl Guide event. "Of course! I should have seen the relationship as soon as I met you."

"Didn't you meet any of my sisters?" asked Gus. "It's quite hard to avoid them. Except for Amanda who is married with a proper job, they hang around costing poor Father a fortune in traffic fines. Polly works in a stables and is optimistically saving up £50 a week to buy a racehorse, Jane went to Angelina's wedding and ran off with one of Nick's dubious friends but every so often she comes back like a broken yo-yo. Diana wants to sail around the world with a school friend. They are not very experienced but if they can make it to Antigua they'll drop anchor and stay until they pick up a local expert to take them on the next leg of the journey. Father says the time has come for them to start living off their wits. I may have to auction them off: I'm sure I could if I had time to organise a proper marriage market: any bidders for three good-looking, sexy young women of very argumentative and contrary dispositions, singly or as a set? I might even make a profit out of them, then Sibylla and I could afford to live together with Willie in some semblance of married bliss independently of Father and the Deathridge curse."

"I expect your father wants you to get properly qualified first, it's his way of keeping you motivated to work. My father would do the same," Clare said with a great show of sympathy and understanding.

"It's not every father who'd let you have his Filippina to suck your cock by way of compensation," I said, breaking up any show of class solidarity between them that might exclude this cunt across the table.

Giulietta stared, doubting if she understood properly, and Clare blushed but Gus laughed unabashed and said, "I'd much rather have my wife do it. So come along to bed, sweetheart."

"Not yet, beloved, let's have our sticky ginger pudding and ice-cream first to get us in the mood. By the way," I said, "I nearly forgot to ask what your mother said when you told her you were married."

"Exactly what you'd expect," he said, "'What!' she said, 'married to that Irish slut, that hussy! Catholic too, no doubt, a trap for life. You poor boy, how will you get out of it? Your father must be mad to allow it.' Of course she'd heard the rumours of his own lapse of probity having Evita living-in, but how could he condone it in his son? etc. etc. and on and on. I just let her talk herself to exhaustion. Then I delivered the coup de grace. We've a baby boy, I said, another young Wittersworth for the firm. She was speechless. For the first time in my life I saw her at a loss for words."

"Goodness!" I said. "I hope she gets over it. I don't want to be the wicked daughter-in-law for the rest of my life."

"Don't worry. She changed tack to start bemoaning the fact that, with Amanda the only child, Father William went off to war saying he was the last of the Wittersworths and when he came back she'd had to endure three more before he got me, as if I were to blame for Father William's shortage of X chromosomes."

Clare went to speed up the service, as gratified as if she had discovered a nugget of gold amongst the potatoes. Where did that leave Nick in her estimation?

Adam, who had said nothing since his attempted defence of Nick, probably because he could see it was a lost cause, declined pudding and went out to smoke a soothing pipe in the garden before retiring, while Tomàs rescued Giulietta and took her to meet the Germans where she could help out with her superior language skills.

I found myself in a head to head with Gino.

"So, you are going to sing for God and Giulietta to-morrow?" I asked him, sliding into the seat vacated by Giulietta.

"I'm not much in the mood for singing," Gino said. "I keep thinking of Christmases at home, especially when you were there and I sang for you, remember *'quae est ista que consurgens ut aurora rutilat?* who is she who rising, shines like the dawn?' That was my best solo piece but I can only do it now when I'm alone in the van."

"I remember how beautifully you sang, it brought tears to my eyes, but how was I to know it was for me?" I said. "You never liked me."

Gino turned away to look after Giulietta. "You never gave a damn anyway," he said.

"Giulietta appreciates you," I said. "You should wear a wedding ring, Gino, you'd be surprised what a difference it makes to how you feel."

I held my fist up to his face with its coupled bands of gold and diamonds.

"You incite me to murder, Sibylla."

"Let me sweeten your temper," I said and offered him a spoonful of ice-cream at the same time pressing my knee into his thigh. His smile lost for a moment its slyly hesitant look and its openness reminded me of Gianni's.

"Gianni needs a woman like Giulietta. Don't let them meet until you're safely married..."

"I can't talk with that stuff in my mouth." Gino stopped me making any comparison.

"You know I never listen to anything you have to say," and I continued to spoon alternate mouthfuls of sticky ginger and ice-cream while he squeezed all the way to the top of my leg.

"You have horny hands," I said "I hope Giulietta doesn't find them too rough in her tender parts."

He looked over his shoulder, unwilling to be caught with his fingers in the pie but, like a greedy monkey in a monkey trap, unable to let go.

"Tomàs will keep her busy for a bit," I said. "You are lucky to have found such a good friend."

Gino smiled again, broadly. I had seldom seen him in such a good mood.

"You are like Gianni when you smile," I said. "It's a pity I never see it when you fuck, you are so fuckingly intense about doing it, as if it's the devil dragging you down to hell by way of my cunt. It's not love you are after, it's the rush of committing a mortal sin."

Gino gave a sharp jab with his fist. Involuntarily I gave a cry, of shock even more than pain, and tears came to my eyes, which I hastily endeavoured to hide.

Giulietta and Tomàs turned around to see what was going on at our table.

"It's time we went home," Giulietta said, giving her hand to Gino so he had to stand up. He remained defiantly silent at her side while she said good-night and Happy Christmas to everyone, then he followed her out.

"What was all that about?" Gus asked as we strolled back to our apartment.

"Nothing much," I said. "To-night was a bit frustrating for Gino. He would really like to kill me but since he can't he wants to fuck me instead. Alternatively fuck first and kill after — or visa versa. Naturally he gets a bit moody."

"You do go out of your way to provoke him."

"You say yourself that is no defence in law."

"Neither is it, my vixen, but Adam is worried that you allow Gino abuse you out of sheer perversity."

Gus was transmitting Adam's opinion without declaring whether he agreed or not though I suspected he was using Adam as a mouthpiece for his own anxieties. Then, his legal intelligence discussing it with his philosophical, he went on:

"We all have the same equipment for fucking with. One assumes the sensations transmitted neurologically are much the same. It's how we respond to them that makes the difference. I've never had a problem with self-control so maybe I have an unfair advantage but to me Gino is an idiot. I would not let any woman provoke me the way you entice him, shaming him and reducing him to an emotional wreck. I would turn my back and walk away."

I was surprised by this gratuitous comment on my sex life; was this a reflection of how the men talked about me with one another?

"That's what Nick does; every time I upset him he walks away. But you are all different," I said, not defending myself nor excusing Gino. "However, if anyone exploits my beauty it's Adam, he only fucks for art's sake."

17

"Adam is naturally paternal, at his age." Gus dismissed Adam's worries with these words. To Gus I was a competent person, capable of looking out for myself.

"Luckily Gino has sober, sensible Giulietta to drive him home and take him to bed. I hope she enjoys it while she can before I finish him for good."

"I can see my mother is right," said Gus. "I'm saddled for life with an Irish witch, my beautiful banshee. Come on and provoke me and see what you get."

Laughing we climbed the stairs and the evening ended in a joyously bawdy romp. The love we shared as husband and wife had nothing to do with the politely dispassionate cock-sucking of Evita or Nick's passionately demanding fuck episodes. I was content that Gus was the man I'd spend the rest of my life beside.

Adam arranged numerous excursions with Gus who obligingly took all the photos he needed for his compositions, sometimes me alone, sometimes with the children as figures in a landscape. Gus also made a record of the new work to show Gillian and he promised me a large print of Eve and the vineyard serpent. I did not tell him I wanted it to remind me that confronted with lust I must be cool like Eve to prevent its love-bites turning to poison.

The castello itself provided plenty of scope for Adam's deconstructed nudes and luckily the gastronomic tourists had departed for the Amalfi lemon fiesta so Clare had no need to get worried about her reputation. Tomàs came to join the artists in contemplating the castello walls from below and thought my body arched under a doorway-to-nothing added a touch of post-modernism to his ancestral ruin.

"It's still a happy home," he said. "There's enough of it left to live in."

"Angelina doubts you'll ever get us a house as good as hers," I remarked to Gus, thinking of our future together as we walked back up to the courtyard.

"She's quite right," said Gus, "the hobbit holes the Wittersworths dwell in don't compare with a cool London townhouse."

"I'd rather share a horse hair sofa with you," I said. "When I came to the obsessively orderly house in Stratton Square to be Nick's nanny-for-the-fucking-of, I was amazed that under that surface of refined elegance lurked a whacking great man-thing that hopped up incongruously out of the master's fly to shatter my modest expectations of love. I had no one to compare him with — so I squirmed, wishing he'd get done with it and get out of me before I died. Until Dr Tsang came along I had no idea that not all penises are quite so taxing — and that dying his way is the ultimate death wish."

"And of course it was the sexy wriggling that made it even more exciting for Nick," said Gus. "He thought he had chaos under control..."

"According to Meg he keeps chaos locked up in his safe," I said with a sudden insight into the puzzle of the safe.

"... until you came and let it escape."

"Like Pandora, except that the last thing left in Nick's box is not Hope, it's a gun, God help us!"

"Father has been writing about guns ever since that silent presence at our wedding. One can legislate till the cows come home but that won't stop mavericks like Nick. I didn't tell him I asked Nick to sell me one of his..."

"Whatever for?" I asked, shocked.

"... But he won't let me have one as if only he has the wit and the skill to use it properly, with his pretence of being über-Swiss. All I want it for is to display in a glass case in our archive."

I was relieved to hear it.

"What I am trying to figure out," said Gus, "is what Nick is really up to. His affairs get more and more obscure. As executor of the Furzy estate he and Shackleton are pursuing N. D. Deathridge for maintenance of the Nickies, for whom N. D. Deathridge, that tricky shit, declines responsibility. Nick says he's doing it to confuse his mother-in-law who wants to sue him for embezzlement, accusing him of using the socially awkward Furzy scrap metal fortune for his own profit."

"The mind boggles."

"Nick won't save himself," grumbled Gus. "Even in his own defence he won't cooperate. He says no to everything, so that may develop into a really nice paternity suit over the Aunties' babies: Nick's unholy horn versus the

Holy Spirit in the form of White Dove Tsang. But if anyone can get Nick out of it, Father can."

Adam continued with his worries: "With these potentially huge costs hanging over him, he seems hell-bent on spending every spare penny he has. Angelina was complaining that he is having work done on the house — she can't imagine why, it was perfect as it was and the builders are a great nuisance."

"The last time I spoke to him," said Tomàs with a smile, "he was grumbling that the council won't let him cut down a few trees in Stratton Square — if he could land there it would be worthwhile keeping a handy helicopter in his factory yard — I think that must be a flight of fancy, not to be taken seriously."

"Sibylla's ring and Gianni's legal fees and the horse he doesn't ride are all part of a pattern," said Gus. "He has Father and me and Toby all involved and the Furzy solicitors but until I can see a clear picture of where he is going I don't know what line to pursue."

"Nick is very prudent with money," I said. "I don't think he'd get into a legal battle unless he were confident of winning."

"He'll end up making fools of us all. Nick would consider it money well spent for the pleasure of causing us maximum annoyance and embarrassment."

"It must be truly embarrassing for Angelina," I said, "her husband making a fool of himself with her two giddy aunts; what has the Sisterhood to say about that?"

"Father is impressed with Angelina: calm, dignified, no reproaches. He says Nick is damned lucky to have such a serene, intelligent wife."

"Nick says luck doesn't come into it."

"The really interesting question," said Gus, "is: will Deathridge & Wittersworth defeat Deathridge & Shackleton? Any bets?"

Gemini! Nick playing against himself running around the chessboard — and cheating on both sides.

❧

Survival
Techniques

It was May's third birthday in February. The treat Adam proposed for her was to take her to Florence and let her walk across the Ponte Vecchio.

"I'm not sure May will see the point of it," I said, "but having a special outing with her grandfather will be a treat. I'm sure you'll have a lovely time."

"We can buy a coral necklace in one of the little shops over the water," said Adam. "Even a three-year-old will see the point of that."

In spite of the fuss Nick was making about May's legal position, which at that time had not yet been resolved, she had not seen her father since last September when she stood with him and her brothers in a family group, with Angelina looking painfully embarrassed at being cast in the role of wicked step-mother.

"After all the talk and arguments," I said to Adam. "I think Father William may have succeeded in fending Nick off."

"As you don't love him it hardly matters," was Adam's dry response, "as long as he keeps paying the rent."

"I miss him," I said, but I couldn't admit what this must mean.

Gus had gone home to bury himself deep in exams, taking my comfort and security with him. As long as I had him, Nick's silence was a minor irritant at the back of my mind but now it was growing into an emptiness that cried out to be filled. I wore his pseudo-wedding ring as confirmation of a tie to a man who was unpredictable to me, no matter what Gus said about him being reliably consistent in his idiosyncrasy.

I phoned Meg.

"Are they still using condoms?" I asked.

"That's none of your business," she said.

"Does that mean no?"

"He's in a foul temper, swearing at the government for incompetent fools and the banks for mismanaging the money supply — not that he seems to be going short. Last week he went off to Switzerland grumbling that he is singlehandedly keeping the economy afloat. He doesn't half fancy himself!"

I reported this to Adam for his interpretation.

"Don't ask me to explain what he's up to," he said. "Nick understands money, it's in his genes. Even his screwed-up beauty of a mother for all her moodiness knew how to keep us going on the Dumez money while I was trying to build up my post-war career."

"Nathalie Dumez," I said, confident that I knew what he was talking about. "Nick told me."

"After working for the government in antiquated dock-yards, I was planning to build yachts with all the refinements I'd been dreaming of throughout the war. But as soon as I had my beautiful prototype finished and ready for the Boat Show to take orders and go into production, Nathalie came out of her self-imposed isolation — she wouldn't even walk down the road to be told by Nick's nice teacher what a brilliant son she had — for the launch. She named her *Espérance* and seduced my deckhand into sailing away with her, simply disappearing, until three years later Espérance was found adrift in the Caribbean with no-one on board. Nathalie's body washed up in St Barthélemy not long after, too eaten to reach any certain conclusion about the cause of death."

I was astounded: the mother who drove a Daimler in the war? The boat that had crossed the Bay of Biscay in bad weather with Nick clinging on by a rope!

"I thought of her as an absence no more significant than my mother in a béguin enclosure in Belgium — Nick doesn't talk about her."

"When she ran off and left him motherless at the age of eleven he didn't even ask where she was. Counting his grandparents, she was the third person who abandoned him. But three years later when her body was found, the gossip and speculation about the possibility of murder made the whole affair a nightmare for us."

Nick's nightmares! Was this where they started?

"Then there was the business of getting the cursed Espérance back. Nick was fifteen by this time and desperately keen to go over to claim our property and sail her home, the two of us in defiance of the world, but I couldn't face the scandal and felt it would do Nick no good either to be exposed to such publicity head-on — especially not Nick with his fiercely confrontational atti-tude; they would have had a field day with him. The 'redhead rebel' or 'firebrand son of tragic heiress' or some such — it would have stuck to his reputation forever. I had to keep him out of it. He sulked for months after that."

And created mayhem at school instead, according to Toby.

"Whenever I tried to talk to him he'd turn his back as if he hadn't heard," Adam continued his unhappy story, "and imitate Louis Armstrong doing *Mack the Knife* — how could he be so callous! Knowing what happened to his mother, to go around singing about the shark biting and blood spurting! Once he had me down he didn't even have to voice the words; he'd do a Satchmo trumpet with his lips — you can just imagine that rubbery lippy pout — it gave me gooseflesh. He would have been easier to deal with if he had expressed his anger but he never said a word so it was impossible to reason with him."

Toby had laughed at Nick's sulks, coming back to school complaining he'd had rotten holidays because he hadn't been allowed to go sailing in the Caribbean. But like the youth Percival in Paul's story of the Holy Grail, Toby had failed to ask the right question. It cast another light on all the Tales Out of School I'd heard from Toby and Frank. It seemed that the schoolmasters were more tolerant of Nick's quirks, moods and irrational behaviour than his friends. It was easy to see how the whole squalid affair must have cast a shadow over his schooldays, how it kept coming back to haunt him. Not easy for a boy to live down a run-away mother who ended up a corpse in the newspapers! So it was just as well he could be so tough about it — as when throwing the tape with her name on it out the car window. Toby punched him in the arm in a gesture that looked punishing but was probably one of compassion if only I had recognised it.

I thought back over the last three years and more, and the times we'd had together: taxi rides in New York; dancing the tango at a château on the Riviera; I knew his friends and relations and through them I thought I had more or less pieced together the whole story of his life: childhood, schooldays, his career and marriage. Occasional mention of his mother, including the fact that it was not after all rugby that had scarred his face but some childish altercation with his mother, but otherwise no significance was attached to her absence.

Adam's revelations opened up a chasm before my feet. What else did I not know? What other chapter in the story was missing?

"My boat was in a sorry state when I got her back," Adam went on as if in the last couple of minutes nothing had happened to alter my perception of the world as I knew it. Grey velvet mamelons. The virtuous Angelina. Adorable poppets fighting for the privilege of holding on to his prick in bed. They all took on a distinctly different meaning in the light of a horribly dead mother.

"It took time and money to get it back into pristine condition so I could show or sell her," Adam went on, unaware of the knock on the head I had just taken. "In the school holidays Nick occasionally spared me a few days to come and lend me a hand. He wanted us to do the Fastnet to give her a racing pedigree — that would enhance the value considerably, but the financial situation became quite critical and other things intervened so Espérance had to sell."

Other things? Nick's saga of mishaps and misdemeanours.

"Yes," I said, "I heard you talking about that. Nick thought you didn't make enough money out of the sale."

Adam gave a rueful laugh. "I thrashed it out with Penn Shackleton. I had mounting debts and legal fees and I needed a quick sale to raise some capital. I see now I should have let Nick have his say in the decision, but it never occurred to me that that obstreperous seventeen-year-old who failed abysmally at school would turn out to be a financial wizard like his grandfather."

I looked at Nick's ring and wondered if I should think of the sweat, blood, and pain it cost to produce a thing of such purely symbolic significance. If anything it represented the tears Nick spilt over me and was a warning to myself not to love him so despairingly. Gus thought the ring was part of some elaborate hoax Nick had set up, which seemed to involve spending as much money as possible in the most pointless way, in complete contradiction of his reputation for good management. This undermined my pleasure in it even more than my suspicion that it was only a ploy in getting me to agree he could have May. Gus's main concern was that Father William wouldn't be made the dupe of Nick's double-dealings. Possibly we were both fundamentally misjudging his sincerity, but how could one tell?

I concluded I would be foolish to expect to see him again except when he came to claim his winnings. But still I missed him; in the most tranquil of moments his quizzical smile would float across my vision like the damned Cheshire Cat that he was and the purely physical pain of his absence would strike like a knife in the gut.

My sense of loss proved premature. The morning of May's birthday I stood with her in the yard outside Adam's cottage while Adam tried to persuade her it was necessary to wear shoes to go to Florence. I refrained from using my nanny skills and let him deal with it: it was his expedition. Though I heard the motor approaching I was too preoccupied to think what it meant, but had enough warning, however subliminal, not to be surprised when the Jaguar drove into the yard and came to rest beside my Alfa. Nick got out and, without looking directly at Adam, May and me, with something of a Tsang-like gesture, took in the whole scene as if it were exactly as he anticipated. My head swam and the sight of him danced before my eyes, dizzy with emotion at being once again within the compass of this man, no longer a chimera lurking in my imagination a thousand miles away.

25

In the momentary hesitation before he faced us I read his anxieties: fear of disenchantment, fear of rejection, fear that his own courage would fail him.

I stood my ground, waiting for him.

Adam dropped the shoes and said to May, "Well, look who's here! it's your Daddy," and led her over to him. May probably remembered the wedding and, holding on to Adam, she let Nick take her other hand and told him "I'm three."

"I know, my precious," he said, "I came to see how big you're growing."

He opened the boot of the car and lifted her up to show what was inside.

"The boxes are your birthday presents," he said, "but not the cases," and put her in the boot to lift them out to Adam.

While they were busy with that he came slowly over to me. His apprehension showed more nakedly in his face now. I recognised Nick's hesitation from the time in New York; he no longer assumed the right to impose himself on me. But perhaps I was simply more aware of his sensitivities now I knew that he been left unloved by his mother and understood the pain of rejection when he threw Nathalie out the car window. I held out my hand to him, showing him I was still wearing his ring.

"I didn't expect to see you again after the way you dropped me out of the plane," I said, "and threw my bag down after me... a pretty conclusive dumping, having got what you wanted off me, you incorrigible cock!"

But when he put his arms around me I cried, "Oh, Nick, you take possession of me as if there is no other woman in the world and I fall for it every time."

The boxes with toys were being sorted on the ground by Adam, and May, after struggling with a long, leather-bound canvas bag she couldn't lift, had managed to unclip the strap and was standing in the boot shouting "Daddy, Daddy!"

Nick went over and helped her hold up by the muzzle a rifle as tall as herself.

"Nick," I shrieked, "What has she got?"

"Not that one, precious," Nick was saying, smiling at her excited pink cheeks, brilliant hair and party dress. "That's Daddy's."

Adam joined me in protest at the madness of travelling with a serious-looking gun in the boot of the car, but Nick was unconcerned.

"I never move without my SIG 510," he said. "The best weapon in the world. Traditionally one keeps it in the bedroom wardrobe but Angelina doesn't like it in the house so I keep it in the motor instead."

"My dear son," said Adam, "I am dumbfounded by your reckless disregard for the law."

"A matter of interpretation," said Nick and lifted May out of the boot to carry her high on his shoulder to Adam's cottage, leaving Adam and me to trail behind with the piles of presents.

"I had a profitable career in armaments," Nick said as we went. "I gave up a well-paid job making the damn things because I wanted to make babies instead. Quitting SIG was the biggest risk of my life — besides, I liked the 510 as it was, heavy and chunky. No need for idiot-proof. We're not Russians."

Maybe SIG was happy to see him go, like his headmaster — an extraordinary talent but too hot to handle. I thought of the Taxi Driver film we saw going to New York. What appealed to Nick must have been the gun dealing.

"After five years of hard work and happiness," he continued, "I suggested to my sweetheart it was time we started a family. She said no, so I left the virtues of the good citizen in its last redoubt where it belongs — and see where that gamble has landed me —"

His expansive gesture took in the Jaguar in the castello yard, May holding on by his Tintinesque quiff, the sun on his mordantly smiling face... I couldn't stop my heart thumping in awe... you are not in love with this man, I told myself severely, he is admittedly a splendid fuckster but, elusive as quicksilver, you can't hope to hold him beyond what it takes to satisfy his restless cock — until the next time. I might see him with altered perception but he certainly hadn't changed.

When Nick heard of Adam's intention to give May her birthday treat in Florence he said, "I'll take you. I'll go and pay off the marble palace I slept in last night — assuming that Mrs Wittersworth will allow me share her bed tonight."

He didn't wait for my answer.

Nick's excuse for not having a child seat in the car was that the only damage he had ever suffered while driving had been several years ago when he crashed deliberately in a fit of suicidal pique.

"At the speed you go you might have to brake suddenly," I protested.

"Anticipation," he said.

Nevertheless the Deathridges drove away down the hill at a sensible speed, no Monza manoeuvres at the hairpin bends, moderation no doubt being imposed by Adam though I could imagine how May would scream with delight at being flung around on the well-padded back seat of the Jaguar and Nick telling her to sit back and allow the G-force hold her in place.

I wandered around aimlessly with Augusta and Willie. It was my turn to be apprehensive. The afternoon dragged on endlessly. I did everything I could think of to do with the children to amuse them and myself but we missed May who was the instigator of our games and I sat glumly on the wall with Willie while Augusta knelt in a flowerbed picking a rosemary bush to pieces. In a moment of panic I thought how easy it would be for Nick to kidnap May; he could just wind his devious way with her and his big gun up through the snowy passes into his spiritual homeland. No one would stop him. By the late afternoon I was convinced it really was May Nick had come for, and if he bothered to return at all he would again take me for what I was, an accommodating cunt for him to pass the night in. Only my faith in Adam's good sense prevented me becoming completely distraught with anxiety.

Trying to distract my mind from this worry I thought of the remark dropped so casually by Nick about his girlfriend. Was I really stupid enough to mind that a dedicated stud like Nick had been spending the prime time of his twenties with some unknown woman while I was still a child eating furry green gooseberries under a bush in Ranelagh Road?

I was as simple-minded as Angelina, when obviously there had to have been others: the Eugenie Nestor had teased him about, and the glamorous wife of his apprentice master at his wedding party whom Meg said Nick was fucking barely out of sight behind the study door, indeed, Nestor and the

Heini girls betting on Nick's marriage to the glacial Angelina not lasting beyond the first night. The implication, which had disconcerted Nick, was that they had set him up to show what they perceived as his true colours. No wonder Nestor smiled while Nick looked mortified. Even a true friend like Nestor couldn't help enjoying a little Schadenfreude.

The interesting aspect was that Nick went looking for a wife because he wanted children, so in spite of the machinations of his friends and colleagues he had achieved his objective, the model family. Angelina made much of their social standing and Nick's status in the business world, but it struck me as funny that Nick's entrée to the royal circle was as side-kick to an African chief in fancy dress, the fellow prankster from his schooldays, who made it an embarrassment to Angelina rather than a well-deserved honour.

It was dark by the time the Deathridges came home again. Nick distributed his gifts amongst the children, including Clare and Tomàs's Marco. I imagined him walking imperiously around Hamleys with assistants trailing behind trying to advise while he picked out items that took his fancy, all quite unnecessary as the castello children were adept at amusing themselves with pebbles, mud, twigs and the games Adam invented for them. The pleasure was Nick's in the buying, which May demonstrated, rejecting all her clowns and puzzles because the gun was missing. That was the first time Nick was confronted by his equally obstinate daughter. He was enchanted.

He held the rifle in front of her to let her feel how heavy it was.

"When you are strong enough to lift it like this you can have it," he said. He demonstrated how high it would have to go, and she imitated his stance, peering along a make-believe barrel — a promise I failed to honour on his behalf many years later, lost when the kaleidoscope of his life finally disintegrated and dispersed in an ever-changing, ever-expanding cloud of random pieces: an armchair, a piano; a blood-stained rugby shirt; a pair of Light Walking Boots Army issue; the Nagant 1878 revolver he promised to leave to Con — the instruction was to guard it with his life, making sure he saved the seventh bullet. The red crocodile disappeared without trace.

"Nick," I said, shocked at how he looked, "by raising the gun, your face changes from indulgent father into a killer's. It's uncanny, scary."

"Thank my Dad," said Nick. "for passing on his Deathrage eyes, though knowing him you'd never think the men of Bamburgh once intimidated the whole island of Britain; he never intimidated anyone with as much as a frosty glare..."

It's not the chill in his eyes, I thought, it's the readiness of his trigger-finger.

"You are infuriating," I said to him. "You've been here a couple of hours and already you've captured May's imagination with your iniquities. Luckily at her age, after you've deserted us for another six months, she won't remember you."

"Of course she'll remember me," said Nick. "I can remember my third birthday, it was the precise moment when I stopped wetting the bed."

"How can you possibly remember that?"

Nick looked at me as if I had asked a silly question but I wanted to know such a vital piece of nanny information.

"I remember my willie letting go," he said, "and feeling the wet flood seeping through my pyjamas and realising what it was. So I didn't do it again."

"Oh, Nick, I can just imagine the whacky kind of little boy you must have been. I wish I had been your nanny, I'd have brought you up properly."

Nick dismissed my claim that I'd have made a better job of him.

"Bonne-Maman getting me into dry clothes in the middle of the night was a game," he said. "I remember her trying to pin me down, tickling me and making me laugh. I'd crawl over her body finding a position of comfort to sleep with my face in her shoulder and she'd hold my hand to stop me sucking my thumb, but when she held my left hand I would turn my face and suck the right one instead — the advantage of being ambidextrous, or maybe that's how I became so. So the lavish praise I got for staying dry was a puzzle. Even at three I knew it was quite undeserved since I wasn't doing it to please her but because I had discovered how my sphincter worked. I let it go again a few times deliberately so she'd make a fuss but it's as well I found out how not to before she left. She was infinitely patient with me. Maman plus wet pyjamas added up to the slaps, tears, mutiny and mayhem I suffered later."

Nick spoke with such compassion for his child-self, I could see Clare was swayed again in his favour, a complete sucker for his charisma. She insisted on us dining with them, dispatching one of her girls to baby-sit for us. Nick agreed so readily it seemed he was deliberately postponing the moment when we would be alone together, like the time he played loud music in the car rather than face up to talking to me, to avoid giving me any hint of his intentions or the purpose of his visit.

I sat by as Clare tried tactfully to find out the same thing, cynically recalling her social manoeuvrings with Gus. Tomàs got straight to the point, asking Nick outright if his workers were on strike.

"Good grief, no," said Nick. "I got rid of the troublemakers years ago, now we work together nach Treu und Glauben, in mutual good faith. So we are just keeping quiet; there's not a lot we can do while no one else is working. Eggerswil keeps the machines ticking over and Gladys is having a lovely time reorganising the stock and colour-coding the filing system. I tell her to go and get a career in interior design. Luckily I have my filing system in my head because no-one will find anything ever again."

I couldn't even begin to imagine what it would be like to work as Nick's secretary. I doubted he would play games on her the way he did with Meg and the household affairs.

"I feel like my grandfather during the war," said Nick. "Every day he would dress as if he were still going to the City, then he'd sit down in his chair and light his pipe, waiting for some unspecified hour to strike. He could recall the details of every financial deal he had ever done, with the name and life history of everyone involved. His books and records had gone up in flames but, he said, he had it all in his head. I would sit astraddle the arm of his chair — you know how broad that is, Sibylla, from the many happy hours you spent there waiting for your cock to come home to roost — I was a cowboy on a bucking bronco but when my whooping got too unruly or I fell over on top of him he would push me off, shouting 'get to hell out of here, you whoreson bloody nuisance!' telling me to go and find Bonne-Maman even though Bon-ne-Maman had never come home and we were alone in the house. He had quite a range of esoteric curses, that's what got me into trouble when I went to school. When he said 'It's time your strumpety cunt of a mother quit lantefantering around town and did some war work in her own home for a change,' I knew from his tone of voice that was bad language — I must have been six or seven. As soon as Maman came in I slid down the curvy Lutyen-sie banisters into the hall yelling 'what's your war work, Strumpety Cunt?' and wasn't surprised that she slapped me quite hard. On the contrary, I was delighted to have learned a really good bad word. I loved the sound of it, funny and wicked at the same time. I'd repeat it under my breath and grin at her. It drove her crazy. 'Stop saying that,' she'd say; 'What?' I'd say. She couldn't slap me for not saying it. When I was sent to bed I'd bounce up and down shouting it, hoping to lure her to come in to shut me up, but she never gave in on that point. I could be as awful as I liked behind the door of my warlord's lair. Whenever my army went on manoeuvres down the stairs and across the hall she'd tell me to confine my unholy death-traps to my hell-hole. We'd have to beat a hasty retreat up to our redoubt in the mountains to avoid being sent down into the deep dark dungeons."

Poor Nathalie Dumez. I wondered if she had ever heard of channelling a boy's naughtiness in a positive direction and not reinforcing it by over-reaction.

"The charlady was allowed in to clean it out once a week and anything smaller than a ping pong ball would disappear into the Electrolux and never be seen again. I'd listen anguished to the death rattle as a brave soldier went to his dusty grave through the snake's horrid maw. Clumsy fat-arse bum-bessy, I'd shout at her — that's what Grandfather called her when she disturbed the dust in his room — but she only laughed and made a swipe at me with her duster, easy to dodge... so I learned very young the value of having a filing system in one's head instead of in boxes."

"It was Babylonian tax collectors who invented record keeping," said Tomàs.

"And that stupid bastard Moses had to write down a mere ten command-ments," said Nick. "If there were fifty or more one might have to start making a few notches on a stick."

"Gus said you pass the time shooting rats," I remarked. "Do you notch them up on a stick?"

"Yes, it's a competition. I've trained a great team of sharpshooters for the job. I told them how during the siege of Paris rats were an essential part of the diet so the boys were experimenting with barbecued rat in the yard. It's a pity their mothers objected so it's back to sausages and onion soup for them while the delicious rats go to waste in the incinerator."

Nick could turn anything into a game.

"The Renaissance Women seem to have survived the spiders in Yucatan," I said.

"Like you said: they learned to live with the spiders, and the birds were spectacular."

"Just as well you weren't there to shoot them," Tomàs remarked, serving the Friday fish.

"Carp!" said Nick, stopping Tomàs from putting any on his plate. "Pre-digested mud! I'll have Mozzarella with olive oil and you may even decorate it with sprigs of greenery if your aesthetic sense can't bear to see it naked on the plate... any effort to save the earth is only a temporary victory. Never-theless, it has given the Renaissance Women a purpose in life. Angelina came home full of enthusiasm."

"You're lucky I didn't stay," I said. "You would have been rather embar-rassed between two rival Mrs Deathridges."

"I dare say I could manage that situation more than adequately. I'd have made quite a satisfactory bigamist if only you had cooperated. I had it all set up when you ran away with the gigolo: a mews flat over an unconverted stable, with a nice friendly horse below. I was sure you would be delighted with it, and May could have gone riding in the park. I cursed Dad for letting you go but he wasn't terribly helpful."

I was so devastated thinking of what I had missed by running away with

Gino when I might have had a horse for stable mate to share with Nick that I said no more, while Nick went on entertaining Tomàs and Clare with horror stories from London about striking grave-diggers and no ambulances: the sick, the dead and rubbish piling up in heaps all over the place.

"I offered the council a cold shed to store coffins in but they turned it down. As usual they think I'm up to no good, though they could hardly suspect even me of barbecuing bodies. But the rats and the dead kept Tsang's alleged Virgin Births off the front page, it was relegated to a bit of comic relief on page three."

"Dr Tsang must be annoyed to have his science belittled by a sensational press."

"He tries to maintain Confucian calm about it though he was a bit upset that, just to prove that lorry drivers picketing the ports weren't going to stop me going anywhere I want to, I took my rented Cessna to give my sweet poppets a joyride across the channel —"

My fault, I concluded. He had that Cessna handy because I needed to get to Heathrow in a hurry...

"Actually it was darling Angelina who said too much and betrayed me to the press. She went to Yucatan to escape the embarrassment, only to be accosted at Miami airport by some journalist from the financial news who asked her if it were true I'd made a killing selling my sperm selector in India — the Indians say it's for breeding a better class of holy cow but I know they'll use it with Tsang's formula for getting their Nickie equivalents, little Krishnas with a mathematical genius — Angelina told him she knows nothing of my affairs but when he showed her the photo of Rose and Violet draped around me in high heeled boots, short slinky dresses and mink stoles, she was startled into admitting the pair of hot floozies are her aunts. Naturally he passed that gem on to the gossip page. I don't know why she blames me for her own blunder..."

"Oh, Nick, so they got you in the papers at last! You've lost your cherished low profile now," I said, delighted at the growing chinks in his armour.

"As no one knows what I look like..."

"... I find that hard to believe!"

"... I'm good at remaining incognito..."

Yes, I knew his 'not here' look.

"... and in leather cap with chin-strap and goggles, posing as a WW1 fighter pilot about to take off in defence of the nation — my enemies in the union call it strike-breaking — you'd have to recognise my very distinguished nose. Makes quite a nice picture though:

Virgins on Honeymoon with Mystery Sperm Donor in Bizarre Love-Triangle!

They have it in a silver frame on their mantelpiece to show off to everyone who visits."

"A look that makes a pantomime of the whole story," I said, "Why do you have to make a mockery of poor Dr Tsang? You can't still be cross about your itchy penis."

"It's entirely a consequence of how bloody uncooperative you are," he said.

"It has nothing at all to do with me," I protested. "And Tomàs's carp is really delicious. Why don't you try it?"

"No, thanks. How can I enjoy any kind of satisfactory love life when all you do is tantalise me with a few sublime fucks and then go, refusing to be my wife in spite of my rather splendid wedding ring? — I'm glad to see that at least you are wearing it."

I did not explain that it wasn't a ring's value I appreciated but the tenderness of his hands when he wrapped me in his scarf against the cold.

Also the way it went rather well in tandem with Gus's.

"What had Angelina to say about finding her aunties in her bed?" I asked, more interested in the complications of Nick's love life than the trials of his business affairs or the imminent collapse of civilisation.

"Nothing I do surprises her. She was content to get her bed — and me — back from them and she'd consider it undignified to show annoyance at their attempted coup. So I took them home to Surrey and our wonderful Nickies. I have never seen such enchanting babies; even while I was polishing the Nagant, thinking of where to put the bullet for instant death without spoiling my looks — my grandfather made a mess of it, I never fond out what weapon he used, when I asked for it back, admittedly twenty years later, the police claimed they'd mislaid it — I was thinking what a pity it was to deny myself the pleasure of seeing how my little experiment in mass production would develop."

Tomàs might have questioned Nick's loyalty to the White Goddess — me, in other words — but he removed Nick's empty Mozzarella plate in silence and emphatically made no offer to replace it with anything else, just as he pointedly ignored Nick's wish to preserve his death's head image with a neat bullet hole and no mess.

"How does Angelina explain the Virgins to the Renaissance Women?" I asked.

"The Women have been a great support. Ever since I had them hypnotised to go to the Yucatan they are entirely on my side. The Virgins and the Nickies fascinate them, they are a rich source of speculation and surmise."

"You are remarkably fortunate with your wife," said Clare, "she must really be an angel."

"Angelina is enjoying it all; she is in prime position as Head Wife and can boss everyone else, which she does with beautiful tact and delicacy. She's the rock on which my domestic happiness rests. I knew I was making the right choice when I married her though it wasn't immediately obvious why — even I didn't foresee all the complications that would arise. It's character that counts, then all the rest will come right."

"I wonder if she says the same about you," said Tomàs.

"She complains over minor inconveniences such as having to play Russian Roulette with my naked dick — I refuse to gag and smother my little buggers but I compromise by withdrawing before the final rush, a gratifyingly high-risk gamble every time... if only you'd come back to me, Sibylla, my life would be perfect."

"If I were in Angelina's shoes I'd get myself knotted," I said. "You don't need any more children."

"If she castrates herself I'll cut her clit off and make a complete job of it."

"My God, Nick, you are disgusting!"

"Are you jealous?" Nick asked, his unashamed amusement revealing his intent to provoke me.

I'd had quite enough of Nick's unselfconsciously implied sexual prowess. "I am happily married to Gus Wittersworth," I said, "so bugger off — not only did you dump me in a wilderness of small planes and baggage buggies a long way away from Alitalia..."

"It was as near as I could get."

"You can't deny that you did push me down on the bed to force-fuck me..."

"You had a tough Catholic hymen: how else was I going to get it in?"

"You could have waited till I was ready for it..."

"May proves how ready you were, that egg just shouting for my gang of squirmers to come and get her. All I did was hold out my hand to offer a polite welcome to Miss Sibylla d'Art, you gave me a heart-stopping smile, hesitatingly eager to take it...

"I'd never touched a man's hand before, we don't shake hands..."

"a captivating gesture that went straight to my balls but, on my way to see my baby coming, I could only kiss it in passing. But Angelina didn't want me to see her in distress and what's more, I didn't want to either, it would spoil the image we both have of our relationship — so I turned back to explore the smile and provocative eyes..."

"I sometimes wonder, Nick, if you and I are living on the same planet," I said, still puzzled how Nick's memory of our first encounter could be so different from mine. "Gus talks about parallel lives and I can't deny you may be right. What I remember is your strength holding me sprawled on my back with your weight pressing down on top of me."

"It always works better if one of a couple has a clue how to go about it. You were fortunate to get me: straight up the cunt and no juvenile phaffing around..."

"A little phaffing around might have been nice..."

"... and bang! you got your baby."

"You mean you got your baby."

"Yes, I am a pretty reliable stud; by the time the Wittersworths got you, you were well broken in..."

Nick infuriatingly always spoke of the Wittersworths in the plural. Did he mean as a family or was he implying my innocently incestuous intercourse with Father William?

Clare returned to put a dish of coconut meringues on the table with three plates, carefully avoiding the teasing mischief in Nick's eye.

"It seems to me," she said, addressing me in her most Edinburgh voice, "quite inappropriate to bring up accusations against your lover at the dinner table..."

"It's his favourite topic of conversation," I snapped back. "You heard what he said. I was the best thing that ever happened to him. Until he met me he was in a straightjacket of propriety, performing his Perfect Husband act for the benefit of the Renaissance Women, now he flies off to Paris to act out his own opéra comique with his giddy aunts-in-law."

"May I please have some of that nicely ripe Gorgonzola," asked Nick humbly. "And I'm sure Tomàs has the perfect Gewürztraminer to go with it."

"I have my own perfect wine to go with it," said Tomàs. "I prefer a deep, spicy red."

"Oh, all right, if you insist," said Nick.

Equilibrium restored over the dining table, Nick continued his albatross tale as if there had been no interruption:

"The Renaissance Women believe Tsang's Virgin Births a noble effort, no matter whether it's true or false, and consult him all the time — no virgins amongst them but they are excited by his rejuvenation techniques. They are all using angelina foam, adding modestly to our profits."

"I haven't seen it in any pharmacies," I said.

I had looked for it after Meg's description of the fake ivory box.

"It's exclusive to Tsang's clinics, not available to the common herd except by post from Hong Kong. We offer a choice of green as well as pink now; the green has peppermint oil in it and acts as a stimulant rather than a relaxant: Angelina's idea, she actually asked Tsang herself to alter his formula for her.

She likes the way it tingles. Personally I prefer to fuck au naturel but it's very popular. We've a plantation of Mexican yams to produce one of the essential ingredients so we can keep strict quality control; all I aim for is washed hands and clean overalls but that's not good enough for Tsang, he's inclined to overdo it with the phases of the moon, though interspersing the crop with little votive fires may well keep the stinging insects at bay. I just pay the wages — whatever it takes to keep my wife's love and loyalty."

Love and loyalty were tributes Nick could command in abundance: Angelina's was unconditional, mine given under protest. Every fibre of my being ached with desire for this transient hero, while he jousted with Tomàs...

Oh God I can't be in love with a man who comes and goes, and talks on and on, of love, despair, cheese and wine, bullets and babies...

"Tsang had to stop coming to London, mainly to escape the Women..." Tsang's tribulations clearly didn't concern Nick unduly... "quite apart from being hounded on all sides by questions from the medical ethics committee and the Furzy legal dreadnoughts. So the Women are now on a mass visit to Hong Kong to attend his clinic, being worked over by his assistants, and hope if possible to save the other half of the planet while they are there. I found a Chinese marshland of no economic value — no gas or oil rights — I'm allowed to lease from the state, where the Women can save the frogs from extinction without compromising me with the government. They may even do some good though the frogs may well end up being a welcome addition to someone's rice — that's one thing I didn't learn to cook, a pity really..."

Nick paused to consider his loss.

"I'd have had a marvellous time catching them but the only frogs on the Sandy Heath were in the Boggy Bottom and I wasn't allowed to go there. That was a D-word. Grandfather took me to a spot above it and told me to look at a muddy white post half sunk in the middle with red letters on it. 'What does that say?' he asked. The first letter was a D for Deathridge. 'Yes,' he said, "it's also a D for Danger; they go well together. What it means is: Dunce Deathridge will be D for very unpleasantly Dead if he goes down there or anywhere near it.'

"He told me to make a lasso in my head and lasso that post, then holding my end firmly in mind run around in a circle, ignoring the trees and bushes that got in the way, and come back to him. All the frogs were safely inside that imaginary circle but I understood it was a line I could not cross — he never told me what Escoffier says about frogs."

"If you took up reading you could find out for yourself," I said, my patience with him exhausted.

"I'll leave that to you."

"I've Tomàs's grandmother's cooking notes," said Clare. "I'll see if she has a good recipe for you."

"Don't bother," said Nick. "If the occasion arises I'll do them à la *Balinaise*: catch your frog, swing it to detach the legs, toss them in a wok, salt, pepper, lime juice and a dash of sambal on the side. Nothing simpler."

"How's the horse?" I asked, closing my eyes to Nick's casual gesture of swinging a frog by its back legs though I understood he was merely mimicking what he had seen done, without prejudice.

"I can't persuade Frank to go in for racing," said Nick. "It's that damn woman. I regret ever introducing them. He was quite dynamic when he had a gang of stable boys to admire his style and good looks on a horse, but Nancy got rid of them and she's content to just muck around, so Frank has gone lazy; it's easier to sell a few dozen wine now and then to his nob friends who come to the hunt. He has a very good eye for a horse: a wasted talent!"

"And in your fine suit you could join the Turf Club in the Royal Enclosure," I said.

"I'll take you along in a fly-away hat to meet the Queen," he said.

"That's more Angelina's kind of thing," I said. "Or even better, the Virgins: one on either arm in truly fantastic hats, egret feathers. Oh, Nick, that would be your moment of glory. But not me; Gus will introduce me properly when I'm Lady Wittersworth. Then she can safely say, politely, that she always had a soft spot for the Irish and I'll do as if I believe her."

Nick gave me one of his scathing looks, then said to Clare: "Even if

Red Rum does run again this season the odds are too short. Frank says to try Lucius."

"No, Nick," said Clare laughing at him, "like your friend we've something better to do with our money than throw it away on horses."

"You are throwing it away on this bottomless pit of a ruin," said Nick. "The best thing that can happen to this place is an earthquake, then you can rebuild it properly from scratch with the insurance money."

"It's not insured," said Tomàs. "Too expensive."

"You'd better try to explain your financial plan to me," said Nick, his raised eyebrow suggesting a world of tolerance at the ineptness of other people with their money.

"We do have an accountant, you know," said Clare, peeved at Nick's presumption that they needed his expertise.

"I'm not interested in petty cash," said Nick. He stood up and gestured Tomàs out into the yard saying: "I'm no good at reading balance sheets, what you can discuss with me is your philosophical framework. I'll give you the Züri gnome treatment — gnome as in first principle, not troll."

Tomàs opened the profligate box of twenty-five Hoyo de Monterrey double coronas that Nick had brought for him and with deep satisfaction selected one. He paused a moment at the hearth biting off the tip and spitting it into the fire and, picking up a suitably glowing spill from among the ashes he lit it and, ready to lend an ear to Nick's gnomic wisdom, followed him out.

I groaned inwardly.

I'd been waiting twelve hours since he made my head swim this morning, and still he had to go and get into a theoretical discourse on his second favourite topic with a man who was well able to hold his own in any debate and all the leisure in the world to enjoy it.

"I might as well give up," I said to Clare. "I'll never get him to bed now. They'll stay up all night again discussing money and sex, sex and money."

"I don't know what you are complaining about," said Clare. "You have no worries about paying the bills; you've fallen on your feet with a man like Nick to take care of you — and a charming husband as well!"

41

Clearly she was finding this discussion of money deeply offensive; she would never normally allow a hint of criticism appear in her dealings with me and my men.

"I'll go and let the babysitter off the hook," I said getting up. I had no wish to get involved in any conflict between the three of them.

Clare walked with me to the door and we stood a while where we could see through the archway Nick and Tomàs as they appeared and reappeared, walking past, up and down, their voices rising and falling, Tomàs explaining, Nick interrupting, asking questions and, judging from his tone, making his dryly sarcastic comments.

"You brought this on yourself," I told Clare. "You offended him by laughing at his tip for the races when he was trying, quite altruistically, to pass on useful information. The only time he got me to place a bet I didn't take him seriously either but I won quite a lot – I know there is no logic to it, it seems pure chance but he is such an intuitive gambler that as often as not it comes off. I think you can trust him."

"I'll take your word for his sincerity though I can't imagine how philosophy is going to help Tomàs financially. But anyway, Tomàs finds Nick quite amusing so he won't at all mind spending the evening in what is entertaining but ultimately idle chat — at least I hope he isn't tempted into any mad scheme."

I left Clare to her own devices at that. If she was so determined not to be advised by someone who overnight could turn the simplest idea into a golden egg, there was nothing more to say to her.

As the babysitter left I told her to go to Nick and ask to be paid. This had the desired result and not long after he came in.

"Well, have you solved Tomàs's problems for him?" I asked.

"Even I can't sort out the muddle of three centuries in an hour," said Nick. "But at least I got him to submit his lack of financial insight to scrutiny. I'll fix him before I go."

With that Nick retired to the bathroom where he spent another half hour, no doubt wielding his cutthroat razor amid clouds of soapsuds. Nothing could be further removed from being practically raped by Gino in a sweat, this obsession with cleanliness! I hadn't been consciously aware of Nick's smell until the afternoon I returned from Christmas at the Grati and he entertained me in his room for the first time. When he had done he put on a clean shirt and in a fit of temper at something I said he threw his befucked one at me. I held it to my nose and realised I could identify his smell. A revelation! Dry, an oak tree with ripe acorns and russetty leaves, a bees nest in its roots, honey with the sting of pungent male sweat: if only I could bottle him!

When eventually Nick decided it was time to give in and come to bed, Willie was doing his Wittersworth best to make sure the Deathrage invaders would get nowhere, sucking with determination to keep the milk flowing. Nick took him for a walk around the room, patting him on the back until he burped, then put him back in his cot. Now Willie was a recognisable little person Nick was happy enough to adopt him into the tribe, the Deathridge-Wittersworth tribe as he described it when buying the ring that united us.

When he lay down beside me, I thought: pistachio flavoured Turkish Delight. Must be his latest bespoke shaving soap.

"Haven't you noticed anything different?" I asked.

"What?"

"The mattress. After all your complaints I got a new one."

Nick ignored such irrelevancies; all he wanted was to fuck, now.

"November!" he said, "I've been waiting since November for this."

"Well, so have I," I answered. "And this has been a very, very long day."

After my day of painful uncertainty, his attack when it came was like our first time together when I clung on for dear life hardly able to contain what was happening to me, being pummelled by this phenomenon of a man.

"Good Lord," I said, "all that hard work on your pretty poppets seems to have made your cock toughen up prodigiously."

"It can't be that," he said, resting on his elbow. "They have the tightest little cunts imaginable; I have to keep it really soft to get into them at all: Tsang's Ancient Chinese Soft Entry. It works on the little pussies — but you know how slow I am at the best of times and that way takes me twice as long — and the two of them work in tandem, bumping each other off, so I have to keep it going at the same pace for both of them. Fucking them takes forever. Not that I'm complaining!"

"Ow, Ow!" I grumbled, "God help me, you might as well be Meg's elephant!"

"My cock's delight, you fuck to the limit, like snappy elastic stretching to the perfect fit."

I took it that that was meant as a compliment.

While I endured his alternating fierce humping and breathless pauses, my mind wandered: Nick's complete lack of concern when demonstrating to May how his rifle worked, his naughty philandering with the so-called virgins, also the casual references to the unknown women who populated his past, who had been hovering in the background of my consciousness, possibly ever since I had first known him if only I had been aware of it. And what about his runaway mother? The mother who left him physically and mentally scarred? What story could possibly explain why she would have deserted her little boy only to come to a ghastly end?

"Oh, my Sibylla, this is what I live for..." he went on moaning with almost unbearable ardour. No hint of fun, naughtiness, laughter; this was pure passion.

He loves me, he really loves me.

Nick rolled over on his back, damply perspiring, open-mouthed and panting.

"The mattress is certainly less back-breaking," he said when he could speak again.

"It was always my back that was being broken on it," I said.

"Well I don't know why it took you so long to get a new one," he said, recovering his wits enough to start another argument.

"Gino bought it for me in Sienna; he brought it in his van."

"The Jag isn't made for carting mattresses around," said Nick, refusing to be needled into either jealousy or guilt.

"When I came back married, Gino tore my wedding dress and forced me quite violently. Then the louse went off to sing evensong with the Carthusians as if that absolved him of his sins."

I tested Nick's limits of tolerance just as he tested mine.

"That is one way of dealing with you," he said, coolly. "Mine is more stylish. I dress for your wedding as if Death were a gentleman, and carry my pistol next to my heart, leaving it to the inspiration of the moment if it's you, me or both of us I'll kill — *Boda de Sangre* — Paul must have remembered we saw Lorca underground in Madrid so he stuck close to me throughout to make sure I didn't overact my part, and Wittersworth is so perceptive, he distracted me from anything but the pleasure of dicing with him over you — figuratively dicing with Death."

Nick's posture with the gun under his coat had certainly kept Paul and the Wittersworths on the alert for the possibility that he might use it. I recalled his eyes fixed on me and baby Willie across the lawn; he had much the same expression now: a wry challenge, a stop-me-if-you-can look.

"I assumed our *Liebestod* was one of your romantic notions," I said. "I wondered why you didn't kiss me, it would have been traditional in the circumstances, but when I kissed you I felt it and knew how near I was to death."

"With me you are always within arm's reach of Death."

Nick, lying beside me, presented a dignified pale profile gazing at the medieval rafters of the roof above us, a finely sculptured face, every line and curve sharply chiseled.

"After you'd been raped by the Grati gang, I watched you come up the stairs to me," he said, "looking quite pitiful. That's when you ceased to be the silly girl I was mindlessly in love with. I saw your vulnerability and recognised the enormous responsibility I had taken on, trapped into loving you forever."

"It wasn't very gallant of you not to go and cut up my rapist."

"Don't be absurd. I don't get my hands dirty with pointless gestures. Taking you to Abb's Head seemed the best solution until I could think how to stop you witlessly getting yourself fucked by any opportunistic lecher. Tsang assured me all you needed was more time to learn some sense, but you didn't give me the time. When I found what I was looking for, you had gone."

"You didn't give me your time either," I said.

Nick was silent.

"I didn't wait around to be your part-time cunt."

"You don't believe that I love you," he said.

"No."

"And you don't love me?"

"Not loving you is misery enough, for heaven's sake, if I loved you I'd go out of my mind."

"I'll watch out for signs of insanity any day soon," said Nick, unimpressed.

"You do have terrific balls," I said, weighing them in the cup of my hand.

"It's time you let them give you another baby," he said, following up with a perfunctory hump, then settled back, prepared to go on arguing.

"Not just now," I said. "I'd expect your undivided attention, like you gave me with May, so get back to me when you've settled the issue with Angelina, the Virgins and Dr Tsang — and that just now was a nice one; you do better when you're not trying too hard."

"Goddamn you for a contrary cunt," he said and went to sleep.

Lolling in bed drinking tea from the Sienna pottery mug Nick disliked — too thick — was sheer contentment, in the dawn after a hard night. While Nick was in the kitchen Augusta and May came in and climbed on the bed, not normally permitted when Nick was in the house.

"Daddy says he's sending in the clowns — that's us," said May. "Why?'

"Ask him," I said.

"That's what you do when things are going wrong and you need to create a diversion and make people laugh," he said when we sat down to black pudding, obviously scrounged from Donna, with butter-fried apple rings.

"The children actually prefer porridge with raspberry jam," I said. "And why do you need to send in the clowns?"

"Because you say you don't love me," he said. "Though your strumpety cunt is willing enough to exploit my love for you."

"You hardly need me now you bask in the adoration of your Virgins —

though surely they can't still be called virgins after Paris, even if they were before."

Nick sat back to consider this proposition.

"Now they've given birth it's open to question," he admitted. "That's Tsang's problem, for his sake it better be true. He is a bit nonplussed that he is expected to act the part of the Holy Spirit to the bastard baby Jesuses. But why not? The Archangel Gabriel didn't have to pay for the privilege of getting the original Jesus."

"Really, Nick! You twist every Bible story to suit yourself."

"I spent five years of my life strenuously resisting Papi Bott."

"I have the impression you are inordinately proud of the little Nickies, however you or Gabriel got them. Do they have red hair?"

"They wear little hats made from baby sealskin. And bootees to match to keep their little tumptytumtoes warm. They have taken up residence at the back of the north wind where my turbulent emotions struggle to survive."

"Oh, Nick, you are making up fairy tales!"

"Even the militant seal-pup protectionist Renaissance Women haven't the heart to protest. Genuine Baby Jesuses couldn't be more adored. Mother Furzy and Great-Uncle Harold believe firmly in their miraculous nature, virgin birth or not."

"That can't have come from either you or the unholy Virgins. It must be the Zen influence," I said.

"From me, without a doubt," said Nick, not allowing Tsang had any part in the miraculous births. "No village church christening for them. They were taken to Harold's holy hideaway to spread a bit of miracle dust, which apparently worked a wonder. The Order received a huge donation to reconsecrate their disused Lady Chapel and a beautifully restored English harpsichord, which sends Harold into raptures. He is dedicating it to the Holy Innocents and hopes to attract pilgrims he can entertain with his own compositions, and the monks chant occasionally as a concession to Hildegard of Bingen. The order has two new postulants to fill their dwindling ranks and visitor numbers have increased tenfold so far. The monk-chef is baking special little sugary ginger-babies to encourage donations from believers and sceptics alike, but of course only the believers receive the spiritual benefit. The abbey should do well out of it and they actually taste delicious, according to Con and Joe. I haven't tried them myself."

"Who gave the chapel money?"

"The donor wishes to remain anonymous."

"About as anonymous as the sperm donor," I said.

"They refer to it as the Shrine of the Blessed Nickies — we just can't get away from that name," said Nick, "it drives Angelina to distraction as everyone is giving in to it. I lent them my Great-grandfather Yussupov's Nikolai Chudovorets to hang over the altar — patron saint of children as well as of cheats and swindlers."

"So it will be you they are praying to, you cunning bastard," I said. "You can place a box for petitions beneath it and have the satisfaction of deciding which miracles to perform to keep the spark of faith alive for your sons until they can manage their own wonderworking enterprise."

"Where would I be without you, Sibylla? You do occasionally come up with a brilliant idea, the advantage of a youthful training in the ways of Mother Church."

Was any fancy too ridiculous for Nick not to take advantage of it?

"Pity I can't work miracles for myself," he said. "My love life is a complete disaster. No one loves me enough to give me what I want."

"For heaven's sake, you consummate fuck-artist," I said, "you've a catalogue of adoring women: what more do you want?"

"The love that eludes me. You."

"Yesterday when I heard your Jaguar growl its way up the hill, I could hardly believe you weren't a figment of my imagination. I was overwhelmed with wonder at how real you really are — I'd given up hope of getting you in my bed ever again."

"I'd gladly spend the rest of my life in your bed... Tsang is full of a new plan, marginally more practical than the Virgin Birth madness, so I agreed to work with him just once more. No matter how much I moan for love of you he expects me to be on stud duty on command, splendidly unsympathetic; no chance of him undermining one's machismo with mis-placed pity."

"What does he do?" I asked. "Give you monkey glands?"

"No thanks, not after the last time. He recommends a daily thirty-mile walk to keep me fit to go on producing healthy sperm. I said I had no inten-tion of doing a Long March even for the sake of generating more Nickies. The occasional climb on the Mont Maudit is exercise enough for me. He was not amused."

"How many more Nickies is he likely to need?" I asked, not taking him seriously.

"Half a dozen; I'll take to the hills to work up the energy."

So, in spite of maximum expenditure of energy in bed, most days Nick would go on long walks, wearing the red crocodile. Seeing him stride across the valley in the distance I said to Adam who was leaning on the wall beside me: "There goes a blot on the landscape."

Adam looked at me in surprise. "I was just thinking how Uccello: a flash of red is just what this tranquil landscape needs."

I reconsidered. My first view of the hills had indeed suggested Boccac-cio: knights in armour, runaway maidens, pursuit and rescue.

"Well," I said, "he'd better look out. If there is any dragon-slayer about he'll make a prime target."

"He makes a not bad-looking dragon," said Adam. "It will take a tough knight in very shiny armour to slay Nick."

Nick borrowed a shotgun from Tomàs, to my relief leaving his up-dated William Tell assault weapon in the boot of the Jaguar, and took May out shooting pigeons. I had to ask myself if the pleasure of his company was worth the anxiety it caused me.

"You can't carry the child over rough ground and a gun at the same time," I objected.

"Yes I can," he replied with the mildest of sarcasm, "In case you haven't been listening again, let me remind you: I am a professional gunsmith, not some peasant out taking pot shots on a Sunday."

Gunsmith still seemed so improbable a profession for such a dude that the argument carried no weight.

"You could trip and fall with her."

"I don't fall," he said.

I half expected my objections to trigger his departure but, rather to my surprise, he gave in to my fears and handed the shotgun back to Tomàs. My peace was short-lived however when he produced his pistol instead, saying it was his civic duty to keep up his target practice and pigeons would do. Typical of Nick: the alternative he offered by way of concession was worse than the conceded.

I could still visualise him standing around at my wedding, the long curve of his coat hanging loose but when he was saying good-bye he was buttoned up with his curly brimmed hat held in the crook of his arm against his chest. It was only because I kissed him he opened his arms to me and I felt it.

"I thought it was bigger," I said when I saw it in his hand.

"That one was," he said. "This is a SIG P210: officers, for the use of. Out of production now, it's still the most accurate there is. As a result it's worth quite a lot to collectors. I'm probably the only man who can still produce something as good as this."

The pistol went neatly in the inside pocket of the crocodile and I thought the only reason he doesn't always carry it around with him is that it would spoil the line of his close-fitting suits.

I had to give in. Shotgun pellets were after all less lethal than the pistol and I had to admit it was unlikely Nick would be careless enough to shoot his daughter.

I hoped that was the last of the surprises he would produce out of the Jaguar's capacious hold.

Nick and May came home from the hunt, May with a couple of pigeons in her fist and Nick with rabbits dangling. Nick cut up the pigeons to remove the breasts for May and Augusta's supper and while I was putting them to bed he went to Adam's to share his swag with his father. A day of solitary painting left Adam in the mood to have a skirmish with Nick and Nick obliged by reporting the latest news he had picked up on his car radio.

"They haven't the nerve to call an election," he said. "They know they'll lose. In the meantime we are all losing money — you as much as anyone, you dim-witted socialist, as our shipbuilding goes down the drain. The country will be bankrupt if this nonsense goes on much longer. Toby and I went to endless meetings of the CBI — my proposals for a completely new pay structure were dismissed as fantasy but it works fine with my old men, and the apprentices can put up with it or leave. Eggers takes the flack for me, the boys call him Herr Flick... and they are beginning to see the point of having to pay into our own savings bank and credit union, it gives them the chance to buy motorbikes they'd have to pay exorbitant interest on anywhere else."

Adam listened with composure, avoiding conflict. "Nick," he said, "is infuriatingly always right, even when he is morally in the wrong. My generation believes in good and evil, right and wrong, but those are concepts that seem to have a different meaning for men like Nick."

"My moral integrity is not open to discussion," said Nick, "so get on with chopping the parsley."

"And like all war babies, he is obsessed with food," said Adam.

Whatever the explanation, Nick was an enthusiastic cook, if somewhat basic in range and execution. I had enjoyed his robust preparation of almost raw beef and the pink lamb chops he served with his Château Petrus to celebrate our baby, so his patient simmering of rabbit stew with carrots and celery, rosemary and bay leaf came as a surprise.

"I learned to prepare rabbits as a child," Nick remarked as he dished up aromatic ladles full. "Grandfather had them brought to the back door, I don't know if they were black market; we paid for them with the ten-shilling notes he kept in the dresser drawer. He would sit at the kitchen table reading out the recipe, telling me what to put in the pot. All we had in the garden was bay leaves and rosemary. Famille Dumez never got around to digging for victory. It was the charlady who brought us the odd onion and carrot — she queued for our rations as well as her own. Grandfather didn't like to get blood on his hands but I took pleasure in the whole process. He told me how to cut the rabbits up by putting the knife between the joints, and which bits of gut were edible, very satisfactory as long as I didn't nick my fingers and get hell from Maman for sticky plasters spoiling my touch on the piano. He showed me how to hold a screwdriver and with a small hammer give it a smart tap to split the rabbit skull open so I could eat the brains. It's hard to believe I wasn't quite eight when he died; my whole life is based on what he taught me."

"You've a very selective memory, Nick," said Adam, spitting out shot. "You forget you had me too, and longer."

"I taught you to cook, not the other way round. If it had been up to you to feed us we'd have lived on kippers," said Nick. "But I don't mean just cooking *à la mode d'Escoffier;* I mean it philosophically."

"You certainly taught me to be philosophical," said Adam. "The only way to outlast your havoc-making was to cultivate the garden of Epicurus."

"That didn't add variety to our diet either. You were better at fishing — did Epicurus fish?"

"Probably, supposing he didn't have slaves to do it. Fishing is a very philosophical occupation, no wonder I took it up."

As I listened to them it struck me how they disagreed — philosophically — about nearly everything but in perfect amiability. They treated each other with good-humoured respect.

"I grew up eating fish and chips," said Adam, "and never wanted anything better until Conrad took me to dinner in the Savoy to introduce me to the money men who might invest in my boat building. I was astonished at how well they ate even though we still had serious food shortages."

"It's a pity you didn't learn anything else from them," said Nick.

"I remember that there was no lack of brandy and I was impressed at how different Conrad was amongst his colleagues, quite convivial, evidently well-liked. I can see his influence on you."

Adam was comparing Nick's social skills with his grandfather's.

"His death altered the course of my life." Adam was still annoyed.

What about Nick? I thought. Finding a bloody corpse must have been a life-changing experience for a child too even though as adult he spoke about it without emotion.

"I was touring the south coast at the time," said Adam, "looking for a suitable boatyard and incidentally to find somewhere to live. I was resigned to continued separation from my wife and child, a common enough situation after the war. But the terrible old man forced me back to Hampstead by shooting himself, condemning me to ten years of unremitting worry on your behalf, wondering what trouble you'd get into next, and failing to get you educated."

"Wrong kind of education," said Nick.

"I went back to sort out the mess he left behind, prepared to make a go of family life," said Adam, sticking to his own version of the story. "But your mother needed me there only for your sake because she couldn't cope with you single-handed. She had no wish to resume any kind of intimate relationship with me even though we got on well enough."

"Maybe you should have tried harder to understand what she had been through; you weren't the only one doing war work, you know."

"That was Nathalie's trouble: she never got over the excitement of the war, which as far as I could judge consisted of driving Dumez's Daimler around Whitehall, picking up and dropping off the big brass — shagging for King and Country."

"She looked great in khaki with a cap," said Nick, "a short skirt and a jersey Bonne-Maman knitted to shape in fine merino wool. She took me with her a couple of times so I could pretend to be a general sitting in the back. One time there was a real general and he made me sit on his knee and put his big cap on my head. He called me a cute little ginger-man. I told him I didn't like his smell. He said it was Old Spice but that wasn't it, it was something else as well, something that made me hold my nose... some Dutchman gave her margarine and she used it for putting a gloss on her bare legs: no one could be expected to eat the stuff, she said. I quite liked it. It went well with rabbit. She also brought home tobacco for Grandfather, best Cuban smuggled in for Churchill, and all sorts of funny things for me to eat, left-overs from off-the-rations banquets — one time it was snails and afterwards I went out with a bucket in the rain and collected all the snails I could find. Grandfather read out what to do with them. It went on for about a week; I loved them: feeding them, washing them and catching them when they escaped, then boiling them in several changes of water. They were horrible to eat though, chewy bits of rubber. Grandfather explained that was because we had no garlic, no butter, no parsley and we couldn't get the oven hot enough."

"Your mother was able to cruise around town because she had Dumez to look after you, and for a morose, bitter old grouch you must have been a welcome distraction."

"I don't know why you call him that, we had fantastic times together. As soon as the raids on London stopped he'd take me into the City to search for things in the ruins."

"St Nicholas and his golden balls," I interrupted, remembering how he had scooped up my scatterbrained windfall earnings from the exhibition and stuffed them in the lizard. The gesture of taking control had offended me at the time but I had to admit it was the moment that put my finances on the path of fiscal probity as befits a New Renaissance Woman.

"I found my future in the devastation of the past," said Nick, "but we never found what he was looking for. We often had to dodge the bomb disposal people, going places we weren't supposed to be."

"He was quite mad," said Adam, aghast at this latest revelation about his father-in-law.

"With him I was the happiest boy in the world. Imagine what my life would have been if he'd rebuilt his City office and took me to work with him — we'd have plotted and schemed and done deals of Dickensian complexity. I'd have been a millionaire at fourteen instead of wasting my best years at school and having to struggle on until I was nearly thirty..."

"Dickensian just about describes you, Dumez and Grandson, a right pair of rogues."

"Only it didn't stop him shooting himself as soon as my back was turned when Mother let me go to jolly St Oswald's to join the gang. And then you came along and took me away from my home."

"I know you didn't want to leave Hampstead but, after she left, you and I living there on our own always had a kind of temporary air about it, as if we were camping in a mausoleum. I rescued you out of that artsy Lutyens time warp..."

"It was my enchanted castle from which I sallied forth every day to conquer the world. Besides, I expected them all to come back, not just Maman but Bonne-Maman in the red Schiaparelli coat she was wearing when she left, smelling of the last precious drops of her Shocking. She gave me the Mae West bottle to keep, to stop me trying to hold on to her when she went out. They just disappeared, one by one, it's not as if they died natural deaths and were buried up the road in the graveyard."

"Your grandfather was, but remember, you ran away — that was the first time — and we had the funeral wondering where on earth you had got to, as if we didn't have worries enough! Nathalie thought at first you were just hiding, then with the help of the police patrol on horseback we spent the rest of the day searching for you all over Hampstead Heath until she was exhausted with grief and worry. She was convinced you had sunk without trace in the Boggy Bottom in spite of being warned not to go near it. You turned up in the evening beaming and jumping for joy, shouting — you had such a loud voice for a small boy..."

"Yes, that was my strength, I could out-shout anyone on the playground."

"... because Arsenal had won by some amazing score. You were such a little dynamo, always buzzing and humming about the place, but to take the bus all the way to Highbury on your own, we'd never have thought of that!"

"I asked you to take me but you weren't listening."

"Can you blame me? As if I didn't have enough to occupy me. I still don't know how you got in..."

"It was easy. I just attached myself to various groups who were all going the same way, darting along from one to the other, and of course I had the tickets Grandfather bought for us. When he was putting them in his desk drawer he said it was an historic occasion to see the Gunners champions again as if the war had never happened, that's why he wanted me to be there to hear the crowd cheering them. I thought he must have forgotten about going or he wouldn't have shot himself before the match. What's more, he promised to take me down Petticoat Lane on Sunday morning to get something I'd seen the Sunday before, an *Enfant de Marie* medal exactly like the one Bonne-Maman wore when she went out to be blown up, so I was very annoyed he killed himself instead. I wouldn't let it stop me going to the match. I had to climb in his window to get my ticket because some fool had locked the study door."

"How did you do that?" Adam asked with a resigned sigh, gathering rabbit bones in a little heap, arranging them in a pleasing pattern around the edge of his plate.

"It was a game I used to play on him; whenever he chased me away in a bad mood I'd be Tarzan and swing myself up by the ivy on to his window ledge and make faces at him through the glass. I discovered that I could open it from the outside by kicking the wooden frame at the bottom. That jerked the latch out of its socket. A bit dicey, I had to hang on and be nimble to swing myself in as it swung out, not to be left dangling out over space. I fell down a few times into the hydrangea bush. When I succeeded Grandfather said 'well done, but remember always to keep your centre of gravity — that's your head — forward so you don't fall backwards, and visa versa of course, use your brain for balance.' I remembered him when I went climbing in the Alps."

I remembered the unlucky boy Toby said fell off the tower during one of Nick's games. Toby didn't say what became of him. Nick may have been training his juvenile followers in risk assessment but seemed callously indifferent to the fate of those who failed. But then, he didn't believe in luck: you gambled, you lost, you suffered the consequences.

"I knew he would want me to go to the game anyway, even though he couldn't. I kept his ticket in my pocket so that his seven and sixpence wouldn't be completely wasted, sentimental little sod that I was."

Nick shook his head over his childish self.

"You were too much for your Mother," said Adam. "Your exuberance and irrepressible jumping around and cheering all evening was more than she could stand, dribbling up and down the hall, dodging around being Denis Compton, scoring thudding goals against the front door, shaking it on its quite substantial hinges, counting up to eight at the top of your voice and then starting all over again.

"'Why?' she cried, exhausted with grief and worry, 'why did Papa abandon us to this green-eyed demon of a child?'

"But I thought you had done the right thing. If I had listened to you I would have gone to the match with you; a more fitting farewell to Old Dumez than that dreary graveyard."

"Yes," said Nick, "you could have got me into our regular place where I could see properly, not with that smelly great hulk who picked me up to see better. He didn't mind my bouncing and screaming on his shoulders. He used to have a little boy like me, before the war, he said."

Nick got up from the table and went to look at the pile of drawings on Adam's desk, standing with his back turned to us.

"If you had listened to me — and, what's more," he said, keeping his voice low, "the house was mine. You had no right to allow strangers in to sit in Grandfather's chair, play Bonne-Maman's piano, sleep in my bed. I would have kept it safe for them. When they came back they wouldn't know where to find me. I even lost the Mae West perfume bottle when we left. Someone must have thrown it out."

"I'm sorry," said Adam defensively, "but we needed the money. The rent paid for your quite absurdly expensive school."

"When you came home from the war I wasn't convinced of the need for a father," Nick said, shuffling together the selection of peaceful Tuscan hills, "until you drew pictures of battleships for me. I was fascinated by the slow, logical way you constructed them, how they grew, detail on detail, to fill the paper."

"The ones you drew for yourself were far more exciting, all guns blazing and men running around the deck shouting, falling overboard, bubbles coming out of their mouths," said Adam. "And all those cut-out trap-doors and things going on below decks, fire in the engine room and bombs exploding through the hull...

"Yes, my imagination needs to create layers of meaning."

"Your sheer inventiveness as a child was astounding. I envied it."

"But you never listened to my opinion. I know it was difficult for you having a boy like me to care for. Thirteen is a wretched age for a boy, wanting so much and an overriding sense of helplessness. I should have been left in my natural habitat to fight it out with my own kind — I belonged to the posh gang, the Ham and High: we fought the Yids from Golders Green and the Paddies from Camden. I was bereft of everything that made sense to me."

Adam looked stricken. "I did my best. Remember that lovely summer you turned fourteen and we spent it fishing for mackerel off Chesil Beach; you loved those glistening, stripy fish, you liked killing, gutting and grilling them on the stones. You said they were the best thing you'd ever eaten."

"The very thought of it now makes me sick," said Nick.

"I taught you how not to drown at sea..."

"What to do if my ship were torpedoed, a situation I've managed to avoid so far, though I suppose if I had run out of fuel and ditched on my way up the Adriatic it might have been useful... then there was the time Papi Bott tried to hold me under after I capsized his boat and we weren't able to salvage it, little did he know you had done the same to teach me not to panic... yes, perhaps it was quite useful after all..."

"I was at a loss that after a fine day on the beach you would spend the night curled up clutching your balls, whimpering."

"My balls ached and I was homesick."

"Most people feel homesick in their heart, not in their balls."

"An association, not cause and effect. I couldn't understand why you took us to live in that god-forsaken place."

"It became a county sport: spot the Deathridge boy as he ran away from home! People would phone me with the latest sightings. You had instant notoriety, the boy racer in your cap and sunglasses — you were such a fantasist, a complete show-off. Our nice local policeman kept telling me that if I couldn't control you he'd be obliged to 'take steps.'"

"The motor was dead easy to start. It was your precious Morgan with the strap over the bonnet and the leaky fold-down roof that they rescued for you; no one gave a damn what became of me."

"Well, you'd leave the car abandoned and disappear."

"There was never enough petrol in the tank."

"But you invariably turned up again. So you'll appreciate what a relief it was to send you to school where fighting the other boys kept you out of worse trouble."

"Talk about time warps! medieval filth: indecently communal cold showers and damp towels, wading through slime, the noise — and the food! Cabbage! Beans on soggy toast! I nearly starved."

Mrs Shackleton and the lobster!

"It wasn't a bad solution to a tricky situation." Adam was unapologetic. "You seemed to make friends in spite of the rows and the tantrums."

"They all hated me, I was a child using his wits just to survive. Grandfather counting out how many *pesos de oro* would buy me a high quality female slave in Havana in 1790 hadn't prepared me for the dullness of what passes for education. At St Oswald's I learned how to kick the shit out of anyone who dared call me names, that was the most useful skill that helped me adapt to the grimness of boarding-school life."

"Adapt?" Adam laughed bitterly. "Not before you and your fellow monkey Joey Madigan ran away together. As well as the usual search parties and dredging below the weir we had police watching Heathrow thinking you might try to stowaway to Tel Aviv, Joey's usual route home. You might well have found a sympathetic Israeli to come to the aid of a fugitive Afrikaner boy. It's an identity not easy to mimic: in Joey's company you'd have got away with it."

"I should have consulted you," said Nick with regret. "We never thought of that. All I wanted was to go home to Hampstead. We would have climbed up into the garage loft and hidden out there, stealing blankets and food — I knew all the secret places. But Joey wanted to see *Blackboard Jungle* so we went to the cinema first. It touched our souls — a lesson in how to be truly awful. Our benighted school was tame by comparison."

"You were gone for days. I wasn't really worried; it was the school that made a fuss. I knew you'd turn up, as usual."

"The best bit was when they smashed the master's jazz records because they weren't rock and roll. We stayed in the cinema until we were thrown out for being rowdy. There were lots of other kids outside so we spent the night rocking around the clock in Leicester Square until the police came and told us all to go home."

"Why didn't they spot you then, they must have known there were two fairly conspicuous boys missing...?"

But it was only another example of Nick's chameleon act.

"We were afraid they'd rumble us in our school clothes but all the boys looked much the same as us only smarter with better-cut coats and terrific skinny trousers. I swapped ties with a guy who had red hair. He said if I wanted to get off with a girl I'd have to scrunch my hair up like his but I said I'd rather do without a girl than look a fool, so he chased me."

Great-Aunt Kathleen could deal with boys like Nick. I never really noticed how she did it, she just liked them, the way Nick liked his boisterous apprentice boys.

"We ran but it was the wrong way for walking out to Hampstead, so we dodged into a hotel on the Strand where Joey had stayed with his mother. I was so high on the music I don't clearly remember, I can't visualise how we got inside but I think it must have been the Savoy. Joey had his American Express but the reception insisted on phoning his mother in Johannesburg to check it was all right. His mother, Josie Teeuwen — you never faced meeting her, you were such a useless shit of a father — wasn't at all bothered, just told him to get back to school first thing. We had a very grand room with a huge bed but I couldn't sleep so we spent the night jumping out of bed to practise dance steps and ordering everything on the menu from room service — they even brought us champagne, we drank a bottle each. After another day in the cinema where I fell asleep during the silly bits, waking up for the fights, we stayed the next night in the park with a gang of boys."

I was glad I'd remembered my Montessori-trained aunt, maybe subconsciously her example was helping me to cope with Nick. Now I was aware of it maybe I'd do better in future. Survival techniques!

Nick went on describing his own survival: "When it started to rain we wandered into Covent Garden and Joey treated us all to breakfast: pots of inky black tea with lots of milk and sugar, and pork pies; then we decided we'd better get back to our Colditz to serve out our sentence before we were caught and had to face the firing squad. Rock and roll gave us something to live for. A defining moment in my life."

"And in mine," said Adam. "I had to go and negotiate with the school to persuade them to keep you. And Joey's mother sent me a letter saying she had no objection to paying for you to share a bed with her son but the bill you'd run up on room service struck her as excessive. That struck me as Boerish meanness, so I wrote back that I understood you were there as her guest. After that it would have been awkward for me to have to meet her in even more controversial circumstances."

"It has nothing to do with meanness," said Nick. "It's *billijkheid* — what's reasonable and fair. Freeloading is heavily frowned upon. Joey and I shared everything equally; I trusted him with my life."

Nick seemed to be forgetting that they played Russian Roulette.

"Fortunately not long after the Blackboard Jungle incident you took up with well-behaved, sensible Frank Buckley — what he saw in a hothead like you I don't know — and doing cavalry charges over the downs from *Quatre Bras* to *La Haye Sainte* absorbed much of the wildness."

"Frank has no imagination; he needed me to add a bit of interest to his boring rides. I identified with le Rougeaud. When it snowed I led the retreat from Moscow; I was a real hero fighting off the nightmare Russians single-handed. That's when I lost a horse, very realistic. Horse-meat lasts only a few days: one needs a live horse to make it home on. You never told me you'd paid for the wretched nag."

"It wasn't much; I didn't have a lot of spare cash."

The silence that followed this remark suggested they were both holding back from saying what was on their minds, the remains of the meal on the table in front of them. I was tempted to start dutifully clearing up, but hesitated to move for fear of disrupting the conversation at a critical point.

Adam and Nick talking of the past sounded as if they had never discussed it before. Maybe they needed my presence to deflect damaging confrontation between them. I was the catalyst that released them. So much was said and implied in that understated exchange between father and son that it took me months, maybe years, to appreciate the full depth of it, to complete the picture of how and why we were now all three eating rabbit on top of a Tuscan hill.

"Well, as Nick is always telling me, I'm a bloody useless father."

Adam was the first to break the deadlock.

"I never caught up on the lost years of the war. Even as an eight-year-old he already outgunned me and by the time he was seventeen he was beyond my powers of reasoning. For both of us setting out to sea for Monte Carlo was a relief, breathing space between troubles left behind and those to come, and Nick was utterly transported by his sense of escape, as if nothing could touch him ever again. I don't know how he survived the voyage. If I hadn't made him clip on his harness so I could winch him back every time he threatened to go overboard, he'd have drowned himself."

This was another slant on Nick's version of their flight into his future, his rite of passage. He gave Adam no credit for keeping him alive. On the contrary.

"I didn't want to be the *Flying Dutchman*, condemned to sailing around the earth forever on the off chance Sibylla would come along to release me from the nightmare and let me die."

A Sibylline shiver of fear went through me but Adam ignored this fantasy and stuck to the facts.

"Throughout the negotiations over selling the *Espérance* he fidgeted in the background, in a state of sulks and silent fury about how it was going, only speaking up to act as a walking-talking currency converter."

"Yes, as soon as I saw we were being paid in Swiss franks," said Nick. "I had to try and intervene. The franks were going up by the minute while sterling slumped, it was our chance to make a killing. You should have held out for half a million but you settled far too soon."

"I was dubious about exchanging my years of hard work for a piece of paper with, to me, a meaningless number of noughts on it drawn on a bank with an incomprehensible name I'd never heard of."

"It is only the most solid bank in the world — they financed the Swiss railways."

"Then you took my wallet with the last of our real money and went off to buy our tickets home. It was one of the most worrying moments you ever inflicted on me. You'd been running off and disappearing since you was seven years old and I fully expected this time would be for good. However, an hour later you returned, not with a flight home from Nice as planned, but rail tickets to Basel."

"I was thinking of Grandfather Dumez with his piles of paper money telling me that the the only notes with sufficient gold reserves behind them were the Swiss, and I wanted to see our boat converted into lovely gold."

"I may have had the paper in my pocket but you already had the money in your head. Once we were on our way I wanted to discuss how we'd start again with our bit of capital but you just stared out the window."

"I was missing Joey"

"I was worrying about the difficulties you'd face back in England... "

"It wasn't the Limpopo."

In spite of Great-Aunt Kathleen and for all Miss Pinkerton's training, I could easily imagine myself one day having the same kind of conversation with May.

"Changing trains at Geneva International was when I finally lost control — everything changed. At first it wasn't obvious to me that we were entering a different world with apparently familiar vine-clad hills passing by, but you felt it and instead of sitting glumly silent as in France you went and sat across the aisle and started a conversation with a young man who was stashing his bag beside ours in the luggage rack..."

"He said '*Exgüsi!*' and sat down beside me. I needed a new friend and with only a three hour train journey ahead of us I had no time to waste."

"Your competence in dealing with the French wasn't surprising but this unexpected switch to German showed that you hadn't been quite so hopelessly idle at school as we thought."

Nick stood up and removed Adam's plate, putting the rabbit bones in the bin outside the back door along with the empty bottles. He'd endured Adam's paternal jeremiads enough already.

Adam refused to be deviated from finishing his story and continued telling it to me:

"The young man was in uniform and his heavy backpack had a rifle attached so I concluded that was what attracted Nick's interest — another cause for worry I had to face up to: the fighting in Aden and Nick's failed plan to skip off with Joey up the Limpopo to avoid being conscripted for National Service."

I might have guessed that the romance of the Limpopo had a down-to-earth expedient to it.

"On arrival in Basel they finished their conversation on the platform, then shook hands with friendly formality. However, when I asked Nick what that was all about, all he said was that the young man told him he'd had a great time on manoeuvres — and he'd been to the top of Mont Blanc, easy, he said. At home in Basel he was apprenticed to an instrument maker.

"'I'm meeting him at his works tomorrow morning so he can show me around,' he said.

"'It's hardly the right time to go larking about,' I protested. "'We have to go to the bank and get the money home as soon as possible.'"

"'The money is safe where it is,' said Nick. 'I have to fix my future first.'

"So that was the end of the line for Nick and me. He had found his safe haven. He stayed behind with our hard-won *Stützlis* to build a career for himself while I went home to find peace and contentment in Abb's Head."

Gus phoned asking to discuss some legal matter with Nick but Nick said to tell him to go to hell.

"Nick seems to have settled in for a long stay," I said, 'though, given the lure of the little Nickies, not to mention the tantalising prospect of getting Angelina pregnant with the help of his angelina squirties, I expect that any day now he will announce his departure and be gone."

"Angelina told Father that the secret ingredient in Dr Tsang's green foam is the extra strength spermicide he formulated for her to neutralise the onslaughts of Nick's super lively little wrigglers. She leaves the ethics of not telling Nick entirely up to Tsang — it's the obverse of his work on fertilising the virgins..."

"... and Tsang's thwarted attempt to produce red-head Chinese," I added, delighted that Angelina had found a way to foil her husband using his own weapon against him. Very satisfactory!

"... but she's tired of people ringing her to ask where he is as if she should know. Father advised her to get an unlisted number. I didn't tell them that the Master Cock is in Italy fucking my wife."

"Yes," I said, "happily his tumultuous lovemaking has settled down into a highly satisfactory once-a-night rhythm. He is doing brilliantly as substitute husband."

"Don't delude yourself, Mrs Wittersworth. It's a strategic withdrawal, he's only keeping himself fit for the fight while here the bantams peck at one another. He'll come back in due course to clean up."

"I know it, damn him. I hope Evita is keeping you happy," I said.

The Curious Incident of the English Visitors

The first I was aware of people turning up at that unseasonable time of year was during a late dinner Nick and I were having alone in the dining room after a long day in Assisi, the ultimate hilltop town, which made Nick smile with derision.

"Quarrelsome bloody Italians," he remarked, expressing a pitying contempt. "Ginos and Giannis, the lot of them."

"Except," I said, "it also produced St Francis."

"One pro hundred mille, not a great score!" said Nick.

He was still smiling his sardonic smile when an elegant couple was brought in by Clare and shown to a table across the room from us. Nick, who normally ignored tourists, surprised me by standing up and making a nod in their direction, formal and dismissive at the same time. The gentleman gave a grave nod in return and they both sat down without a word being exchanged.

"Do you know them?" I asked.

"I met him at a reception at the Residence when I was in Bern — Bern is a great place for meeting people on neutral ground — something of a contradiction: the beating heart of minding your own business and a breeding ground for spies."

Clare and Tomàs's guests came by personal recommendation, mostly German and Austrian, so a Swiss connection was not surprising. What did surprise me was that Nick's mouth had that twitchy down-turn that indicated he was quite intrigued by their presence and instead of frostily shunning any intrusion I caught him transparently looking at them.

"Nice sable," was all he remarked.

I had seen without any particular interest that a long fur coat was draped across a spare chair beside them. The big dining hall with its stone floor and high ceiling could be quite chilly, but the newcomers had been put near the fireplace which Tomàs had stacked with a generous supply of logs.

"Angelina was wearing hers; it must be the season."

Nick clearly attached no importance to what he was saying; it was a cover-up, but seeing my sceptical look he added, "Do you want one?"

"No, thanks."

The last thing I wanted was what Angelina and some diplomat's wife were wearing, season or not.

We had finished and were leaving while they had barely started; Nick put his arm around me in his overt display of possession and gave them a poker-faced good evening as we passed their table. I could tell he was amused by the situation. He murmured as we went out the door, "She looks familiar. I believe I met her at a funeral, or maybe it was her sister... it was a long time ago and I was somewhat distracted at the time."

In the morning I asked Clare who they were.

"Mr and Mrs Bolus," she said. "He seemed interested to know about Nick. Last night after you left he asked me. I was discreet, just told them his name and vaguely his business and that he usually stays a week or two. I said nothing about you and they didn't ask."

"I expect he was trying to remember where he met Nick before. I suppose diplomats need a good memory and he'd be embarrassed if he couldn't recall who he is."

Visitors to the castello tended to melt away in the daytime; one seldom met anyone around so that afternoon when I heard voices below I looked over the gallery and saw it was Nick in the courtyard chatting in a suspiciously friendly manner to the English gentleman, while Mrs Bolus was being nice to May who was hop-scotching on the flagstones beside them. My impression of Nick's secret enjoyment was reinforced when he came in and said in an ostensibly casual way, "They've invited us to have dinner with them this evening."

"It's better to avoid English people when they're on holidays," I remarked. "I hope it's not going to be an evening of name dropping and 'do you know the Dorset Lambs?' Nothing could be more boring. Clare does so annoy me when she does it."

Nick's eyebrow suggested he might actually be looking forward to a bit of competitive namedropping.

"What tricks are you up to?' I asked. "What did you say to them?"

"Don't worry, they are leaving again to-morrow. I merely reminded Bolus where we met, actually more than once. When I was flying some stuff out to East Africa he fixed the paperwork for me. He remembered that perfectly well. He recognised me immediately, he was just being careful, uncertain about you. That's why I took May down to introduce her so they would understand our relationship."

"You were flaunting your balls, as usual," I said, laughing at him. If Bolus knew him from Switzerland he possibly knew about Angelina too so I knew I had to play along in my role as trophy cunt.

"You should have lived in the days of codpieces, then you could have had a massive bulge sticking out of your doublet and hose, cerise pink like the King of Spain, intimidating the competition."

"Quite," said Nick. "Put on your sexiest dress — the smokey-blue Armani without the underpinnings is just right, subtle and stunning."

"At close quarters across the table that may put your friend off his food."

"He isn't here for the food. Give him something to live for."

"His wife looks quite capable of doing that for him, she is really lovely."

In manner not unlike Angelina, I thought, only a lot more fun judging by how she had been playing with May.

"She is an upper-class lady of refined sensibilities," said Nick approvingly, but his words contained an undercurrent of irony.

Nick was out to make a good impression; he stopped short of full evening gear as inappropriate but took a shirt to Donna for extra ironing lest the slightest wrinkle mar its creamy perfection under his sky blue tie with inky squiggles, and streamlined navy suit that looked inky black by lamplight.

He had me tighten the buckle at the back of his waistcoat so it was snugly taut across his torso.

"You are not leaving any room for your dinner," I said, resisting the urge to hug him around his slender flanks and ruffle up his pride in his own stylish panache.

"When would I ever eat anything bulky or bloating?" he said. "I shall have lambs' testicles *alla pizzaiola* without onions, a steamed trout with lemon, and chunks of fresh Reggiano with English mustard. As it will be Tomàs's wine I shan't be tempted to drink too much."

"You've already discussed the menu with Clare?"

"I have no faith in chance; it seldom favours the unprepared."

"Except that really you did fall on me the minute you laid eyes on me. Was that premeditated?"

"That's the difference between us, between being prepared to act on intuition and being gormless. Wittersworth was quite right to accuse me of abusing my authority but if I hadn't, common sense would have asserted itself: you would have remained a modest nanny and I a boring boss. My life took off into the stratosphere in that one inspired moment."

Nick believed his story as firmly as I believed mine. But then, he had also ditched Adam on the train to latch on to the guy with the gun and so secure his future: what was that if not intuition?

I hoped Mrs Bolus wouldn't come to dinner in a neat blouse while I was in Nick's favourite revealing dress, but happily she was even more startling in a bias cut gown in broad black and white stripes slanting dizzyingly around her tall body, and her floppy dark curls tied up off her naked shoulders. She received us standing by the monumental hearth in hostess mode. Mr Bolus sat beside it looking rather tired and, it seemed reluctantly, stood up as we advanced towards them.

"Good," I murmured to Nick, "some challenging competition at last."

"Heirloom diamonds," he pointed out, not troubling to lower his voice as we crossed the room, referring to her parure of necklace and dangly earrings. "Wittersworth hasn't been forthcoming in providing you with anything similar."

I thought that Nick was referring to the fact that the only precious jewels I had were gifts from him, not my husband.

"All I need from Gus is my wedding ring," I said, refusing to rise to his quite uncalled for taunt.

Tomàs had a medieval pile of logs burning for us on this late frosty evening. The table was a large round one, laid for style rather than intimacy, so the conversations tended to split into a series of separate duos as we had to turn to one side or the other to talk.

"You and Mr Deathridge have a lovely little daughter," Mrs Bolus said to me. "Leon and I have two. They are at home with Mother who loves having the opportunity to experiment with discipline — not that her efforts did much good with my sisters and me. We ran rings around her as I'm sure my two little angels are doing right now."

She had such a mischievous twinkle in her eye that I liked her immediately.

"I have a second daughter too," I said. "She will be two in August"

"And a little boy?"

"Yes, he is six months."

"Goodness, you have been busy. You must let me see them in the morning. I can see why you like to bring them up here, the surroundings are so pleasant. It's a pity about the cement factory down the valley."

"I don't notice it's there," I said. "It's down wind from us."

While she chatted on amiably about the pleasures of Tuscany, Leon Bolus said to Nick:

"It must be difficult for you at the moment; do you think these sanctions will affect your business?"

"Given this damn fool government, who knows?" said Nick. "I'm here to escape the CBI expecting me to lend weight to their negotiations any longer. I've already offered my solution to the nation's problems to blockheads who won't listen. I walked out saying I'd rather engage my wit and energy in a cockfight with my favourite cunt."

Oh, Nick! So Gus was right; that certainly threw cold water on any illusion it was my irresistible charms that kept him at my side. Why did I believe in love stories?

"Anyway," I said to Mrs Bolus, bringing to an end any romantic fiction about lovers in Tuscany, "I don't expect to live here for long; my husband will get us a home of our own soon. I keep rejecting Nick's nonsensical proposals to whisk me and the children off to an island in the South China Sea..."

It was distracting talking to her as I couldn't help hearing at the same time how Mr Bolus was bent on grilling Nick about the Swiss arms industry, wanting to know the reality behind official statements on to whom what could or couldn't be exported. I wondered if this information was the reason for his show of interest in us, trying to find out how far Nick was implicated in the trade, legally or otherwise.

"You were there," said Nick, "when I had that nice little atelier in the Kügelgassli. It was handy for the various blacks and latinos who liked to drop in for a chat."

"No," said Mr Bolus in emphatic contradiction, "I knew nothing about that."

Nick's pause expressed his polite disbelief before he went on, "I was doing well there but I decided I'd have more scope in the free-for-all of London's multitudes. Now I'm the Savile Row tailor of the gun world, it's what I amuse myself doing while my men are producing the bread and butter stuff that keeps the taxman happy — my Luddite approach is surprisingly profitable; it's extraordinary what people are prepared to pay to say their piece was fitted and finished for them by Totenkopf himself. They visit me at my bench; they watch my handiwork and discuss the survival of the richest. It gives a quaintly Leonardo quality to the industrial shambles of west London."

What a fantasy! I recalled leaning over the banisters to see the unfathomable Mr Deathridge down in the hall checking in the mirror the perfection of his tie before going out the door. I had imagined he would spend his day in the City with equally impeccable gentlemen. Now I could more readily believe in a secretary called Gladys holding the line of defence on the phone and a Mr Eggers doing the donkeywork while Nick was kicking a ball around the yard with his juvenile rat catchers.

Mr Bolus too looked sceptical. The questioning had left Nick unfazed; he was apparently quite enjoying it, but given his talent for bluffing and talking nonsense, would Mr Bolus realise how much it was open to interpretation? Nick's bluff — or otherwise — spiralled into even dizzier heights as he launched forth into the intricacies of gun-design, clearly putting an end to this discussion by driving his interlocutor to bewilderment with an excess of irrelevant detail.

"Do you do any more flying in the little Pilatus turboprop?" Bolus asked, quasi-casually, not to be completely put off by Nick's diversionary tactics, aware of Nick's smokescreen.

"No!" Nick's air of finality echoed Bolus's earlier emphatic denial as if mocking it.

"I quite enjoyed that slightly hair-raising spin up the Grünhorn Pass you took me on — though we seemed to deviate a bit off-course. I'm not sure if it was intentional or not..."

Mr Bolus looked at Nick for confirmation but Nick was giving nothing away, no more than mildly amused at giving his passenger a fright — that he had a licence to fly suggested that Nick might, after all, have put his artfully contrived illiteracy aside for the sake of buzzing fearsomely through Alpine gorges. The Bolus question also suggested that our host knew Nick rather better than Nick had implied. I was about to turn my attention again to Mrs Bolus when as an afterthought Nick added:

"The fuselage got a bit damaged on the way back from *notre cher ami*. I didn't mind taking his diplomatic bag on board for him and I didn't ask what was in it but I resented the gorillas who came along to keep an eye on it. I decided they were too much dead weight slowing me down so I left them to the vultures in the Drakensberg. But the diplomatic pass that came with it was useful."

"You don't say!" Mr Bolus refused to be shocked by this, "A bit risky, don't you think? Losing his minders must have annoyed Gabriel."

"Not when I phoned him from Zürich with a number and code ... "

Nick's teasing, taunting attitude suggested he knew he had again got away with — murder? — and there was nothing Leon could do about it. Or maybe anything Leon would wish to do about it.

Mrs Bolus asking me about the chance of finding truffles made me miss the rest of this duel but even she had to pay attention to the men when Nick, upping the ante, turned tables on the relentless interrogation he had endured and began to describe in excruciating detail a banquet he had attended recently at Windsor Castle, going through the menu, the wines and a seemingly interminable guest list as if to test the diplomat on his acquaintance with the inner circle, a technique he must have learned from listening to his grandfather's monologues while he picked off marauding Indians with his great-grandfather's original Belgian Nagant: White Army, officers, for the use of. Mr Bolus looked more and more exhausted with the effort of keeping his end up, until eventually Mrs Bolus rescued her husband by enquiring of Nick whether he had ever been hunting in these parts.

"Nothing worth mentioning, but Tomàs has invited me to come for the boar next autumn."

I hadn't heard of this, so it was quite a useful piece of information. It reminded me again how uncommunicative Nick could be. One only ever found out something from him if it were strictly relevant to the moment. He planned well ahead but he didn't allow anyone else get there ahead of him.

With Nick turning his full attention to Mrs Bolus, Mr Bolus remarked to me:

"I gather Deathridge is not your husband," which didn't strike me as a very diplomatic gambit though possibly a flirtatious one, maybe the effect of barely covered nipples across the table stimulating a mildly sexual advance.

"I suppose you must know Mrs Deathridge," I said, countering his indelicacy.

"Not personally," he said, "but I met her father when he came to Bern to find out how reliable were the rumours in the City that Deathridge had made a substantial fortune when working there."

Angelina's Daddy determined to see her married to the Right Man before he died!

"I didn't know Deathridge," Mr Bolus went on, "but when I asked around, it appeared he was quite well known around town, well integrated in more local activities — the Swiss are very clubby, he did all the usual things: skiing, shooting and he played piano at a jazz club. The flying was for his skydiving club. So no inexplicable wealth but a highly skilled, presumably well-paid job — salaries are strictly confidential — and even more importantly, there was no mention of any complications with women."

After Nestor's stories about Nick and the Heini girls, this surprised me, but Mr Bolus continued: "I didn't think it quite appropriate to report back to Furzy that when I introduced myself to his prospective son-in-law the first thing he asked me was if I'd like to buy his wickedly expensive Porsche. Now that he was getting married, he said, it broke his heart to part with it as it had taken the place of a woman in his life."

This seemed in complete contradiction to Nick's remark that he married Angelina when his Swiss girlfriend refused to start a family with him.

"So I was confident my account would be to Furzy's satisfaction, nothing about exceptional wealth but he'd be getting a responsible, industrious young man for son-in-law. My wife was interested to hear about the engagement since her younger sisters went to the same school as Angelina and when the marriage finally took place after these lengthy negotiations, one of them told us what fantastic fun she'd had at the wedding reception."

She must have been one of the many girls Nick flirted with on the dance floor. The whole account of the wedding was far more likely of the Nick who had flirted with the Heini girls than the sober jazz-playing citizen of Mr Bolus's description, which matched the 7:45 one I knew in Stratton Square. How to reconcile the contradictions?

"Oddly enough," I said, hoping to coax more facts out of the diplomat, "Nick says he remembers her from a funeral — an unlikely mix-up."

Mr Bolus made no comment. I looked across the table at Nick deep in conversation, sharply etched laughter lines around eyes and mouth banishing the customary frown. I felt confused; this connection with Mrs Bolus was a complication I hadn't allowed for. Maybe I had misread the situation.

"My wife's lovely sisters, and now you ... all these subtle permutations of

7 5

beautiful young women," Mr Bolus sighed. "I'm afraid it is too late for me to enjoy them, but I can see the attraction for a man like Deathridge, in a position to pick and choose and vigorous enough to make the most of the opportunities on offer."

"Why shouldn't you?" I asked. He seemed more than attractive enough in spite of his somewhat faded appearance.

"I'm under a death sentence," he said. "I have a desperate longing to squeeze all the pleasure I can out of life before it's too late. My dear wife is very understanding."

I couldn't think that this was anything other than a proposition I would have to wriggle out of as politely as I could. I glanced again at Nick who was thoroughly absorbed in his affair with Mrs Bolus. I concluded that it was Mrs Bolus Nick had dressed with such care to impress, noting how the high-cut starched collar of his shirt set off the long curve of his jaw, and the blue in his tie brought out an unexpected blue glint in his eyes. Without his weekly barber's appointment his hair was longer than usual and, even more unusual for him, he had run his fingers through it with some lotion, which ruffled it up and made it shine copper in the firelight. He looked terrific.

To remind myself of where my loyalty lay as much as to inform Mr Bolus I said, "I am completely devoted to my husband but I had Nick's daughter a few years before I married Gus — a child is such an indestructible bond, it's more than marriage."

Even as I said it I felt a surge of happiness. Fuck me, fuck, fuck, fuck, no matter that your cock compass is pointing firmly at charming Mrs Bolus just now...

"My husband doesn't worry about him," I said, "His rampant outbursts pass like a summer squall, usually leaving me in tears, but Gus says Nick has a short fuse and will self-destruct in the not too distant future — Gus will be a doctor of philosophy as soon as he gets his thesis finished; he refers to himself as the long-distance runner; he'll outlast all the others."

Mr Bolus leaned back observing me, not eating: as Nick said, he wasn't there for the food.

"They are lucky men to have you," he said.

This was not a proposition; it was a simple statement of fact.

"I'm the lucky one," I said. "They are both prodigious fuckers."

Mr Bolus looked hard at Nick who was displaying such a concentrated interest in his wife.

"I had actually forgotten all about my brief encounter with Deathridge," he said, "when a year or two later my wife and I had an invitation to the wedding, not from the Furzy family as one might expect, but through Hein, Deathridge's earlier employer. He and Mrs Hein dropped in to see me at my office. He introduced himself as the owner of the Pilatus Porter and thanked me for facilitating Deathridge's undertakings in Southern Africa. I had no idea I had done any such thing ..."

Any more than Adam knew he had given his permission for a teenage marriage.

"I'd merely mentioned the names of a few people I'd met when working there, as one does, when he told me about his proposed solo flight to test the latest model Pilatus ... which is why I foolishly accepted his invitation to that scary spin that nearly ended my career, skidding and bumping down a glacier — the Swiss may think nothing of risking life and limb in their beloved mountains but it never appealed to me... "

Frank and Toby had mocked Nick's African adventure which seemed a follow-up to his fights with their old school comrade — I assumed Chief Babutu's string of ridiculous titles was an invention of Nick's — but now there was Mr Bolus's *cher ami* as well. I wondered who that could have been. Was he another with whom Nick traded guns and gold? Or the source of the pink sapphires Nick said he 'picked up' on Madagascar?

Mr Bolus was equally foxed, it seemed.

"Until Mr Hein's smiling innuendos it never occurred to me there might be anything dubious if not downright illegal about Deathridge's venture. I wondered if that perilous buzz on the glacier hadn't been a veiled threat to scare me to keep my mouth shut — maybe I wasn't very good at my job not to have been more alert to the possibility — but just look at him... that appeal, that earnest sincerity, who wouldn't be persuaded?"

Indeed.

"Before I recovered from the shock of that sudden insight, Mr Hein gave me the details of a Fokker Friendship he was chartering to take the Swiss contingent over to London for the Deathridge wedding. I declined. The last thing I could afford in my position was any suggestion I had a personal involvement with what could have been a huge diplomatic scandal, though it wasn't until a visit to Pretoria and meeting another friend of my wife's that I learned the extent of his activities and knew I'd really had a lucky escape — not that it matters now; my career is over."

I must have looked blank at this. Why was Mr Bolus talking to me as if I were a trusted confidante? Was it the effect of Armani clad nipples? I knew about the Swiss at the wedding causing Angelina considerable distress and about Nick's Tintinesque fascination with small planes, but what did this jumble of disparate elements mean? I saw an undercurrent of bitterness as he eyed Nick again — maybe not so much jealousy as envy. After all, Father William had commended Nick for a negotiating skill that went beyond diplomacy, adept in situations where more of an iron fist was needed inside the kid glove and a less scrupulous concern with protocol.

"Hein urged me to reconsider my refusal," Mr Bolus went on, "saying my part in getting Deathridge splendidly married off to an English beauty warranted a place of honour among the rest of the merry band. This added to my consternation, so imagine my chagrin when Mrs Hein, a Nefertiti of a woman, exquisitely beautiful and quite terrifyingly dynamic, said all his colleagues considered Nick quite mad to exchange a highly successful career for a venture into the unknown in a dysfunctional British industry — and that she was curious to meet his new wife, casually mentioning that she had been the first Mrs Deathridge."

I could feel Mr Bolus's shock go through my own body.

Mrs Hein! The First Mrs Deathridge! The study door with Meg goggling in amazement at Nick jerking his arse and her red knickers on the floor and laughing over his shoulder! Close harmony at the piano!

It was her he left because he wanted children — well he had certainly achieved that — I felt quite sick even though Clare had kindly substituted chicken pieces in a gentle tarragon sauce on my plate instead of the lambs' testicles.

"That was when I realised I should have extended my enquiries further back to his earlier career before he moved to Bern. When I opened up that can of worms and heard about his lurid disputes with his ex-father-in-law it was too late to warn Furzy I had made a mistake. I could see that he might not appreciate playing second fiddle to Jacob Bott."

I smiled at the irony of Nick exchanging a good-natured, generous father like Adam for a fierce Patriarch ...

"I saw them safely away to their car," said Mr Bolus, his expression indicating how relieved he was to be rid of the Heinses. "Outside was the latest model Espada, spotlessly bright white, and looking out the rear window was a little boy with red-gold curls. I had a moment of apprehension: failing to inform Mr Furzy of a brief early marriage might be excused, but a son? That was surely an oversight too much. However, Hein took the child on his arm to show him to me saying he was their little Roger. Besides, at no more than about two, he was clearly too young to be Deathridge's."

Nick had described Papi Bott as a giant with a grizzly red beard, so any similarity between Bott's grandson and Nick could be coincidental. Was Mr Bolus possibly trying to undermine Nick's merit as my lover? Compensating for his own disadvantage by casting doubts on Nick's integrity?

Nick was evidently succeeding with Mrs Bolus; she was flushed and sparkling at him and his face was creasing up even more with suppressed laughter, a carnival mask that didn't hide his machiavellian delight in courting her.

Dear sweet Jesus! this is how he looks when he is throwing all his wit and energy into captivating a clever woman. He has never done that for me.

Clare came and put her best Edinburgh cut glass bowls with her luscious chocolate mousse in front of us, including Nick, daring him to make a fuss in the presence of his hosts. At this challenge Nick's mask broke and he smiled at her broadly enough to show his crooked tooth. Acknowledging her dare he requested coffee, Blue Mountain with fresh cream. He left his mousse untouched but when Clare returned he stood and pulled up a chair from another table, insisting she took his place. Sitting down beside her, he told her to eat her own poison while he drank his coffee.

"You were curious, Leon," he said to Mr Bolus, "how I survived my epic flight by bush plane into blackest Africa..."

I knew tall tales were on the menu.

Having already semi-demolished Bolus with the Queen's equivalent of a medieval feast for her lords, knights and favoured foreigners at Windsor Castle, Nick now continued the joust, including Clare amongst his sparring partners, recounting how, flying over remote scrubland, circumnavigating past tropical storms — no weather warnings — he took what seemed a reasonably safe opportunity to land on the hard salty crust of a lakeside to refresh himself and, sitting in the scant shade of a baobab tree to let his body, shirt and underpants dry, elephant gun to hand, being puzzled how, out of an apparently deserted landscape, he was slowly engulfed in a tide of children and girls, giggling and pointing, and being convinced that it was not so much the colour of his skin or his hair that amused them as the bush of flamboyant red framing his imposing pink penis —

"The more they giggled and edged closer the more it sat up and took notice of them," he said, 'so I had to pack up and go, fast! I had no wish to be gang raped by a horde of irresistibly mischievous youngsters — the boys at school used to bet on who could entice me away from Mrs Dyer; silly asses, it was her bosom I wanted to weep on, my uppity prick was quite content to jiggle away in solitary fulfilment..."

— and remote refuelling stops that also functioned as caravanserai where tough bearded nomads gathered to watch his meticulous shaving, his skin lubricated with oil in the desert conditions —

"decent people, there was no attempt to rob me; they were more rapacious about my Jermyn Street shirts than my offer of rand or dollars in payment — no wonder I arrived back in Zürich nearly naked —"

— and so on, his stories culminating in a description of the all-night feast

Frank had envied, in a tent under the stars, presided over by the chief, with great hunks of unidentifiable animal served on silver platters he claimed were gifts from Queen Victoria, while the main hazard was how politely to decline having sex between courses with his possibly syphilitic serving-girls. Nick told his tale, eyes downcast with fake modesty, then with a look of faraway longing: "A jig with his superb, equally enormous wife would have been much more to my taste, I'd gladly have swapped him my elephant gun for the privilege — if only I had half a dozen condoms handy. A missed opportunity."

Bring on the clowns!

I didn't doubt that Nick's stories were loosely based on fact but I knew how he could shift the vanishing point of truth to suit the mood of the moment. Tonight, for the Boluses, the point centred on sex and a career beyond the limits of the law.

"Considering how you reject my food," said Clare, laughing at him, "I can hardly imagine you enjoying the food of savages."

"Quite wrong, Contessa," said Nick, "I eat your savage food too, slabs of Florentine beef, rabbits, trout; I'd eat locusts dipped in honey if you served them — but chocolate mousse makes me sneeze and my eyes water: definitely not a sexy look for a man with love on his mind."

Nick's look of love encompassed all three of us women.

"Being married with a family alters one's perspective on risk taking," Mr Bolus remarked, reflecting on Nick's hazards in general, not specifically syphilitic.

"Not necessarily," said Nick. "There's still plenty of excitement to be had, though admittedly the attraction of exploring the rosy depths of a giant black cunt isn't so deliriously urgent now I have Sibylla's to sink my dick into."

With that he stood up and offered me his arm. I was sorely tempted to refuse to take it but I hadn't the heart to spoil his exit so I let him hold his arm around me while he solemnly shook hands with all, thanking everyone for a delightful evening.

"It has been a pleasure meeting you, Mr Deathridge," said Mrs Bolus, matching him in solemnity.

"You surpassed yourself this evening," said Clare.

Leon Bolus saw us to the door.

"Your humble servant, Mrs Wittersworth," he said and kissed my hand with a bow. He said it as if we had formed an enduring friendship, unlikely but flattering.

To Nick: "Goodnight, Deathridge — are you never troubled by ghosts?"

Nick smiled noncommittally.

The challenge I heard in Leon's voice which at first I had assumed was of a purely sexual nature I now guessed was a more general testosterone driven rivalry, from one who had spent his life, now near the end, following a safe, prestigious career, for a man who had taken colossal risks and was reaping the rewards and looking forward to an even more fulfilled and prosperous future. Maybe after all it was Leon Bolus for whom Nick had dressed up, to impress him as a gentleman not out of place at the Lord Mayor's table, not just a daredevil sweating in the angst and heat of the African veldt.

Diabolical Nick, embracing me with such demonstrative passion he was practically inviting them into the bedroom — for whatever reason, it was enormously important to him to show the Boluses his triumphant possession of the woman he loved: Sibylla, in his eyes so beautiful, the mother of his child, dressed in the dress he bought, wearing his jewels. He was determined there should be no doubt in the Boluses' minds about the conquering power of his love.

Nick woke up in the morning groaning.

"My head! I must have got carried away and drunk too much of Tomàs's god-awful wine."

"It wasn't the wine," I said. "You were talking too much."

"My cock was so worked up it kept me on edge all night."

"You were lusting after that woman..."

"I have a superstitious dread of syphilis. I should have risked it; she was probably perfectly all right and anyway it can be cured nowadays..."

I giggled. "You mean the black cunt; I was thinking of..."

"She liked me. Every time she leant over to offer me a delicious morsel of tubercular cow lung her tits brushed my arm... shit! I'm such a headless chicken, look at this stupid cock! I swear when I face the firing squad Dick will still be standing to attention — lie down and shut up," he said, addressing his cock, which was looking for notice as if it hadn't had more than enough homage paid to it the night before.

"What were you and Mrs Bolus talking about?" I asked.

"You, of course," he said.

"Me? That must have been pretty boring for her."

"Oh, no. She was quite intrigued. She started it by mentioning the fox-hunting controversy so I told her how I took you to a hunt but you went home to bed with my best friend instead. You know I can be quite diverting when I put my mind to it. I got myself quite twitchy bragging about what a fantastic cunt you are, how many adoring lovers you've left expiring of broken hearts, your fame as muse — I offered to show her Dad's paintings but she declined — I described our fuck-fest in New York in graphic detail, I said your wedding was remarkable because you were the most ethereal of brides, ravishingly appealing, and having been laid by every one of the men guests, singly and in groups, including the groom's eminent father, no-one could quite believe you had chosen to marry that pedantic young man with the wild hair and the totally misplaced confidence in his own cleverness."

"Oh, Nick, how could you? It's all very well for you and Paul to make fun of me at the Furzys where no-one knows me and I'm no more than a good story, but in front of people I've just met and I would like to like me, that's unfair, and your description of Gus Wittersworth is way off the mark. Dreadful."

"It's passed the evening nicely," said Nick, unrepentant. "I like talking about you. Otherwise I'd have had to listen to her going on about her horse, her dog, life in Salisbury compared with life in Nairobi or some such rubbish. She loved it; sparks flying across the table indicate the slow burn down below — what a lady!"

"I'll be acutely embarrassed to meet her again. She expressed an interest in the children so I said I'd be in the garden after breakfast and if she had time to come and see them before she goes that would have the opportunity. Now it will be too shameful, especially what you said about my wedding; that was really unnecessary."

"Not a bit, that was the *clou de la soirée*, in fact the point of the whole story."

Nick talking bawdy to an attractive woman was not surprising. I didn't mention what Leon Bolus had told me about not flying with the First Mrs Deathridge to Nick's wedding and his suspicion about the Heins' too young redheaded child. If for whatever reason Nick didn't tell me himself I certainly wouldn't force the subject on him.

Leaving him to brood on his missed opportunity and console himself with sweet-scented soap suds from Santa Maria Novella and his fearsome razor, I went down to let the children play outside, deciding I couldn't be put off my routine by Nick's iniquitous exposure of my love life to a stranger. It occurred to me that in the telling Nick had come to see my multiple lovers as an enhancement of his own self-image as Top Cock.

Mrs Bolus came to join the children and me, looking prim in what was then conventional English county gear: pressed clean jeans with a navy reefer over a white blouse and Gucci loafers, eternally familiar. There was nothing in her attitude that suggested she was shocked by Nick's revelations, but then she was a diplomat's wife so should know how to keep her composure in the most testing of situations, however refined her sensibilities.

She picked Willie up and sat with him on the low wall watching the girls run around. May had a long stick with which she was shooting people. Nick had promised he'd take her to town and buy her a 'real' gun in the afternoon. I did not approve but I was no match for Nick and his daughter. Sweet Augusta was hopping around in circles over the whitewashed stones that marked out one of the neglected flowerbeds, singing to herself, being a blackbird.

Mrs Bolus held Willie, stroking his head of silky dark curls with great affection, and said, "Leon and I always wanted a son, but poor dear, it isn't going to happen now. The doctors give him about six months. I hope he didn't say anything inappropriate to you last night. You looked so radiant coming in with Nick — Leon can get so full of resentment at other people's happiness he nearly loses his sense of decorum."

"Oh, no," I said. "I was flattered that he spoke to me so frankly. You seemed to be getting on all right with Nick. If anyone can be uncompromisingly forthright, he can, but only if provoked, which of course is unlikely to happen with someone like you," I added, challenging her on what I considered her frivolous encouragement of Nick at his worst.

She smiled broadly and I wasn't sure if she winked at me or just twinkled. "Oh, I realise he was going out of his way to scandalise me but I'm fairly immune to men with balls. I have a brother who is not that much different — in fact they have a remarkable lot in common ..."

"Willie is our baby," said May, taking aim. "You can't have him."

"I know, you horrid little Deathridge," said Mrs Bolus laughing. "I have a little brother of my own."

"I have lots of brothers," said May off-hand and ran away to ambush the cat.

"Nick thought he might have met you before," I said, "but Mr Bolus says it was your sister."

"It was my youngest sister Jane who went to the wedding," she said. "But actually I met Nick years before that when he was about to leave school — not officially, he just walked out — I'm sure that last night he was particularly out to impress me how much he is no longer the boy who stood isolated in misery in the funeral chapel with an utterly forlorn expression on his sweet face, pink and pouting, twitching between laughing and crying and terribly shy. One wanted to hug him, such an appealingly bashful bad boy. Now he is such an invincible stud he wouldn't want to be reminded how nakedly vulnerable he was back then."

Well, he had certainly succeeded in impressing her, so that would be a satisfaction to him, adding to his conceit — as if he hadn't cause enough already.

"You must come and see us when you're next in England," she said. "I'll give you our phone number."

She tucked Willie back in his stroller and fished a card out of her pocket.

I glanced at it, just Mr and Mrs Leon Bolus and an address in Wiltshire. Well, I thought, if one were going to Abb's Head one might possibly go that way. But with Gus, not with Nick.

Then she went away to the car park where her husband was waiting beside his magnificently old-fashioned Humber Super Snipe and Nick was saying, "I hope you get home with fewer hazards than I faced — unless the French are on strike you shouldn't have any fuel problems. Take a spare can of petrol in case you run into trouble."

"I don't think that will be necessary," said Leon smiling. "I don't expect any pirates either."

"Easy landing, Leon," said Nick, shaking his hand and quite solicitously seeing him into his seat, saying before slamming the door on him, "Don't let me be a burden on your conscience — if you have one."

As the Boluses drove off I joined Nick who was looking after them with a deeply satisfied smile. Sweet face, indeed! Any sweetness had long gone — though when he smiled as now one could catch a glimpse of how engaging he might have been as a youngster.

"A successful visit from your point of view," I said. "You must be very pleased with yourself."

"Yes," he said. "I played my part, keeping my end up splendidly. Don't you know who that was? I was waiting to see how long it would take you to work it out but you never did. My sweetheart!"

He hugged me tight against his body, shaking with a combination of love and laughter.

"That was your sister-in-law, Amanda Wittersworth."

The sheer duplicity of the man! Thinking that after four years I knew the worst of him, I was still astounded at how he could deceive me. I pushed him away.

"You are a complete bastard. Why didn't you warn me? My God, you set me up to look an utter tart in that dress, telling me to leave off the appropriate underwear and got me propositioned by my brother-in-law, and all that swaggering with your cock practically on show and parading May in front of them — you are totally shameless."

"You performed brilliantly," he said, hardly able to contain himself with glee. "I bet it was the formidable Lady Wittersworth who sent her daughter to spy out what you get up to in Italy while poor Gussie is slaving away in Lincoln's Inn. What a stroke of fortune I was here to act as agent provocateur. One up to Deathridge, I'd say, winning on points so far."

"How did you know who she was."

"I wasn't sure at first but I knew from Angelina that Bolus was married to one of the Wittersworth girls. When she mentioned that she quite liked the lambs' testicles — that she'd had much weirder in Africa — I knew she had to be one of the gaggle of girls I'd met before in a rather unfortunate situation; she must have been about nineteen, a year or two older than I. I was so conspicuous in my awfulness she had to remember me but neither of us would admit it, a double bluff."

"Now I see why you were so obviously out to impress her. I thought you were seriously flirting with her."

"Well, I was, like mad. Talking sex with a gorgeous woman over dinner is a prelude to getting into bed with her – one can feel it coming. Given half a chance I'd have done it, if only to fuck Gus Wittersworth — but I couldn't fuck Leon Bolus; wittingly or not, he was a huge help to me in my life of crime."

Infuriating man! God preserve me from jealousy, but I could see how he would enjoy trying out his fuck apparatus on such a challenging woman. I was almost sorry for him that he hadn't had the chance.

"Those Wittersworths are all the same," said Nick. "You can tell she's his sister. I'm amazed you didn't see that."

"That's why she was so interested in Willie."

"That will teach young Wittersworth to try and rob me of my daughter," Nick said, "asserting he has a right to all your children. His mother will give him hell over the promiscuous whore whose bastards he is proposing to bestow the Wittersworth name on. And Willie, the precious son and heir, with diversely illegitimate sisters."

"Oh, dear God, Nick, you are cruel. Utterly heartless! Oh, and all that stuff you told her about me; Jesus Christ, what you said about the wedding — and we didn't even invite her to it! I can't believe how you could do that to me. Did you really say that about Father William? When you knew perfectly well he is her own father? That is truly the pits, the worst thing you could have done."

Nick caught me, lifting me off the ground and perching me on the bonnet of the Jaguar with his arms around me. May instantly clamoured to be put up too.

"Don't worry," he said. "You were beautiful and charming and as you obviously hadn't a clue they couldn't think you were acting the honey for their sake, completely genuine and lovely. And Wittersworth must have learned by now how to stand up to his mother. Besides I'm sure Amanda will use her discretion about what to pass on. Probably not the bit about the wedding. But she'll have plenty to tease young Gus about. I hope she makes him squirm."

"That's not likely," I said. "Wee is not much given to squirming. When the Italians make horns at him he swears right back at them — the advantage of a classical education. And Father William loves me," I added, reassured. "You were right, he really did want to steal me away from you, only he is too decent. I'm sorry he didn't go through with it; I'd have had a lovely life with him and Gus."

"Yes, now they'll know the shameless gusto with which the great Wittersworth enjoyed you; what could be a better guarantee of quality, even in whores?"

"Oh, get over it, Nick. It's been more than three years, the last time just before May was born when we feasted on caviar in Angelina's drawing room. I boldly helped us to a bottle of your champagne; it was wonderful, even better than the Taittinger you gave us on Paul's birthday."

"So it should; it cost considerably more. I chose the rosé because I wanted to see how the pretty pink bubbles would look when you put the glass to your adorable pink lips ..."

"My God, Nick, that's almost a compliment, coming from you, I'd never have suspected it ..."

"But the bottle you snatched was a Dom Pérignon '66, an exceptionally good vintage. It must have added considerably to the lubrication of your cunt. I hope Wittersworth appreciated it. Actually I can't think of a better use for it. When I saw it was gone I only wished it had been me."

"Meg disposed of the empty bottle," I said. "There were so many I didn't think you'd notice one less."

"I have a ledger of a mind; I don't need a cellar book to know exactly where every bottle is. Besides, there weren't many 66's, it was rather hard to come by. If I'd known you could taste the difference I'd have celebrated you and our baby with the vintage rosé — or maybe not, the colour mightn't have matched quite as well and it was the aesthetic delight I was aiming for, exactly that fresh, tender, rose-petal pink. Damn it, Sibylla, I wish I had you back home. I would give anything to go back four years and start again. What's the use of a sharp mind when I can't think how to hold you? You're quicksilver, impossible to grasp — stop dancing on the bonnet, May, you're making dirty footprints all over it. Sit down and I'll polish it with your bum."

He grasped her under the armpits and, to her great delight, slid her on her knickers, with her bare feet kicking in the air, up and down the long, curved length of metal. I wandered off to find Augusta still chanting around in circles and occasionally feeding Willie bits of biscuit from her coat pocket. She had been strictly forbidden to try him on pebbles, leaves or insects.

I rescued Willie from his sister's ministrations and gave him my breast instead. He was practically weaned off it, but it was a comfort to both of us to have a cuddle now and then.

While Nick took May shopping for guns I had a chance to talk to Gus even though it was not encouraged to phone him at work.

"Your sister and husband were here," I said, "they've just left and they didn't tell me who they were because Nick is here. He knew them but he didn't let on and just let me blunder on while he had fun telling her the most disgraceful stories about me."

"The sneak," said Gus. "I expect Amanda egged him on; I can just imagine her and Nick getting on fine."

"She was terribly nice, only Nick was really appalling. I am so embarrassed."

"Outwitting the Wittersworths, as usual! Don't worry, Amanda probably did it as a great joke; she's well able to deal with Nick's scurrilousness. I bet she is in stitches all the way home. I'll phone her when they get back and sweetly ask for news of my darling wife. That will take the wind out of her sails. Can't talk now, too many listeners-in. Bugger off!" The final expletive was obviously not intended for me but someone eavesdropping at the other end.

It was a relief what a calming effect a few words with Wee had. By the time Nick returned I was ready to tackle him again on his general outrageousness: bringing May home equipped with a lifelike rifle as big as herself; playing up to Amanda; and all his innumerable other offences past and present, but as usual without getting the least satisfaction, not a glimmer of remorse or an apology, indeed the more exasperated I got with him the more he enjoyed it until he had me on the bed and smothered my complaints in a barrage of triumphant fucking.

~

A Blip
in the
Economy

I woke up late next morning to find that Willie had been parked in the bed beside me and Nick and the girls were missing. A pot of coffee still warm indicated that Nick had had some breakfast before going out and I sat down at the table to enjoy a cup and brood over how easily he got the better of me.

"My Daddy says the bee-eaters are coming over from Africa," said May bursting in, "and we can go paddling in the sea."

"May's Daddy," said Augusta. "Bee-eaters."

Carefully enunciated, she spoke like Gus already, her personal best Daddy.

"Where is he now?" I asked.

"In the car listening to the goddam news."

Nick came in not long after and went rummaging in the wardrobe where there were clothes that got left behind between visits.

"I feel like a swim," he said producing a pair of blue and white boxer shorts in lieu of his missing swim trunks.

"The sea will be freezing, bee-eaters or not," I said.

I guessed the news hadn't been what he wanted to hear and he needed to take drastic action to calm his impatience.

It was a fine, sunny spring morning and Nick followed the compass to the coast until he found a stretch of sandy beach where he could park at a convenient distance for the children to walk. He strode off ahead of us and as we came down from the road we saw him plunge into the shimmering sea and by the time we sat down and took our shoes off he was no more than a dot in the distance rising and falling in the swell until completely lost from view.

The whole length of beach was deserted but for a couple with their dogs walking briskly away, and voices from distant fishing boats floating across the water was the only sound punctuating the tranquil scene.

May and Augusta ran down and hopped up and down at the water's edge with the surf breaking around their ankles, shrieking that it was cold and chanting "Da-dy, Da-dy" scanning the water to see where he had gone. I sat nursing Willie, enjoying the mild sea breeze and thinking how hardy Nick's body was; for him the satisfaction of pitting his strength against the elements cancelled out the pain; I could not possibly find any pleasure in willingly immersing myself in that cold nothingness, beautiful as it appeared on the surface.

The shouts of 'Daddy' became suddenly more excited when Nick's head unexpectedly reappeared out of the waves quite nearby, and to my horror May, followed by Augusta, floundered out towards him and fell in completely head under where the sand shelved away under their feet.

"Nick," I called in panic, putting Willie down and rushing to the rescue. Luckily their heads were bobbing and Nick was in time to scoop them up before I had to sacrifice my dress to my life-saving nanny skills. I wished I had a camera to record the image of Nick with a streaming wet little girl on each arm.

"We went swimming," said May.

"With your clothes on," I said, stripping them off.

Nick chased them up and down the strand to get warm again, laughing in spite of chattering teeth, then I dressed them in their jumpers and their spare dry pants, and feeling very pleased with themselves they got back in the car. Nick hadn't brought spare underpants so he drove sitting on a towel to protect the leather from his damp bottom, the cotton cling-wrapping his body, heating on full blast, and set out down the steady line of the Via Aurelia through the tunnel of trees to Pisa. There he stood

in the car-park putting his trousers on over almost dry shorts, quite unembarrassed, and made us wait for lunch so he could climb the tower before it
closed.

He bought the girls ice cream to keep them quiet and I stood with them
below in the square, watching for him to reappear. At the top, in defiance of
instructions not to drop anything down, he took a bundle of 100,000 lire
notes and chucked them one by one into the wind and watched them float
away for the pleasure of seeing how far from a straight drop they would land.
Before he got to the ground again they had melted away like snowflakes in
the sun.

"Did you catch any?" he asked. That was as much as he'd said to me all day.

"You didn't expect me to compete with boys and beggars, did you?"

I was indignant when I understood he had nothing left for a meal. He
bought the children more ice-cream with coins from the pot of car-parking
money and went on a walk around the baptistery while they stood and
licked; no drips, spills or crumbs allowed in the car.

A fast Jaguar ride brought us back to Clare, very hungry.

Though Nick made no comment on our day, he looked happy, still glowing from his swim. And the vicarious thrill of being penniless pleased him.

Ever after the Pisa experience I took care to have enough cash in
my bag to buy food in case Nick decided to gamble all on some other ridiculous proposition.

After dinner Nick as usual spent an hour sitting on the wall while Tomàs
smoked his evening Havana, continuing his philosophical discussion on
wealth and how it's created; assets, their actual and symbolic value, scarcely
mentioning something as ephemeral as cash.

"My grandfather used to complain that they wouldn't consult him on how
to win the war," he said when he came in. "He told me to look behind the
Punch and Judy show on the stage and spot how the money is moving.
I know just how he felt — not that I'd want to waste my time on a pig-headed
government doomed to failure. With Tomàs I may get some positive result."

What kind of result had he achieved when he threw handfuls

of paper lire into the wind and watched them waft into the insolvent hands of children and beggars below? That could only cause an unsustainable blip in the local economy. I could understand Clare's anxiety that he would influence Tomàs equally foolishly.

~

Rain
Dance

Early in the morning I came from the bathroom in two minds whether I wanted to go back to bed or not, undecided between getting the children up to start the day and the pleasure of being there when Nick came crashing back to earth from his eternal wanderings in the darkness of his soul. As always time was running out and I knew his departure must surely be imminent. And the really annoying thing was that Angelina with her safety-net of green foam to ease his formulaic home-coming marriage rite didn't appreciate his oh so desirable matitudinal stiff willie. For my part, having him beside me to fuck the day awake was probably what I would miss most about him when he went.

Nick however was sitting on the side of the bed inspecting the sole of his foot — one of his obsessions was the condition of his feet — and while he did that his genitals were dangling idly for once. Observed impartially, I considered that they were only marginally more bulky than for instance Father William's, but then Father William was a bigger, altogether more substantial man. Or Gianni who was so harmoniously proportioned in all his parts. Nick's appeared all the more prominent because they sat so self-aware upfront, the centre point of his slender figure. His years of dangling on ropes above precipices, inching his way across sheer rock faces didn't show so much in his lean arms and angular shoulders as in the athlete's thighs, strength I was made aware of when he gripped and bent me to his will, fucking to high heaven. Dressed by his tailor's skill in slim fitting clothes he was nevertheless imposing. It's all posture and attitude, I concluded.

I knelt on the floor beside him and when he was satisfied that his feet were blemish free, uncontaminated by the Tuscan earth, I laid my cheek against his tender inner thigh and hugged him.

"You are beautiful," I said.

"No-one has ever said that to me before," he said.

"I've never seen anything more godlike than how you appeared, emerging from the sea, a colossus in wet shorts, with the little girls screaming with fearful delight in your arms..."

"Oh, Sibylla, that is the oldest cliché in the world for impressing a woman: save her babies from drowning — none of my other women presented me with such a golden opportunity."

"I can't believe that with all the stories of your girlfriends fighting over you, none of them told you how splendid you are just for being you, no heroics needed."

Nick dismissed that. "My relations with women have always been too contentious. None of them took time off from skirmishing with me to tell me they actually like me. Until I saw you looking down at me as if you had been there waiting for me all my life, I had no idea how sincere, unconditional love looked. I saw it in the concentration of your eyes on mine. Even when you say you don't love me I can feel it in every touch, every gesture; I see it in your smile. I am yours."

So different from his agony of desire when engaged in his fuck heroics, this humbly tender declaration moved me to tears. For once Nick overcame his prickly prudishness about being touched to allow me bury my face in his crotch, snuffling like a truffle pig around and between the hairy base and balls of his powerhouse. There I found a gourmet feast, a delight to smell and taste: not only earthy truffles, but oysters, caviar, ginger, vanilla, honey, snails in butter. Between breaths, smiling to see how my kisses incited him to swell and stiffen into his usual impressive size, I said, "This is straight cock worship."

Nick's face expressed pure delight. Possibly he had never before submitted it to being kissed.

"This might be devil worship," he said, "if your traditional devil is a man like me. Lucifer was thrown out of heaven for having better balls than Jesus."

I laughed. "The bible according to Deathrage! As a girl I spent my time praying for the opportunity to commit a sin or two but I didn't succeed until I met you. It took you about five minutes to convert me into a mortal sinner. The enormity of it was thrilling."

"So you finally admit that your reward for pious virginity was getting your first fuck from a cock as good as mine."

"That's not what I said..."

"My friends laughed at me for talking about a girl as if I had never been in love before — which was true, never like this! I was functioning in a trance from one fuck to the next, in a state of constant cock-hardiness challenged by these quasi-modest eyes and your enchanting smile luring me on. Yet every time I responded and came to you, you acted as if you were startled to see me but were too polite to say no."

"This whole business of sex puzzled me. Meg kept asking me what was going on as if having you do your see-saw between my legs until I cried was only something for Meg to make fun of over teacups in the kitchen — the weirdness of it kept me on edge all day and even asleep at night I was dreaming mad dreams about it."

"Fucking requires no explanation. It takes seven days to form a habit; I should have thought that after a month of it you would have known what to expect."

"Knowing what's coming wouldn't make nightly torture sessions any easier either," I said.

"I've spent my life not being afraid, but you scared me witless, a fragile girl with the power to break me — I can't tell you how disconcerting that was, and utterly disarming."

"I can't tell you how disconcerting it was being fucked in grim silence."

"What was there to say? My hardworking cock was doing the talking in the most effective way possible."

"You just wanted to get it done and not to be distracted by my silliness."

"Good grief, if silliness were going to put me off I'd have given up years ago. Cunts don't talk, mercifully. Did I ever mention how much I am enslaved to you, the more fool I?"

"Possibly, but I never believe you."

"Kiss me some more," he said, leaning backwards, chin up, supported on his hands, surrendering himself and at last I grasped the pleasure of being the driving force. Often enough I had felt his explosive energy erupt inside me, but this was the first time I saw it happen. Well, I thought, Dolly Miller could dismiss that as so much superfluous body fluid, but to me it was his vital essence, what made him the man he was.

It was persistent shouts from the children's room demanding to be let up that made us come to our senses and get off the bed, still dazed and dizzy.

The effect on my humour was a feeling of swimming through a sea of sublime contentment; I was at last in full command of the art of loving. It didn't matter to me at all that surrendering his cock to me left Nick quite exceptionally cantankerous, drained of emotion.

He stood at the stove and scrambled half a dozen eggs, piled the resulting mess on a plate, covered it with Donna's rich tomato sauce and, with a fork, and a tea-towel as tablecloth, took it away to go and eat in the car.

"He's gone to the goddamn news again," said May.

She spoke with such well-developed Deathridge derision in her three-year-old voice I had to laugh.

"No date for the general election yet," Nick remarked when he came back, "but it's quite amusing to see the unions self-destruct, taking the government along with them."

He made a second helping of scrambled eggs and tomato sauce and sat at the table eating it absentmindedly, clearly unaware he had already eaten a more than adequate quantity. It rather slowly dawned on me that he was enjoying the political chaos from a distance, and his delay in going home was because he was waiting for some signal that would trigger a welcome return to the fray when his participation might actually be effective.

Hands deep in the pockets of his red crocodile he spent the morning wandering around the vineyards in the wake of Tomàs, the cellar master and, surprisingly, Gino. Nick drifted idly along, seemingly not paying any attention to their discussions, his eyes scanning the horizon as if he were more interested in the possible appearance of a short-toed eagle winging over from Africa, than the closer-to-home prospects for the grape harvest as judged by the buds on the vine stocks.

"It's a rain dance," he said when I came to sit down beside him in the pergola where the workers gathered for their midday meal. "White magic. I'm lending my weight to their worry quota."

In spite of his ridicule of activities in which he took no part, I was reminded of him in the betting shop near Abb's Head when he had me read out the horses' names while he apparently idly observed the other punters. I never knew by what white magic he settled on the winner from the names I suggested. I had a feeling something similar was now taking place in the greater objective of getting Tomàs to think more creatively about his money problems.

I remarked that whenever Gus came to visit he became enthusiastic about the possibility of producing his own wine on a south-facing hillside in Kent, to which Nick said, ignoring any probable offence to Tomàs:

"Well, I wouldn't take this mishmash of a set-up as a starting point. Tell Gus to consult me and I'll do him a system that is simple and efficient."

Then conceding something to Tomàs's sensibilities he added, "It's easier to start from scratch with no hereditary burden of past decisions and other people's mistakes. Tomàs here gets by on his taste and blending ability but the method is patchwork. I doubt Wittersworth would have a sufficiently developed palette to do that — but you could."

"Me?" Such a thought had never entered my head.

"You'd do better to listen and learn from Tomàs so you might be of some use to your husband rather than parading your cunt so inopportunely for Gino to chase."

It took enormous self-possession for me not to die of shame on the spot in the presence of the men. Or at least blush.

"I'll inform my husband of your valued opinion," I said with as much dignity as I could muster, feeling I had been reprimanded by a responsible adult for the immature frivolity of my ways. Nick had effectively made it impossible for me to show my face amongst the men again. The bubble of my vanity was pricked.

Since Nick had driven into the castello yard and into my bed, his presence obliterated every other, so why should he see fit to drag my indiscretions with Gino into the open now? But how could I have supposed that the men wouldn't gossip about me? Or that Nick wouldn't have picked up their jokes and sly comments on what Gino and I did behind the shed or down the lane? It was certain that Nick would not regard Gino as a worthy rival.

Gino, confronted on his own ground by the legendary Nick, was both resentful and curious, but would have avoided a confrontation. Nick however wouldn't let him escape unscathed.

"Your sister Elsa is doing well in Hong Kong," he said, raising his brows at the heap of spaghetti in front of Gino as if it were beneath contempt though of course it was what all the men were eating. Nick had a few slices of Parma ham and some black olives on his plate. Maybe he just wasn't hungry after his dozen scrambled eggs. "She seems to be the intelligent member of the family."

Gino stuck his fork defiantly into his pasta and shovelled it in, trying to ignore Nick's tone of voice, which insinuated that he didn't think much of the Grati, and Gino least of all.

"She is superb and quite fearsome," Nick persisted in the face of Gino's silence. "She runs the Tsang clinics, keeps the girls in check and sorts out the patients. I imagine her ancestor must have been a Madam in a Roman brothel, just what Tsang needs to control his over-enthusiastic clients. It was a stroke of genius on his part to marry her."

"I'm glad my match-making turned out so well," I said.

"She's a useful asset to me too," said Nick.

"She was always keen on you," I said, resentful of his praise of Elsa after being so rude about my uselessness as a wife.

Nick stared at me with his blankest look.

"If you think I have to fuck her to get her cooperation in dealing with tricky Orientals you are quite wrong. Elsa gets her satisfaction out of being a successful businesswoman; she has no interest in leaping in and out of bed with all and sundry."

There was so much implied insult in Nick's words, I got up and retreated in a huff back to the house. He was probably looking for an opportunity to pick a quarrel with me, mentally getting ready to leave.

It was doubly effective because it made Gino determined to steal a march on him.

Clare quite innocently made it possible when, waiting for the traditional Friday evening supper to be served in the dining-room, she engaged Nick in a discussion of how to improve my apartment, Nick fending off any suggestion I should pay extra rent to cover the cost of the restoration work, while Tomàs and Gino were outside in the ablutions scrubbing their hands after their work in the vineyard. I came in through the hall from seeing to the children and as I passed, Gino grasped my arm and indicated the water closet.

I hadn't been alone with Gino since the Christmas incident but my fury with Nick at belittling me for a vain, irresponsible cunt made the idea of eluding the watchful eyes around us appeal to me and with it the possibility of making a fool of Gino, so without more than a second's hesitation I went and waited for him to slip in behind me and lock the door.

"This is a new experience," I giggled as he silently dropped his sap-stained trousers and fumbled with my fanny. "I'm glad you washed your hands but they are still slimy."

"I'll show that arrogant bugger," Gino muttered. "He thinks I'm a stupid peasant."

"Well, so you are, Gino, that's your chief attraction, a free-range animal of a fucker. You don't have to rape me, you know, I'm cooperating as best I can, stuck in a loo."

But Gino was beyond reason, working himself up to a frenzy while I clung on. Reaching for support I grabbed the chain and a flush of water from the tank above gushed around me. I laughed again at the absurdity of it, feeling like Nick's Lorelei, clinging to a rock being battered by waves that threatened to sweep her away into the arms of the river god. In the awkwardness of my position I quickly had enough of Gino's clumsiness and failure to finish.

"They'll all be outside waiting for their turn," I said. "You might as well hang a notice on the door saying 'queue here for free fucks.' For pity sake, stop."

I stood up, wringing out my wet skirt while he pulled himself together. Visibly distressed, he tried to escape out the back door but I wouldn't let him go and made him walk with me into the restaurant, which he did, glowering and daring anyone to make remarks, while I strolled, demonstratively smiling at the other diners. It was hard to tell how much had been heard or surmised. Tomàs would surely have noticed, and Clare's flushed face suggested disapproval, but Nick was talking to Adam and neither showed any sign of either curiosity or displeasure. I sat down beside them while Gino sought refuge on the far side of Tomàs, unnerved by his own folly in provoking Nick.

"My dress is a bit wet," I said, "I had a little accident in the lavatory."

Nick raised a quizzical eyebrow but made no comment, continuing what he was saying to Adam about packing some of his smaller paintings which Nick was prepared to take back to Gillian.

"I'll see to it she sticks to the straight and narrow in the framing department," Nick said, but Adam looked at me, without displaying too much interest, and remarked:

"It's probably not the first time that happened."

"Well, it is," I snapped back, "I've never done it in a loo before."

Nick took my hand and looked at it, and for an eternity of dismay I thought he was about to take his ring back, but all he said was a mildly sarcastic: "you are very fetching when you're angry."

And when I cry, I thought, as tears came to my eyes.

"It's high time I left," Nick said, with an off-hand gesture passing me his handkerchief to wipe my face. He finished the meal in silence while I cursed myself for being so childishly offended by Nick's uncompromising opinion of my folly that to hurt him I had succumbed once again to the intensely pleasurable but self-defeating desire to torment Gino.

Walking through the courtyard back to our apartment Nick put his arm around me but I wasn't reassured, it was the same instinctively protective gesture from the day of the Sea Pigeon when he was getting ready to leave me to fend for myself with a bank card and my winnings instead of himself.

We went out through the archway and leaned on the wall overlooking the misty land below. We seemed to have run out of anything to say until, turning to go in, Nick broke his silence:

"Don't think I won't settle with your fucking peasant. It will be easy enough to fix a hunting accident when we go after the boar. It will give me the greatest pleasure to put a bullet through him where it hurts most. I'll blast his balls off."

Nick took aim down the valley with an imagined rifle.

"We used to practise from our réduit positions who could score at 400 meters," he said. "Just knowing we could do it was enough to win the war."

A war of nerves, I presumed, rather than in actual combat.

Holding me close as if to shield me from the mythical demons of the Italian landscape, he led me up our stairs to bed, but when we got there we were both too drained to do anything but lie side by side in the dark. I could already feel the pain, anticipating the emptiness he would leave behind when he got into his Jaguar and drove away down the zigzag track that led to the rest of his life.

"May said you were listening to the goddamn news. She is learning the same bad language your grandfather taught you," I said.

"You drive me to goddamn despair," said Nick. "Once again, for a moment you trapped me into thinking that you might love me, but obviously nothing has changed... every morning the first thing I do is stretch out in my desire for you and you are not there; I wake up in your absence. The exquisite pleasure of having you beside me is multiplied by all those mornings of emptiness. I am leaving tomorrow."

"I'm used to being left."

Adam joined May and me to say good-bye to Nick as he departed. Adam, I thought, looked unusually pensive. It occurred to me that I might look like that in thirty years time when May drove off into a world beyond my power to protect or influence, when I would just have to accept whatever choices she made for herself.

"I always thought it something of a miracle," said Adam, watching brake lights disappear around the bend of the road, "how I got as remarkable a son as Nick."

"He's a remarkably puzzling lover," I said.

"It's understandable that a lull in the Blitz was enough for two young people to fuck away their fear of imminent death, but what were we thinking of to have a baby? We considered a termination — Nathalie knew a good address — but Dumez père was delighted to have her pregnant, thinking that would keep her at home, and told me to get to hell up to Glasgow where I'd been posted, but Nathalie's mother would have none of that and insisted we get married and leave together, more to get Nathalie out of London than any moral consideration. I counted myself extremely lucky on all fronts until she decided that if she were going to die in childbirth in the middle of an air raid it might as well be in the comfort of her father's house and not in slummy digs with me. So that's Nick: the wonder of conception and birth in the midst of death and destruction."

Lucifer falling or Phoenix rising?

"The evening when you came through the door with Gino," Adam went on, "I saw how Nick's hand closed on the steak knife, balanced loosely, prepared to strike. Yet by the time you reached us he betrayed nothing of his killer instinct. I was truly impressed by such passion and such self-control."

I didn't say that Nick had merely replaced one lethal plan with a better one. He was calm because he could afford to wait; when he hurts he does it with cool precision.

"Nick is in a rush to get back to London," said Adam. "Now the government is going to the country at last, he'll be there to add to the pressure on the new chancellor for a more laissez-faire monetary policy."

Oh, Adam!

Clearly Nick's sessions with the car radio were his rain dance and had achieved the desired result. He could go now and lend his weight to the nation's worry quota.

"If he gets what he wants," said Adam, "the world will become once more one big melting pot of riches. Not that at the worst of times the law ever stopped Nick happily juggling doubloons, dollars, his precious *Stützlis*..."

"Like chucking lire into the wind off the top up the Tower of Pisa," I said, bitterly disillusioned.

~

The Consolation of Philosophy

6

Shortly before Easter Gus came to spend his term break and the happiness of being with him reminded me once again why I had married him. Tweedledee needed no explanations, we carried on from where we left off as if there were no time or distance between us.

Our little tribe was complete again. Even May, disconcerted that it wasn't her Daddy being hugged with such joy, allowed herself to be caught up in the circle with Augusta and Willie.

"You're not Daddy, are you?" she asked him and he had the wit to understand her confusion.

"I'm Augustus Wittersworth," he said, "and you can call me Gus. All my best friends do."

"Gussie, Gussie, Gussie," May chortled, delighted at having this question of identity satisfactorily solved and as he went flying down the path to the vineyards holding Willie aloft like a mini aircraft with outstretched arms, she raced after him not to be left out of the fun. Augusta and I followed at a pace more suited to little legs.

When I caught up with him, Gus said, "The Deathrage phoned to tell me that my divine wife is rolling in the shit with the vineyard satyr. 'You are very kind,' I said to him, 'it's so nice to be kept up-to-date with the latest reports from the fucking battlefield. Do I understand that you retired hurt?'"

"I'm afraid he did," I said. "Did your sister tell you about meeting him?"

"Amanda congratulated me on getting the most alluring, captivating, amiable girl in the world to be my wife and Willie, the most gorgeous baby she ever saw, except for me of course, and why on earth we hadn't invited her to the wedding, so I had to do the usual grovelling. Then she said she was thrilled she had the chance to see the Deathrage in action again after so many years so she could tell her friend Maddie Madigan the latest gossip about him — including the riveting detail that he is madly in love with and furiously fucking her dazzling new sister-in-law: Maddie, she claims, will be jealous!"

"Oh Lord," I sighed, "not another one!"

Gus went on: "I was fascinated to know in what episode of his mysterious past might this jealousy be rooted and Amanda said she'd tell all when we had time to talk. Unfortunately Leon's condition got worse and we didn't have the opportunity with Mother fussing around and getting worked up about Leon's pension. Amanda did say that Leon's meeting with Deathridge affected him profoundly. He was brooding over it so much on the road home she had to drive all the way; at the time she thought it was the journey, now she blames Leon's catastrophic collapse on Nick for making him feel an utter fool. I was tempted to say Nick is such a merchant of death it's not surprising the cancer cells jumped for joy at the chance to do their damnedest but I thought that might be tactless so I held my tongue. Poor Leon, the last thing one needs when at death's door is Old Nick giving one a kick in the arse."

"Nick was remarkably nice to Leon," I protested. "He did his absolute best to amuse him and saw him off with a gently understanding farewell."

"I'm not so sure I'd like to have that diabolical con artist being kind to me when I'm not feeling too good," said Gus. "A bit like the Walrus and the Oysters."

"When Nick arrived for May's birthday he was in such awe-inspiring Nickishly splendid fuck-form that I fell in love with him all over again," I said. "It was when Amanda came and reminded him of things he'd rather forget, such as the acutely unhappy youth he was when she first knew him, that he started to be difficult. Whatever it was that they were both not saying, that's when the devil got into him. He was brilliantly awful while she was here, entertainingly outrageous, then for the rest of the time quite impossible. He was in a testosterone driven fury that nothing could appease — I was on my knees. The annoying thing is that he gets ever more maddeningly sexy the more he is driving one to despair with his contrariness."

"Nick uses sex to control his despair, it seems to me," said Gus. "Fucking is his alternative to killing himself."

I didn't like to hurt Gus's pride by making comparisons, but couldn't resist saying Nick's sperm fountain was quite the most impressive thing I'd ever seen, positively monumental, it would make a fine addition to the Villa d'Este gardens.

"Maybe he'll let us cast him in bronze for the garden when we move into our house — pour épater les tantes as Nick himself would say, spurting sky-high and streaming down in cascades."

I hugged Gus again in the sheer relief of having such a sweet, reasonable, generous man for husband.

"Adam thought he was frustrated by the news from England because of the financial situation. Nick kept on throwing it at Adam as if it's all his fault..."

"So it is," said Gus, "men of Adam's generation won the war but messed up the peace."

"But," I went on, "what was really interesting was the discussion he and Adam had about Nick as a boy. They have such a different perspective on what really happened. I wish I'd known sooner that the circumstances of his mother's death were so distressing for him."

I told Gus the gist of what I'd learned, but to my surprise he knew all about the scandal surrounding Nathalie Dumez's disappearance.

"You could have mentioned it to me," I said.

"We law lords deal in truths, not conjectures," he answered loftily. "Father says some rag newspaper reporter happened to be in the West Indies when her body was recovered and sent a story back as a bit of gory gossip of little substance; it was picked up by other papers — people love gruesome details and someone made a connection with her father who shot himself, so that started the speculation he did it because of his daughter's war record. It was just conjecture made with hindsight and probably not true. They went digging in the dirt to find her sexual partners in St Barth's but no one there would talk to outsiders. Other than that there was nothing in it. No murder mystery."

"But, Wee, that is quite something to Nick — why he was so unhappy at school and why Adam wouldn't take him to rescue their boat, to keep him away from such hideous publicity. Neither Adam nor Nick will talk about it, they both circle around the subject."

"That's their affair."

"But it is mine too when Nick is being extremely unpleasant to me," I protested, annoyed that Gus was dismissing it as of no importance.

"Just deal with Nick as he is; knowing how he got that way makes no difference."

"Oh, yes, it does; it explains why he is so unpredictable."

"He's not unpredictable," said Gus. "I'd say he is remarkably consistent. Your expectations are out of step with his reality."

"Dr Tsang said the same to Angelina." I remembered from the scene when May was born when she finally had to face up to the knowledge that Nick did not match her illusion of the perfect husband.

"The odd thing is that when Nick and Adam were talking about bombs and black-market rabbits I had to laugh; the way Nick tells it, it sounds positively comic. With his clownishly deadpan expression, only by the odd blink or twitch revealing what he's thinking, he interprets his whole life as something of a joke, so that his grandfather blowing his brains out is more of an unfortunate contretemps that nearly stopped him going to a football match than a crisis that altered the course of his life. He seems to think that growing up in a large gloomy house on the edge of Hampstead Heath with a crazy grandfather and a war on constitutes a blissfully happy childhood. Where does that leave Miss Pinkerton's theories of responsible child care?"

Gus laughed. "Nick and I have a lot in common," he said.

"That's what your sister said," I said. "But now I think of it, what you have in common is me."

But now Nick was hors de combat — if only temporarily.

I was glad that Gus would be here for Gino and Giulietta's Easter wedding, but quite surprised when Gus said, "Elsa isn't coming but Tsang will be. He is visiting the Vatican and he'll be here any day now to see how you and his babies are getting on. He asked as a special favour if he could spend a night with you. I told him to fuck off, that any such decision is yours. He reminded me that I'd said I'd like to see the Sex Guru in action, I said that he had missed his chance at the Gang Bang."

"Good," I said. "The pills he sent me to try out for him seem to have worked against Nick's invasive little buggers; if I stop taking them I can probably trick Tsang's into doing their job and giving me the sweet little China baby I wanted"

"That's not what he has in mind," said Gus. "It's sublime Zennish fusion of body and soul he's after."

"Maybe that's what he'll get for himself, but all I want is his sperm. I know it means you'll have to lay off, not to get my eggs too confused, but you've surely had enough of Evita sucking you off to last a while..."

"Actually no," said Gus. "Now I'm a grown-up professional gentleman I've put such youthful indiscretion behind me."

"It seems a pity to waste Evita's talent to please," I said, not to be too blatant about how pleased I was to hear it.

"She regales Father with horror stories of what she had to put up with professionally, it makes him feel virtuous that all he wants is a reasonably uncomplicated fuck. I had to tell her to just let me do it and not talk to me. I'm not totally Zen but I like to enjoy it with a pure mind and not be put off by sordid details. Nowadays I take long lunch breaks in the Bunghole with the chaps and work late. Cycling home dodging taxi-drivers after a long day is all the exercise I need."

"So mindless sex with Evita has been filed away with fastidious Catullus in your archive of what not to do," I said, laughing at him. "Nick was ecstatic when I kissed his cock but after it he was fiendishly moody. He didn't get it up again before he drove off home in a huff."

"I suppose he was mortified that he let a flighty cunt like you take control."

"I must confess I went out of my way to annoy him even though Mr Big is quite immensely satisfying."

"I've moved beyond Nick being my exemplum of the Erasmus-Socratic hero to the Hegel interpretation. It's all about Selbstbestimmung, the freedom and sovereignty of the self…"

"Maybe," I said. "If so, Nick's sovereignty is in his balls…"

"More likely it's buried under the Paradeplatz with his gold," said Gus. "There's nothing like a nice hoard to enhance one's Selbstbestimmung and stiffen the cock."

"My nemesis is that my Selbstbestimmung crumples at the sight of him. Perhaps with Tsang I'll really get to the bottom of understanding life; the Tsang Art of Fucking is surely the path to enlightenment."

"My dear Sibylla, if your cunt were the path to enlightenment you'd be the wisest woman on earth."

"Well," I said, "you do say I am the Sibyl."

The stable-yard apartments had been booked by the Grati family for the wedding. Biba and Luigi came and brought Xin, the Number One China Baby. I studied Biba for signs of Dr Tsang's influence — one could hardly imagine what it must have been like for her cocooned in her flowery apartment as his queen bee — but the Hong Kong experience had left her apparently unchanged. She looked happy, coming to her son's wedding; a good Italian woman was the next best thing to the church and she hugged and thanked me as if I had anything to do with this satisfactory outcome.

Luigi said nothing, but the glances we exchanged behind Biba's back said it all: mutual gratitude and forgiveness.

While they took the opportunity to travel south visiting relatives, Biba agreed to leave Xin with me so Dr Tsang could have a few days with his daughter. I thought this was taking a big risk. Gus had already kidnapped Augusta. How did they know Tsang wouldn't do the same? But then, Biba might not want to have to explain to her grandmother and aunts how she and Luigi came to have an obviously anomalous China baby.

Dr Tsang arrived all the way from Rome, where he had been speaking at a Vatican seminar on fertility, in a very large white Mercedes seated beside an affable Monsignor who blessed us all impartially and distributed holy medals amongst the children. His chauffeur unloaded Dr Tsang's luggage and carried it through the archway before they departed again on their way to Paris.

"Usually I have my masseur fly to Rome for my nose," Monsignor explained, "but this week I am making the trip instead, saving him the trouble of the journey and at the same time taking a little holiday."

He had a very prominent fleshy red nose so evidently the weekly massage wasn't doing much to cure it. My irreverent thought was that maybe a large red other body part was doing better out of it.

I noted there was no futon carrier in the neat row of bags and cases. Dr Tsang, standing there in the sunlight in the courtyard observing the children, the stone wellhead, the doves basking on the roof-tiles, was substantially present in his solid flesh, a golden Buddha. He bowed to me with his usual reverential politeness, and I was surprised at how strange it felt to embrace him again. The first time it was a lesson in the Art of Fucking he undertook at Nick's behest but finished by asking me to go home with him. I had rejected all his offers to go just as he had resisted my requests for sex; this time I hardly supposed he'd come for an idle fuck, so what did he want?

Gus came with Xin on his arm to say hello, handing her over in to her father and took Willie from me in exchange, leaving me to get on as best I could. I felt he was handing me over too: allowing me Dr Tsang was his quid pro quo for my acceptance of Evita.

Xin, who was a year old, looked a proper China baby, not a hint of Grati about the calm way she took to Dr Tsang and continued to observe the world from the vantage point of his arms.

"I have Nick's redhead imp, the Grati beauty, Willie the Wittersworth with a feather in his cap: a China baby would add nicely to my score," I said.

Dr Tsang merely smiled his politely inscrutable smile and followed me up the dark stairway into my apartment. He looked around the living room with some surprise but seemed pleased enough. Then I led him into the bed-room. The plank bed with its feather mattress must be at least as comfortable as his futon on the floor so he could not complain.

"It is not quite as lush as Nick's Chinese Chippendale,' I said, "but I think you'll find it comfortable enough if you care to share it with me."

Dr Tsang eyed me as if calculating the degree of comfort I was likely to provide him. At least it wasn't his manner to get on top and hump me into the flat earth the way Nick did.

My nervous babbling seemed to pass over his head as he took in all the details of my life. In his serene presence I had an uncomfortable feeling that my memories of intercourse with him were no more than the lurid obscenities of my imagination. I thought: he is such a Buddha, transcend-ently indifferent to the material world. He comes trailing the clouds of heaven with him; I had visions of skyscrapers floating above the mist, sparkling in the sun, untouched by the crowded squalor beneath.

Dr Tsang put his clothes-bag down on a chair with an air of having arrived where he wanted to be and said "I have been anticipating the pleas-ure of having this time with you. You are looking very well. How old is your baby now?"

I knew he knew perfectly well that Willie was seven months.

"I might well get pregnant again," I said, "Nick does his best but thanks to you I've managed so far to elude his furious little wrigglers— even you haven't succeeded in depleting him with your demands — are you here to try out how active yours are?"

Dr Tsang shook his head and smiled, saying:

"Wittersworth is your husband now; you have made your choice. However, I offer my services in a non-reproductive capacity."

I had to make the best I could of that because, putting Xin down in the middle of the bed, he unfolded his spare suit from the suit carrier, draped his black silk robe ceremoniously across the foot of the bed, then requested tea, leaving me still confused about his intentions.

We went out to the garden, and Tsang devoted the rest of the afternoon to playing with the children. Gus and I sat side by side on the low coping around the fountain and remarked on how he could squat on the ground at toddler level and remain unruffled and perfectly dignified under the delighted onslaughts of the little ones. Xin sat on his knee and batted off the others who were trying to storm the castle and take her place. Did she know that she and Dr Tsang had something in common not shared by the others?

"I'm pleased he married Elsa, she suits him. He'd never have done for me. It will be interesting to have sex with him again but there's no thrill in it. If it were Nick I'd be a quivering jelly of nervous anticipation."

"Dr Tsang is so formal and polite," said Gus, "it's hard to see him as a lover, but as a father he is doing all right."

"It does seem a pity he can't have his only child," I said.

"He should have thought of that before he used up his one shot at paternity on a scientific gamble instead of confining his effort to his wife." Gus was unimpressed by Tsang letting science get the better of common sense. "But there's no reason for me not to emulate Nick and get half a dozen — if I can get my wife to cooperate."

"Not until you can provide a house to accommodate us all."

'Don't worry, I'll get you a glorified hovel with enough room for your wildest extravagances."

"Nick said I wouldn't be able to trick Dr Tsang into giving me a baby. It would be a triumph if I succeeded."

"I don't suppose there is anything against a Law Lord being putative father to a Chinese child," said Gus, quite unperturbed.

"Well," I said, "you have Willie."

"We'll have to take him to meet Mother. Polly has gone to Ireland to go into partnership with a racehorse and Jane is off to Bahia to find creepie-crawlies in the Mata Atlântica so it's getting a bit quiet at home. Mother will be pleased to see you and Willie."

"In spite of Amanda's report, based on Nick's scandalous revelations?"

"I told Amanda she needn't believe a word Nick says but she says she can see that perfectly well for herself but it's too good a story not to be true.

I indicated it would not be wise to repeat anything he said to Mother. I said 'talk to Father instead.' But of course she can't, she can hardly ask him if it's true he joined in gang-banging his lovely daughter-in-law."

"Nick is pitiless — it's his revenge on me for forcing him into such a situation — gosh, I wish I could do it over again; I was shaking and shattered after the three of you but he took me on and made me finish it. He is magnificently uncompromising."

"I'm glad I had the chance to see him in action,"said Gus. "I was so young, I could hardly believe he'd do all that — in his fancy evening gear, what a spectacle!"

"I am absolutely mad for him but I can't forgive him for telling Amanda." I said. "It's such a breach of confidence."

"Amanda won't tell. She always protected me from the other three Harpies. Now they have gone it's safe for you to come home and face the Gorgon. You won't turn into stone; she is harmless really. Father is even making plans to take Evita home with him when he retires to concentrate on his writing, though he hasn't mentioned that to Mother yet."

"Good luck to him," I said. "If anyone can get away with setting up a ménage à trois with a Girl Guide supremo and a Filipina sex slave it would surely be Father William with his reputation for prudence and good sense."

"Paul wanted to come with me but when I told him Tsang would be here he backed off."

"Good grief, that would really have been an embarrassment of riches," I said, shocked at Gus's off-hand announcement. "He has been marvellously conscientious about my further education, sending me stuff to read with notes attached like 'this will tickle the brain cells' or ' this is to titillate the imagination' but he says nothing about his own love life."

"He wants you to meet his fiancée but he could see that with Tsang around his presence wouldn't be given due importance so regretfully he chose to stay away."

"What happened to the night-club hostess Nick was talking about?"

"This is her."

"Has he given up the idea of going into politics then? I doubt his local committee will select an unsuitable wife."

"On the contrary. Madge is the driving force behind him, an ambitious Australian, skinny girl and sharp as a pin. She'll goad him to the top all right. They got together over the goat. Paul was telling his friends the antics of the goat and Madge chipped in with advice because she grew up surrounded by frisky sheep. Paul invited her to come home with him but she said home visits to clients were not part of her job description. Nick manoeuvred them into it. He went to meet her at the club. Gianni introduced them so she knew he was bona fide, otherwise she would have been staggered at how he questioned her. She says it was like a very stiff job interview: her qualifications, her intentions, her relationship with Paul. 'I mean,' she said 'he even asked me how often we had sex, like, on a weekly average over the last three months!' She told him she was a hostess not a whore. Paul thought this was pushing big-brotherliness too far, but Madge took it all as perfectly reasonable when at the end of it Nick proposed she move in with Paul, with a clear statement of terms and conditions: she's allowed to keep a dog as long as she looks after the rest of the menagerie that's accumulating in the back garden. So after a trial period living in sin on the top floor where Paul used to sleep with you, Mrs Furzy was presented with a fait accompli and they are officially engaged. It won't be quite the county wedding she envisaged but in fact it's highly suitable. Madge has a degree in economics."

"What on earth was she doing acting as hostess in a night-club then?"

"Selecting a suitable husband, I suppose."

"How rational! How glad I am that you selected highly unsuitable me, Wee dear! Without you my life would be sheer chaos."

Gus kissed me. "The best of luck with the Chink," he said, his eyes twinkling with mischief. He seemed to take the whole Tsang thing as a joke. I thanked my lucky stars for Evita.

Dr Tsang made his silent ritual of invocation to whatever spirits he wished to enter him prior to getting into bed with me. His approach was as decorous as when he came to deliver my babies, as solemn as Holy

Communion. I thought: he has it in his power to give me new life. After all, I asked him to do this often enough and here he was at last; what more was there to say? All I had to do was lie down with my knees up and let him get on with it.

"One thing puzzles me," I said, "why you have been so resistant to me when you do it all the time with others. And at the Grati you were busy getting Biba to have your baby when you should have been saving me."

"I am governed by reason and scientific curiosity," he said. "I could give you any number of rational explanations for why: I could say that I tried to get you to listen to me but you had to make up your own mind."

It was only when he'd gone to the bathroom, which he converted into a haven of sybaritic repose, scenting the air with his lotions and oils, that I realised he hadn't answered my question.

The Sex Guru was in abeyance. Dear Dr Tsang had come more modestly as friend and lover, which seemed appropriate for our future child if we had one — and I felt it might be a real possibility as Dr Tsang was quite un-Zen-like in expressing pleasure. I was the one who felt detached from the moment. Que sera, sera!

I was woken up in the early hours before dawn by the sound of jazz music, someone playing the piano very loud with a teasingly insistent beat, and I lay listening, trying to think what that tune was, until I realised the music was in my head.

It's Nick, I thought, he's mocking me again.

"You want erotic? You want ecstasy? You want a baby? He's a Chinaman for pity sake, how do you imagine he has the balls to give you what you want? You poor goose, that's what you had me for, no one does ecstasy better than I! You broke my heart, you killed me, and now you're in bed with a fucking Chinaman! Use you wits, woman, if you have any."

His voice was so clear in my head I could hardly believe he wasn't there at the foot of the bed, holding forth in that tone that was beyond sarcasm.

Shut up, Nick, I answered him in my head. Just go away and shut up. If I broke your heart, it's because you were tearing the life out of mine.

Nevertheless, the tune haunted me, insistently, tormenting me because I couldn't put a name to it. If only I could interpret it properly I'd understand the meaning of life. But I had to acknowledge that he was right, Nick had the answer, not Tsang.

I couldn't sleep so I got up and had a shower. When I came out Dr Tsang was sitting with the China baby on his lap letting her smell his apothecary bottles and telling her the names of the ingredients in Chinese.

"We'll go and find new scents out there later," he told her, pointing out the window to the hills beyond the vineyards.

"Well?" said Gus when he saw me.

"He is certainly a very competent lover," I said. "But I still don't know why he's here."

"He looks positively happy," Gus remarked. "It's only a fraction more expressive than his normal attitude, but perceptible none the less."

"But actually," I said, "I am concerned that he sees sex as spiritual fulfil-ment, which is not what I need, not after a whole glorious month of Nick giving me his abundant all — if I don't get my China baby I'm going to be so cross."

Gus stayed close to me all day, while Dr Tsang again busied himself with the children. He called on Marco and the castello's older children to get their go-carts and loaded the babies into them on cushions, and the proces-sion set off, disappearing into the distance with the little ones toddling bravely after him. Biba might have been shocked to see her precious China bumped along over the stony ground but she was no less precious to Dr Tsang and he wasn't worried.

We didn't see them again until late afternoon when they trailed back, hot and tired but smiling, with bunches and wreaths of wilting flowers; hands, feet and faces stained. "Rites of Spring," I thought and wondered what initi-ations into what mysteries had taken place out there in the hills.

At dinner that evening Dr Tsang and I gathered with Adam, Gus, Clare and Tomàs. Clare thanked Dr Tsang for the good time Marco had enjoyed with him. According to Marco's account of the outing they had stopped at a farm for bread and cheese, played games in the wood and rested in the shade.

"Children notice and remember what is appropriate to their age and interest," Dr Tsang remarked, noncommittally.

"And the botany lesson?" I asked.

Dr Tsang smiled his deprecating smile, saying, "children learn the fundamental facts of life like flowers that unfold in their own time, at their own pace."

"I wish I had known Dr Tsang when I was a child," I said. "When I think how I was left to blunder along in ignorance with my great-aunt telling me my best friend is Jesus in heaven!"

I explained to Clare: "Dr Tsang is my guru. He initiated me into the true facts of life, as well as coming all the way from Hong Kong to help me giving birth to my babies."

Clare, as if suddenly enlightened, glanced at Gus who was unperturbedly picking the bones of his guinea fowl.

"He's the Number One Fuck Artist from the Orient," he said between mouthfuls. "At least Sibylla says so."

After dinner we gathered in Adam's studio and Dr Tsang admired Adam's recent works and his work in progress. Dr Tsang's preference was for the stark black and white of the drawings, murmuring phrases like 'direct communication of the inner nature of things' and 'a clear perception of the truth'. I wondered if there were anything he couldn't talk about in such terms. He understood Adam's difficulty in keeping the misty-eyed softness of the land and culture out of his own vision.

"That acrobatic couple is approaching Tiepolo," he remarked.

I was shocked to realise this must be a recording of something he had seen. My image had escaped my control, any passer-by could take it away from me in his head. Uncanny! But it explained what had always disturbed me, how I had no control over the men who fell in love with whatever it was they saw in me.

"I know," said Adam, "I'm disappointed. Softened by the cold distance, it doesn't show the dangerous edge that I wanted to give it. The question is how to make it factual, unemotional and also erotic. I will have to do it over again."

"It is the same as in my work," said Dr Tsang. "It is the passion, the devotion to the subject which is so intense, that make the results bitingly sharp and produces the unsentimental image."

"With this one my vision was troubled..."

Troubled it should be, I thought but didn't say, for intruding into my personal life. Way back in Abb's Head posing for the artist had made sense of my existence. But could one own one's own image when anyone can see it?

Dr Tsang courteously acceded to the request from Adam and Gus to pose naked for pencil and camera. He sat so immobile in his Buddha pose that Adam could make a very detailed drawing, down to the last wrinkle, fold and twist of pubic hair, and when he was satisfied Tsang invited me to take my place beside him.

"Observe," said Tsang. We stretched out on the floor on our sides, facing each other, whereupon Gus grabbed his Leica and Adam sat back, content to look and leave Gus the Recording Angel to do the work.

"A living art exhibition," said Adam, his fingers itching already to get started on a great new work.

"Splendid," said Gus, "the photos will be superb. Thank you, Dr Tsang. That was a fine performance, Sibylla. The Oriental Fuck Artist meets the Hottest Cunt in Christendom, what a title for a show of our work, Adam! I am going to develop and print these myself," he said, carefully sealing his roll of film in its canister. "I won't trust them even to my friend at the forensic lab. I can never quite rely on him not to steal copies for his private enjoyment, not that he'd ever dare infringe my copyright; he knows I'd skin him alive if he did. Figuratively of course."

"Well," said Adam, "you have to allow him enjoy them in his own way. After all, the people who buy my pictures have their own interpretation of them. Whatever my intention might have been, once they have gone to their new owners I have no say in how they use them. When I painted Sibylla on the chaise it was a study in form and function, not Sibylla the harlot for Nick to fuck out his emotional distress on."

"Is there an objective reality that is the same to all men?" Gus asked. "Looking at Sibylla I don't think so, all the men who fuck her experience her in their different ways."

"So I don't have an objective reality!" I said, exasperated at that male chauvinist statement.

"Sibylla is a rainbow," said Dr Tsang. "Men chase after her thinking to pin her down to the earth with their pricks, but when the prick is withdrawn there is nothing there, the rainbow has shifted position, the weather has changed, the illusion has moved on."

"I feel real to me," I said.

Dr Tsang re-robed himself in his Shantung suit, converting himself from archaic naked Buddha into world renowned doctor on holiday in Italy, and went out to meditate in the garden.

"What do you and Adam talk about all evening?" I asked Gus while Adam was tidying up his work.

"All the usual topics," said Gus. "Philosophy, mechanical engineering, crime, the meaning of life, chickens and how to cook them, women and how to fuck them. Don't worry about us, we know our place in the hierarchy of your lovers, we are not at a loss to amuse ourselves while your Tsangsi-pu entertains you."

"*Mack the Knife*," I said, suddenly remembering.

"What does that mean?" asked Gus.

"I wish I knew," I said. "Nick tormented Adam by persistently singing that when his mother's remains were found; I heard him play it when I woke up this morning, with such fantastic embellishments I didn't immediately recognise it. It was about half past four; it would have been half past three in England so he must have been awake half the night again..."

"You were having a Sibyl moment," Gus said. "I must remember to ask him, to find out whether it was telepathy or a hallucination."

"Trust Nick to turn up out of nowhere and spoil the party! I'm sorry now that I succeeded in foiling his determination to get me pregnant. I think he's right that Dr Tsang's spiritual approach to sex won't produce anything as matter-of-fact as a baby. Oh, dear," I said, suddenly tearful, "I'm beginning to feel I've made a dreadful mistake; Nick would have been a more sincere, a less fanciful choice — even though his enthusiasm for getting little Nickies out of his Virgins is rather annoying — but then almost everything Nick does is annoying..."

"It's back to the consolation of philosophy for us, Adam," said Gus, sighing with mock resignation as I brooded on the likelihood that Nick would find consolation from my intransigence with his more than willing poppets. Did erotic ecstasy on Tsang's spiritual level come anywhere near the vital satisfaction to be had from Nick's hardy cock? Tsang's complexities made me realise how I adored Nick's lack of fancy footwork in his fanatically straight fucking. The realisation I had alienated him for the sake of Dr Tsang's embellishments was unbearable.

But when we joined Dr Tsang outside he said to Gus, "it's time for me to regain my peace of mind and hand your too beautiful wife back to you. I've achieved what I came for."

"I doubt Sibylla got what she wanted though," said Gus, severely putting the doctor in his place. By Gus's estimate, the duty of reciprocity was out of balance.

Nevertheless, during the following days Gus continued to engage Dr Tsang in conversations that took them, with their trail of attendant putti, for walks around the fields, discussing Gus's thesis for his PhD.

"It's about reading Zeno in the light of modern science, with a nod to the Sceptics," he explained. "The academics thought Zeno totally daft to say that consciousness is a material substance anchored in the body; only with electrodes attached to the brain and the knowledge of how hormones trigger the emotions has his theory become indisputably true, two thousand years too late. But that's where Dr Tsang's scepticism is useful; one needs a degree of doubt to prevent putting a full stop to further questions and castrating research. I admire how he evaluates the evidence in a way that is entirely non-judgemental. Because I am interested in making good law I tend to the dogmatic, Tsang with his open mind teases me out of any complacency."

This surprised me. I would have thought Gus was the one with the open mind and Dr Tsang the dogmatist. Obviously I knew nothing about philosophy, whatever about the Advanced Art of Fucking.

~

Boda de Sangre

7

The parents of the bride, after parking their light blue Lancia, I presume unwittingly, beside my red Alfa Romeo, came into the castello as if taking over for the day. I resented this as an invasion of my home, for no better reason than that I resented losing my best enemy before I had finished with him. Dr Tsang may have hypnotised me out of my fear of the rapist but it had left me with an unrelenting desire for revenge. Marrying a nice young woman was as if he were escaping me.

"Gino claims to be the father of my baby," I said to them, showing off Augusta, sweetly pretty in the party dress Biba had brought for her. "Actually she comes from Gianni, his brother. When he arrives you'll see how much more handsome he is."

Gus came and introduced himself as my husband and, taking Augusta on his arm, carried her away out of the cockpit.

"You are a mischief-maker," he remarked mildly. "Most parents are not as liberal as Father William, they won't like their daughter's husband's lover turning up at the wedding."

"But I am not actually carrying a gun," I said. "Besides, Gino is not my lover, anything but. He's a blindly fucking idiot."

"Did Tsang not tell you about Giulietta?" Gus asked. "Giulietta introduced herself to Tsang as his sister-in-law. Tsang thought that quite charming and to satisfy his professional curiosity — knowing Gino's record with you — he asked some leading questions from which to get a picture of their love life. To his surprise Giulietta quite openly responded that she lets

Gino spend the night in her bed but they don't do sex. She says she is proud of Gino's spiritual qualities and was particularly pleased because she was able to boast about his virtue to her uncle the Bishop, and now to Tsang as well it seems, thought why she should think the sex guru would be impressed by that I can't imagine."

"Gino didn't show any spiritual qualities when he was fucking me behind the shed," I said. "And then he comes complaining to me that I'm the reason he can't do it with Giulietta! My God, what a shit!"

"I thought it quite a good act. He can impress Giulietta with his restraint because it's you he lusts after."

"And half raped me in the loo; I wish Nick had stuck that knife in his belly."

"Nick is no fool — and you gave Gino the opportunity to act as he did. Tsang offered him a sedative and advised him not to rape his wife on their wedding night."

"It's really strange to think that Tsang is Gino's brother-in-law," I said. "I can't think of two men more utterly different. I hope Gino takes his advice — for Giulietta's sake."

"As long as you don't provoke him too much at the wedding."

"Don't count on it," I said.

Gus gave me his knowing Wittersworth smile.

"So you'll be the banshee at the wedding feast, imitating the Deathrage! He was splendid at ours — and splendidly outrageous, death threats and all. The idea that he might just possibly do it only added to the appeal. Personally I took it as a compliment, wholly apposite. Father had no choice but to call it quits especially as they had witnessed each other at the infamous gang-bang. What a stroke of genius that was!"

"The gang-bang story seems to improve with time," I said. "Even Nick is coming around to seeing it as a triumph salvaging his pride rather than a disgrace and humiliation."

"Not one of my photos came out, but why should I be surprised? Nick doesn't record on film. If only I'd been able to capture it I could study it over and over — I'd winkle out the last delectable morsel of meaningful detail, every gesture, every sigh or groan, every fleeting expression could have been recorded and frozen in time."

"Every clench and thrust of your four bare bums," I said, "Yes, I'd like to see that, that's the aspect of it I never see, the far side of the moon."

"We stupidly call it the Gang-bang ," said Gus, "but you know it was really the Sibyl's Halloween party. You got what you wanted, your four worshipful lovers prostrating themselves for you. I still get a buzz out of it. Paul too; I expect he'll put it in a play if he ever gets his career off the ground, though with Madge as well as his mother pushing him into politics it may take a while."

Gino had come early and was wandering around looking lost until Tomàs came to his rescue, taking time off from his more urgent tasks to sit Gino down with a glass of wine and some cheese, rightly assuming he hadn't had any breakfast.

Gus watched them from a distance.

"What a stupid idea to have Gianni over as best man," he said. "Gino needs a friend, not an enemy."

"The whole wedding here is stupid." I said, my anger, fear and disappointment in the Grati boiling over. "This is where I'm happy with you and our children, I don't accept they have any right to be here too when it cost me so much to get away from them."

"Clare can thank you for the amount of money she is making out of them," said Gus. "And why isn't Gianni here yet, to pretend at least to do the right thing? Good grief, those Grati piss me off."

I thought of Gus and Paul spraying each other with fifty-pounds-a-bottle champagne; Nick and Father William shaking hands; Paul buttoning up Nick's coat, smiling with brotherly love knowing what was concealed inside, putting his beautiful curly-brimmed top-hat into his hands to give him something else to hold. Mine was the best wedding ever!

Julie arrived with a garment carrier over her arm.

"I brought you a dress," she said, her tone implying I would let them down by wearing some rag if she had not done so.

"Good," I said. "Gino ripped my wedding dress trying to get it off me so that's no longer fit to wear — unless I put it on just to shame him."

This gave me an idea, but I let her hang the new dress, which was decent delphinium shades of blue, nothing to rival the bride, in my bedroom beside Dr Tsang's best suit which he had left hanging where it wouldn't get creased.

"Whose is that?" she said. "It's too small to be Gus's."

"It belongs to China's daddy," I said. "With luck he'll have given me a China baby of my own. It's now or never, it has to be Gus from now on."

"Don't tell me your man Deathridge has given up lusting after you. That would be a miracle — and a blessing."

"I put Nick off by letting Gino try to flush me down the lavatory — maybe that was Gino's way of getting rid of me before his marriage."

Julie was disgusted; it was so easy to shock her one could hardly resist. I hugged her; she was the nearest I had to a real woman friend.

"Where is Gus, then?"

"Taking pictures, as usual, collecting evidence. Where is Gianni?"

"No idea; I suppose he'll show up eventually. He went into Florence because he decided on the way over that his first and fatal mistake was to let you go on wearing Mr Deathridge's engagement ring instead of selling it and getting you one of his own. He says he got his priorities wrong; he was saving for a house but the symbolic gesture of commitment was more important. I love having him live with me; he is good company — except that he still eats his heart out over you. You missed a good husband there, you know, it was very ill-considered of you to walk out on him."

"Gus asked me first, and got me pregnant."

"But so did Gianni, he was your fiancé long before anyone else."

"Only because he was standing in for Nick, taking on his role. If I married Gianni, Nick would still regard him as nothing more than his substitute, a surrogate husband standing in while the real one was busy elsewhere. You were quite right to advise him against it. As you said, I'd make him miserable — on the other hand, is he any happier without me?"

"Men!" declared Julie with scorn. "They make such a drama out of love.

Gianni likes being the romantic hero claiming to be faithful to his ideals; I say it is being too obstinate to admit he had a lucky escape — from you and from Nick Deathridge, that unscrupulous devil; please God he won't turn up here today to make a mockery of the whole thing. Getting Gianni and Gino together is difficult enough."

The chapel had been transformed for the occasion with candles and flowers so it looked quite festively different from the usual gloom. I looked up at the painted ceiling which had a few more cracks in the plaster than when Nick and I were doing the devil's work on the altar steps in defiance of the pains of hell hanging over our heads. I hoped my floor wouldn't come through and cover the congregation in dust even if that would be a great inspiration to Adam with his present interest in ruins. Julie is right, I thought; if Nick were here he would think nothing of engineering a small earthquake to make a fitting climax to the Grati story. I regretted the lost opportunity for Nick's sake.

Studying the ceiling I nearly missed the entry Gino and Gianni made, striding side by side up to the altar, both in handsome dark suits. They stood motionless in front of the altar like a pair of modern knights in armour; I was transfixed by this view of them, wondering how the cut of their backs could be so alike and yet so different, and decided it was literally in the cut of their suits, Gianni's more structured one making him look tall and upright beside Gino's fashionably slouchy Italian.

Giulietta's uncle the Bishop was waiting to conduct the ceremony and eventually Giulietta with her father and little sister simpering with the veil in her hands walked up the aisle to join them. Julie cast a critical eye over her dress.

"No good," she whispered to me. "Too plain, in frightfully good taste. Doesn't bode well for Gino's happiness."

"She's a pharmacist," I replied. "What did you expect?"

I tried to picture her and Gino lying side by side in bed and came to the conclusion that though she was by far the stronger personality of the two, for all his so-called spiritual qualities Gino was still my free-range rapist: happily, now someone else's problem.

Dr Tsang and Biba were sitting side-by-side with their disputed baby between them, and Adam held May standing on the bench beside him so she could see the action. Gus sat beside me with Willie while Julie kept a firm hold on Augusta who wanted to join in the procession to the altar.

"They should have let her be flower girl," said Julie. "She could have done that; she'd look sweet."

"The Capulets wouldn't want Gino's beautiful bastard stealing the limelight," I said.

"Well, Gianni wouldn't let Gino have her either," said Julie. "I can understand men fighting over a woman, but these two really fell out over whose baby you had. Don't think they are putting on a good show of solidarity, Gino didn't want Gianni here, Gianni didn't want to come. It was Mama who insisted they behave with decency and bring a blessing on the family after all our troubles."

"Gianni has put on weight," I remarked. "It becomes him to be more statuesque. It doesn't spoil the melancholy looks. My God, but that is a sharp suit he is wearing."

"Ever since Nick came to the night-club to talk to him about Wittersworth and the children, he was determined to have a suit by the same tailor no matter what it cost. And the shoes. He was hardly listening to the practical details of what Nick was proposing to him, too busy thinking, 'this man has it all, style, attitude and my woman.'"

Julie sighed in despair for her poor deluded brother. "That man has the most detrimental effect on him."

"Nick doesn't give a damn for Gianni's opinion," I said. "All he wanted was to make use of him."

Heads from the other side of the aisle turned in our direction, disapproving of our whispering, but Julie and I were more interested in our discussion than in the wedding service, which to us was irrelevant. May too was causing something of a distraction that ended when Adam dragged her firmly behind him out of the chapel, Adam no doubt glad of the excuse to escape.

I smiled at them. May had a long way to go before she achieved the same level of disruptiveness as her father.

"The tailor must have enjoyed having such a fine figure of a man to show off his work on," I said. "But even though Gianni is well built he has nothing like the terrific personality that Nick gives to everything he wears."

Julie looked at me with bewilderment. Obviously she had never considered such a comparison between her beloved brother and the man whom she saw as a malevolent influence. She quickly covered up her shock however by saying: "Gianni is really wearing it to show Gino up for a peasant in his Sunday suit."

The sound of the wheezy little organ was drowned out in my head by the memory of Gianni's sentimentally vulgar *Comparsita* as we danced the dance of pimp and whore in the shadows. But again, Nick had put his stamp on that memory too, ridiculing my regret over Gianni by his insolently cool pleasure in his own virtuoso command of the dance floor: desire and antagonism in equal measure. Where Gianni brought tears to my eyes, Nick's exaggerated sense of the absurd made me laugh. Yet it was Nick who turned it into a dance of death with the help of the French violinist who made the music wail and shriek so Nick could strut his stuff with death defying bravura.

Seeing Gianni here, his physical presence was all the more disturbing because in my mind he was already past tense. Why?

I vowed to keep a grip on myself.

I took Gus's hand.

"I really thought I might have married Gianni," I whispered to him. "It's strange to think it might have been me and Gianni before the altar."

"No chance," said Gus. "Gianni was never more than a romantic dream, as Tsang explains by the mysteries of science."

"I am severely disillusioned with Tsang's science," I said. "I can't help feeling there's more to love than evolutionary imperatives and hormones."

"This chapel would have suited you. A registry office didn't have the powerful magic needed to stop your unorthodox fucking around." said Gus.

"I've finished with all that anyway."

"If you like I'll marry you again. Bell, book and candle and all that, and we'll invite Mother to really upset her."

"I'd need a new wedding dress," I said, "and we could get Nick and May to dance upstairs until the floor comes down on us. Wouldn't they love that! Look after Willie, I am going away a minute to rig Gino's final downfall."

Just before the end at the blessing I slipped out and up my stairs. I took off Julie's new dress and stood naked before the mirror for a few minutes, thinking of Gianni and Gino, asking myself what future there could possibly be for us after what had been our past. Then I took my wedding dress out of the box where I had hidden it, put it on and carefully arranged the torn folds to the best advantage. The flimsy silk Julie had used for her creation was not intended to last for more than a day's display, like the fragile wings of Nick's butterfly, unlike Angelina's museum piece structured as if to last genera-tions. No wonder it ripped so easily when Gino wrenched it off my shoulders while I protected my breasts. It was better to let him have the freedom of my cunt than bruise Willie's life-sustaining nipples.

I looked out over the gallery to see how the party below had fallen into place in the sunshine of the courtyard. Drinks were being passed around by Tomàs's cellar men in their colourful Palio costumes and the maids with trays of snacks to keep people happy until we were invited in for the breakfast. The children played in and out of the garden and the vari-ous family and friends of the bride mingled happily around the bride and groom. The London Grati, outnumbered, stood in a solid phalanx. One could almost see their shields and double bladed swords glinting in the sun. I went down to join them. I sidled up behind Gianni and laid my hand on his upper arm, the way I held him when we danced. He swung around as if stabbed in the back, and went white when he saw it was me, swallowing hard.

"I thought you'd like to see me in my wedding dress," I said. "You didn't come to wish me well."

Gianni didn't answer, hardly breathing, unable to speak.

"It's somewhat the worse for wear." I turned around to let him admire the effect of the little rosebuds, some hanging by a thread, the crumpled silk skirt, a nipple showing through the shreds of the bodice.

Julie came to wail over the destruction of her fine work.

"Look at the state it's in. Whatever happened to it?"

"I told you, Gino tore it to get it off, he hated it and hated me for wearing it."

"You look so lovely in it, even now, Primavera, my ideal of beauty. Oh, dear Sibylla, you would make a saint weep. I was fulfilling my own fantasy when I made it. Poor Gino, that dress is a deliberate incitement to sin."

"That's why he tried to get it off, so he could fuck me naked but I held on and wouldn't let him."

The Grati clustered around me, protecting me from the critical eyes of the other guests. Gianni, still speechless, took my elbow and held it in a vicious grip.

Gus, with Willie on his arm and Augusta by the hand, came and saw it too. May had always known that Nick was her father; Augusta never recognised any other but Gus and he was keeping her firmly in his grasp in the presence of the full contingent of Grati with their competing claims. He was absolutely resolved that she should not become a pawn between Gianni and Gino, but in truth neither of her possible fathers was in the least interested in her; what counted for them was their rivalry with each other, not the child at the centre of it.

Juggling babies and camera, Gus snapped the group, then said, to no one in particular, "I see pseudo-Achilles has come out of his tent at last."

Paul wasn't there to share the joke, only Adam, who was saying to Tsang what an admirable work of deconstruction I looked in my rags, an inspiration to be noted though he feared it would lead to a Hogarthian view of the world... and went away grumbling about his purity of vision being ruined by sordid reality, and Tsang advising a return to Abb's Head. Gus picked Augusta up on his other arm and followed Adam with Tsang who was holding on to Xin as if he would never let her go. The Magi, I thought, seeing them remove themselves from the scene. The wise men from the East: gold, frankincense and myrrh.

"You and Gino looked lovely together at the altar," Biba said to Gianni. "I am so proud of my sons." She looked pointedly at how he was holding on to me and added, "Children are a blessing; it's time you found yourself a good woman and started a family like your brother."

"I have one," said Gianni.

The children trooped off to be entertained by a clown while we moved into the dining hall and sought our places. Biba and Luigi, Julie and Gianni were to sit on Gino's side, but as Gianni had his arm around me and seemed incapable of letting go, Julie, to avoid a fuss, gave me her place. She went to sit with Gus, Adam and Tsang, Tsang being forgiven for the China baby and the abduction of Elsa in the light of the current crisis. I could see them with heads together talking amongst themselves while Gianni and I sat in silence, pretending to eat, hardly even drinking. Julie said Gianni had come to finish his quarrel with Gino, and his reaction to seeing me indicated that I was still the fulcrum that connected the brothers.

The chatter of Italian voices from Giuletta's family and friends made a background din to the silence between Gianni and me. This was the nightmare of a wedding party I had so mercifully avoided with Gus and Father William. I could feel the antagonism from Giulietta's side of the table reaching us, a pall of ill-will towards Gianni the Magnificent, with his Primavera in tatters. Gino was drinking to ease his nerves, no doubt bitterly regretting that he had given in to his mother's desire for peace between her sons. Gianni, who had always outshone him, was now sitting there for everyone to make comparisons, and me sitting beside him flaunting my torn dress to shame him. Pimp and whore perhaps, but also Hero and Diva.

I thought: this is a fatal mistake, and wondered how I could get Gianni away before the storm broke. Seated as we were at the head of the hall facing the guests like apostles at the Last Supper there was no obvious escape. Eventually Gianni's mood thawed and he came to life, responding to his surroundings. He inclined his head towards me and murmured. "I am not leaving here without you." Then, having apparently resolved in his own mind what to do about me, he stood up to do his duty and propose the toast to the bridal couple.

He spoke for what seemed like a long time, amusingly, telling the traditional family jokes, tales of their shared boyhood. To the uninitiated it was all harmless fun, but the aware could detect the hidden barbs, it was a speech larded with fishhooks to stick in the flesh. He concluded: "As children and boys we shared everything, but now it is over. Gino has his bride — how fortunate for him I no longer share his interests."

I thought of Gianni weeping with rage and humiliation the night Gino raped me. Was this really to tell Gino that he had not the least interest in returning the compliment? The insult hidden in the humour of his voice would not be lost on Gino, and possibly one or two others: Luigi, Julie, Gus. The fatal stab came at the end when instead of the bride, Gianni turned to me and said, "To the last love we shared, our only truly beloved, Sibylla, mother of our child."

A murmur of incomprehension went around the guests when he put his last-minute purchase of a ring from Florence on my finger.

My only thought was that it would do nicely for Augusta later and wished I had had some small token of acknowledgement from the random sperm who was my father. Did he even know I existed?

Gianni sat down amid a babble of talk, and the clink of glasses and some nervous laughter covered up the confusion. The majority of the people in the hall had no idea what that was all about, but Gino responded, audible only to those around him, "I'll kill you."

Biba sat with tears running down her face and Luigi holding her hand in an attempt to control her, and his sons. Giulietta looked puzzled and dismayed at this outburst of incomprehensible emotion from the Grati side, her parents were flushed with anger. The reverend uncle and others close enough to follow what was happening looked either fascinated or shocked as they tried to figure out the implications of Gianni's speech. Everyone looked at me. Gus came to my rescue. He stood up and came over to me and said with his courtroom enunciation: "Come along, my darling wife, we'll go and get a little fresh air outside."

Holding myself with dignity in spite of my blushes before a sea of hostile eyes, I sailed out past the assembled guests on the arm of my fine young husband, deeply grateful for who he was and enormously proud of him.

Once we were outside, sitting by the fountain, Gus's laughter bubbled over.

"That was superb, I wouldn't have missed that for the world. My God, Gianni, what a speech, what a splendid way to get his revenge! The vendetta of the Grati! and what a clever trick for you to wear the dress. That was justice for us. Brilliant! When I saw it first I thought you'd taken leave of your senses, but you never told me what happened to it. That was a mistake. You must tell me everything otherwise I mightn't be prepared to act, I might miss the right move to defend you."

"I didn't tell you because I was so hurt that Gino ruined my wedding dress and I didn't want it to hurt you too. If anyone was going to rip it, it should have been you, not that jackal."

"Seeing it in public like this is more of a shock than it would have been if you had just told me."

We remained sitting there peaceably together when the guests started to trickle out, still murmuring, falling into awkward little silences when they saw me, then moving away into the garden. There was no sign of the Grati. Eventually Julie came out and grabbed me.

"For God's sake go in and talk sense to my brothers."

Gus wanted to come too but I begged him not to, not to risk getting mixed up in a violent confrontation between the Grati, to let them sort out their own quarrels.

"Go and see Willie and the girls are not being scared by the clown," I said and went back in with Julie.

The wedding party was still standing around at the head of the hall, arguing furiously. Again, silence fell when I appeared.

"So this is the whore you've been fornicating with?" said Giulietta's father, backed up by his holy brother.

"Watch your language," said Luigi, standing up to his opposite number.

The mother was on the verge of screaming, Giulietta almost fainting, little sister skipping around in high excitement, Biba clinging to Gianni and weeping. Gianni handed her off to Julie to free himself so if necessary he could defend himself against Gino who looked murderous. I took Gianni by the arm and said, "Let's get away from this madhouse. I want to talk to you."

I guided him out, not through the door into the courtyard, but through the steaming kitchen where the washing up was in full swing, up into the deserted front hall of the castello so we could go out the grand entrance and down the slope to the meadows below.

"Poor Giulietta," I said, "that's an unlucky name. You have started a feud that will never heal. Montagues and Capulets. And Gino, his marriage wrecked before it even started."

"His Eminence says they can get an annulment, say she was deceived. Then we'll be back where we started, fighting over you."

"Is that where you want to be?" I asked.

Gianni stopped, knee-deep in the long grass.

"No, but that is my life for ever, a constant replay of the same old pain, the same longing for the same elusive happiness. I should have killed Gino that very first time, when it was still possible."

"I should have married you that first time, when that was still possible. You were so obviously the Right Man. My mistake was I thought by putting my body between you I had succeeded in reconciling you. Gus saved me out of that trap or together you would have destroyed me — your new trousers will be ruined here in the grass, let's go up the path to the barn. There'll be no-one there to-day."

Hand in hand we walked up to the barn where the farm workers kept their tools and ate their midday meals in the shade of the vine-covered pergola.

"I am so used to looking at your photograph," said Gianni, "that I'd almost forgotten how you really look — Julie is right, you are more of a Primavera tripping through the flowery meadow with a twinkle in your eye and a wicked smile than that dreamy seductress in Gus's photo."

"I may have looked dreamy when I had nothing to do but lie around being fucked stupid by you and Gino. Since then it's a constant battle of wits with Nick and Gus and making the right kind of home for my children. Of course I've changed."

We sat down on an abandoned rug and it was the easiest thing in the world to embrace and lie together, reliving all our happy hours, until the sun was sinking lower in the sky.

"I used to think the shelter on the North Sea strand was our best fuck ever, but now it must be this," I said.

"I could die happy now," said Gianni, but his words made me shiver as we watched the shadows gathering.

"I never believed a word you said," I explained. "I never understood that men took love so seriously."

"It was Gino who said 'girls are all just cunts'. Sure they are, but we are not animals to fuck any cunt we can get into. Even Gino isn't that stupid, see what a nice little wife he has found for himself. Well, good luck to him with her. But I won't compromise, will not debase my love."

I could see no solution. I would go back to Gus, Gianni would go back to loneliness; we would both be burdened with sweet memories for the rest of our lives, full of bitter regret.

"You'll come home with me," he said, "we'll get a place of our own and raise our family, as we always intended. We can start again."

"We had better go back," I said. "Your Mama will be out of her mind with worry that you've committed some folly — like running away with this wicked temptress."

Gianni, who had been lying on the rug with the presence and grace of Mars conquered by Venus, naked, with no artistically draped rag across his middle, began to dress himself. His beauty came into sharp focus, that exquisite profile, the way his dark hair curled in the nape of his neck. Seeing me shiver he gave me his shirt to wear over my rosebud dress. He slung the jacket of his dark suit with its silk lining over his shoulder as we went, exposing his magnificent torso to the sun's dying caresses. He sang as we strolled through the valley, humming a silly love song, pausing to point at the sky where a pallid montgolfière was losing height against the rising moon and kiss me again and again before we reached the end of the climb up to the castello. I offered him his shirt back before we went through the porch, but he said, "keep it" and buttoned his jacket over his bare chest with the collar up like a gangster in a film.

"You're a star," I said, kissing him for the last time.

At first the place seemed deserted, but we heard voices coming from the dining room, and went in to find the Grati parents and Julie, Gus, Adam, and Dr Tsang sitting around a table stripped of everything but a few half empty bottles of prosecco slowly losing their sparkle. Surprisingly Gino was there too, standing at a distance, glowering.

"What are you doing here?" said Gianni, his ebullient tones in sharp contrast to the subdued mood among the party at the table. "Have you abandoned your unlucky bride already?"

"You bloody wrecker, while you were out there fucking Sibylla I've been through the wringer with my in-laws. What I'm doing here is waiting to kill you."

Gino threw himself at Gianni who, laughing, backed out into the courtyard, the trained fighter moving with ease away from his blindly furious brother.

"I won," he teased him. "Go and chase after your Giulietta, she'll forgive you. You can tell her I came all the way from London to stop you getting to fuck Sibylla on your wedding day. She can thank me for that."

"You fucking shit," Gino shouted as he blundered on, "I'll see you in hell first."

Facing the fury of Gino's onrush Gianni continued back, enticing Gino to attack him while not a single blow hit the mark, and on through the arch at the other end of the courtyard, out into the garden, where he sidestepped the onslaught through the labyrinthine twists and turns of the knot garden and laughed as Gino fell headfirst over the box edging into a rose bed.

Gino's drunk, I thought. The other men looked on bemused; no one thought to interfere, Gianni was clearly in command of the situation, demon-strating his skill, enjoying his triumph, teasingly humiliating his lifelong rival.

Gino picked himself up, sobered, and approached more cautiously where Gianni was waiting for him by the wall.

"Stop, Gino," I cried out in terror. I could see he was being lured into a trap; I had seen Gianni's fighting techniques in the gym. Gianni glanced in my direction and smiled, momentarily suspending time. Then inexplicably he disappeared from view. We rushed to the garden wall and looked over. Gianni's body was lying far below on the cart track.

"Good God, what happened?"

"He fell, he tripped," said Gino, expressionless.

No one believed him. Gianni was so surefooted, he would never lose his balance like that in a fight. Dr Tsang, Adam and Luigi were running down the winding steps to reach the track below. Gus was holding me, Biba was screaming at Gino "You killed him!" Julie just sat down and held her head for a moment, then followed the men down, casting off her high heels as she went, followed more slowly by Biba.

I saw what Gino held in the hand that hung down by his trouser leg: an iron stake from the rose bed. He saw me looking and dropped it back behind the box hedge from where it came.

The last glimmer of light was fading from the springtime sky as Gus leaned perilously over the parapet and took pictures of the group below, Dr Tsang kneeling low over the body, then sitting back on his heels.

"Forensics can enhance it," said Gus after doing his best with the settings. The scene below was so motionless that even a long exposure seemed likely to succeed. Gino too stood frozen at the top of the steps, waiting. When Biba's wail told us the worst he turned and walked away, disappearing into the night.

Gus and I waited above while Luigi, Dr Tsang and Adam somehow man-aged to carry the body slowly, painfully, up the steps, Julie helping at the bends. At the top I handed her Gianni's shirt. She would need it to dress him decently before he was laid out.

Gus and Dr Tsang took me away to bed. That night the three of us lay in the four-poster on the mattress Gino had bought for me, Gus with his arms around me, Dr Tsang lying on his back, looking up. They were guardian angels keeping vigil.

"He was probably dead before he went over," said Dr Tsang. "A single blow to the heart."

"They shouldn't have moved the body," said Gus.

When he said that I understood why he hadn't gone to help the three older men. "But no one will blame Biba and Luigi," he added.

"What difference does it make?" I said. "We all saw what happened: a wedding, a drunken fight, an unfortunate accident. Nothing unusual."

"It is a Grati affair," said Dr Tsang. "They will solve it. No need for any other involvement."

"He was fucked out and laughing when he died," I said. The tears were running down my face, but I said, "I'm not sad, he was splendid in his Savile Row suit, the most handsome man in the world. He said he would die happy and he did."

Dr Tsang talked quietly in the dark:

"I was nine years old when I saw my father die," he said. "He was shot standing at our door from a passing car and was dead on the spot. We lived near the border where hundreds of Russian refugees were coming over. I didn't know then that he was a spy, but he had passed on to me his principle, not to live in fear of death, saying 'do what you believe in and take the consequences'. So I suppose he knew what was coming and accepted it. He was a hero of the revolution and happily for him he didn't live to see the stupidities that followed. He said to my mother she could never possess more than she could carry, including one child. Luckily as by then she didn't have to carry me she was able to take her Russian violin along and earn a living playing revolutionary dance tunes without having her personal opinions questioned. It was unfortunate for her that she ended up, not the widow of a hero, but the mother of a traitor. But you see even that wasn't the end. Death isn't the end. Even I, who saw my expectation and hope for a one kind of future lost in the birth of Augusta Grati, I can see that Gianni lives in his child and in our memories of him. He didn't have a revolution to die for, but he died for love, which in the light of history may be a more noble cause."

No one questioned our account of what happened, backed up by the famous Dr Tsang. Tomàs produced an antique painted chest as coffin from the unlimited resources of Castello Giugno for Gianni, whose fine suit was now a fitting shroud, emblematic of his style, his charm; its stains: blood, Tuscan mud and semen no more than footnotes to his life. Luigi, burdened and at the same time restored by the responsibility he thought he had shuffled off for good when Gianni took over the business, loaded the coffin into a borrowed van with cooling system, piled a consignment of castello wine in crates on top and drove it, together with Biba, Julie and China, back home, unblinking through the customs to whom he was a familiar figure.

The bloodless white shirt Gianni had lent to keep me warm covered up the hole in his heart, stabbed through with the metal rose stake.

We stood at the top of the hill watching the departure of the Grati. May held on to Adam, her expression showing her satisfaction at the departure of the China baby, then she grabbed Augusta with the other hand and dragged her away, followed by Adam. The Deathridges had not enjoyed the invasion of the Grati.

Gus was impressed by the independence of spirit that risked the illegality of the undertaking. No sordid police investigations to sully Gianni's passing, no bureaucratic mutilation of his beautiful body. Tsang on the other hand was calmly confident.

"Even if caught they'll probably get away with it," he said.

Gus and I listened to him and heard the voice of someone who had risked far more as a fugitive crossing a continent: shot or drowned or a life wasted in prison.

Then as we turned back into the garden I said: "Did he die because I distracted him, shouting?"

"Or carelessness and arrogance because he underrated Gino?" suggested Gus.

"It could have been his own death wish that he didn't sidestep an obvious lunge," said Tsang.

Or possibly all three, who can tell?

Tsang cancelled his pending appointments, probably losing many thousands in cash terms for the sake of staying with me a few days longer until the last ripples of Gianni's departure died down. I took him for a walk up to the vine-covered shelter where I had spent the afternoon with Gianni. We sat where Gianni and I had sat, looking at the sunlit hillside across the green-gold of the valley. I wondered how many generations of lovers had passed idle hours there before us, and left as little trace of their presence behind.

"It wasn't meant to happen like this," I said, trying to find words to express the dismay I felt. "I had no intention of murdering Gianni. It was Gino I wanted to suffer. I planned to leave him emotionally crippled and his prick permanently disabled so he'd never find love or satisfaction ever again. Gianni was my ideal man. The afternoon we spent here on this hillside was the culmination of our life together. I knew it was our last, but I had no way of knowing it was a prelude to his death."

"You achieved your objective with Gino," said Dr Tsang. "That Gino murdered his brother has only incidentally anything to do with you; you may have been the catalyst but you didn't do it any more than Biba did, any more than Eve is to blame for Cain and Able."

"I lied to you about the contraceptive," I said. "After all my mistakes and misunderstandings I was hoping my next would be a China baby."

He chuckled, "I know, but you can't fool your Dr Tsang. I told you, you need a young man, but it's a pity about Gianni. I'm afraid it is beyond our control. The autonomous, subconscious system is way ahead of the conscious mind when it comes to decision making."

Dr Tsang was being as cryptic as usual.

"So I'm not going to have your baby?"

"Definitely not. You may well be pregnant but it won't be mine. Perhaps Gianni's genes reading the signals that portended his death, had already decided it was time to move on, and made sure some essential part of him would have a future. I told you why I came here: you are the one woman I can lose my head over, the one who releases me from my conscious control. What better way to test out my ritual Chinese vasectomy and make sure I can still function satisfactorily without my sperm ducts."

"You had no trouble resisting me when your sperm ducts were working," I reproached him, feeling a terrible emptiness. No wonder Nick had made fun of me with his insider knowledge. Gus too, I thought. He wasn't worried that he might have to bring up a China baby. Men! how they ganged together to fuck and fool me!

"There is a higher level of command, it's in the brain, not in the testicles."

"Oh, Tsang Jun, you used me; I am just one of your guinea pigs like all the others."

"In this case I myself am the experiment, not you. You are the nearest I know to the matrix, the touchstone against which all truth is tested. As such you are the most precious thing in my life. The right to love you is the one thing I would willingly die for."

"Oh, no! That's what Gianni said and see what happened."

"Now the Grati circus is wound up it is time for you to go home with your husband."

"Have you no more experiments in mind?"

"I can think of one or two. I'll let you know. Comrade Nicolai is my go-between."

"So you can fuck me by proxy? I am part of your zoo? Well let me tell you, I refuse."

Tsang made a sound that was the nearest he came to laughing out loud, but he made no response to my accusation. Instead he said:

"You can talk to me any time, you have my number and I will never fail to answer you."

"You said that before, but long distance conversations with you are like talking to God in heaven, the answers are cryptic and highly unsatisfactory. You are a very perverse man; you made Biba have your baby just to prove you could, and you refused to give me mine because it wouldn't prove some scientific point you happen to be interested in. All I'm good for is fucking; I've had enough of you men."

"I repeat what I said," said Tsang Jun patiently, not in the least annoyed. "Your husband is the man to father your children."

With that he got nimbly up off the ground, striding purposefully across the hillside leaving me clutching air like a disciple trying to hold on to the lord as he ascended into heaven, and I had to jump up and run to catch him before he disappeared from view.

We met Gus prowling around the garden 'collecting evidence' and Tsang said, "My friend Wittersworth, I am leaving to-morrow. This woman is destroying in me a lifetime of equanimity in the face of fortune."

"I've had the advantage of a classical education," said Gus, as if that explained me. "I'm going to fly home and fix things with my Grand-mamma, then I'll come back with the Bentley for Sibylla and the children."

"Good," said Tsang Jun. "I'll go now and have a talk with Adam before I leave."

"I'll come with you," said Gus and the two of them went off together to go and set up their male conspiracy in Adam's cottage.

I remained behind thinking: they will discuss how best to deal with me, a team strategy, but I have no one. As a woman I am frighteningly alone, utterly dependent on the myth they have created around a perceived beauty which I cannot see. I cannot see myself either as Gianni saw me, Primavera walking barefoot through a flower-studded meadow, tossing dog roses to the zephyr, or as Adam's vineyard Eve, an icon of lust.

They would conspire to maintain my mythological status and Gus would witness and record their conversation. I remembered the first time I became aware of how men regarded me. It was at the dentist when Nick put his arm around me, shamelessly demonstrating his possession in a way that surprised me at the time. Now I recognised that that was the moment that created me, when I was elevated into this fabulous creature of whom they all wanted part.

Gianni had been caught up in the wrong story. He should have been the

romantic hero, the knight-errant in black armour who galloped to my rescue on his motorbike and snatched me away from the cruel lord and master
who held me enslaved. He should have protected me from the pirates and
the rapists on our mystical journey, taken me to his stronghold and married
me. We should have lived happily ever after. In the traditional fairy tale
version of events Nick, pursuing us, through his own wickedness should
have come to a bad end — not that it mightn't still happen, but it wouldn't be
because of Gianni.

It wasn't Gianni's fault that I turned out to be *La Belle Dame Sans Merci*
who enslaved him instead and sucked him dry, leaving him on the cold sea-
shore, alone and palely loitering. I rather fancied cavorting with pirates and
kept looking back, dropping my gloves, my veil, my jewels to leave a trail by
which Nick could follow and find me.

The magician Dr Tsang saw from the start that, even if Gianni was a nice
enough young man, our stories didn't match.

The Sin Eater

8

After the departure of Dr Tsang and Gus, Adam and I spent our time walking the hills, lives in abeyance until the next thing.

"I have all these great drawings," Adam said, "but such a sense of futility, I can't start on anything big."

Tomás, who had been a stalwart in helping Luigi get Gianni shipped home with a minimum of fuss, came to discuss terminating my rental agreement. Usually this was Clare's territory, but she was upset by a death at one of her normally successful functions and left it to Tomás to deal with the aftermath.

"I shall be leaving with Sibylla," said Adam. "The spirit of this place is too tainted with droopy-eyed angels and sweet Madonnas to suit someone who spent his childhood playing among the austere ruins of Lindisfarne."

"Will you go back to Abb's Head?" I asked.

"My hermit's existence will seem a bit empty now," he said despondently. "I hope that Gus finds some place suitable for you and the children — he seems confident enough."

"Nick was talking to me last night," said Tomás, "— actually at about three o'clock this morning. He is on his way. He made some rude remarks about Gus from which I gather he is anxious to get Sibylla home before Gus does."

"Nick can't have me," I protested. "He has wrecked my life too often already. I don't want to see him now; he'll make a mockery of the whole Gianni tragedy and if he expects to steal me away from Gus he is mistaken.

It's only a month since he drove away fucked out and furious because I had the temerity to tickle his balls, so why is he coming back so soon?"

Nevertheless, I felt a surge of optimism at the prospect of Nick's acerbic wit reducing the whole dreadful Gianni affair to fit his own eccentric scale of values.

"He says he is getting exactly what he wants from the new government," said Tomas, "so I suppose now he can give his mind to getting you."

"I expect he is coming to claim May," I said. "I've known he would ever since he bought her off me with his bogus wedding ring."

I frowned at the quite absurdly extravagant circle of diamonds. No matter how furious I was with him I hadn't taken it off since he put it on my finger that bitterly cold morning in Bond Street.

"Did you ever get any benefit from his financial advice, Tomas?" Adam asked.

Tomas gave a rueful laugh. "Maybe," he said. "It seemed to make sense at the time, now I feel it has drifted away from me, like the smoke of his fine Havanas. However, I do find I am asking myself questions that mightn't have occurred to me before, so I suppose there is some lingering influence."

"If Nick comes by car," I said to Adam, "you could go home with him — I certainly will not."

"And leave you here alone?" said Adam. "I think not."

"Nick may see Europe as an exciting series of mountains and rivers to cross with his internal compass set to Italy, but luckily all I need is a simple road map; I can put my children in my car and drive them home to Gus."

The loss of Gianni, my knight in shining armour, left me knowing I had to fight my own battles. But I spoke with more bravado than I felt. Since I saw Gianni disappear over the parapet I felt shaky and sick, also I had to admit that without Nick I would never have achieved the status of New Renaissance Woman with a bright red Alfa Romeo.

"Nick," said Adam, "left it too late to scrap the past and its mistakes."

"Nick never admits to a mistake," said Tomás with the kind of head-shaking acceptance all Nick's friends sooner or later adopted. "He never lets go, he accumulates, piling up layer upon layer of possessions, friendships, women, children, and especially love. But as he finds it hard to trust that anyone loves him, he can never have enough — of anything."

"I dare say you're right, Tomás," said Adam. "The irredeemable despair of the abandoned child..."

"*Papà e arrivato!*"

May had pretentiously taken to talking only Italian and I could hear her shouting below in the courtyard. I ran downstairs and found Nick talking to Adam with May dancing around him singing her song of triumph that it was her turn to have a Daddy. He was wearing a dark suit and a very pretty swirly bright pink, turquoise and emerald tie but I had never seen him looking so dishevelled, Though the suit was exceptionally beautiful, even for Nick, he had probably slept in it. Beside him was a tiny red Ferrari.

"Good Heavens! where did that ridiculous toy come from?" I said while May climbed behind the wheel, thinking it was another present for her, like the gun. He had left the key in the ignition and May was delighted that she could make it hum.

"I picked it up at Milan airport, a super-fast fuck machine, my dear — Sunday morning on the autostrada, heaven on wheels. Do me a favour, Dad, keep an eye on the children," he said to Adam, "I'm in desperate need of my Strumpety Cunt."

He walked briskly away towards my door. Adam and I looked at each other wondering what Nickish bee was buzzing inside the chestnutty brain-box now.

"I think you may have written him off prematurely — again!" said Adam.

"I'm not so sure," I said. "It depends on what he's really here for."

Turning to follow him in, I surrendered any pretence I wasn't insatiably in love with this man whose stud potential I had turned down for the sake of getting a China baby. Idiot! Dr Tsang had shown me how to receive the gift of love; it was Nicolai Dumez Deathridge who gave it.

"Have you had any lunch?" I asked, trying to judge the meaning of his unusual appearance.

"I can't remember," he said. "I'm not hungry so I must have had something."

Taking the suit off and hanging it up he said, rather surprised, "That's what I put on yesterday morning for the Grati funeral. I can't have had time to change."

"Not with that tie, I hope," I said thinking even Nick couldn't have had such a lapse of good taste, notwithstanding the evidence of the red crocodile.

He put his hand in the pocket and took out a narrow silk knit black tie and looked at it bemused.

"I didn't think you'd go to Gianni's funeral," I said.

"I'll tell you about it later," he said.

"Have you come to settle with Gino?"

"For pity sake, shut up and lie down on the bed so I can relieve my balls."

He was laughing at himself, deprecating his own urgency. Gone was the arrogant mastery with which he had held me down onto the bed that first time, fucking as if there could be no alternative but to do it, there and then. Gone too was the holding back of New York, and the doubt of the blue lizard. He was inviting me to lie down with him, confident my desire for him was equal to his for me. Balance achieved.

The genius of Nick: all the hurt, resentment and frustration he caused melted away in the pleasure of seeing him. How was it possible that the first three months, when daily intercourse with him had been a duty I couldn't wriggle out of, Nick had succeeded in hiding his amazing charisma under a bushel, so all I felt was his willpower pressing down on me, the weight of his balls? Until the night of the Taittinger dinner! If only I'd been strong-minded enough to say no to Gianni at that turning point I'd have saved my deluded fiancé from a hopeless love. Meg said I'd be the death of him — she may not have meant it quite so literally.

Nick groaned furiously as if fucking were sheer agony but gradually he wound down and by late afternoon he had exhausted himself. He sat up against the pillows, his humour restored.

So was mine.

"Sibylla, you witch, this is what you do to me. Until I met you I was perfectly happy: I did my work, shot clay pigeons as my civic duty, played chess at the club and slept peacefully in bed with my lovely wife. Then you came along and since then I'm in constant turmoil; I find peace only in moments like this, emotionally and physically drained."

"Obviously you thrive on turmoil," I said, laughing at how he was looking both utterly spent and immensely pleased with himself. His image of himself was as much an illusion as my first impression of him had been and even Angelina admitted her Otherwise Perfect Husband did not sleep peacefully.

I got up to make tea and leave him to come to his senses.

When I returned he hadn't moved, still totally relaxed, at peace with his world.

"*Ecce homo!* What are you like, Nick Deathridge, you indomitable stud! Where would we be without you?"

"All my friends say that," said Nick, without either modesty or conceit, and closed his eyes.

"I can't imagine why," I said and put the teapot on the table beside him.

"Julie gave me a letter for you but I forgot to bring my bag from the car," he said.

I went to get it and to relieve Adam of the children. Clare was already giving May and Augusta their tea so I took Willie, and Adam, too curious to hold back any longer, came up with me carrying the squashy leather bag Nick travelled with to avoid airport delays. That was in the days before cutthroat razors were banned from First Class cabins.

Nick was asleep when we came in, but immediately opened his eyes and said, "I need something stronger than tea. I haven't been to bed since the day before yesterday though I suppose I must have slept on the plane."

"Soundly, I should think," I said, "since you didn't find time to shave — and you smell fantastic."

"Or wash," he said, "forty-four hours worth of fatty acids, glycogen and androstenole."

"Bottle it as an aphrodisiac," I suggested.

"I'll put it to Tsang," he said, "you can be his Nose and make your fortune."

151

Adam opened a bottle of wine and cut up some salami to keep us going until dinnertime while Willie munched on a rusk for his gums.

"Clare is giving the children cheese fondue," Adam remarked. "Would you like some?"

Nick groaned. "That will give them indigestion, poor defenceless infants. I had enough of that in Basel until I persuaded our friends that beef fondue — a contradiction in terms — is marginally more palatable and less likely to cause instant death. They laughed at me and said they thought instant death was my goal in life to which I said, yes, by being pushed out the window by an irate boss, by avalanche or friendly fire, or even eaten by piranhas, but not by stomach ache."

"Lucky there are no piranhas in the Rhine," said Adam. "I've never known a so-called expert yachtsman fall overboard quite as often as you. You are the reason for my advanced design in MOB equipment."

"I gave up sailing after I capsized Papi Bott's boat. I had no trouble in getting out when it happened – you taught me that off Chesil Beach — but when he dragged me back into the water to see how it could be salvaged he thought he could keep me under long enough to lose me — he is a bear of a man, twice as heavy as skinny me, with a murderous rage lurking under his skullcap — but with my vast experience of fighting my way through tackles it would take more than a somewhat affronted Papi to dispose of me. I kicked him in the balls and swam for the quayside. After that I went skydiving with the guys instead, far more exhilarating."

Nick shut his eyes again, perhaps feeling the wind on his face, Lucifer falling, falling...

It struck me that Adam was dryly dismissive of Nick's watery adventures; he had suffered enough as father from Nick's recklessness, but I remembered Leon Bolus remarking on Nick's lurid quarrels with Jacob Bott, so the drowning episode was probably more significant than Adam appreciated.

"I heard from both Tomás and Tsang that Gianni was killed at his brother's wedding," Nick went on. Considering his own expertise in avoiding murder he probably thought it sheer incompetence to lose one's life in such simple circumstances.

Unless one had a death wish.

"They were very non-committal about what happened, Tomás said it was an accident, Tsang said it was a fight, but you know how cryptic Tsang can be, and Tomás was singularly unforthcoming too. You, Dad, never even mentioned it to me."

"My consolation is that you weren't here when it happened," said Adam. "So it has nothing to do with you."

"Gianni knew better than to take me on in a fight or he'd have had his pretty face smashed in the dust much sooner — I've dealt with more vicious thugs than he..."

Nick's confidence in his own fighting skill always stuck me as sheer hubris.

"I" — his emphatic ego — "kept our exchanges on a strictly business footing and honoured my side of the bargain. He was the one who betrayed my trust. I wouldn't have gone to his funeral but Elsa phoned and asked me to come and stand by her. Then young Wittersworth said he wasn't going, but would I meet him after and tell him all about it. I had no idea what was going on so I was pleased enough to meet him and hear what he had to say — my daughter's step-father, so by some twist of fate he's almost my brother — it excused me the unpleasant duty of having to go back to the Grati house for the funeral sandwiches and Madeira seed-cake, pretending to be sorry there's one fucker less in the world."

Nick was not good at polite pretence.

"The Grati seemed proud of how Luigi drove with the corpse all the way from Italy to the parish church and got the cooperation of the priest to keep it quietly in the lady chapel for a couple of days while the family gathered around. Elsa got there from Hong Kong looking absolutely stunning, a real Madam. The London clan was overawed by such style."

"I'm glad my flippant advice to Elsa to get Tsang to teach her sex turned out so well," I said. "Greatly relieved, considering all the other blunders I've made."

"That she wanted to hold my hand throughout the service was to be expected, I was next best thing to Tsang, but I was embarrassed that Gianni's mother seemed to think I was a good friend of his; she clung to me, probably to fill the gap left by his brother's absence."

"I wonder if Gino went back to Giulietta," I said, "or if she wanted him back. Italians react differently about insults and honour…"

"To make up for Gino not coming to sing a requiem," Nick went on, not distracted by my speculation about a story in which he had no interest, "a girl from the choir who says she used to sing duets with Gino volunteered to sing; she said it would be a great privilege but rather to Mrs Grati's dismay off she went into Dido's lament, just imagine, that pagan at a good Catholic funeral! I thought it was surprisingly appropriate — *when I am laid in earth, may my wrongs create no trouble in thy breast, remember me, but ah! forget my fate* — a pure voice with only a few chords on the organ for accompaniment, very moving! Not a dry eye in the church. If I were a dog I'd have howled; I could make Bonne-Maman's French bulldog howl by singing at it in just such a tone of voice, we'd sit in bed and howl together — I was sure she would come back for the dog if not for me."

A lonely little red-head in the big bed Paul and I came to share 30 years on…

I thought it ironic that this was probably the same 'chick' about whom Gino made lewd jokes. I remembered him going about his work humming bits of Purcell and could well see him as the unfaithful Aeneas seducing his Dido, toying with the alternative of a life singing duets in domestic harmony but choosing instead to stay as an impediment to his brother's happiness. Unlucky girl! It shed a new light on Gino's secret life, the one I gave him no credit for having. Maybe the cause of the 'trouble' Julie had hinted at.

"Biba said: 'If Gino were here he would sing me a decent Stabat Mater —'"

Perhaps, but I had a blinding vision, which I had not considered in its significance before, that when Biba screamed her despair at the moment of Gianni's death, Gino, waiting at the top of the steps for confirmation, had turned and walked slowly away into the dark, and he was smiling. Whatever remorse might come later, he felt joy in the moment of his victory. Virgam virtutis tuae, he sang quietly to himself as he went. I had heard him sing that before; I assumed it was something to do with the Virgin Mary at her vespers. It was only afterwards that I realised it was his psalm of revenge; his hand had grasped the iron rod and used it to destroy his enemy. No doubt he sang it all the way home in his rented car with the inappropriate white ribbons. He could have gone and sung it at the funeral, no-one would have been any the wiser; he could have stood up and justified himself before his friends and family, not slunk off to the Carthusians the way he did when he destroyed my wedding dress, as if his sins were only between him and God.

Gus would say: God doesn't come into it.

"Somewhat tactlessly," Nick went on, recounting with dry humour the unexpected part he was called on to play in his despised rival's funeral, "I said I could do a Pergolesi better than that braying ass Gino — we had a fairly High-Church choirmaster at school, though nothing like as High as Great-uncle Harold — anyway it was an excuse for me to escape Biba's clutches and have a little fun reliving my choirboy days in falsetto with exaggeratedly lugubrious quavers insulting the intelligence, and the Dido girl chiming in with the descant covering up my cod Latin — I was such a dopey youngster I slept my time away during Latin lessons. Actually I surprised myself how easy it is to pick it up. After a little conference with the organist I decided to cut the Counterreformation crap and do it as *opera buffa*. We got a bit carried away, finding great rapport over the music — I could have fucked them both for the pure pleasure of it — whatever the rest of the congregation thought of our rather exuberant interpretation, more triumphant than dolorosa. It was a terrific send-up of that fucker Gianni, and, for inspiring that moment of musical mayhem, I forgive him his trespasses against me."

"Really, Nick, did you have to make fun of Gianni even at his funeral? You are such a clown."

"I do rather well at funerals — even my grandfather's that I didn't go to but spent my rage screaming my head off at Highbury, ruining it for my mother."

"Poor Biba, I'm sure she was grateful nevertheless. She has lost two sons,"

I said, "after striving all their lives to keep the peace between them. Dr Tsang's experiment in polyandry didn't help either, it turned normal sibling rivalry into murderous jealousy."

"It was your experiment," Nick pointed out, "Tsang was interested in the outcome only after you initiated it; he is still interested in how Augusta turns out in evolutionary terms. It's a long-term project. Science gives no moral weight to grief or happiness."

"Well it's not much comfort to know," I said, "that it's insignificant to the human race whether the Grati killed each other or that we'll all live happily ever after."

Nick continued: "The martial arts club carried the coffin, muttering their hatred of women who drive good guys to their deaths. It wasn't exactly cowardice not to challenge this point of view on your behalf: they looked rather menacing and there were quite a lot of them — not that that ever daunted me before and a nice fracas would have provided a fitting disruption to the ceremonial exit of your failed lover, but I didn't see the point of sacrificing myself in such unworthy company. Your friend Mary shared their feelings, condemning you as the witch who held the brothers under a spell and left them helplessly enthralled while you flitted on — there was an element of class bitterness against me there; I told her she'd have made a great tricoteuse and asked if she is aware that civilisation has moved on since witch-burnings."

Class awareness was not something Mary brought over from Ranelagh Road; she must have picked it up from her Bobby. She didn't have a Great-Aunt Kathleen with backbone behind her.

"On the way out Julie cornered me for a private chat at the back of the church. I was afraid she would try to stop me escaping, but it was only another attack, to let me know how much she blames me for the way I interfered in Gianni's life; in her eyes I am the real culprit — an absurdly irrational conclusion."

Nick rummaged in his bag and produced an envelope, which he handed to me.

"This is what Julie wanted to discuss. She found it in Gianni's room after she got home. It's addressed to you; presumably if he had come home he would have destroyed it. Julie was rather annoyed that he left nothing for her. She read it to me but she didn't want the others to know about it. She regards it as a suicide note."

"It can't be," I said in protest, handing it back unread, tears in my eyes. "We all saw Gino kill him. You read it."

Nick shook his head, almost apologetically, and I realised it was the kind of thing he wouldn't be able to read. Adam took it instead, rescuing us from emotional deadlock.

"*My Beloved,*" he read, "*I am dying for you.*"

"That's a common enough expression," I said, "that doesn't mean anything sinister."

"It depends how you emphasise it," said Nick. "'*Dying*' or '*for you*'."

Adam continued reading:

"*You promised me so much happiness I can't believe how I came to lose you and my baby, and the life we could have had together.*

When Mr Deathridge brought you to meet me I thought, this is the girl for me. I completely misunderstood what was going on between you and him.

I accepted his money and he has made me repay it ever since in shame and mockery – I should have known that such love and loveliness were beyond me.

Time does not heal.

Julie, bless her, tries to save me from myself, but without you there is nothing worth saving.

To-morrow I hope I may see you, even at a distance, so I can die happy. Gianni.

PS. Gino thinks he has escaped me but I'll settle with him once and for ever."

I listened with dismay.

"I would have preferred not to give it to you," said Nick, "after all, I destroyed the other letters he wrote you. It is obvious that he went to the wedding knowing he and Gino would fight — again, and this time he intended to finish it."

"But," I protested again, "we spent the afternoon making love; Gianni was perfectly happy when we walked up the hill to the castello. He was smiling at me when Gino struck him."

I kept silent about him saying he would not go home without me. It had nothing to do with Nick: Nick was an irrelevance between Gianni and me. Gianni never understood that his real rival was Gus, that I was never going to leave Gus.

"Gianni could still have stepped aside when Gino went for him," said Adam, studying Gianni's letter.

"In his position," said Nick, "if I were going to let Gino kill me I'd have made sure I took him down with me."

Well yes, Nick wouldn't go quietly.

"What makes his death a somewhat comic story for me," Nick went on, "is how ready he was to be seduced by the offer of a pretty girl for a night. He made it too easy for me."

"How much did you pay him?" I asked, pursuing what I believed lay at the heart of the matter.

Nick shook his head.

"It would be unethical to reveal the financial implications of our arrangement."

"I just wanted to know the cash value the two of you put on a pretty cunt."

Nick ignored that.

"Dr Tsang says that by bringing your money and my alien beauty into their ordinary lives we sowed the seeds of destruction," I said.

"Beauty doesn't kill," said Adam.

"Neither does money pull the trigger." Nick looked at me with such contempt that I blushed, though his response puzzled me.

"Or in this case the rose stake Gino picked up from the flower bed," I said, wondering why Nick used a shooting analogy, unless it was that Nick was the person who came to a wedding with a gun under his coat, not Gino. Was this the question of moral responsibility I hadn't read in *The Chronicle of a Death Foretold* when Gino came to take me away from Abb's Head?

Both Adam and Nick were looking at me with surprise and I realised no one else had seen the iron rod with which Gino had destroyed his enemy. It hadn't occurred to me to mention it before — in fact none of us ever discussed the details of what happened. We all believed the evidence of our own eyes, assuming we had all seen the same thing.

"Nevertheless, when introducing Gianni to your enchanting Sibylla you could have anticipated the consequences for the unfortunate young man," said Adam.

"I'm not responsible for what happened to the gigolo," Nick replied. "And how could I possibly think my Sibyl would leave me for that guy; sure, he was good-looking, that was his stock-in-trade, along with charm and good manners, but how can that be enough? What kind of life was he offering you?"

"A happy family, something I had never had. He may have been a professional charmer but he was faithful — to the death; he didn't have a wife and God knows how many other women in his life."

"Monogamy is not exactly your strong point either, Mrs Wittersworth," Nick remarked drily, not disguising his amusement at my failure to win any argument with him.

"What exactly was in that contract you made him sign?" I asked.

"Good grief, I don't know. Toby does all that — I tell him what I want and he makes it happen."

All I remembered of that meeting was that while I sat there dumbstruck by gorgeous Gianni, neither of the men seemed to focus on me at all. Having negotiated the initial introductions they sat back exchanging views, apparently more interested in the prospects for a team of such talented players as Arsenal getting their act together enough to start winning a few matches again, in equable agreement that it was time Bertie Mee moved on. How could a conversation so trivial and utterly irrelevant have initiated the tragedy of Gianni's end?

Nick continued: "After he met you he phoned me to ask if sex was included in the contract. I said that was entirely your decision, it was not for me to say. I was outraged that he took that to mean I would pay for your pleasure but I was too proud to say no. It goes to show once again what a complete sucker I am as far as you are concerned."

"You continue to amaze me, Nick," said Adam. "You reduced Gianni's love to a commercial transaction; that was iniquitous. It was bound to end badly, though not necessarily the way it did."

"I tried not to see his motorbike chained to my railings but I had to look every so often to see if it were still there, realising I had done a deal with the devil, the more fool I. I can't tell you the satisfaction it gives me to know that the indignity I suffered that night was worthwhile after all, it made Gianni my stand-in, that he took the blow that was destined for me."

"The Sin-eater!" I said. "The fee for a Sin-eater is five silver shillings; is that what you paid him?"

"Quite possibly, or the equivalent," said Nick, but now he was laughing at me for still half believing in Great-Aunt Kathleen's fire-side ghost stories, just the way I half believed in the devil.

"I never cared for morality plays," said Adam, "but this is the nearest I've come to a Faustian bargain in real life — and by my own son!"

"Gus will gladly negotiate for you in any further bargains with the devil," I said to Nick.

"It will be signing my death warrant if young Wittersworth has any hand in it. There's nothing he'd like better than to see me trip myself up and go tumbling into the abyss. But now Gianni is dead," he went on regardless of my mocking, "I believe I may live. Death has passed me by — for now..."

Dear God, I thought, men certainly know how to make a drama out of love — and all I have to do is lie on my back and let the boy-ohs fuck me...

"... so my state of mind after the funeral when I made my escape from the grieving family was one of relief. Driving down to the station to meet Wittersworth, I saw him from a distance standing there. In his new three-piece suit and umbrella as swagger stick, it struck me that he has the presence to match his ambition. He looked like a man who won't waste his time waiting for the hereditary ermine to fall on his shoulders. He has positioned himself to win his own."

It pleased me that Nick was showing a glimmer of appreciation for Gus.

"He made a great show of squeezing into the Jag, 'not as generous as the Bentley' he remarked, politely not complaining, the pompous young ass — the absurdity of it, there isn't a more comfortable driving seat in the world — 'My favourite passenger is your eminently fuckable wife,' I said. 'She seems to be pleased enough with what I can do for her but maybe it's getting too stretched for your satisfaction. Where are we going?"

"Not that I've noticed," said Wittersworth. 'If you can spare an hour or two, head down the M20 for Maidstone and I'll direct you from there.'

"I still had no idea what was the purpose for this journey à deux, but he wanted to talk about the details of the funeral, so I told him: who was there, what was said and done. I handed over Gianni's letter to read. He agreed with Julie about its meaning. He said the reason he couldn't go to the funeral was because he knows what really happened and was afraid his conscience would get the better of him. Like being asked at a wedding if one knows of any impediment — he thought he might feel compelled to blurt out the truth as soon as they started chucking earth on the coffin, burying the evidence. When he told me the whole story I said I thought it a pity he didn't, it would have been a moment of high theatre. It wouldn't hurt me to see the Grati in the shit. I can see why Tsang had to stay away too: no need for him to compromise his reputation. Still, I have to admit it took some nerve to go to such lengths to avoid an inquest: smuggling the body, forging papers and deceiving the priest. I'd have done the same myself."

The highest possible praise from Nick!

Flexing and relaxing his limbs in a state of post-coital contentment Nick rearranged the pillows, took another glass of wine and settled comfortably. I wondered how Adam could resist getting his pencil out, given what he could see of Nick's naked body lounging with angular grace in front of him: Nick who never removed his protective armour of fine tailoring! His feet pressed together with prehensile toes caressing each other, it was impossible not to be riveted by the way his genitals rested on his drawn-up inner thigh, Nick's worry bunch that were carrying on their own internal conversation, nodding and nudging away amongst themselves, keeping grumpily busy until Bossy Brain told them to be quiet and behave themselves. Seeing him so exposed, I wondered what had cracked the shell of his emotional reserve.

"I am sorry I missed the Grati drama," he said. "I would have enjoyed that."

"Everyone said what a blessing it was that you didn't come," I said. "It was bad enough without you here to complicate matters."

Adam merely groaned at the prospect of Nick getting involved in the fight. There might have been more than one fatality.

"Unfortunately, I was otherwise occupied," Nick said, shifting his weight around uneasily. "Wittersworth and Toby insisted that Dunce Deathridge remain sitting in the corner while they thrashed out my legal and financial position, versus the Furzys who were pursuing me on a completely trumped up charge of embezzlement, and against Tsang who said I'd cheated on him professionally and brought him into disrepute. Needless to say I got the better of them all, but you see," Nick concluded, with an air of modest triumph, "I've been rather too busy to concern myself with *The Death of a Gigolo*."

"Oh, don't torment me, Nick! I so wanted Gianni to be the right man, I could have married him only for you."

"And Mr Wittersworth?"

"Gus belongs in a parallel universe, he's my other reality."

"Gus Wittersworth didn't waste years of his life reading philosophy for nothing," said Nick. "He can untangle the twisted logic of the Sibyl. It's sincere fools like Gianni and me who are destroyed by it."

Nick closed his eyes and looked as if he would fall asleep with his face half buried in a pillow, but as soon as Adam stood up to steal away one eye opened a slit to look up and Nick said, "Dad, it's payback time..."

Adam paused but didn't turn round.

"When you left me standing at the railway station in Basel to find my own way in the world, you sensibly rid yourself of your unruly son. It cost you the modest profit of your boat, but however unlikely it seemed at the time, it has proved a wise investment. Now, after surviving the Furzy onslaught, I can return your wildly speculative outlay, with thanks."

"No, thanks," said Adam. "And that isn't exactly what happened. With singular lack of gratitude you taunted me for my ineptitude with money so I handed it over to you together with our debts. You kindly paid my ticket home. Penn Shackleton thought me extremely foolish and accused me of evading my duty to you, but really, after all the trouble we had been through with your mother, I was sick of the whole Dumez drama — and honestly, of you too. I certainly don't need your money now."

With that he walked on towards the door.

"Hold on a minute, Dad. Listen to me — it really annoyed me that I was burdened with such hopelessly incompetent parents; Grandfather shouldn't have shot himself until I was old enough to take on his responsibilities. I was powerless: my mother wouldn't let me take care of her and you didn't."

"It was irresponsibly selfish of your mother to sail away into the unknown. She stole my only asset and left me the cost of maintaining her hugely expensive house that we couldn't afford to live in and of bringing up her talented, engaging, but quite impossible child."

"She was entitled to take the boat; you built it at the expense of her life," said Nick.

Adam re-considered his actions.

"No, Nick," he said, refusing to accept Nick's judgement. "Nathalie made her own mistakes."

"Penn Shackleton allowed his personal opinion of me influence his application of the law," said Nick. "I could sue him for malpractice. The *Espérance* was in my mother's possession when she died; legally it was mine, as was the house that you sold. So that 1ˢᵗ June 1959, my eighteenth birthday, when I saw you off on the Paris Express I actually had every right to keep the money. But there you are, Dad, you cast your bread upon the waters and it has come back to feed you."

"Where on earth do you get these weird expressions from?' Adam stood at the door, distinctly irritated with his son's interpretation of their mutual rights and obligations.

Nick looked puzzled. "It must be from Papi Bott. He spoke in riddles of biblical proportions, the tiresome old man; he was always trying to catch me out, the male equivalent of Mother Furzy only infinitely more clever at it. What I mean is, take the money while you can before I gamble it away in some fantastic enterprise, which may well end in a big bang. My self-destructive tendency gets stronger with age — only that it's offset by my Gemini ability to outwit myself. So if you think the Dumez mother and son treated you badly, make sure of your fair share now while we are settling old scores."

Was that what he had come for?

"I don't want any of it," Adam said.

"You'll live longer than I," said Nick. "You'll need it."

Clearly he knew the Sin-eater Effect was only a temporary reprieve.

Adam came back from the door to explain his point of view.

"Nathalie took fright during the bombing of our shipyard in May '41 so she risked your life as well as her own by setting off alone for NW3. I had spent the night fire-fighting and when I got home the neighbours said they saw her driving off in an ambulance. Once I established she was driving the ambulance herself and not being transported in it in premature labour I didn't expect to see her ever again, but a few weeks later her voice at the end of a crackly phone line told me she'd see me after the war and by the way I had a son — but having a son four hundred and fifty impossible miles away was too abstract to get excited about when I was working twelve hours a day, and half the night on fire watch. Conrad and Anna Dumez gave you a better home than I could have in the circumstances."

"I may be 50% Deathridge genes with whatever dormant potential they bring with them," Nick answered, "but it was Anna and Conrad who were the triggers, who made me what I am. While you were busy winning the war my grandparents were vying with each other to cherish my peculiar genius.

I spent the first few years of my life perched on Bonne-Maman's left hip. She lifted me up to protect me from Coco, her French bulldog, who nipped my toes when I was crawling around and I never let her put me down again until the day she —"

Nick looked as if he were about to fling his glass in a Taittinger gesture but I put out my hand and took it before he could spill it. He hardly noticed but clutched a pillow to his chest.

"Grandfather would rant at her, 'you're mollycoddling that little leech,' and how right he was! I was thoroughly, blissfully mollycoddled; every child should have it so good. She played Chopin with me sitting on her lap, so I picked up polonaises like a gypsy child repeating what I heard. Maman told me to keep on practising so that when she came back I wouldn't disappoint her — a cruel deception but that's how they coped with me."

Miss Pinkerton's answer to highly emotional children was cool commonsense from Day One, a quality clearly lacking in the Dumez household once his grandmother walked out the door.

"I didn't see the point of leaving me to sleep alone in Bonne-Maman's empty bed, but Maman with her paranoid germ phobia wouldn't let me get in with her; we had terrific rows every time I tried. I'd howl loud enough to disturb Grandfather and he'd come storming in yelling 'Useless bloody mother, get the child to shut up before I throttle him.' 'Go along and sleep with your grandfather,' Maman would say, but he'd dump me back in the bed where he used to sleep with my grandmother before I came between them with my weeing willie. They got me to go to sleep by saying she would come home in the night. I realised that it was a lie when they let me take her dolls to bed with me, but it was a comfort to believe them and I told the same lie to Coco. He would lie crouched on our bed and every so often he'd sit up with his cocky black ears spread like bat's wings, as if expecting her to come in. When he disappeared they told me he had gone to look for Bonne-Maman. I accepted that that was as good a story as any to explain what was going on. It wasn't until I went to boarding school that I knew it definitely wasn't going to happen."

Still squeezing his pillow, Nick was unselfconsciously rocking it between his thighs and I could see why he looked so anguished when fucking: it had started as a form of self-comfort when his distress became too much to bear.

"Coco the Clown and Little Nickie!" he said. "It was a circus act we put on either to raise a smile or raise hell depending on the mood of the audience. The only person who invariably laughed was the charlady. And we could get her to be the Fat Lady by running off with her feather-duster so she'd chase us."

Send in the clowns! He had sent in May and Augusta because I outwitted him by marrying Gus Wittersworth, the one rival he couldn't outmanoeuvre. Gus had advised me to take Nick for who he was, that knowing how he got that way made no difference, but I didn't agree: I wanted to hear Nick's own version of his story. It was time I emptied my mind of my illusions and fantasies to see him with open eyes, as he was for himself.

The early summer sun had moved away from our side of the courtyard and the bedroom with its small window was getting dim. Nick stroked his jaw and chin saying, "I'm badly in need of a shave. I don't think I've ever attacked my Strumpety Cunt in quite such caveman style before. And I stink. Rather nice. That's how thin a layer civilisation is, forty-eight hours not washing and one's primitive instincts come to the surface. Maman and Grandfather used to argue over the stupidest things, a recurring topic for a good fight was Mother taking double her ration of bath water because, she said, there were two of us using it. So when she had finished I was allowed in — you remember the enormous tub and the excitingly explosive copper geyser, it was as good as a swimming pool to me — and when she went off to do her war-work Grandfather had to come to make sure I didn't drown in it or flood the house. He'd shave at the hand basin in his vest and braces, stropping his razor up and down the leather, scowling in a fearsome way."

I tried to picture an elderly Nick with a thin furrowed face etched with a permanent frown but in my imagination Nick refused to grow old.

"He'd slap his hand with the strap and say 'this is what grandfathers use for beating disobedient little boys; and Disobedience is your middle name,' but I knew he didn't mean it because when I tried to be a submarine and hide under the water he'd test my endurance, seeing how long I'd hold my breath and just when I thought I'd burst or choke he'd catch me out by the feet and dangle me upside down. My lively little prick would bob up and down and that made him smile, 'Nickie and his maggot, our hope for the future — if we survive at all.'"

Nickie's maggot sat up quietly pleased with itself being discussed. Knowing how sulky it could become, I wondered if this posing naked was a provocation, a dare or an invitation. In the tiny teardrop that glistened in its eager eye I saw the embodiment of his whole self, the Aleph of his existence. My head spun with yearning to contain him, his whole life, within me.

"I knew he cracked the leather only to see if I'd flinch. It was a game. He never actually hit me though I often felt the wind of it swoosh past me. I got my education from him: swearing at me, making me dodge his blows, taking me for long walks across the heath and down town, making me the receptacle of his lifetime of experience and knowledge. When he was dead the first thing I did was run to the bathroom to retrieve his shaving gear and hide it before Mother thought of it. It was a smart move — I still use it — though having such a lethal razor-blade at school was risky, I would have been expelled in the row over that if it hadn't been for trouble of a different sort intervening."

"It was playing those reckless games that got you into trouble," said Adam. "I still can't get over the Russian Roulette — that old man had a lot to answer for."

"He wasn't that old," said Nick. "Younger than Churchill. 'You are my real war work,' he said. A dispatch rider would come with papers he had to work on, and we'd sit down at his table together. He put me across from him and made me write my name over and over: N dot D dot Deathridge, it didn't matter that it wasn't legible as long as it looked good. I could never be sure of getting it right — I still can't — the letters keep mixing themselves up. I never learned anything as basic as the alphabet, just N for Nickie and D for Dumez, but also D for disobedience. I understood the D was making fun of me. Dunce was another of his words: 'Dunce Deathridge, that's what you'll be signing as your name, bloody ignorant little nincompoop, no use to us at Bosanquet & Dumez; you can go and work at the Bank of England, they won't notice the difference.'"

N dot D dot Deathsquiggle seemed to have been enough to get by on even if the D's got themselves mixed up. I smiled at the vision I had of a boy Nick in black suit, wing collar, perched at a table with quill pen scratching away in a long ledger by the light of tall tallow candles. Enough to get him in evening clothes with Angelina in her diamonds at Mansion House dinners.

"He put me off paperwork for ever," Nick went on. "'Dummy war work' he called it, 'a sheer bloody waste of time to shut me up and keep me out of the way.' Every now and then he'd get so annoyed he would screw up a ball and throw it against the wall. 'Goddamn them, they take my motor, make a poxy whore of my daughter, and condemn me to shuffling bits of paper around. I, Conrad Dumez! We came over from Amsterdam in 1815, trading in wool. Time enough you'd think to earn a little respect.' On a bad day the floor would be strewn. When Churchill was in Yalta, furious that he hadn't been invited along, he sent one straight out the window into the front garden where it stuck in the holly bush. 'Run down, Nickie,' he said, 'go and get it back before some traitor or spy picks it up.' I had to climb into the prickles for it. When I brought it back he said 'traitors and spies get shot. I may well die by the bullet but I am not in either category and wouldn't want to get it in the neck by sheer carelessness. I'll choose my own time' — which he did a few years later.'

"It was only after he shot himself that I understood why he'd hug me and say 'God help us, Nickie, how is this going to end?' and 'what will become of you? I wish I knew.'"

"1948 was a very low point," said Adam. "If only he had stuck it out a bit longer..."

"Bonne-Maman wasn't going to come home... but I wish he had stayed around longer for me," said Nick. "He wouldn't be too disappointed after all in how Dunce Deathridge has done... he fought with Maman over letting me stay at home playing the fool but she said that it didn't matter that I didn't read when I showed amazing command of Bonne-Maman's music..."

Nick, lying back, stretched out his strong, supple fingers in front of his face, marvelling at the prodigy he once was. I could picture the little hands skipping up and down the keys, feet dancing to keep up.

"She was so proud of you though you were a little hell-raiser, even the time you ran away to watch Arsenal instead of coming to your grandfather's funeral."

"Well, going to Highbury was quite an achievement for a seven-year-old," said Nick, still proud of himself, thirty years on. "Instead of hitting me she should have let me work off my excitement and taken me to bed with her, then we would both have slept in peace. I tried so hard to make her love me — it's a pity you didn't act your part. Even eunuchs know how to look after their mistresses."

Adam shook his head, bemused at this latest slur on his adequacy as husband and father.

"Nathalie wasn't much good as a mother though she was quite foolishly fond of you. As I remember it, the pair of you would spend the evenings reading from the *1001 Nights* and getting immense entertainment out of discussing the nonsense of it, Nathalie in fits of laughter at how you repeated the silly love poems with your solemn little face. I was shocked: it wasn't the version I'd heard as a child..."

"What fascinated me was how the stories within the story proliferated: death deferred, a seduction scene set up by a witch for a handsome young man or the rape of a captured maiden postponed while the characters told of some other improbable adventure; the thrill of recognition when the thread of diversions unravelled back to the beginning until eventually the sexy bits came to a happy climax — Maman explained the ridiculously ambiguous language to me so I wouldn't be confused for life thinking a night of coupling meant that the prince got the lady to lie on the bed and put a stick of Brighton Rock in her mouth for her to suck all night long — quite a plausibly nice idea for a nine-year-old but Maman assured me that ladies like doing it with willies almost as much — and when the numerous lost boys and lonely young men wandered bug-eyed through market places, pomegranates and pears stood for breasts and bums, and if the hero paused for Friday prayers before going in at the narrow gate it meant he was empty-ing his mind of all thought so he could enter the tight slit between his beloved's thighs with a pure heart — I still do that. I loved deciphering the puzzle of things not said."

The enigma of Nick himself was beginning to unravel.

"Then I started to have wet dreams — what a thrilling revelation that was! Wow, I could hardly believe that something so sensational popped up out of my willie, my great little, wonderfully lively getting amazingly bigger little maggot. Grandfather would have been proud of me — he gave me such con-fidence in my prick that all the teasing I got at school couldn't diminish its pert up-frontness. It was my excuse to go and climb on top of Maman, the way I did with Bonne-Maman when I wee-ed myself, complaining that I needed clean pyjamas."

"Why didn't you come to me?" asked Adam, shocked. "That's what fath-ers are there for."

"What fun was there in that? It had nothing to do with you," said Nick. "I told her I dreamt she opened the gate to let me into her garden of delights, that I was the *Unbinder* of unhappy wives come to release her from her misery with my sugar stick — this wasn't really true, I was using the Arabian nights to explain my messed up pyjamas. I was astonished but it was all the more exhilarating that instead of playing along with my version of the story she called me a *merdaillon* and slapped me. She stopped reading to me but I knew all the stories anyway and her fury when I woke her up night after night to tell her another changed what had been childish fantasies we shared into a sweetly risky dare to challenge her. As I persisted I knew I was being truly, thrillingly awful; at ten or eleven I didn't understand quite how cruel I was to pester my adored Maman with my 1001 nights of wet dreams — actually only about 501; I wasted a lot of nights waiting for it to happen before I worked out I could will it to come by thinking up a good story first. Like Scheherazade, I hoped to keep her enthralled."

"Well," said Adam, "I suppose making your mother explain the nonsense she was telling you was one way to get a sex education. Would you mind putting some clothes on? I find it singularly disturbing to hear you discuss your precocious sex life with your virility so blatantly on display."

Nick's amusement hardly bothered to be secretive any more. He brushed a smile aside with the lightest of touches and gave his penis an encouraging rub before telling it to lie down and shut up — as usual treating it as if it were a tiresomely frisky and demanding pet dog.

From the little shakes of his head and the sighs of disbelief or disapproval, I could see that while Adam was listening his eyes were focussed and moving in a way that was drawing in his head what he saw in front of him but Nick was not only exposing his body to our scrutiny, his unusual frankness about his mind games was forcing Adam to hold an inquest on his part in his son's childhood.

"When Maman was unhappy and ill I took care of her but when she was feeling feistier we had terrific tussles and shouting matches. She'd either wail like a banshee or hit me. I was having a great time: I had St Oswald's to go to for the fighting and gangs and I had Hampstead Heath to roam around and Grandfather's old lady friend in Highgate to visit. She saved up her sweet ration for me, bars of Cadbury's with a kind of goopy jelly inside. You came home with your blueprints and laid them out flat on the table and I had to stand over you and check your calculations to make sure you weren't making any mistakes. Grandfather told me about his friend who drowned on the Titanic and I didn't want you to make that kind of idiot blunder."

"You can't even read a roadmap," I said, "how could you read a blueprint?"

"I hope May has my brain," he answered. "Sometimes you are quite extraordinarily simpleminded. My whole life's work consists of turning ideas into reality; I learned how from imagining how Dad's drawings would work bobbing around in the waves hitting icebergs. You were good at explaining them, Dad, it's a pity you were so preoccupied with that or you might have noticed how your wife and son tormented each other — you might even have asked why."

"You dramatise yourself, Nick; you weren't to blame for your mother's misery," said Adam impatiently. "Neither was I," he added, since Nick was implying some colossal failure on his father's part.

"I have half a dozen children; I take responsibility for them and for their mothers."

Nick's statement didn't dramatise his authority but nevertheless one had to understand it as a criticism of his father's failure with one wife and one child.

"I saw she was becoming more and more unstable, but really, discussing the Arabian Nights with a young boy and going off with..."

"It must have been a wonderful escape for her when you employed a black dick to man her flying carpet into the setting sun: a story worthy of your bawdy illustration," said Nick, mocking Adam's denial of responsibility. "Your art makes explicit what the poet clouds in words."

"We never found out what happened to my deckhand after she sailed away with him; he was an paradox, a strikingly handsome black African with beautiful manners and a posh voice..."

"He worked for a West African embassy until he was left stranded by civil war back home. Your boat with my mother on board was a convenient stepping stone on the way to America for someone who had lost his country."

Nick interjected this as a piece of information of no great import, simply to complete the record.

"You are curiously well-informed considering you were a child at the time," said Adam.

"By osmosis and deduction, I saw what was going on but I lacked the key to make sense of it. Pauvre Maman! All the men in her life let her down and as a child I didn't know how to deal with such a relentless crescendo of catastrophes. I was eleven when she left. My best efforts only succeeded in driving her away."

"Your mother ran off with an African in my boat — it had nothing to do with you..."

"An engineer should have a better grasp of cause and effect... she could go because you were there to protect me from interfering busybodies and do-gooders; that's what fathers are good for, though you cured me of any love of football by taking me to Wembley to see England thrashed by Hungary. If Grandfather had taken me we'd have won."

Nick's mouth drooped and he looked sorry for himself, reflecting on the uselessness of parents. In spite of Adam's protests, he lay with his belly exposed, looking vulnerable, almost submissive — but not for long.

"... though actually, if she had consulted me I'd have told her I didn't need you, I could have managed perfectly well on my own."

He rolled over to consider the delights of being a Dickensian orphan all alone in a big house with the ghosts if not the actual skeletons of his grandparents, mother and dog around him and a Bum-bessy coming in now and then to flick away the cobwebs.

"I dare say you would have. You'd have gone on living in your little world of juvenile gangs and catapults, a charming but completely wild boy who couldn't read or write. All I could do was to try to get you educated — with no cooperation from you."

"You must admit that though the education you subjected me to was adequate enough for Dunce Deathridge it wasn't quite the one the Dumez-Yussupov genius might have had some benefit from," said Nick and, leaning on his elbow, he held out his glass for a refill. Lying so candidly naked, he was asking his father and me to recognise his otherness, his Nickiness, granting him what Gussie would call his *aidos*,

"You say that with such an air of gracious forgiveness for your pathetically stupid father that I am tempted to empty this bottle over your conceited prick," said Adam, but nevertheless poured it into the glass.

"I'm well used to defending my prick from assault, male and female; don't take advantage of my respect for my dear unworldly Dad."

Adam put the bottle down and walked away, stopping in front of his picture of Gus and me. Maybe he was reconsidering his refusal to do one of Nick. I hoped so: the more disturbed he was the better his picture was likely to be, venting his frustration. Nick was by now well in his stride opening up the various cans of worms that constituted their joint history.

173

"My career in music got lost when you left my piano behind," he said, opening another.

"For pity sake, Nick," said Adam, returning to the fray, "Give it up! that monster was a symbol of Dumez prosperity: they always had a house big enough to contain it. Remember when we went to the cottage the front room hadn't been built; there was just a small room each, a kitchen and a bog. It was practically derelict because it was off limits during the war. That's why I got it so cheaply. I had to do the best I could."

"A hideaway from the scandal of my mother's death," said Nick.

"I was convinced she had been murdered," said Adam, "That Dennis... he was far too well-spoken for a deckhand but he seemed to be what I needed to talk to clients at the boat show..."

"He was a decent chap out of a job — what choice did he have? He gave my mother the help she needed. You must have a guilty conscience," said Nick, the submerged rocks of his accusations breaking the surface again.

"Of course not," said Adam. "The local police wanted to close the case and hush it up, so I had her flown back home."

"They were quite right. There was no evidence it was anything but an unlucky accident. She slipped anchor and drifted. Mother couldn't sail her back singlehanded..."

"The dinghy was missing..."

"The money she had with her could all be accounted for; you may not have approved of what she did with it but she wasn't robbed," said Nick. "Exactly the conclusion the English coroner came to after months of specu- lation and publicity and a complete waste of time and money."

Both men spoke with such detachment they might have been discussing the weather yet I was aware it was a game of chess in which Nick was attack- ing and Adam, defending, was having his pieces relentlessly picked off.

"Shut up in school I had no escape from the malicious rumours spread by the gutter press," said Nick. "They relished such stories: that her brain was affected by syphilis she got from fucking around in creole bars and dance halls, conjuring up sordid images of debauchery, an English lady taking drugs with the black women and getting screwed by their men — it wasn't true but it was a good story. Even Toby, who had shared a room with me up till then, moved out and left me alone."

"Mr Dyer reported to me that you seemed to be coping very well," said Adam. "If you had gone quiet he might have worried but the fights went on much the same as usual, neither was there any reduction in the rowdiness or sulks, no change really."

"I was so touchy the least sexual innuendo sent me into a rage."

"Which, according to Toby, the others thought very funny, especially given your own wide-ranging command of indecent language," I reminded him.

"Babuto tormented me worse than ever, and every time I tried to get away by myself Joey came pestering after me. When we stopped fighting we'd hide under the bridge chewing biltong of which he had an inexhaustible supply, or he'd have a new record and dance to it knowing I couldn't resist joining in. So I learned to hide my suffering even when I knew the boys were making smutty jokes behind my back about shagging black cocks. I targeted those I suspected of spite with an extra hard elbow or knee in the groin at rugby but I was deeply ashamed that I couldn't bring myself to speak up in defence of my mother; I had no words to describe the shame I felt or the pain of losing her. I wanted to stand up to the whole school and scream at them: 'it's all lies, you ill-bred, ignorant louts.' I fought with fists and kicks but I choked on the words."

Toby's observations suggested that Nick had endured quite a bit of physical chastisement in his childhood before being abandoned but Nick's own words suggested something far more complex. Nick the man spoke as if Nathalie Dumez running away with a refugee African was merely an acting out of their Arabian dreams of romance and adventure. Nick granted his mother her *aidos*. It was Adam who was bitter about her failings as wife and mother.

Willie began to cry and I realised that while I was listening to Nick's story he had demolished a whole packet of rusks and was trying to shred the paper.

"And that's why you wouldn't take me to the hunt," I said, wiping Willie's face and hands and rocking him to sleep. I pictured the gathering in Frank's yard, the crowd with their horses and dogs. "You were afraid your horsy friends would laugh at your silly young cunt the way the boys at school sniggered about your mother."

"As if it mattered," said Nick, letting go at last. "You cured me of that vanity. You deserted me for a mere gigolo. And now the gigolo has paid the price. The Grati were right to bury him quietly. There is no such thing as justice for the dead. It's the living who count."

I had to acknowledge that, though I accused Nick of treating me with high-handed disregard for my feelings, on the contrary he had consistently done what he could to preserve my self-respect, from the party escort that cost him so dearly, to the blue lizard, by way of New York; I was the one who lacked the virtue of *aidos* towards him.

"I wasn't any help to you, Nick, " Adam said, conceding that he too had failed. "I didn't know what to say to you to explain how she could have done what she did."

"You wouldn't read the coroner's report to me," said Nick, pointing out exactly where this particular failure lay. "You wouldn't read it yourself. You said the brutal forensic details couldn't tell me if my mother loved me. But I had to know, after the way I harassed her for love, if my over-eager willie was why she rejected me. The nightmare of it haunted me. I imagined her being eaten alive, I'd wake up in the night rigid with disgust that I had a faceless corpse in bed beside me and without daring to look I'd find myself fucking it: my punishment, the most hideous of wet dreams. It sickened me and I did my best not to ejaculate into it but that only prolonged the torture. What a mess I made of myself!"

"Toby didn't desert you in trouble," I said, marvelling at Toby's sympathetic discretion when he was telling me about Nick's nightmares and I was ashamed to think how lightly I had dismissed them. But how could I have guessed he was troubled by anything as horrifying, considering that he was so self-contained, dominating me with his willpower?

"Toby told me he felt the decent thing to do was to withdraw and leave you to hump your nightmare in private. He didn't say whether he knew the cause of it."

"It can't have been hard for him to guess," said Nick. "After all it was Toby who stole a copy of the coroner's report from his Dad and read it for me. Toby didn't want to know all the horrific details but he did it because I couldn't. After he read it, when I shut my eyes it repeated itself over and over again in my head like a scratched record. Toby's support was the brightest light in a dark world. Even when he asked to move out he never told the house-master why: good fellow Toby, the most honest chap on earth — and he is forever having to tell lies for me!"

"You never let me find out that you knew about it," said Adam. "And when I went to Mr Dyer to discuss your hopelessly bad reports he just smiled and said, 'Nick is a fine boy, we can put up with a lot of nonsense from him. He'll do very well when he finds his feet.' So I left it at that. What more could I do?"

"Mr Dyer is a decent man, he respected my privacy," said Nick. "On a clear night he'd let me out in the yard to look at the stars through his telescope. He wasn't much good at it but he had diagrams and he'd read the names for me, with a flask of tea and a bar of hazelnut chocolate. Monsieur Michel was the person I talked to simply because one can say things in French one can't say in English. He told me all boys come in their pyjamas — not necessarily because they dream they are doing it with their mothers though that's pretty normal, he said, there are much weirder things than that. He suggested I try thinking about shooting at the rifle range or kicking for goal instead. It was also a help that he'd spent a few summers working at a bar on St Barth's and could talk about what kind of life Maman might have lived there, nothing like the vulgarity of the stories being reported in the papers here. The French Creoles are pretty civilised. He went back there later to run his own language school. That's why I chose to go there for my honeymoon."

"You figured out your own strategies for surviving, even though it meant risking your neck on Frank's horses and all that tomfoolery at school," said Adam, his failure to address the problem of Nick and his wet dreams clearly still troubling him, "I can even forgive you for wrecking my Morgan motor-car, the first thing I ever spent a substantial amount of money on — it might even have been what seduced your mother, more sporty and dashing than Daddy's Daimler."

"It was falling to bits by the time I got to drive it," said Nick. "Even I couldn't fix it any more, it needed more than a strap and a bit of bent wire to hold it together."

"Still, there was no need to drive it into the stream and abandon it there."

"It was supposed to be a fording place; I could see it was deeper than usual after days of rain but I was curious to find out how deep it would have to be to stop the motor and if I could still get across. A misjudgement, when it stalled I might have been swept away; though just over knee deep, the con-crete bottom was slimy, hard to stay on one's feet with the current pouring down off the hills."

"You always had a tendency to overestimate your own strength; it would have been poetic justice if you lost your life where probably it started — it's highly likely the Morgan is where you were conceived," Adam said. "I'd been given a ration of petrol to get myself and my gear up to Glasgow and I was saying good-bye to your mother. I might never have seen her again but for you popping up between us."

Nick looked at his father as if for once he had surprised him, and his eyes had a gleam of genuine delight.

"I wish you had told me that before, it would have added to my enjoyment of the moment. As it was, I was so wet and cold I sat under a hedge and cried, watching the old motor being pushed downstream and crashing into the bank. I had to walk miles uphill to get to the main road and hitch a lift home."

"You were lucky a passing neighbour recognised that Deathridge's boy was running away from home again; no stranger would have wanted a filthy wet savage like you in their car. Sad end for the Morgan though!"

"Not really," said Nick, unapologetic, "quite a fitting end for a brave little motor."

"I don't know how you got by at school with your unashamed crying, all that weeping and wailing in paroxysms of self-pity. You were an embarrassment to me."

"I was an embarrassment to everyone but myself," said Nick, allowing a glimmer of well-polished teeth to show in what could pass for a shame-faced smile. "Besides, I could deliver a pretty vicious slicing kick to the kneecap: London boy! I learned how fighting the Camden Town gang."

Adam and Nick were silent as they adjusted their views of the past and of each other. Would their account ever be settled?

"I didn't get over my hay fever until I went to Switzerland," said Nick, surprising me with another of his apparently inconsequential statements, but followed it up, saying, "one of the minor blessings of getting out at a time when being British was an embarrassment. My eyes dried up and I didn't have to cringe every time we gave in to the brutally obtuse, treacherous Yanks. We beat the shit out of Nasser and then let him get away with it."

Nick sat upright with a sharp intake of breath.

"Oh, Christ, I have such great balls."

He gripped them between his hands, squeezing with a grimace of satisfaction.

"The wheel of fortune is spinning for me," he said. "I've spent most of my life defying death to come and get me and getting away with it. Paying Gianni to fuck for me was the shrewdest thing I ever did. I'll be thirty-eight on the First of June. I was born out of the Blitz and survived everything life has thrown at me since and I'm in prime shape, never better. I have cheated fate. My Faustian pact with Death seems to be holding."

"If my Great-aunt Kathleen hadn't died so unexpectedly," I said, "I'd have stayed at home with her in Ranelagh Road and been a Montessori teacher: then marrying someone like Gianni would have been the best thing that could happen to me — there was an Italian ice-cream parlour I passed on the way downtown with terribly good-looking boys, they went to the Christian Brothers, dashing in their red blazers but scary. Meeting the irresistible force of your prick and marrying Gussie Wittersworth were unwarranted turns of fortune. Sometimes I wake up in the night and wonder how it happened."

"If you can make yourself decent, Nick," said Adam, "we'll go down to dinner. We've had quite enough of your digressions into the misfortunes of your youth. It's time you told us the real story."

~

The
Inquest

9

We sat down to dinner in a corner of the dining room where the ill-fated wedding feast had taken place, where a few months earlier Nick had done his best to seduce Amanda Wittersworth. Clare had made her special lobster bisque in her own game of culinary flirtation with Nick and, while the maid served it, she came to talk to him and say how sorry she was we were leaving the castello. I said they would have a more peaceful life without us but her expressions of regret were sincerely forgiving. Tomás came and poured glasses of oloroso sherry to have with the bisque — very Edinburgh, said Nick — and kissed me on the cheek by way of moral support. Probably he felt it was safe to risk his tribute to the White Goddess now I was leaving. Then they moved on to the seasonal gathering of Germans, letting us get on with our meal.

Adam said, "Well, you left us on the road with Gus at about two o'clock yesterday afternoon. Presumably something happened to precipitate you turning up here in a state of disarray twenty-four hours later."

Nick tasted the sherry, then emptied the glass into his soup and stirred them together saying it might make them both more palatable. Having spoilt both the soup and the sherry he pushed his plate aside and proceeded to tell his story:

"Yes, following Gus's directions we left the motorway, went through several villages and finally turned into a drive and down a gentle slope. Pausing as instructed around a bend under the lime trees, there, on a slight elevation with the countryside rolling away beyond it, sat the prettiest little Palladian villa — souvenir of some ancestor's Grand Tour, no doubt.

"'Will it do?' asked Gus. 'It's rather bijou, has all the trimmings on the *piano nobile* but upstairs the smaller rooms have been turned into modern conveniences so there are only five decent bedrooms, not counting the ground floor of course, but even so it should be adequate for all our children, yours as well as mine.'

"I looked at him to see if he was taking the mickey with me," said Nick, "or was he being genuinely modest. I can so easily imagine him tricking his victims and misleading a jury with his double-edged questions. 'Why?' I asked, 'Are you thinking of buying?'

"'Fortunately, no,' Gus said. 'My grandmother is living here. It's called the Malcontenta after the villa it's rather inaccurately modelled on, on a more modest scale luckily. It does have frescos of the Virtues: Continence, Fortitude, Prudence and so on — rather a vain hope, given my wife's infatuation with the Wrong Fucking Man.'

"It didn't seem to perturb him unduly," said Nick. "Remarkable young man! In the circumstances I'd have done Deathridge in and disposed of the body under a blackberry hedge. He wouldn't be the first man to try getting rid of me — including my own father."

"Gus is a modern Stoic," I said. "He believes that the autonomy of the individual includes women. He did mention we would have a miniature palace to live in but he was only joking. Then with the trouble over Gianni I forgot to ask him any more about it. If his frescos are too insulting I'll whitewash them."

"Major works of art," said Nick, "more the scale of the Carracci than Tomás's Giottos. Double flights going up to the loggia and massive oak doors, the proportions slightly disconcerting to one whose natural frame of reference for domestic harmony is early Lutyens."

"Arts and Crafts fakery," was Adam's disparaging comment. "Dumez could have had Max Fry for the same money building for the future."

"Spare me," said Nick. "Who wants to live like a goldfish in a glass bowl? Max Fry never built a fortress against the Wicked World. Gus's villa is the next best thing. 'There's a cabinet of curiosities,' he informed me, leading the way in through the cavern of a hall, 'you may add a few of your more esoteric inventions to the hilarity of future generations.'

"I was tempted to give him a kick in the arse," said Nick, "but we were met by Grand-mamma Wittersworth who was not surprised to see us, so obviously Gus had planned the visit without warning me of his intentions.

"'Goodness,' she said. 'You look like a pair of undertakers. Not to carry me away, I hope, or not just yet.'

"'We've just come from a funeral,' said Gus.

"'An unfortunate comparison in the circumstances,' she said. 'No disrespect to the dead.'

"'No need to apologise,' said Gus.

"'I didn't,' she said.

Nick excused himself and left them sparring, remembering he had a spare tie in the car as he and Angelina had a dinner appointment later. He went and put that on and presented himself again, looking rather more appropriate to being received by a gracious lady in her Palladian hall.

"'We were laying to rest Sibylla's other life,' Gus was explaining to his grandmother when Nick came back. '*The romance of Gianni the Magnificent: a tragedy in three acts.*'

Nick said: 'alternatively, an *opera buffa*. Just like *Salome*, it would take the comic genius of Oscar Wilde to do it justice.'

"'When am I going to meet this amazing wife of yours William tells me about?" said Grand-mamma. "I simply cannot comprehend the discourtesy of not inviting me to your wedding."

"Do I have to eat dirt for the rest of your life?' asked Gus. 'Blame this man. Nick Deathridge was Sibylla's first lover. She was already expecting his baby when I met her. The rivalry was acute — it still is! I had to get her to the registry office fast when I could, no time for the niceties. If you and Mother were involved, expressing your contrary opinions, I would have lost my chance to nail her. I am just showing Nick that when I get his precious bastard here she won't be living in a hovel."

"So that was the purpose of my visit," said Nick. "Gus was showing off the handsome old woman, the Roman antiquities, the Venetian chandeliers, the classical proportions of the life my daughter will be subjected to, and indicating that there is nothing I can do about it. Except refuse to let him adopt her. Maybe he was hoping I would see the futility of my gesture."

I had seen nothing of this yet, but already Nick describing it to me was shaping it in my mind. I was glad I hadn't met young Gus against this background but in the bachelor squalor of Marylebone where we made love on a horsehair couch and our bicycles got tangled in the narrow hall. My precious Tweedledee: little did I appreciate what a treasure I had secured.

"Grand-mamma insisted we had tea, then walk around the romantically unkempt park, then drinks, then something to eat, then another drink, another snack, a game of bawdy Scrabble: who could produce the rudest words. I did rather well on that one," said Nick.

"I didn't know you could spell," I said.

Nick looked at me, surprised that I doubted him, but continued unperturbed:

"I could see where Gus got his wit and charm from. They kept me entertained until after midnight. I had to phone Angelina to cancel our dinner date, to her great annoyance — she hates having to apologise for me — but I was entranced, there was no way I could escape, or even want to. I knew I was being manipulated, but I was happy to go along with it, to be diverted, to be captivated."

I could understand Nick's pleasure in being challenged and how he loved to play games, apparently even Scrabble, which considering he claimed he had never learned the alphabet was mildly surprising. He probably shuffled the pieces in much the same way as he picked winners at the races.

"All the way back in the car we did our best to bore the other to death," he said, "or at least despair. I thought I had quite a talent for that, but I'd say Gus won hands down by reciting Latin poetry for what seemed like hours on end — except that I found it quite entertaining, no worse than Scrabble; I suppose I must have absorbed some understanding in spite of my passive resistance in the classroom."

One could see how Nick could hold the floor interminably at meetings, unwelcome when everyone else wanted to have their say but entertaining at long dinners where gentlemen could sit back with brandy and cigars and just listen with effortless attention, Nick resilient enough to withstand the comic relief of heckling — he went on:

"I dropped him off in Marylebone sometime around dawn and went home. After the best part of a day and a night battling with the Wittersworths over you I was so fucking mad my balls were fit to burst. I just picked up the appropriate passport and matching driving license and went to Heathrow to catch the first available flight to get me anywhere near to you, actually early morning Alitalia to Milan, hence the Ferrari. But of course Wittersworth hasn't won. And telling me how he had successfully kidnapped Augusta only upped the ante. Does he think I can't do likewise?"

I could tell Nick was not only bursting in his balls but mentally totally immersed in this game of wits with Gus in which I was the Cunt Queen to be captured, May my pawn. But since the Grati had already fought this battle with deadly outcome I had to take it seriously.

"What really pisses me off," said Nick, "is that that house of Wittersworth's is something money can't buy. Granddad Deathridge's ancestral home would need to have been something better than a fisherman's hut in Sea-houses smoking herrings — in itself a bit of a come-down for a Viking— or maybe that's what Vikings did in their spare time between the fighting."

"If Gus already has a house for Sibylla," said Adam, unmoved by the dig at his modest background and accepting a scoop of soured cream in his second serving of bisque, "she doesn't need you to buy her one."

"I wasn't in a position to buy anything while the Furzys and their team of dreadnoughts had me cornered with my D for dunce's cap on," said Nick. "Mrs Furzy started the whole thing, thinking she'd catch me out in a swindle and make me pay fantastic compensation. Holy Harold put that idea in her head and she was only too ready to believe the worst of me. Why someone with a vow of pseudo-poverty and a lifetime of irresponsibly protected living thought he could advise her — he must have had a hint from some malevolent source looking to make trouble on my behalf. The Virgins too are constantly nagging for more money because of the Nickies, which I refuse to pay, so Wittersworth dragged Tsang into the case. That complicated the whole thing beyond what their simple minds could grasp. I told my unloving mother-in-law that, contrary to her delusions of unlimited wealth, I have impoverished myself to maintain her pretentious lifestyle."

"You can't expect us to believe that you were seriously deprived," I said.

"While they started legal proceedings against me I escaped once more with Rose and Violet on what they considered a soirée of high culture: *Les Contes d'Hoffman* at the *Opéra Comique*. The darlings, I so enjoy their thrills and burblings! They loved it all; for me it's only that one song, *elle a fui, la tourterelle* — I dissolve in tears, longing to expire on the Shackleton's divine bosom."

I could hear the echo of Toby saying, "Leave my mother out of it!"

"Having my Poppets on either side to dry my cheeks and hold my hands made it doubly exquisite an emotion." Nick sighed with pleasure and Adam raised his eyes from his soup with corresponding displeasure. "I had the audience around me shouting '*bis, bis, bis!*' so I got them to repeat it three times, humouring the mad Englishman with his gorgeous lady loves. Love is taken seriously in Paris."

"When you were sixteen you might well blame it on hay fever though you could certainly weep on the slightest provocation, but you ought surely have got over your infatuation with Hannah Shackleton by now." said Adam. "And a night at the Opéra Comique can hardly be your financial ruin," obviously not taking into consideration Nick's propensity for expanding any simple event into a major extravaganza.

"Next morning we did the Galerie Lafayette, which used to be their favourite shop before they had my wallet at their disposal, but except for the cosmetic counters where they made clowns of themselves while I stood by like a horse sleeping on my feet, they skipped the rest of the vulgar display for the fun of exploring a new level of service in more exclusive boutiques — people complain how rude Parisians are; it's something I've never experienced, they combine charm and manners with good business sense. I even went to the extreme of eating macaroons — though I draw the line at drinking chocolate — at Ladurie with my sweethearts for the look on their naughty faces. They believe they are seducing me with their wickedness, trying to get me to buy them ocelot coats, the scatterbrained poppets. I asked how they were going to turn up at anti-hunt demonstrations in Surrey wearing ocelot, but they couldn't see the connection."

"Well, if they succeeded in impoverishing you, you must have been spending on other outrageous things, if not ocelot," I said.

"You know I have no trouble spending money."

Nick's gravity was in itself suspicious.

"Paris is the one city where one isn't embarrassed to go round town with two flighty ladies in their forties hanging on one's arms and telling everyone I am the father of their babies. I enjoy being made a spectacle of by such ridiculously silly women; happily with their trim little figures and slim, lively legs they don't look too ludicrous in fringed gold lamé shifts that enhance their adorable Nickie-round tummies, a pair of flappers in monkey fur jackets and with their four inch high heels expecting to be carried squealing with excitement on and off river boats for romantic moonlight cruises with specially chartered gypsy violins to swoon to."

I smiled, remembering Paul's description of Nick chasing them with the mucking-out broom and Rose skidding in the shit in her pink silk knickers. I supposed that Violet would go for mauve underwear. Gipsy violins suggested that not a lot had changed in his attitude to them: a loving mockery of two darlings who gave him enormous pleasure because like dolls he could do what he liked with them.

"They are such a pretty contrast to me in my most formal gear and unruffled dignity: I defy anyone to laugh at us. We spent a couple of weeks at the George V — I was a bit coy about taking them back to the Ritz after their brilliant performance there the last time. They dragged me across the road to Hermès to buy a hat so they could flirt with the hatter. He fitted me out really rather handsomely but I managed to lose it before we came home —

I need a wide brim to balance my chin but the gangster image would undermine my standing in the City. So you see, it all adds up."

"But you are singularly good at keeping the tally," I said. "You must have
known exactly what you were doing."

"Of course," he said.

"So what were you really up to?" I asked.

Nick shrugged off such a silly question.

"Ostentatiously running up bills."

"Lucky Virgins at the receiving end."

"I brought them home to face the music, the Virgins showing off their
quite absurdly useless acquisitions to the fury of Mrs Furzy and Angelina,
and me penniless, pleading poverty and unable to pay out Mrs Furzy's
quarterly revenue. She was having to pay for her groceries with a credit card.
I'm good at not laughing."

"You can be unbelievably malicious, Nick," I said.

"Just teaching fools the facts of life," he said sharply in response, then
went on with his storytelling: "It has put the Furzys in a quandary," he said.
"The outcome is exactly the opposite from that which they expected. Having
initiated proceedings against me on some completely unfounded suspicion
in Great-Uncle's head, thereby losing my unpaid work and goodwill which,
when it proved false, made me appear the victim of their greed and left them
much worse off than before."

"Sitting in Fred Furzy's chair and drinking his wine..." Adam started to
question Nick's claim to doing unpaid work but Nick went on:

"I sat dumbly by while Toby produced the evidence that in the face of
a falling bond market for years I've been subsidising any shortfall in my
mother-in-law's income, and though the Virgins arrived home from Paris
staggering under the weight of my gifts, that was no more than generosity
on my part and even though the children are genetically mine that doesn't
relieve Tsang of responsibility for his experiments that produced them.
Angelina is beside herself with annoyance. But, however awful I am, she
blames her mother most of all for dragging all this into the public eye and

what's worse, altering the dynamics of our family life. Without my subsidy Mrs Furzy is having to sell her house. Angelina was terrified the same might happen to hers."

"You can't mean it!" I cried, "Her house is all the world to Angelina. You can't have squandered that away."

"That's not what I said. I told you, I was the dunce sitting in the corner with my face to the wall. I said nothing — until it was all settled and agreed, the dreadnoughts quite intimidated by the Worthy Witters and foiled by Toby's meticulous record keeping. They tailed off about their business; there was no case to answer, nothing they could charge absurd fees for. The family gathered in Wittersworth's chambers to listen to his fatherly admonitions and commiserate with one another, and even, begrudgingly, with me though it was clearly all my fault for being so wildly spend-thrift and wasting a whole year, when I could have been earning a proper living, on Tsang's mad schemes."

"I still don't believe that diamond rings and a stay at the Ritz can add up to more than petty cash for you," I said, knowing how difficult it was to drag out of Nick the whole truth. Adam must have thought the same. He said:

"Why am I thinking, Nick, that this claim to poverty is all some sinister plot? How did you persuade anyone to believe you couldn't raise the odd few hundred thousand to pay off your debts..."

"Why are you surprised, Dad? You and my friends have been telling me for years that my wealth is so ephemeral I am bound to come a cropper sooner or later. My house of cards, Wittersworth calls it. And Angelina isn't surprised we are suddenly penniless because she never could understand how the weird little twiddly bits that come out of my workshop can add up to anything significant. Young Gus is the only one who is perceptive enough to have faith in me; he knows that most of my ready cash has gone missing on Death Row."

"Death Row? You're saying that to mystify us," I said.

"Eggers is quite annoyed about it. His ambition is for a self-perpetuating cycle of chunky new machines making more chunky new machines in the

Swiss aesthetic, so I told him to buy me out and get to hell back to the bear pit where he belongs...... a few years ago a gang of boys invaded the yard and landed their football on my desk amid a shower of glass; I swung down the fire-escape after them and ran them to earth hiding out in a row of deserted houses..."

"Your rat catchers?" I asked, wondering where this diversion was leading.

"Their older brothers, it was well before the rat crisis — that was when I first got them organised and playing proper games with goalposts instead of my windows. My chase into the hinterland alerted me that this area was scheduled for demolition and I persuaded the council that instead of some outmoded tower block they should let me rebuild the street to the original footprint, only better, for my workers. They agreed begrudgingly because there is no public money to do it themselves though they were reluctant to let the likes of me provide social housing, it smacks too much of patronage and no kudos in it for them. That's what Toby and I spent most of last year doing — that rubbish with Tsang was nothing more than divertimento con brio. My staff name it Death Row because they could see our profits going down the drain on this pointless act of philanthropy."

"Philanthropy?" said Adam. "It sounds more like a shrewd investment."

"The one doesn't exclude the other — so, having extricated myself blamelessly from a tight corner and weathered the Furzy threat," Nick carried on with the fiction of his financial ruin, "I simply closed the books on my factory and Toby kept it quiet that he had signed a contract on my behalf with the development company that built my houses. The terms are satisfactory: the sheds will be knocked down and replaced with luxury flats for which I shall receive an annually inflation-adjusted ground rent. Keeping my old men at work on such a prime site on the fringes of respectability was my really sound investment. They don't have to wait for their carriage clocks now but can go off and open up little repair shops in shopping arcades if they have no allotments to attend to. I'll take a bet on not one of them sitting around on his backside on the dole — I do include going to football or the dogs as being gainfully employed —

and of course they have my nice little houses as part of their well-endowed pension fund."

"You would almost drive me to believe in the devil, Nick," said Adam. "They say he looks after his own. Someone must be looking after you and it can't be God."

"Who looks after me," said Nick, "is Me. Moi. Myself. Maybe I am the Devil; I certainly look after my own. Darling Angelina has nothing to worry about. She can go on entertaining her Women in style and educate our sons according to her fancy."

"Where does Paul stand in all of this?" I asked, thinking of how Paul had his arm around Nick's shoulder during the peace conference, as if he felt a protective urge that was a role reversal between the brothers-in-law.

"I told Paul to stay well out of it. Neither he nor Angelina has any interest in inheriting a phoney Tudor mansion with leaking gutters and out-of-date plumbing — their father bought it with the intention of demolishing it for scrap, only Queenie Furzy took a notion to live there in delusional splendour. It is up to Paul to find something better for himself when he can afford to move out of my attic. I suggested that she move into the Virgins' pretty little gingerbread cottage, and pay them a proper rent for the privilege. And her friends will tell her how sensible to downsize, it's all the fashion."

"What about the Virgins?" I asked. "I loved the stories about them and the goat in their little house with the cuckoo-clock."

"The Virgins did look a bit bemused until I said they should move in with Angelina and me and bring the Nickies where Angelina can see to it that they'll get a sensible up-bringing."

I could see the point of that. The Virgins, with or without the goat, were unlikely to be very reliable mothers, but while Nick went on about his domestic arrangements I wasn't listening, still feeling the piercingly sharp sensation of embracing his naked body... what did I care about the drawing-room where Angelina entertained her Women friends though it seemed a pity when Nick said he was replacing the Steinway with a nicely bouncy bed for her Aunties to shriek and giggle in to their hearts' content.

"Your lovely piano, Nick, you can't throw that out!"

"It's no good," he said, dismissing my objection. "I can't play in a ladies' tea-room... I've had an architect in to join up the guest lavatory and cloak-room on the landing into a bathroom and dressing room for them..."

Angelina's complaint about builders explained: Nick must have been organising this move well in advance despite Angelina's objection to what appeared quite unnecessary work on her house. Equally he must have been drawing up plans for his Death Row a few of years before needing to move his workers out in advance of demolishing his factory, confirming Adam's suspicions. Nick Machiavelli!

"The Nickies are already quite at home in the nursery — there have never been such yummy babies, I could eat them. The little darlings, Angelina sees that having ready-made Nickies spares her the indignity of spreading her legs to let me in and my offspring out. Con and Joe play with them as if they were a pair of puppies. They are still known by the generic name of Nickies. Angelina is doing her best to get them properly christened but the Virgins are content that Tsang registered them as Furzy A and B. I suppose any future Nickies will be C, D, E and F with bracelet name tags to identify them."

"Oh, Nick, you can't be serious!"

Nick's total heart-melting love for his little Nickies-with-no-names put both Angelina's and my noses out of joint as the mothers of his more conventionally acquired children.

"Don't your people mind living on Death Row?" I asked.

"No one has survived working for me for ten years without developing a sense of the ridiculous. When they want to be posh they say they live in the Deathridge Garden City — I ask you, the whole thing is little more than an acre or two. How absurd is that! I wanted to call the pub on the corner 'Hell's Kitchen' but they voted for 'The Jolly Roger' with skull and crossbones on the sign. They regretted it when there was an invasion by the local punks who come to sing *Friggin' in the Riggin'* for them but these are only the kids who used to play football in the yard before the present lot, so they've adopted it now as our anthem, they sing lengthy rude verses when they come to watch football on the big screen and I throw a party for them to encourage a bit of anarchy; it keeps the Ancients in touch with their youth and they've taken to wearing similar black jerseys, some even getting skull and crossbone tattoos on the forearm as a sign they belong."

"You too?" I asked knowing he had several black jerseys in his wardrobe.

"Goodness no. They expect me to turn up as a fancy gentleman, bow tie, velvet jacket and shiny shoes, so they can boast to their friends that they are mates with a fabulously rich genuine millionaire who dances the sailors' hornpipe for them, leaping across from table to table while they clap and stand by to catch me when I fall off — pure pandemonium. I tell them they are allowed to do that when they are making enough money to pay for the damage and they start wearing proper shoes like mine. Unlike my colleagues in the City they take my financial advice seriously and have set up a mutual havoc fund."

"How reliable would they think your example if they had seen you standing on top of the leaning tower of Pisa tossing bundles of lire into the wind."

"That is exactly what they'd all love to do."

"Anyway, how can you pretend to be fabulously wealthy when you deliberately throw it all away?"

"Wittersworth and Toby got poor maligned me off paying any costs — everyone vastly underestimated the value of my intellectual property, those sneaky little patents Toby had assiduously filed for me without having a clue what they were worth. To him it was all a great bore, doing me a favour."

Nick looked around the dining room to see if the Germans were eating anything interesting. So far he'd had nothing.

"I can't drink Tomas's raw chianti on an empty stomach," he complained. "I'm randy as hell for another go with my favourite cunt whose dewy lips are beguiling me across the table but I'm starving after the last bout... it's days since I had a square meal, all that flirting with Grand-mamma Wittersworth's dainty snacks made me miss a good dinner chez Hardi: fillet of horse à la Bruxelloise with pommes frites... I'm wax in the hands of a certain vintage of fine lady, forever howling in the dark for my... never mind... my friends and enemies alike were agog with incredulity when the bidding started: Japs and Americans; bless us, even a few Germans; and the ever pragmatic Swiss were prepared to compromise over stuff they say I stole from them — improved as it was by my refinements. So, surprise, surprise! to everyone's annoyance that I'd got away with it again, I came out of a minor embarrassment wealthier beyond wildest expectations. My punks and pirates put up a scoreboard in the canteen as a mini stock market and cheered at every additional killing. They are proud of me."

When I asked Gus later what had really been going on, he said Nick had simply wanted to divest himself of his English liabilities at the least possible cost to himself. The capital valuation on a few sheds and Luddite equipment was not significant; it would take years for the property development to show any profit on the books; and the real immediate gain from the patents simply disappeared *ins blau hinein*, otherwise known as the Deathridge Swiss bank account."

"But the Virgins? How did he get out of that?"

"Tsang says Nick's involvement with his virgin births has made the whole enterprise invalid. Nick says that his purpose in taking them to Paris and spending wildly on their ridiculous choice of furs and shoes was a bribe to persuade them to stop referring to their miracle pups as the Nickies. Nick claims he has absolutely no emotional attachment to them — though having fun with them relieves his anxieties; he only supplied the ginger for Tsang's Mendelian cross-breeding experiment with sperm selected to balance up the rose and violet. It took Tsang six months to find a combination that satisfied him. Just think, says Nick, looking hard done by, what a drain that was on his sperm production."

"Not something Nick normally complains about," I said.

"Sperm selection indeed!" said Gus, "I bet he just fucked it straight up their obliging cunts. The whole thing is a hoax and Tsang will be struck off for scientific fraud. But he is making plenty of money out of his notoriety if nothing else, and Nick was supplying the equipment and technical advice without his name being mentioned. No wonder it was worth bribing the Virgins with macaroons at Ladurie.

Gus's disingenuous Wittersworth smile betrayed his own involvement. "Who do you think," he said, "took the hint to start the ball rolling by spreading the rumour that Nick was in financial trouble and the Furzy estate had been robbed?"

"You?"

"That's Nick's lateral thinking in action. He used to take tackles head-on until he got his nose smashed. Now he knows better how to go about getting where he wants to be. Even the damned Death Row will revert to him when his Ancients die off, worth considerably more than he paid to build it. Nick's apology is that he can't help making money; he blames Toby for bullying him into signing whatever he sees fit to arrange for him — claiming that he has always been at the mercy of Toby of the Ten Commandments."

As if!

The Inquest: 2nd Course

10

The next course was fettuccine with funghi sprinkled with Clare's home-made truffle oil, a favourite with both Adam and me and we were busy with our forks while Nick sat brooding on his misfortunes, not eating, not talking. Eventually he said with an air of mild irony:

"I wonder, what would I have to do to win my father's approval?"

Adam looked up from his plate, apologetically.

"I'm sorry, Nick. Of course, congratulations on a successful outcome to your financial dealings..."

"and outwitting the legal challenges?"

"yes, that too, of course..."

"am I allowed out of the dunce's corner?"

"I never doubted your ability to use your wits to get what you want..."

"and the ingenious solution to the complications of my love life?"

"well I'm not so sure about that — getting babies with two more than slightly batty ladies ten years older than yourself — you can hardly expect me to say I'm delighted," said Adam, giving up any further pretence at agreement. "And you can't expect me to be overjoyed at having a son who, it seems, is capable of making money out of a crisis, deceiving his own legal team quite as much as the opposition. I don't suppose for a minute that your present activities are any less destructive than the mishaps of your unbridled youth."

"I can't seem to persuade you what a great life I am having," said Nick, "— and I don't know what you are calling mishaps; audacious I may have been but not foolhardy and when the unexpected happens I am quick enough to make instant adjustments — the way you demonstrated when you took me sailing."

"Thank you for admitting I taught you something," said Adam dryly.

"Basel is where I got advanced instruction in survival skills; I went along with the rest of Hein's apprentices and found the real purpose of climbing, skiing, shooting and all that. In no time I was hurtling across mountains with a rucksack and a gun on my back like the best of them, falling on my face in snow, shooting at moving targets through trees... I felt justified that Joey and I used to pull horrible faces at each other when we were being lectured at school with nonsense about sportsmanship and fair play: tell that fairytale to an Afrikaner."

"And you escaped the dreariness of square-bashing in Britain..."

"... I might have been killed clambering around the barren rocks of Aden dodging Arab bullets whereas the Swiss sensibly put all their effort and ingenuity into defending the tiny fraction of the earth's surface they call their own. Besides, who needs a lot when what one has is simply the best? I wanted more than anything to be Swiss, but I'd have to wait ten years — unless I could find a Swiss wife. The heroic Fock Apparat der Englischer Bueb was widely discussed among the girls, so I decided to make the most of my only asset and auction myself off. I got numerous offers but, thwarted because Mrs Shackleton wouldn't give me her violin to console me for losing her..."

"Why on earth do you imagine she should part with her father's violin for the sake of a disgracefully badly behaved youngster...?"

"I was in disgrace, not disgraceful, there is a difference... I offered myself to whomever could get me the nearest thing to a Stradivari. But no one could raise enough money for what I wanted. Even when I located a nice Andreas Morelli, 1930's in not bad condition, I couldn't get it. I kept dragging girls along to talk to the dealer, Mr Mug. He taught me Ravel's *Habanera* to impress them — I heard it again a few weeks ago, standing on the concourse at Schiphol messily eating new herring and raw onion, and it transported me instantly to a steep alley in the Baseler Altstadt and I felt again that youthful eagerness and longing tearing my heart — he played the piano to flatter my performance, the only person who ever did that for me, but he wouldn't reduce his price. He suggested the girls form a syndicate to buy it and take turns with me, but though that was quite a nice notion it was obviously no good as a solution to the legal necessity of finding a wife."

Adam didn't deign to respond to this provocation.

"However, while the negotiations were going on it was flattering to my narcissism and quite titillating being courted... I had to fend them off from handling the merchandise so they made a game of it to see if it responded better to cooing or chirping. One girl had a particularly shrill whistle that made it shiver."

Adam remained obstinately silent, apparently concentrating on careful forkfuls of fettuccine while I swallowed my regret that I would never know Nick as he was when young, the look of wounded innocence belied by the glint of mischief in his eyes. I remembered Adèle telling me how he had cajoled her into buying him a pair of fine Italian dancing shoes with no recompense beyond a turn on the dance floor and a love song at dawn — I must remember to find out what he had sung. The only time he sang for me was the Ave Maria when he was making fun of my Great-Aunt Kathleen's Latin — I told him that Dublin Latin was just as likely to sound like ancient Romans as posh English — I'm not a parrot, I told myself whenever I caught myself out imitating Nick's rounded vowels and resonant cadenzas, and the most pleasure I got out of fighting with Mary was hearing an echo of my own voice again.

Had Adèle whistled or chirped to get a rise? It was a pity I didn't know that delightful little nugget sooner or I'd have asked her.

When my attention returned to the table with Adam and Nick, Adam was saying:

"After I had you fixed up with good-natured Mr Hein, little did I think that the raw youth I'd left behind, too shy to talk to girls, would in no time be making an exhibition of himself with the encouragement of apparently intelligent young women..."

"It wasn't like that," said Nick. "Hein exploited me mercilessly and I was relentlessly molested by a pack of wolf bitches competing for my innocent dick..."

"... obviously I don't understand the power of sexual magnetism."

"Obviously not," said Nick, polite concern failing to disguise his heavy sarcasm. "I don't suppose you've ever been in love, Father dear. I, on the other hand, have never not been in love or pining for love, but at eighteen I was nothing but a freshly primed cock, which I sold, not after all for a violin, but to Eugenie Bott when she fixed my citizenship application for me."

"So that's where the mysterious Eugenie comes in," I said. "Not a very romantic exchange after your bargaining with all the other girls."

"It was the best bargain of my life," said Nick. "I gave her exclusive rights to my goy-boy cock, to her Papi's furious disapproval when I turned up on his doorstep, an uncircumcised pig fucking his daughter — I said I was perfectly happy with my cock as it was, I had no intention of having it trimmed — her mother let me in and protected me by reclining gracefully in the sitting room with her coffee pot for company, reading Rilke's Duino Elegies while I put my best effort into getting on top of Eugenie in her mother's bed."

Successfully, according to Nestor's report.

"When I'd done, on my way out I had to thank Mami by shaking her hand and kissing her on both cheeks. She'd smile at me with an air of romantic melancholy and quote something that meant nothing to me at the time:

'always, no matter what we do, we are in the stance
of one departing — as he,
on the last hill that shows him all his past
one last time, turns, stops, lingers —
we live our lives, forever taking leave.'

"I couldn't know what she was talking about; I never thought of taking leave of Eugenie: I was hers for life."

"You've travelled quite a road from Duino," I said, thinking how Nick was forever taking leave of me, and the pain of each departure.

"We took the train to Trieste to go swimming off the rocks at Duino but the caretaker at the castle didn't think two young strangers wanting to make love to the tune of Rilke was sufficient reason to let us in... pity, it would have been a nicely melancholic place for an illicit honeymoon..."

"I never understood why you choose to honeymoon on St Barthélemy of all places," Adam remarked, dismissing Nick's youthful amours as so much frivolity. "You drifted up to your bridal suite looking like a zombie and weren't heard of again. Mrs Furzy phoned me after a few weeks to know what you were doing with her precious daughter, as if I should know. She didn't take kindly to my answer that you were presumably doing what most newly weds do and were too fatigued to report back to Mother."

Adam picked up his fork again to go on with his dinner, indicating to Nick that his fettuccine was waiting in front of him.

"I hoped blue seas and tropical gardens would put Angelina in a receptive mood but she was rather annoyed with me; she's not exactly twinkle-toes, and I'd made her practise a lively Viennese over and over, warning her I didn't want her tripping me up, so she didn't appreciate that I turned our inaugural waltz into a marvellous satire — well, her incomprehension of what was happening to the music added to the success of my hoax. Eugenie said I should have danced it with her, but she'd have been too slick a performer. The whole point of the piece is to end in utter confusion. It worked beautifully."

"It quickly put an end to any attempt on my part to partner the mother of the bride," said Adam ruefully. "On the other hand every one of your polite Swiss lady friends got me to dance with them in the course of the evening. I was impressed by how conscientiously they were set on doing their duty, making it delightfully easy for me..."

Grown-up Heini girls?

Ignoring that, Nick said, "I wanted to borrow our Espérance back from the Greek for a month and take it on a memory trip, but St Barths was a bit far for me to handle alone; obviously Angelina would be worse than useless as crew...

I'd have asked you only I was afraid you'd cramp my style once we got there."

Adam looked aghast.

"I can't think of a more stomach-turning suggestion, Nick. I can't describe how relieved I was to sell that boat and see the last of her. The couple of years I spent doing it up after what she had been through in the Caribbean were the most dismal of my life, between your shenanigans and dealing with the aftermath of your mother's death..."

"Obviously you wouldn't understand why I had to go or what I had to do there, you clueless old misanthrope."

"I'm not all that clueless," said Adam. "Coming back home to Abb's Head alone and empty-handed was pure happiness: no debts, no worries, no son! So raking up the past after all the trouble it cost us to get it safely buried... no, thanks!"

"Angelina's resentment with me for sabotaging the boorjoy grandeur of her wedding went beyond all reason. I was baffled what to do to get her cooperation in starting our breeding programme without further delay. But if it was her intention to make me feel that I was at fault, she failed. I went to a hot salsa joint in Gustavia to make sure it wasn't my internationally renowned fuck apparatus that had lost its drive..."

"Oh, dear Nick," said Adam, shaking his head. "I wish I understood you better."

"My good friend Michel Bon understood exactly what I needed and worked out a plan of action. Though he had been useless to me as a French teacher, he told me the true facts of life, the things a boy really wants to know, and he had lent a sympathetic ear to my unceasing complaints about the awfulness of everything — I can see I must have been a real pain in the arse as a snivelling schoolboy."

Adam and I both refrained from the obvious comment: "You still are."

Tomás brought us a bottle of wine which he promised would please even Nick. Nick produced out of his inner breast pocket an aluminium tube and gave it to Tomás.

"This is Castro's favourite, *muy especializo*."

Tomás transferred it with an equally solemn nod to his own pocket and moved on.

Nick continued as if there had been no interruption: "Michel pointed out this girl, telling me if I had money to spend and wanted to test my cock I should try my luck with her. I got him to negotiate with her for the exclusive use of her cunt for a few weeks; she was inclined to calculate what she could earn without me, Michel persuaded her to regard it as a 75% paid holiday. I'd never had dealings with a prostitute before and I stood by while he bargained for me, remembering Grandfather telling me what would influence the price of a female slave if I were buying one with his bag of pesos de oro."

"He would have been proud of you," I said, smiling at Nick's quasimodesty. I understood, if Adam didn't, that Nick could tell his story only as a marvellous satire of his own invention. To expose the tragedy below the protective veneer of farce would be bad manners.

"I quite regretted that she expected to be paid in French francs," he said, "though that didn't spoil the ballsy feel of it — we hotfooted off to her tidy little green painted, red roofed house, very classy, no sleaze, where she gave me a good run for my money and I proved my dick was in fine fettle. So that's how I kept myself stimulated enough to persist with Angelina without getting either too discouraged or too forceful."

"I can't help feeling, Nick," said Adam, with a slow glimmer of insight, "that scandalous as your story is, you are telling only a superficial truth, that underlying this so-called consideration for Angelina you had a much darker motive."

"My motive was to get Angelina pregnant before we went home."

"Hardly a sensible way to go about it, spending your energy whoring around. At least you don't seem to have caught syphilis in your unholy worship of the dead."

Nick looked disconcerted by Adam's interpretation but didn't deny it. Instead he picked on Adam's pointing out the health hazard of his feral fucking.

"Of course not," he said, "I'm not stupid. But don't forget, the spirochete was equally happy in wartime London along with no bananas and back street abortions."

A light went on in my head too. Was this the source of Nick's phobic dread of syphilis, the reason he couldn't fuck his fantastic African Queen? He had told Leon it was a thrill he still regretted not taking a risk for — he had said it rather rudely but I didn't suppose Leon minded that though he had looked a bit traumatised by the end of Nick's storytelling. Obviously he understood what eluded me in my ignorance. How infuriating it was not to be told the whole truth, to be left guessing!

It appeared that Nick hadn't always been inhibited for lack of condoms. He went on: "I went to St Barth's equipped for an emergency with a few rubbers in my wallet but the whole affair took longer and was more complicated than I anticipated — happily the hotel porter's supply was much more festive than those from the dispenser at Heathrow, delightfully silky super size Magnums. I'd never used condoms before and I loved it; they looked as if they'd been designed by Salvador Dali in one of his crazier moments. It was like dressing up in a very smart tight suit; my cock sat up instantly, very smug and pleased with himself, ready for a night at the go-go. I rather fancied myself in the glossy black ones with crinkly, expandable pink tips but the girls preferred me in sparkly gold with little tufty knobs on."

So clearly Nick went on his honeymoon with the intention of going native, independently of how he and Angelina got on.

"I don't think we need know the precise fashion statement you were making while humping your whores," said Adam.

"Angelina is always telling the Renaissance Women what a perfect husband she has," I said, giggling in delighted surprise at the vision of Nick cat-walking his cock in glistening gold. "How would she explain it to them if she knew the lengths you go to, to achieve such unlikely perfection?"

Nick seemed to take this as a genuine accolade and continued to talk at cross purposes to any comment Adam or I made, determined to tell the story his way, paying no attention to our increasingly startled reaction to his revelations, pursuing his own justification.

"Michel took me around at night to see the hot spots and talk to the permanent population, some of whom remembered the gossip of twenty years ago. I was sorry not to have the Espérance; that would surely have jogged a few more memories. The most interesting came from a healer and a fortune-teller; one couldn't not believe them or rather, believe in them. Their stories didn't quite agree but they both promised me a fulfilled life with many sons. They didn't arrive at the same total; the top estimate was ten! — at the time, considering how things were going with Angelina, that was quite encouraging if not altogether credible."

"Not such an unlikely prediction for a vigorous young man on his honeymoon," said Adam, unimpressed.

"And your tally is coming along nicely," I said, "assuming there is any truth in your story about the Nickies — I'll believe it when I see them, baby-seal hats and all."

"A pair of cherubs, I'll have to keep their little wings clipped or they'll fly away — I got talking to a history student when she disapproved of my choice of Guatemalan coffee, telling me to take Cuban — Creole females are just as bossy as metropolitan French — so I can't imagine how I came to spend an hour or more describing the retreat from Moscow to a pretty young woman, though she was quite taken with the story of French soldiers bargaining with Russian girls with the buttons off their coats."

"It does seem an unlikely topic of conversation with a strange girl in a tropical bar," I said. He never talked to me about anything like that. He simply fucked.

"I thought I should counteract the French bias of the history she was learning," he explained. "I couldn't help thinking as I looked at her bright-eyed face and nicely shaped body that if Mother, when she left home, had done the sensible thing and brought me along to take care of her, this is the kind of girl I might have married. Whether or not she had the least interest in the problem of horses dying in the snow, she liked me well enough to take me to a crystalline expanse of beach where the only problem was not getting sand in one's condom. I was tempted to throw them away but she would have none of it; however much the idea of a chocolate brown Nickie appealed to me, a pinkie one didn't appeal to her. We solved it in the shallows at the water's edge with condoms shaped like slippery fat fish, filmy green scales and long tickly fins. We did it sitting facing each other with our heads together so we could watch the fins floating and the head swimming in and out. It slowed me down even more than usual. She said the whole purpose is to slow down — useful advice since previously I'd only had Eugenie urging me to speed it up — 'just fuck,' Eugenie would say, 'don't make such a performance of it'. Ah, the pleasure of a slow fuck with a black girl in a blue sea!"

"Really?' was Adam's muted response, knowing he was being teased into a cockfight.

"In between times dabbling in the waves, she helped me by flicking through old newspapers for any relevant details and comments about finding my mother's body, which turned up exactly what I wanted. So in spite of the rout I was suffering from Angelina coyly acting the submissive wife while she skilfully evaded my attempts to get us fulfilling our biological functions, Michel and the girls kept me happily occupied."

As Nick told it, fucking in creole must have been the most carefree sex he had ever enjoyed, fancy condoms and all — however strangely he combined it with digging for the truth about his mother's death!

"Admittedly I was run ragged between them all," he said. "I hardly slept while I was there, but even on one's honeymoon one is entitled to take time off for a daily swim across the bay, the only time I got to myself. I would float, suspended weightlessly on the waves, offering myself to any big fish idling by — trial by water. They swam quite close to me but didn't seem interested. They saw me as a bit of worthless flotsam, I suppose. I proved to myself it is possible to offer up one's life the way my mother did and nevertheless survive. It reinforced my belief in the fortune-teller, not necessarily for myself but for my mother. She told her the hideous truth of what life and what death were in the cards for her. Why else let Espérance drift out into shark infested waters for a swim?"

"I don't know which is a worse trial for Angelina: your bumptious cock or your dicing with death," said Adam.

"Making love to Angelina is a privilege and one has to approach her in a calm state of mind; one can't go in quivering with animal passion, better to work that off elsewhere. Now when we go to formal balls, which she loves dressing up for and thank goodness her sense of style has improved beyond recognition, I am careful to keep it slow and not too complicated for her so I can bask in the reflection of her pale beauty without worrying about her feet —and it's the same in bed."

Adam went on with his dinner, indicating to Nick that his was going cold in front of him.

"Are you going to eat that?" he asked. "If not, I'll have it; it's too good to waste."

"Eat up," said Nick, passing over his plate. "Eat for victory."

"You have never gone hungry," said Adam, adding more truffle oil to Nick's rejected pasta.

"Not recently," said Nick

"Your homage to your mother's memory hardly required you to stake your own life," said Adam, focusing on the real business of Nick's sojourn on St Barths. To Adam the girls were irrelevant — but then he didn't suffer from jealousy.

"I had to find out what it was my mother abandoned me for. I put myself through the same experiences hoping I would find her answer in a bois-terous, pleasure-seeking, carefree life. She had fucked for King and Country, as you so uncharitably put it, living like everyone at the time, without thought for the consequences. But for her the aftermath in the England of 1953 was very grim."

"A problem faced by all the women of post-war Britain," said Adam sharply, not conceding Nick's covert accusation, "only she had the means and was egocentric enough to get out — Suicide Banker's Daughter Flees Austerity — nice headline! At least she did have enough common sense to leave you behind."

"Naturally, when it was me she was running away from."

Nick removed the bowl of grated Parmesan from in front of Adam to stop him absentmindedly heaping it up.

"With a certain amount of judicious guesswork I was able to put together the jigsaw of what happened. I can tell you — if you can bear the truth."

"No," said Adam. "That is a whole different story. Let the dead rest in peace."

"It's the living I care about," said Nick. "She had a good war until she lost — as surely as if she's been shot down. My life has been a terrific fight all the way and, whatever the odds against me, I've had a great time."

"No doubt you'll go on having a good time and it's equally certain sooner or later you too will be shot down," said Adam. "I don't think you can count on Gianni's death guaranteeing your survival — or not for long."

"Grandfather's maggot isn't doing too badly in the survival stakes. After all, in spite of Mrs Shackleton's misgiving, you didn't succeed in drowning me in the Bay of Biscay — think of the trouble you could have saved yourself if you hadn't given me a steadying hand — all that quite uncalled for snatching me from the waves!"

"I can't even begin to imagine it," said Adam with an expression of despairing amusement at Nick's irrepressible self-belief, his insouciance in the face of misfortune.

All the suppressed emotions, Adam's anxieties and Nick's resentments, which they had never faced up to before I turned up at Abb's Head to sow discord between them, were at last being confronted. But I felt there was a fundamental misunderstanding between them which wasn't being resolved, quite apart Nick's tendency to manipulate the truth and Adam's inclination to avoid it altogether.

"Having brought my enquiries to a satisfactory conclusion I no longer needed the services of my research assistant either in the library or on the beach, and fucking Michel's tart was getting me nowhere — besides she had the disgusting habit of chewing gum and addressed me disparagingly as Le Petit Prince, though she had to admit my prick, whether dressed in black or gold, was as good as any she'd ever encountered — and black men are big! As became evident, my research into her charms was all a waste of time;

exuberant black sex may have appealed to my mother too…"

"It was what she was there for," said Adam.

"No, it wasn't… nevertheless, my girl was well worth the price she screwed out of Michel. I'd have gladly paid her in pieces of eight, but as farewell present I gave her all the books Angelina had been too idle to read. She was really pleased with that. I don't know if she intended to read them or regarded them as chic decoration for her orderly little house."

Nick looked pleased when a earthenware dish of fragrant roast chicken on a bed of chickpeas, slices of succulent aubergine and whole heads of garlic was placed in front of him. He dismissed the maid and divided it up, selecting some nice pieces for Adam and me and taking the rest for himself, ignoring the chickpeas.

"Not even Clare could tempt me to insult my stomach with gut filler," he said. "Aubergines are pure poison too, but delicious, so I'll die a day sooner, after all I'm not planning to live to a hundred. Besides, one needs plenty of Tomás's good olive oil to protect the stomach from his wine."

"You certainly came back from your honeymoon quite perceptibly changed," said Adam, helping himself to chickpeas to supplement his portion of chicken breast. "Everyone remarked how you seemed to have sobered up beyond expectations, boringly so for those who had been entertained by your eccentricities. We put it down to Angelina's influence and concluded that after a successful honeymoon with your lovely wife you had settled down to being a sensible married man. I would never have guessed anything like the stories you have just told us; in fact I still find them hardly credible. I suspect you of trying to confound your long-suffering parent."

"Of course it was a successful honeymoon," said Nick, getting the wings out of the way first, prising the oysters out of the back before starting in on the well-developed legs of Clare's handsome semi-wild Leghorn cockerel. "I achieved everything I set out to do — apart from getting Angelina pregnant, but considering the obstacles she put in my way I made a good start."

"My admiration for Angelina grows the more I know her," said Adam.

"You mean she wasn't an easy push-over like me," I said.

"Yes, he got exactly the wife he deserves."

"The tropical garden was making her more and more lethargic," Nick went on, not put off by our ironic comments. "She spent her days in her hammock being ogled by the beach boys while she played at sleeping beauty. The last straw was Gladys phoning to get my instructions about an accident in the workshop — I was furious that one of my boys had been injured when I wasn't there to deal with it — after my Armee training, what a waste of a good accident! I went to Angelina and said, 'either you let me fuck you now or I'm going home without you; you can stay here in Never-Never Land. I wasted two years of my productive life to accommodate your whims. I proved my economic worth to your father, so fulfil your contract or I'll sue his estate for every penny you've got for stringing me along on false pretences.'

"In the end, after weeks of forbearance and consideration for her imaginary hurts, I had to bloody well lose my temper before I could get it up that lady's cunt. Not a pleasant experience: me cursing and Angelina crying. I made it clear: 'this is what marriage means: I fuck when, how and as often as I see fit.'"

In theory, perhaps.

I thought of Nick lying with unselfconscious grace on the bed an hour or so ago, with what he called his famous fuck apparatus on display, and quite unembarrassed telling about its activities in a world unknown to me. But then, it had always been so, so it made no difference now. I'd always had it with the sum total of its experience, and its maturity made it what it was, including gold-spangled sandy condoms and sexy hot salsa. After the hunt, at Abb's Head, I had lain in bed weeping inconsolably at the realisation that he was beyond me. Three years on, three years of rapture, grief, anger and laughter, he was still the same impossible man, only more so.

"Can I ask you," I said, as coolly as I could manage, like the men keeping my emotions under control, "if, in her neat little green house, you kissed your prostitute?"

Nick pursed his lips into its primmest pout, reflecting a moment, squishing a garlic clove between his fingers and sucking the pulp out before saying: "No, it was strictly at the business end. I went for a fuck, not to get intimate."

"You didn't kiss me either when you rammed me on a heap of old blankets in your cellar," I said, "I must be very low down on the scale of beings."

"Ah, no, Sibylla. In the pecking order of women you are top cunt. The cellar was your decision, not mine; you chose it to bring me down to earth when we could have done it anywhere you liked, my whole house was at your disposal. You held yourself aloof; you never yielded to me. How could I kiss you? It takes two to make love, to express mutual desire, affection, agreement; if I impose it on you it becomes a mockery, an insult."

"It was a mockery at the exhibition," I said, "when I was posing for Adam and you came to make a holy show of me."

"Let's face it, sweetheart, you do expose yourself to mockery, and that I find very hard to resist. Otherwise, I am such a slave to your caprice there is nothing I wouldn't sacrifice to placate you. Didn't I humiliate myself to kiss your cunt at the Wittersworths?"

"You did that to humiliate me; you reduced me to a jelly totally at your mercy."

"Kiss my cock," said Nick, for once looking me straight in the eyes, "and I place my entire fortune at your feet."

"Now that I don't need it," I said, smiling at how his lip trembled and his eyes narrowed in a spasm of desire, a willing victim to love. "I noticed you left that bit out when you went through your charade with the wedding ring."

Nick, who was deboning a chicken leg with his fingers, put it down, his cheekbones flushed with colour predicting an outburst of temper.

"You are such a liar, Sibylla," he said. "It wasn't a charade; I mean every word I say. You're the one who continually dupes me... what a siren! *'Oh, train me not, sweet mermaid, with thy note, to drown me in tears. Sing, siren, for thyself!'...* what about the blissful hours we spent in Gramercy Park when I couldn't get enough of you? I kissed you for forty-eight hours and hardly paused for breath..."

211

"That's true," I conceded, "and at Eze too, you didn't do too badly then either —but you should have taken Angelina to the château for your honeymoon and lived out your adolescent dreams with your lovely wife instead of Miss Mischief d'Art; toile de Jouey and romantic strolls under the pines would have suited her better than having to compete with Creole prostitutes for your attention, or fending off beach boys while you courted your mother's ghost amongst the sharks."

Nick stood up, furious that I seemed to mock his confidences, and towered above me with clenched fists.

I trembled: the threat in his drawn face was as spine-tingling as a furious fuck.

"Paul says you won bets with your kisses," I said, looking up at him, daring him to hit me. "You can't have been in love with all of those women... the cuckoo-clock competition?"

When Nick understood the trend of my remarks his anger subsided and he sat down again, wiping his garlicky hands in his napkin.

"They were all lovely girls, why shouldn't I let them kiss me?... they were only checking out how lively a cock Angelina was getting... the competition was a bit of fun but Nestor knows me only too well and he wasn't going to waste the time and trouble he spends on his clocks by giving them to anyone I'm not genuinely in love with; it was meant as a huge compliment to me, in fact his wedding present to a man who has everything: favours for my once and future lovers!"

This hadn't been understood as a factor in the reports I'd heard and made me think: the cuckoo joke is more complex than I realised at first reading. Toby said it caused a prolonged period of tension in the Shackleton household when a cuckoo-clock of quite extraordinary size and complexity arrived addressed to his mother. It was now hanging prominently on the back wall of her Help the Aged, Sterilise Feral Cats and Support the Lifeboats collecting shed — his father wouldn't have it in the house — where it is a great attraction for the generous donors, especially children, who use their little gifts as an excuse to come and admire the cavorting couples and goats prancing, cuckoos and owls popping in and out depending on the time of day or night, hooting and shouting cuckoo.

"Well," I said, "the inscription on Mrs Shackleton's clock — something like 'The Deathridge Wedding Games, 1st Prize' — causes much mystification amongst the Friends; no-one associates her with anything improper so think it must be a joke, but Toby and his father are uncomfortable that it means more than a prize in a silly game."

"I had to squeeze years of adoring Mrs Shackleton into the one occasion when it was socially acceptable, a last kiss for my first love. We danced our way through her entire Joe Loss repertoire because that's how she taught me when I was a callow youth. Her love was what enabled me to withstand the onslaughts of the Heini girls. Mrs Furzy thought I was foolish to make such an old-fashioned choice but actually everyone loved it, it's such great music to dance to in the quiet of the night."

"It was half the dance floor for you and half for everyone else," said Adam.

"Mrs Shackleton is a fine figure of a woman," said Nick. "She has a wonderful buoyancy; she just floats in my arms... she needs a big stage to show off her grace. Quakers go in for Spartan simplicity; there was no clutter to clear when we did our stuff in her drawing room but that ballroom... that was ours for flying to the moon!"

"Penn looked on, at first quite relaxed about the way you and his wife were joined at the hip..."

"When I was a boy I didn't have the footwork or the daring to get that close to her..."

"... until he saw you half hidden by the swirling crowd rocking together in a long embrace," said Adam. "I thought all evening that you were rather overdoing the kissing games, but that arse-lock with Hannah Shackleton went beyond decent."

"I'm a slow fucker — even without a frilly condom on."

Nick pressed his fingers to his face in his characteristic act of concealing his mirth, unabashed by the memory of how he had been ridiculed by his wedding-guests.

"Having done your damnedest to mortify me, you came and sat beside me," said Adam, "sweating but otherwise looking as good as I've ever seen you. I was grudgingly forced to admit I was proud of my spectacularly awful son. A starched shirt and evening tails cover up a multitude of sins."

"Not to mention wet pants."

"Oh, Nick, you are such a buffoon! One can't believe a word you say," I said, remembering him at the château dancing in his tails, blissfully moving his legs between and around mine. I could feel the glow of his passion for me and the Habanera but on that occasion its fulfilment could wait for the bedroom.

How misplaced were my first impressions when his short crest of russet hair brushed up off a high, furrowed forehead and pale eyes were completely contrary to my notion of a handsome man, distorted by early exposure to Hollywood in the Metropole on Sunday afternoons with Great-Aunt Kathleen: Ginos and Giannis, not Nicks.

"You'd think a whole chicken would be enough for three people," Adam said plaintively, recovering his voice and looking at the plate of bones being cleared away from in front of Nick while Clare came to the rescue with a bowl of hot water and a towel, "but obviously not when one has to share it with as insatiable a carnivore as you. Tomás's bottle didn't last long either."

"Plenty of chickpeas left," said Nick, drying his hands and pushing the nearly empty dish towards his father with a mock-liberal gesture.

"Remember Penn Shackleton drove us down to the jetty when we left for Monte Carlo?" said Adam, returning the chickpeas with equal contempt. "When I came home from Hein's without you he said how pleased he had been to see your tail-light disappear across the water. 'I never objected to my wife having innocent fun,' he said, 'but that boy can move his arse a bit too effectively for any husband's peace of mind.'"

"It had never occurred to me," said Adam, "that as well as the trail of broken bones and bloody noses you were leaving behind you, you'd been chasing my best friend's wife to add to my embarrassments."

Nick looked positively misty-eyed at the memory.

"I was about fifteen when I was saved from this misogynist of a father by lovely, loveable, liberal, luscious, delectable Mrs Shackleton. She awakened my sensual awareness of how my body affects other people. Immersing myself in a bath of hot water gave me an instant erection thinking how she would like me when I came out pink and steaming..."

"Really, Nick, that's enough about Toby's mother!" Adam sat back to confront his son. "She was only being kind to a motherless boy, I don't know how you can suppose she took any interest in your body..."

"Because she didn't mind seeing my bouncy cock when she chased me out of the bath and stood over me to make me clean it up after me... she seemed to think its crescendos an unremarkable part of a boy's anatomy, which was immensely reassuring to me after being smacked for it by my unhappy mother."

Adam shut his eyes to the image this conjured up of the effect Nick's cock must have had on his kindly hostess doing her best to educate a wayward youth in proper behaviour.

"My wet dreams took a turn for the better when Mrs Shackleton came to replace my mother. It was a test of nerve though; I had to open the coffin not knowing which of them I'd find inside. I'm telling you, it was a monstrous gooey mess of relief every time Mrs Shackleton popped out, lively and laughing."

Nick smiled more openly, amused by Adam's incredulity, "Remember how cross you were when I spent the price of a decent suit on that pair of pale velvet britches? When I tried them on in the shop — a superb new changing room for 1957, all-round mirror and a tropical wood door that swung open at a touch, the first sign of post-war chic — my one thought was how Mrs Shackleton would be impressed when she saw how terrific my legs and my neat bum looked in them. I emerged from the eclipse of school uniform with the realisation that one can dress to seduce. At sixteen I woke up to the fact that a sex education based on the Arabian Nights wasn't much use to a 20th Century boy..."

"You do remember that the suit you didn't buy was to wear at your mother's funeral..." Adam remarked, quite gently.

"You wanted to have her cremated," said Nick. "I refused to go."

"Oh, dear Nick, there was nothing left: to bury a few bones in a coffin seemed incongruous."

For the first time, talking about his wife, Adam looked distressed.

"And her hair," said Nick and I could see in the set of his mouth how he dominated any opposition. His fantasy of his mother's hair growing to fill her coffin, which had so startled Clare and me, suddenly made sense.

"And when Mrs Shackleton dragged me to that other funeral I wore my lovely trousers in defiance of the remorse I was supposed to feel. That's when scary Maddie Madigan fell in love with me — I was fortunate I had Mrs Shackleton to hide behind."

"Amanda Wittersworth too," I said. "You seem to have put on a good show to entertain those girls as well."

Nick continued, as if there had been none of these digression, "While the Heini girls were Strad hunting for me, Mrs Shackleton came to find me and I was sure I could get it from her. I put so much persuasion into charming her pants off I couldn't believe it when she refused me."

The 1001 Nights of Nick's life story, the circuitous route by which it turns endlessly around to question the same uncertainties, again and again: his favourite trousers, the funerals he did or didn't misbehave at, his failed courtship of Toby's mother...

"This conversation is getting out of hand," said Adam. "We've gone from the price of Creole prostitutes to the question of Mrs Shackleton's securely virtuous knickers in a matter of minutes. Nick, do you think you could desist from discussing your sex life for at least the rest of the evening?"

Nick studied Tomas's new labels for his wine bottles. "Too fancy," was his verdict. "The plainer the label the better the wine. Nice drawing of the castello, obviously one of yours, Dad, but really all that fancy gilt lettering and the whole history of the place telling us how bloody marvellous it is... why do Italians have to overdo it?"

216

Then, as an afterthought he added, "Mrs Shackleton is the first woman who let me into bed with her — she was already used to seeing me naked."

"You are preposterous!" said Adam. "I don't believe you."

Perhaps Nick was still suffering from the Wittersworth effect, being teased into the small hours of the morning, and was taking it out on his father. He pretended not to notice how Adam was becoming more and more exasperated.

"I took her dancing in the darkest of dives," he said, "and begged her to give me what I wanted."

Sex or a Stradivarius: it wasn't clear which was uppermost in Nick's mind.

"I pleaded with her — I told her it didn't have to be a Stradivari, anything Cremona, or even a Mittenwald would do. It was no good. She said 'I love you, Nick, but I am not buying you.' She took my heart, that cruel woman, and gave me nothing."

He put his head in his hands, shaking and heaving as if he were still weeping over the disappointment inflicted on him by his unkind mistress. It took some stretch of the imagination to picture a slim young Nick with Toby's tall, well-built mother engaged in a lover's brawl in some shady dance club.

"Only you, Nick," I said, "would seriously expect a middle-aged Quaker lady to take you to bed with her, naked or not."

Nick looked up with red face, half-closed eyes and a faintly mocking smile.

"When she came to rescue, as she thought, her lost boy from the fierce Helvetii who hurl rocks around by way of sport, I tried to impress on her what a hard time I was having — that she was just in time to save me from the fate of Orpheus, dismembered in a frenzy of Heini girls."

"One can easily imagine how you might have flirted by candlelight but..." I said.

"I told you how I pleaded with her and how she cheated me. It was nearly three o'clock in the morning when I escorted her to her hotel so I asked her to let me stay as I had to be at work by eight. Why not? We had just been dancing for hours so what was different in lying down beside her on the bed? Of course I discovered that there is a vast difference: the minute one is horizontal one's muscles disengage from the business of standing and, liberated to move in a different dimension, the autonomous response is to shift fast forward into fuck gear."

"Your muscles did all right standing in the laundry," I said.

"That was terrific; with one's feet on the ground one gets great power into one's up-thrust. That way it's quicker too, convenient for not being late for dinner — nothing like a quick fuck for whipping up an appetite and thank you, Sibylla, for providing me with a whole season of splendid preludes to my nights at the opera. My reputation for after dinner wit rests on the buzz you gave me; that's what I can live off if my house of cards ever does collapse."

"I was working for my wages," I said.

"Sweet Sibylla, I miss you terribly... Mrs Shackleton didn't mind me lying up against her and jiggling a bit but she absolutely wouldn't let me wriggle between her legs. I was at a disadvantage in that I didn't dare use my hands to find the way, I was too in awe of her, but I was so desperate I was bawling and begging her, and she was telling me to keep quiet, she didn't want it broadcast around the whole marketplace that she was foolish enough to allow an obstreperously demanding young cock share her bed.

"'Stop it, Nick,' she said. 'You're behaving like a four-year-old. Grow up!'

"So I stopped. Instantly. She is the one woman whose authority I respect — the bloody Fourth Commandment again, damn Toby! I just had to withdraw and admit defeat."

"That is something to be grateful for," said Adam. "Hannah Shackleton told me very little about her visit to Basel — hearing how you misbehaved with her it's hardly surprising — and I find it hard to forgive you for somehow reducing my dear friend to another episode among many in your disgraceful love-life, twisting her motherly concern into a tale of unrequited love — I thought if anyone could make you act with a bit of decorum, she could."

'So I lay off her and, to pass the time till dawn, I took her gently by the scruff of her imagination into the Heini madhouse. Can that woman laugh! Just as with my earlier tales out of school I could feel her tits a-quiver; I had her delicious plump belly shaking so much I was able to edge my way in pretty damn close to where I wanted to be. It was the best of wet dreams come true. She won on a technicality but I didn't feel I had failed at my first attempt to lay a woman, while she managed to preserve a pretence of matronly dignity. A strong-minded lady, I'm glad she has found a good use for her prize clock. It's just the touch of scandal she needs to spice up her exemplary life. I must find the opportunity to make a generous contribution to her charities, and if she accepts I'll venture a more grown-up shot in her irreproachably virtuous British Home Stores extra-large knickers."

"If you are quite sure that you don't need a dish of bull's balls to boost your confidence," said Adam, standing up, "let me get you some of Donna's ricotta cheese cake."

Nick shook his head, so Adam left the table to fetch some for himself and me.

"Now that you have your Virgins in their boudoir instead of the nanny in the cellar, do I feature in your future game plan?" I asked.

"Why should you?" asked Nick. "You will be Lady Wittersworth and live in a splendid villa. What more do you want? My cock as well?"

Nick's quizzical look belied the rejection implied in his words.

"Yes," I said.

He leant across to me, gave his grandmother's ring an affectionate rub and kissed my hand — no mockery.

~

The Inquest:
3rd Course

11

"**N**ow you're one of the idle rich with no workers to boss around the place," said Adam when he came back with two portions of cheesecake, "what are going to do with yourself?"

"I'm making amends to Tsang for ruining his Virgin Births," Nick answered. "I'm helping him set up a research centre in the New Territories so he'll have it up and running when Hong Kong goes Chinaside. It was slightly tricky deviating my Taiwanese suppliers for him but Elsa manages all that. I have to make sure he goes on making enough money to support the present and future crop of Nickies."

"How does your new life affect Angelina?" Adam asked.

"Since the Renaissance Women have taken up hawking, Angelina is devoted to the peregrine she keeps in the garden. She is very good with it; she looks splendid with it perched on her fist, it gives her an air of quite impressive authority. She was a beauty at eighteen: what she has now is character. I congratulate myself on being so perceptive; she answers all my questions about the meaning of marriage. When we embrace her smile reassures me that there nothing but unshakable love and loyalty between us."

Just like Gus and me!

"The peregrine lives in an aviary attached to the potting shed where the goat is reinstalled for the Nickies. Joe calls her his Mammy Goat; he's possessive because he had her milk first. Madge tells him little brothers always get milk from the same mammy — Con tries to explain to him that it's not the goat's udders that make the Nickies his brothers, it's what Daddy does with his big dick — but that's beyond him: Dunce Deathridge Mark II, he's just as much a baby as I was at that age; Con is far more astute."

I longed for Nick's boys the way I longed for their father, for the life I couldn't have.

"Con takes a keen interest in the Virgins' tummies, he listens with his ear against them and insists he can hear talking inside — when I asked him what they were saying in there, he looked at me pitying my stupidity: it's baby talk of course. Angelina tells him not to be rude, so he mimes it, meaningful looks at the bulging Aunties, buttoning his lips and pointing an accusing finger at my crotch."

"Dear Angelina," said Adam, "a houseful of Nicks! What she deserves is a couple of nice little girls."

"I got a small pony for the boys and Madge takes them riding in the park; she pays the rent by supervising the menagerie and the boys love her amiable bulldog, a charmingly hideous beast who roams about devouring everything that takes his fancy; the Nickies have escaped so far, they only get slobbered on and they are constantly needing new hats to replace the ones he chews. It's beginning look like a slum out the back. At least the peregrine frightens off pigeons and other vermin but Meg objects to the fridge being full of dead mice."

"Who can blame her?" said Adam.

"My incurably pretentious mother-in-law thinks that now I have swindled the Furzys out of their socially embarrassing scrap-yard fortune the least I can do is bribe my way to a title so she can bask in the glory of referring to her daughter as Lady Deathridge."

"It shouldn't be difficult, the new government will be only too eager to make friends among the rich," said Adam with deepest scorn.

"They are certainly not going to give you any gongs for painting lewd pictures."

"That suits me fine," said Adam. "I'm in good company. Art is above social conformity."

Nick flipped his lapel to show a small enamel shield, red with a white cross, matching his father's claim as a free spirit. Nick was an independent republic of one in a loose confederation with his fellow Swiss mavericks.

"When it's orders and decorations on the menu, this indicates where my allegiance lies. No kowtowing for me."

"But you are great chums with the Queen," I said thinking of his dryly humorous accounts of his African and other far-flung friends at the Palace.

"I adore her. But, even if she wanted to give me her gracious recognition for relieving her of over-enthusiastic tributes of jellied eyeballs and zebu cock, I'd have to refuse. It would be a betrayal of all we stand for. Maybe I could get them to give me a Nobel Prize instead..."

"Not the Peace Prize for sure," said Adam, "perhaps a Booby Prize as Stud for wantonly increasing the earth's population in the face of diminishing resources..." but his face had cleared, the lines of distress that had been etching themselves steadily deeper all evening smoothed out again and he looked at Nick with appreciation that at last, after an evening of resisting Nick's provocations, here was something they could agree on.

"I'm concerned for your happiness," he said. "It's not the money; I worry about your state of mind, your reckless heart. You are letting your balls rule your head."

Nick dismissed Adam's concern. "I'm perfectly in control of my balls, my head and my money, dear Father. Your worry is entirely superfluous."

I could feel the deep groundswell of affection pass between the two men though they still looked at each other as if challenging the other's understanding.

"You must miss your wine cellar when you are in Hong Kong," Adam remarked, uncorking another bottle.

"Come home and help me drink it dry," said Nick. "I'm counting on you to take over the garden room; stripped of its Chinoiserie and whitewashed it will make you a fine studio, nice light and opening into the garden. Plenty of store rooms and Sibylla won't need it, she can have any future babies in Palladian style instead. The only question is whether you would get any work done with four grandsons and a free-range bulldog in close proximity."

"Angelina might have something to say about that," said Adam. "With all the other burdens you have dumped on her she may have plans other than being saddled with her father-in-law as well."

Nick looked his most uncompromising; it was clear to see what Angelina had to contend with, notwithstanding his declaration of total devotion.

"I risked my life for that house. It's mine to dispose of as I see fit."

"That's something of an exaggeration, surely?" Adam had relaxed after the truce that seemed to have been reached and wasn't taking Nick's remark too seriously, more preoccupied with gathering up the delicious crumbly bits of cheesecake. "You must have been in a position to buy a house once you got over the initial difficulties — I never understood what your shop steward made such a fuss about, dragging in the union...'

"The bloody fool, he fell straight into my trap," said Nick with his most malicious smile, crooked tooth in full view. "I taught my apprentices to dismantle some guns I'd been working on at SIG to explain the mechanism and after making a few minor adjustments how to get them to fit back together. It was a test of skill and intelligence. They were thrilled and with great glee obligingly passed on a few misleading comments I'd made, convinced that the boss is a master criminal with a stash of illegal weapons. So when the union stool pigeon tried to do an underhand deal with me I was able to dismiss that incubus for attempted entrapment, possibly with a view to blackmail – it was all too easy and predictable. I had a free hand from then on..."

Well, I thought, if anyone was guilty of entrapment, it had to be Nick.

"... anyway, in spite of all that, you could well afford a house," said Adam, not getting deviated into labour relations, something Nick enjoyed so much he could go on all evening recounting his disputes and his triumphs.

"You have a great ability for avoiding unpleasant truths," said Nick. "I couldn't spend my working capital on a house, certainly not a house on six floors in Bayswater, with garden, needing total renovation from a semi-dosshouse back to a gentleman's residence fit for my beautiful Angelina, my new Mrs Deathridge. But you won't want to know that I raised the money with diamonds from South Africa," adding with a gleam in his eye, "Maddie got them for me and Eugenie helped me dispose of them. Papi Bott is in the business, the old crook."

Adam was aghast.

"That was an extraordinary risk to take, even for you, Nick. Their scanning is too good; people get caught all the time."

"I know; obviously I didn't take the usual route. You don't think I'd whistle through customs with a million or two of diamonds in my duffle-bag, do you? Besides, it was slightly more complicated than that; I took the diamonds out in exchange for what my Tintinesque bush plane was able to ferry in..."

Adam groaned. "Stop right there, Nick. Don't tell me any more."

"Cultivate your blissful ignorance, Dad, that's the way to stay alive... have you any of your fig and ginger jelly left?" he said to Clare as she passed.

"I saved it specially for you, Nick," she said, "and some freshly baked biscotti to go with it."

"Don't bother with biscotti," he said. "I'll have it with cheese if the Caprotto is fit to eat. And tell Tomás to find me a digestif that won't ruin my liver, make me fart or give me a headache."

"Have you tried water?" said Clare as she went off to plunder her larder.

Nick unbuckled his million-franc watch and sat winding it with an air of indifference, deliberately ignoring Adam who was looking at him in dumbfounded bafflement as his son metamorphed before his eyes from successful industrialist into international criminal.

"Your Swiss lady seems to be helpful in more ways than one," I said, thinking of Leon Bolus's dismay when he heard Mrs Hein claim she was the first Mrs Deathridge. It occurred to me that Adam was unaware of this well-kept secret. "And not strictly business either. Was she not jealous to see you marrying Angelina?"

"Yes, furiously," said Nick. "When a rival wife came on the scene Eugenie was contemptuous that I adored Angelina not only for her flawless beauty but the immaculate virtue that gives her such a tranquil disposition. In spite of her girl friends' urging, I wasn't going to risk my virgin bride's ideal of love before the contract was signed and the gross reality of *le coq hardi* essential for babies was sanctioned by Holy Harold... As Nestor had such fun telling you, my late love did her best to sabotage my wedding. But she got her 15% out of the diamond transaction and anyway five years on she could hardly expect me to remain faithful to her forever after she so heartlessly divorced me, under the delusion that Hein's fat money bags would satisfy her better than my richly endowed testicles."

In an earlier account Nick said he left her to marry Angelina because he wanted children. His many versions of his life story changed from bitter to triumphant to farce according to his humour.

"Up till then Eugenie had been my first and only cunt — if one discounts my not quite successful attempt to penetrate the Shackleton defences — but when she observed Angelina indulge herself in le Palme d'Or on Knicker-bocker Glories — with a Swiss flag stuck on top instead of a pink umbrella — she taunted me that if she'd had my child, at least hers would have brains.

"'Prove it,' I said."

"But you were still so young," I said, "there must have been other women."

Nick shook his head.

"I'd still be married to her if she hadn't let her Bott prudence deceive her that she needed more than happiness: a husband with a good address in Basel and a chalet in Gstaad, and the newest, longest, slinkiest Lamborghini for purring its way up and down between the two like a snow leopard."

Even Leon Bolus who must have been used to the Embassy motors had remarked on the flashiness of the Heins' car.

I laughed at Nick's prim little pout expressing deep offence. He seemed more annoyed with Hein about the car — cars and watches, the modest Swiss's form of ostentation — than for stealing his wife.

"Well, he must be very well off indeed if anything he offers her is bigger and better than yours!" I said.

"It was a hard slog catching up with him, and damn her for a cunning vixen, she does well out of both her husbands whereas I am singularly badly treated by all my women — a complete dupe to all of you — except for

Angelina, of course, and even she deceived me — fucking for Con was a painful struggle, and it wasn't any better with Joe..."

Nick exaggerating for dramatic effect: I was more inclined to believe Angelina's version.

Adam found his voice. "I'm only your father," he said, restricting himself to the mildest of sarcasm at Nick's latest revelation, "but a marriage is something you might have mentioned to me sooner."

"You must have known," said Nick. "I was nineteen; I'd have needed your permission."

"Don't think you can fool me, Nick," said Adam. "When you asked me to come over to settle some legal matters for you I fully expected to have to bail you out of trouble, as always. I was pleasantly surprised it was nothing more serious than some incomprehensible bureaucratic paperwork needing my signature: apprenticeship, money, residence; how was I to know that included marriage?"

"I don't remember," said Nick. "Possibly I forgot to mention it."

"You have the most convenient lapses of memory for a man who can carry tables of logarithms around in his head," said Adam, tricked by Nick's diversionary tactics, allowing himself be distracted from the dubious means by which Nick had acquired his house. He went on, "Actually, I was quite disconcerted to see how you had changed in a year. You'd turned yourself into the very model of Swissy young man, neat haircut and good shoes, and I went home, believe it or not after all I'd been through with you, with a terrible feeling of regret that I had lost my wild boy. I kept thinking of that sunny day in Taunton when Penn and I sat on the pavilion stand and saw you hit such an accomplished and elegant century. What might have been, if only..."

"... if only Joey Madigan hadn't wrecked my life by getting me to demonstrate the rules of chance by way of Russian Roulette. But it hasn't been all bad. I'd have missed out on crash-landing in the Drakensberg and having Eugenie blissfully nurse me back from semi-starvation — I adored that woman, I simply could not believe it when she terminated my contract

— the Swiss do divorce, as in everything, by mutual consent, but in fact I never willingly agreed."

"I can't think why you didn't consult me about getting married in the first place," said Adam, perplexed and hurt. "Did I ever refuse you anything?"

Nick's raised eyebrows and quizzically sardonic smile dismissed Adam's lack of perception. It occurred to me that the mild disparagement with which Nick treated his father was a mask for a deep-seated anger: anger which he never let overcome his affection, its presence marked only by a momentary hesitation, a silence before carrying on as if it weren't there, what Nick might describe as his natural propensity for syncopation, a missing beat where normally a stressed one would be expected.

"I told you countless times that I sold my cock because I needed a Swiss wife," he said.

"I don't think you ever actually said that, Nick," said Adam "and out of the jumble of disgraceful anecdotes about your girlfriends and the scandalous cock auction, and all your other nonsense, how were we to conclude you had actually fooled one of them into marrying you?"

"I didn't know what was in those papers either; Eugenie put it all together for me. My helplessness on the administrative front flatters her as that's her specialty — out of bed. Eugenie liked the way my prick stands up stiff when I lie on my back but when she offered me that position permanently as husband I didn't accept. I held out until I could get her to lie down under me and let me fuck her properly. At the time you signed the papers I was having this struggle, fucking to the tune of Mami Bott reciting Rilke and Papi Bott swearing he'd cut my penis down to size — I told you all about that, don't you ever listen to me? — and the outcome was still uncertain — a predicament I didn't feel like discussing with my dear Dad. And it was years before I saw you again."

"I spent my time rebuilding my house and fishing. It got annoying how complete strangers would ask me how you were — as if I should know." Adam had the same sense of grievance as Angelina that Nick, who claimed to have no friends, nevertheless had a multitude of anonymous well-wishers. "You never wrote home..."

"I don't write."

"... or called me on the phone."

"There was nothing to say. You had done your bit spiriting me and the Espérance away before the police got after me over that business with the gun and then the Queen requested my help in defending the pathetic remnants of her empire, so you see the advantage of marrying Eugenie: with the flourish of a pen she transformed me into the respectable citizen of a country where controversy is avoided — or at least limited to the iniquity of leaving one's fluff in the communal dryer or dropping a sock on the way upstairs. But, just like Mrs Shackleton before her, Eugenie cheated me. Every time she wanted sex I reminded her she owed me a violin; she refused saying she had no wish to hear me murdering Saint-Saëns, knowing perfectly well that after a sulk of five minutes I'd be begging her to let me in."

I groaned to myself. After years of complaining that Nick had nothing to say to me, now he had started talking it was not so much having a conversation as doing a crazy jigsaw where the random pieces of information only made sense when fitted together. What started as a charming anecdote of a violin and a black velvet jacket became a cock auction and now a battle of the sexes between a very young husband and a bossy wife. What next?

"That's what led to Papi Bott's first attempt to murder me."

I caught Adam's eye and smiled, sharing his disbelief; Nick continued:

"I discovered that he had a fine pre-war Sacconi on top of his bookcase — I thought it was where he kept his service rifle, that's why I was looking — so I borrowed it to see if three years after the Shackleton fiasco I could still make it sing. I spent ages with the help of Mr Mug getting it fit to use; he kindly gave me new strings — his shop with the cat in the window is a convenient front for orphaned goods that trickle across the border to be disposed of — a man of integrity, buyers just have to take his word on questions of provenance. He rings me every so often when he gets his hands on some nice instrument, plays it for me over the phone; I tell him to offer it to Eugenie, she still owes me — so after I'd figured out the Sacconi I surprised the Bott family with a brilliant performance of Ravel's *Tzigane* — with fairly dramatic results. As usual! I can't understand why my fiddle playing enrages people so; I do it very well when I get the chance, indicating the piano rhythms by tapping my foot and knocking on wood but only Mami showed any appreciation; Papi was beside himself with rage. When I asked him if he were criticising my style or my technique he said he could hear echoes of Oistrack but that wasn't the point: I was a barefaced thief to have helped myself to his violin as if it were public property. I said he had no right to hide away an instrument like that when I needed one."

According to Toby, Nick had his own interpretation of the 8th Commandment, as with all the others.

"It was worse than Mr Shackleton telling me I couldn't stand up in public and wiggle my arse so obscenely — Bott's unspeakable meanness is what provoked me to wreck his boat and him to do his best to drown me."

"Your whole life is a game of Russian Roulette," said Adam, not knowing at this stage whether to strive any further to talk sense into his son or give up.

"The violin had been entrusted to Bott by a friend who was gassed so he was touchy about it. I still think it would have been more correct for him to encourage his son-in-law to develop his talent; I was only twenty, I could still have become a world-class performer. And an instrument has a life of its own, what's the point if it isn't played? The bigoted bastard! It's not my fault that my ancestors possibly murdered his in some pogrom a hundred years ago, there should be a statute of limitations on ancestral enmity, especially when I could coax such a terrific sound out of a few strings of catgut and a nice bit of forest. I have steady fingers, I hit the note spot on every time, no annoying vibrato, no fiddling around trying to find it."

I could imagine Nick's earnest frown as he played and it pained me to think I might never get to hear him unless I was prepared to go out and buy the instrument. But like all his other girl friends it was beyond my means to give him what he demanded.

"Eugenie's response to my heroic effort to please her," said Nick, still reliving his juvenile wrongs, "was to say that seeing me play only confirmed how obsessively introverted I am. She refused to let me spend my time like that when she wanted me to go out dancing with her and the rest of the gang. She was a fantastic dancer and so, with my fucking rights established, I gave in and stopped complaining about the violin — not that I gave up asking for it. Staying on top of Eugenie was a finely balanced act."

Nick's love life was becoming a coherent story at last. Eugenie was the girl with the slit skirt and stunning legs who owned the Vespa he borrowed to take Mrs Shackleton dining and dancing in his attempt to get into bed with her, who became the First Mrs Deathridge whom he fucked behind the door to the shock of Meg, defying his wedding guests — or just because he couldn't let her go even all those years after she sent him packing so she could marry the boss.

That Nick had this other woman in his life was no surprise; I suspected as much ever since that early morning telephone conversation in Abb's Head. I had detected it in the erotic tension of his posture: glass-blower indeed! It was clear from the way he spoke that he had never fallen out of love with her and was still securely in favour with his one-time wife.

I had arrived on the scene too late for a man who already possessed everything. And I didn't even qualify for a cuckoo-clock. I wanted to get up and hug him, the way Amanda described that she and Maddie Madigan and all the girls at Joey's funeral wanted to hug him for his appealingly vulner-able sulky face and, in spite of his brave show of defiance, so grief-stricken. But young Nick had turned and walked away from them, out of their lives. I withheld myself from a fearful premonition that he would do the same again, a lonely figure walking into the unknown.

"I gave myself honestly and unreservedly to my brilliant wife, but," Nick said to me, "my sweetheart Sibylla, there is no cause for you to be jealous..."

"I'm not," I said.

"... I was never in love until I met you..."

"Honestly, Nick, whatever you do with your wives, Numbers One or Two, is no concern of mine, and the whole Eugenie story is pure commedia del arte. I can't wait to discuss this latest instalment with Paul — he is still cross with you that her kisses earned him only ten pounds because you wouldn't pay up for the second."

"Yes, I did my duty as guardian and told him the principles of seduction but I should have explained the terms of our bet more accurately before letting him loose in a ballroom full of lovely women to see how many favours he could win."

"You didn't have to explain," I said. "You taught him by example."

"I did nothing improper. I had my bullishness well under control — it was your Sibyl eyes looking down into my soul that sent me into a spin, dizzy with wonder. That's the moment I felt what exquisite fulfilment it is to have this powerhouse of emotion squatting here boldly upfront, quivering with eagerness to be unleashed — by your smile or the memory of your smile."

Adam waited with an expression of pained patience for him to finish. Nick's declaration of love, as usual confounded by incidental anecdote, ended with a fondly approving pat to his well-tailored crotch. But he hadn't quite done.

"I have to take your word for it," he said, "that women enjoy sex but it isn't obvious to me how you can without the equipment to make it happen."

"The evidence," I said, "lies in my willingness to suffer your colossal ego up my cunt."

Not to be diverted from his enquiry by the intrusion of Nick's cock into every hiatus in the conversation, Adam said, "I only went to see you on your 21st birthday because Hannah Shackleton said she'd go if I didn't, shaming me into what she perceived as my duty."

"That's a pity," said Nick. "Maman Shackleton coming to kiss me would have been a good birthday present…"

That casual reference to Mrs Shackleton was a sudden revelation to me. Until Nick saw me, he was the stag to be hunted. Even Angelina had been brought to him by her father. What an insight that gave me! I was the love he had pursued for himself: his personal veni, vidi, vici! No wonder he didn't quite know how to negotiate terms with a girl who did not come dancing out of her corner with wide open arms, inviting him to the fray.

Adam persisted, "Mr Hein told me what I scarcely hoped to hear, that when you finished your apprenticeship he would be glad to give you a permanent position on his staff, so your future seemed secure. Why was there no mention of a wife then?"

"You never asked," said Nick. "Surely any natural father would have enquired about his son's love life?"

"Surely any natural son could have said, 'By the way, Respected Parent, I'd like you to meet my wife'?

"But you did meet her — in Hein's office. You told me you were going to sell my piano, grumbling that you had already paid out far too much to keep it in the Harrods climate-controlled warehouse, so I asked you to hand the bill over to Eugenie and told her to keep up the payments. She shook your hand and said she was pleased to meet dear Nicki's Dadi at last. You were too concerned about paying the bill to pay attention to the girl."

"How was I to guess she was more than any polite young lady secretary?"

"Hein made a joke about needing her to keep me in order. His idea of a funny story was to tell you that when I offered to construct him a robot to do his tediously repetitive tasks he'd refused, saying I was cheaper."

"That didn't strike me as unreasonable."

"You could have pointed out to him, as I did, that I was cheaper only because he didn't pay me what I was worth. Whenever I made a fuss he called Eugenie down to the shop floor to tell her to control her husband. They were constantly giggling about me as if I were a silly joke — discipline by giggles! The Swiss have a very peculiar sense of humour."

"It seems to have worked," said Adam dryly.

"Yes, it made me feel ridiculous."

"Mr Hein struck me as a thoroughly decent chap," said Adam.

"It depends what you call decent. He'd have made a killing in robots if he'd taken up my offer instead of laughing at it. Hein exploited me mercilessly, but I put up with him because he let me fly his buzzy little Pilatus P-3. He designed instruments and he'd sit beside me and explain the workings. He is the best teacher I've ever had because he understood the peculiarities of my learning processes, though he tended to go into fits of maniacal laughter in moments of crisis when I misunderstood what he said.

"'Nicki, Nicki, the sky is up that way!'"

"I see I have more to be grateful for than I realised," said Adam. "I was impressed how fluent you were in that incomprehensible language. Not understanding a word you said was the moment you ceased to be my child and became some stranger. I should have realised it was more than a simple question of language."

"The triumph of Tintin!" Nick was being facetious with his deadpan face on. "Bonne-Maman helping me from beyond. I had to get to grips with the language pretty damn fast just to stay alive. But when I got my licence he bought the new PC-6 Turbo for me to take him cruising over the slopes in search of better snow."

Two daredevils and a small plane: well-matched, they were lucky to have found each other even if Nick didn't believe in luck!

"I'd drop him off as high as possible and wave good-bye as he went yodelling down, not expecting to find him at the bottom in one piece. But there he'd be, drunk on exhilaration and schnapps, tripping the light fantastic with some film star. For me the pleasure was to be alone in the sky, an eagle ridge-soaring, doing barrel rolls in and out of the clouds, then diving to the ground with the mountain streaming past, at the last minute lining up to the ground and feeling the sweet moment of contact as a release in one's belly... Eugenie tolerated my expeditions with Nestor and the other guys but the outings with Hein she regarded with deep misgiving — probably afraid she'd lose her now and future husband in one fell swoop."

"Don't you have to pass exams to get a pilot's licence?" I asked, picturing him as a young man flying between snow-covered peaks and skidding to a halt on glaciers. Leon Bolus's nerve-wracking experience came to mind.

"With Heini behind me merrily making fun of my mistakes, how could I fail?" said Nick. "It's only knobs, maths and intuition, the things I'm rather good at."

Also guessing and gambling!

"Next best thing to a visit from Mrs Shackleton was the very proper 21st birthday treat you gave me, boating on the Genfersee and eating fish grilled at the lakeside. Believe me, I was truly grateful — I am always happy in your company even if you consider me a pain in the arse."

Adam was sceptical of Nick's gratitude.

"You boast that you have broken every single commandment except 4 — but to say that you honour your father while spending two and a half days in his company without mentioning the not insignificant fact that you have a wife makes that a gross exaggeration."

"Spending two and a half days of precious free time with my Old Man when I could have been having a party, dancing the night away with my wife and friends seems pretty respectful to me."

"You seemed to have plenty to talk about, so why not mention that?"

"There was plenty going on: a state of emergency in Paris and on Sunday the worst ever airliner crash; Berlin — Kennedy was saving the world and Khrushchev planning his missile bases in Cuba — Eugenie used to call me Nikita Deathwish, but then she is given to silly teases: she introduced me to her friends saying, 'I married him for his name and his English cock: the Freudian drollness of the first is self-evident; the quite comic magnitude of the second I leave to your imagination.' She selected my clothes for me; she liked to exaggerate my English look by way of advertising the stylishly virile quality of her prize cock... Adèle took a photo of us at the railway station after our wedding, me with a gormlessly youthful face looking absurd under a wide brimmed felt hat, pure 1940's, and Eugenie glee-fully triumphant."

"Oh, Nick, I'd love to see it."

"I tore it up."

And threw her camera in the river, according to Adèle.

Nick smiled at the onyx death's head on his little finger.

"Eugenie gave me this as a wedding ring," he remarked. "Another of her jokes."

"And you still wear it!"

"It's a very Mittel-Europa memento mori," he said, surprised we found anything inappropriate in wearing an ex-wife's wedding ring.

"... rockets going to the moon," he went on, "anti-Apartheid rallies — when I finally escaped from slave-master Hein, Eugenie took me to visit her uncle in Johannesburg. He offered me an excellent salary and a nice house with swimming pool if I'd stay and make myself useful as gunsmith and sharpshooter but so soon after Sharpsville Eugenie decided it was all a bit too exciting for her taste — in spite of her act as stunning, world-weary heroine straight out of a film noir, she's uncompromisingly Swiss."

"I daresay you were more aware of all that than I was," admitted Adam. "I'd had my war and living in Abb's Head I wasn't interested in getting involved in another — though admittedly the idea of basing Polaris so near to Glasgow was a concern. A number of my old colleagues were organising protests, not that it did any good and I thought if there were a nuclear war the distance would be immaterial."

"You are so English, Dad! No wonder you lost an empire. I was much keener on the idea of fighting off the Bolsheviks than shooting blacks. I was tempted by the really big Oerlikons, but I saw more of a future for myself in small arms — not so swanky but easy to trade."

"So how come you are doing medical stuff?" I asked.

"Sheer laziness."

Nick paused, as if still considering his options. Again he was at such a point in his career that he needed to make decisions.

"You ventured forth from your ivory tower to see me once again after I was cut loose from my safe haven in the bosom of the Botts — I can't imagine why you bothered. Guilt, I suppose."

"I needed your signature to release some old Dumez stuff Penn Shackleton was looking into and he made me go, knowing it was waste of time to send you anything by post and expect an answer – it's a mystery how you ever got on in business..."

"That's how," said Nick. "If it's important enough it comes to me."

"You took me to see a mountain rescue team at work," said Adam. "I was duly impressed — I can figure out how to keep an 800 ton vessel stable in a force 10 gale, but the physical effort of your Alpine scrambling in a blizzard seems totally impossible."

"I knew you wouldn't be impressed with what I was doing at the arms factory, fascinating as it was to me. You had been corrupted by Mr Shackleton's pacifism."

"So why didn't I get to know your wife then?"

Nick leaned his elbows on the table, lower lip protruding, looking glum.

"I am so tired of this conversation," he complained. "I want to go to bed."

So did I. This was turning into dinner-table talk of Proustian tediousness, but Adam could be just as relentless as Nick.

"I can't see any reason to be so secretive," he said. "I was worried that the traumas of your mother's death had left you too scarred for normal relationships. Think what a relief it would have been to know you were married to a perfectly respectable young woman: a work colleague, what could be more suitable?"

"Because the painful subject of my divorce was no longer relevant — you'd think being deserted by one's mother and grandmother was enough betrayal for any man to endure, but I thought I had my wife for life. At twenty-four I'd achieved everything: Swiss passport, satisfying work and a woman who was absolute perfection, fun, clever, stylish beyond beauty and marvellously fuckable — those legs! I'd get between them, go to Cock Paradise and die there."

"Nick, for decency sake, spare us the intimate details," said Adam, cracking walnuts as a distraction since it was clear Nick was impervious to criticism and any success in getting him to shut up over his cock was doomed to be short-lived.

Nick flexed his fingers, tapped on the table and looked around impatiently to see where Tomás was with his drink. Adam went to fetch a bottle and poured out a glass of pinky plum liqueur for Nick, his hand resting a moment lightly on the nape of Nick's neck — a paternal gesture, I thought, as if testing for a fever.

"Hein cheated me out of more than my wife," said Nick, acknowledging the filled glass with a nod though he pulled a face when he tasted it. "But he also taught me how to survive in business. After he parted company with his Italian film star — she tried to make it sensational but he bowed out with a polite smile... it must be the giggles that attract women, he never appeared in public without some exotic beauty on his arm — Eugenie decided she'd have him, complaining that Itchy Fingers had been trying for years to giggle his way into her knickers so it was time to make it legal. She is so efficient; she handed me my congé in the morning and had Hein down town to sign up in the afternoon."

Nick's wry tone did not invite sympathy. As usual his insouciance in telling made his life story seem a series of absurd episodes.

"I was to all practical purposes suicidal," he went on. "I might have hung around to make an abject fool of myself at their wedding — the way I did at yours — but Papi Bott generously saved me from that indignity. He was so glad to see the back of me that he gave me the 1965 Porsche cabriolet, the latest model, black with silver leather upholstery, that must have been the most gorgeous auto ever, speeding me on my way with a 'Die happy!' So I drove the Porsche up a mountain and took the straight-on option at a hairpin bend but instead of it doing a graceful nosedive into eternity we made a very inelegant belly landing below among some very startled cows. I'm bloody rubbish at killing myself."

He shuffled restlessly and said: "What on earth is taking Clare so long with the compote? I suppose she is busy wrecking it with dollops of mascarpone; she can't leave well alone... I took idiotic risks and brought them all off quite brilliantly, I'm just not stupid enough to succeed in failing. Even hurling myself into a crevasse didn't work. I had kept my rug-sack on to make myself heavier, I thought to fall faster, but I got stuck on a ledge. I could have just perched there in misery until I froze, that would have been the easy way out, but with my ice-pick, pitons and rope I had to see if I couldn't somehow climb out. After all, if I fell to my death it hardly mattered and climbing kept me from being bored in the meantime."

"Well you hadn't trained in mountain rescue for nothing," said Adam. "It's only right you could save yourself."

"As solo effort it was bloody difficult," said Nick. "When I dragged myself over the edge I was so exhausted I could have collapsed right there and died of exposure; I picked myself up again only because I had to tell Nestor how damned clever I'd been. But he laughed at me so much that I gave up on suicide; obviously it wasn't working. Actually when the Porsche and I recovered from the shock, I drove it for another four years. I cleaned and polished the motor parts so obsessively that when I sold it to help finance my gun-running in Africa it was still like new. I didn't waste my mother's remains either, Dad. I made a handsome profit out of the derisory remnants of my Dumez inheritance you'd failed to squander."

"You took my yacht money... " Adam protested.

"I paid off your debts."

"What did I do to be punished with a son like you?" said Adam, half-laughing, still uncertain how much to believe of Nick's dubious life and death stories.

"You let my mother die in agony."

This was so shocking a response that Adam was silenced.

But Nick's narrative continued, challenging our disbelief.

"Hein let me take the Pilatus — well, he couldn't refuse and anyway he assumed that a solo flight that distance would be near impossible and if I didn't crash I'd end up shot or in prison — a man of limited imagination; he didn't even consider the hazard of Maddie Madigan trying to poison me, so he couldn't be disappointed when that didn't happen either."

The drip-drip effect of slow detail expanding the Africa story.

"He knows I can't resist a dare and he was prepared to sacrifice his precious aircraft to get rid of me, not to mention his pretentiously over-specified Cosmonaute wristwatch which he insisted I took, a sop to his conscience — as if I couldn't see the sun and the stars coming up and going down, with my instrument panel to tell me how far I'd gone at what speed... I'll achieve my life's end without assistance from Hein and his expensive toys."

When Nick discussed the same event with Nestor they were treating their boss as something of a joke with his man-on-the-moon watch.

"It came in useful though, it bought me enough fuel to get me out of Africa — the most expensive fuel ever, considering the exquisite watch-maker's skill and precious metals. Hein was furious."

Adam shuffled with his chair, impatient to get up and go, but couldn't quite make up his mind to do it. Nick, the Ancient Mariner. Next thing we'd be having albatrosses.

"Going was a well-planned doddle," he went on, "the return journey rather less so. I calculated it would take me about two weeks but with all the mis-haps — dropping in on Maddie for resuscitation after my near disaster in the Drakensberg added considerably to the complications; that was dicing with a different kind of death — so I was away longer than anticipated. Hein was quite put out that the Pilatus was somewhat scruffy when he got it back. He has little appreciation of the conditions I was working in or the air space I had to weave my way through, often at dodgy altitudes, no squawking, and the refuelling options were a bit erratic too. How pleased I was finally to see Corfu below me and have the nice clear run of the Adriatic where a Swiss registered aircraft is nothing spectacular and I could reconnect with the civilised world as we know it! The biggest hazard at that point was relaxing too much and falling asleep."

Madagascar, I thought, or was it Mozambique? Bolus mentioned Addis Ababa, Alexandria? Self-conscious in my flimsy Armani gown I wasn't tak-ing in the significance of what he was telling me about these places, and Nick had been having far too much fun jousting with Amanda to care any more about the boring details of his odyssey. Nick cared nothing for the land; even the prettiest of Tuscan settings was of no interest to him beyond what it delivered in the way of food and drink, and in the most picturesque of towns only the evidence of human intellect in the way of science and music. So it was easy to picture him on the long stretches of arid nothing-ness flying in a state of abstraction with his mind empty of anything but the dials in front of him, dodging bird strikes and thunderclouds, rousing himself only at the last minute for the climactic moment of landing and dealing with potentially hostile people on the ground.

"Well," said Adam sharply, finding his voice again after Nick's knife-stab in the back, "a small plane built in the Alps hardly seems suitable for taking into the Rand. Whatever possessed you even to attempt it?"

"Aircraft and pilot performed brilliantly," said Nick with an air of modest self-congratulation. "Equally robust; with our endurance and wits we survived with all our vital bits intact; it's short run and quick take-off saved my skin in a couple of awkward situations. No, the moral of the story is: don't get into a gunfight in a cockpit. Hein never forgave me for the inelegantly repaired holes in the fuselage. However, five years of the master's engineering skill behind me meant I could have rebuilt it from scratch if necessary — and don't forget the hours of highly skilled but unpaid work I put in at the paternal boatyard..."

"I was wasting a fortune on trying to get you educated," Adam dismissed Nick's implied reproach.

"The most embarrassing moment of my return home was when I guilelessly wandered into the First Class lounge at Zurich and realised that in sweat-encrusted khaki shirt and shorts I looked somewhat out of place among the suits. Having made a conscious decision to stay dirty for the sake of being inconspicuous at obscure desert airfields, and my sturdy Belstaff jacket had been sacrificed to repairs — it was that or my sleeping bag and not freezing at night was more important — and my underpants went on an irritating rattle, so it took quite some sang-froid to carry off my state of undress. You cannot imagine the contrast between Zurich and somewhere like Port Sudan, and that was positively civilised compared with some."

"That's the story you told them at the Swiss Embassy the night of the gang-bang."

I was delighted to have that cryptic conversation, when Father William prevented Nick driving off into the London night-traffic distraught with emotion, explained at last. Clever Father William! He possibly saved our lives by that few minutes delay.

"At Eugenie's request I diverted from Belp where I was known and would have blended with the small craft of ski tourists, and landed on Zurich 28 dodging the heavy metal at great inconvenience to myself in my exhausted state; then the ground staff naggingly offering me cups of coffee because I sat there, nodding off, shedding red dust from every crease of my scanty clothing; my boots too: Swiss Army issue, which at least gave me a semblance of credibility — the boots boosted my confidence even better than having a considerable fortune stashed away in a knapsack and a couple of innocent looking kitbags. Gabriel's diplomatic bag was more conspicuous but I didn't really care what happened to that. I can't tell you how relieved I was when Eugenie arrived to pick me up and brought me something bankable to wear — though I had a struggle to get her to hand over the suit carrier; she really wanted to parade me along the Bahnhofstrasse in my Afrikaner disguise as if I were a pet cheetah on a chain — watch out, I said, that's the one feline that doesn't retract its claws. Fortunately I came equipped with exactly what she wanted — and I don't mean my cock, that was temporarily out of action after weeks of living on biltong and adrenaline; even I can't fly and fuck, the arousal is too huge, all one's libido goes into one's affair with the aircraft."

Nick's telling of the same story at the embassy was to prove a point about diplomacy, but for the entertainment of the Boluses and Clare it became a farce and now his laconic complacency in the telling his triumphs sidetracked Adam into taking it with an unwarranted degree of scepticism.

"I had great respect for Mr Hein's judgement," Adam said, "now I'm not so sure. He seems to have got himself quite a liability when he took you on. I can't imagine what possessed him to let you take his plane on such a completely mad expedition."

"Its droll yellow with cocky red tail and wings didn't look at all out of place on the African earth and I was sorry he disassociated himself from my exploits by having it re-sprayed silver with flashy blue and green stripes, covering up the scars of its heroic survival."

Nick seemed to attach less heroism to his own survival.

"I came home from my travels loaded but exhausted. The Botts took me back into the bosom of the family and I slept more or less continuously for a week while Eugenie force-fed me her Mami's chicken soup. I obediently opened my mouth and swallowed on command, though I still had sufficient wit about me to spit out any attempt to stuff me with so-called fluffy matzo balls. In my dreamlike state I associated them with the fat live grubs Maddie Madigan forced me to eat. Her idea of a gourmet delight was to dip them in salt and vinegar to make them squirm in my mouth."

Grubs, oysters, sea urchins? All exactly the kind of thing Nick would consider a gourmet delight. Incomparably better than chocolate mousse.

"While I was recovering Papi Bott stood on anti-fuck guard over me uttering Biblical imprecations — I point out to him he can hardly blame me for Hein's redhead baby when he, the grandfather, has a patriarchal bush of once red beard, but, I said, I take it as a compliment that he gives me credit for it. I think he actually quite likes me."

"Even I quite like you," I said.

"By the time I came down to earth Eugenie had done all the finances and with her skewy sense of humour I woke up to find her placid, large baby sitting on my bed dribbling over the paper that represented my profit from our partnership. A well-behaved child, unlike either of his parents, he handed it over without screaming too ear-shatteringly — it was good to see I hadn't lost my magic touch with the young, though knowing Eugenie had that delightful little fellow all to herself added to my frustration when Angelina wasn't producing any. Unlike his grandfather he raised no objection to me fucking his mother either. The Swiss, tough bastards that they are, have impeccable manners from infancy."

"If you can eat live grubs," I said, "I don't know why you're so rude about Clare's food."

"I prefer grubs," he said. "While I was with Maddie I demonstrated my latest rifle in her back yard to show her how finely tuned and accurate it is. Her gardener Joop's job was to set up the target and he was impressed but Maddie dismissed it, saying that her rubbishy old AK47 was good enough for shooting him with and proved it by putting a bullet in the target within inches of his nose. Joop wasn't at all put out; he said he'd already fixed it to swap with the neighbours' boys who was going to kill whose boss — they didn't quite like to have to knife their own."

"Oh, Nick, it can't be true!"

"You don't know Maddie Madigan! So I gave Joop the new rifle, showed him how to maintain it properly and told him to guard his mistress."

Clare came to say she was sorry for the delay; she had dropped the compote on the kitchen floor and had to go down to the cellar for another jar. Nick was so absorbed in his own story he had already forgotten he asked for figs.

"Get back to your pigsty, you poxy slattern of a cuntessa," he said waving this interruption away, and turning back to Adam: "My rock hard glittering jewel of a wife was quite right to get rid of me: I was a pest. And she knows the English cock is available whenever she wants it extra hard. Besides, I do rather well out of my divorce. After failing to murder or otherwise dispose of me, bossy Hein and bully Bott vie with each other to prove how enlightened they are, really. They've both been better fathers to me than you ever were."

"You mean money-laundering for you?"

"You make it sound illegal." Nick was not disconcerted by Adam's censure.

"I don't suppose you are any better a son to them than you are to me, you fucking ingrate."

"Hein and Bott: it was surviving my battles with them that got me where I am now. You ought to have been in there too — but, apart from fucking my mother, what use have you ever been to me?"

Adam gave a sardonic smile at this rare opportunity to put Nick down.

"I'd say that was the single essential favour ever done for you, what brought you to this table with your stuffed wallet and your bulging balls."

"I must remember what to say when my many sons gather around my deathbed and curse me for a rotten father."

They held each other's gaze, both trying not to give in and laugh.

"The Swiss have a great feeling for domesticity," said Nick, standing up.

"Are you changing the subject?" asked Adam.

"I remember Hein showing you photos of his little boy at my wedding reception. I wonder why."

Nick, who had eaten nothing but the excessively garlicky chicken, turned away to go to the sideboard to help himself from the cheese platter, avoiding any more of his father's probing, and as he went he murmured, smiling to himself, "Every sturdy little Eidgenosse is a national treasure... even one with red hair and a solemn absence of giggles."

I looked at his back and wondered if I understood him right.

Adam kept his eyes fixed in puzzlement on Nick as he ambled away from us, conspicuously well-dressed amongst the Germans in their holiday shirts.

"Nick certainly doesn't get his love of fancy dress from me; the only tie I possess is a black one for funerals. He must have got it from watching that crazy eccentric Dumez getting dressed every morning as if he expected a call from Churchill or the King to come down town to save the country when all he was really useful for was decoding Russian monetary policy, not exactly onerous; it's not as if the Russians had any, letting a few million peasants starve is one way of solving a food shortage, though I suppose decoding anarchy is another way of putting it. Now I think of it, Nick's handwriting must be illegible because of watching Dumez do his Cyrillic script; very likely he never got the two alphabets separated in his laterally working brain. It never occurred to me before."

"And upside-down," I pointed out. "Across the table, creating his own writing code in his head. Nick told me his grandmother took him to Russian Orthodox services in Buckingham Palace Road."

"She went for the music," said Adam to excuse such a lapse in an otherwise intelligent woman. "I suppose I married Nick's mother for the sheer glamour of a Nathalie in khaki. I should have looked closer at Deduschka Dumez, then I'd have known that her flaming mop tucked under a cap, and a tight skirt that shot up to her knickers every time she got in and out from behind the steering wheel were as much an act as Nick in morning-suit, getting Bailey Bubutu to exchange his ceremonial lion-tuft codpiece for a sufficiently folkloresy embroidered robe to be allowed in to offer his so-called respects to the Queen. Playacting both of them, from beginning to end."

I giggled as I imagined the long-suffering Queen's prim face hiding what I hoped was a sense of the ridiculous when confronting Nick in splendidly formal attire, and the image, implicit between them, of Nick's desire to jig the expansive wife of his colourful friend but for the lack of condoms against the health hazard.

Adam's gaze was still following Nick as he moved with light-footed swagger past the other tables and their occupants, responding with an affable grüezi to a succession of Guten Abend's. Taking his time, he was giving Adam time to simmer down.

"It's as well he is so thin," said Adam. "If he had a fat arse that strutting would be positively obnoxious."

I had to smile. To my love-sated eyes Nick was a dancer of consummate grace, waltzing past the obstacles of tables, chairs, and their various occupants who were happy to engage with him, Nick's unapologetic Schweizerdeutsch displaying his credentials as cock of the walk, possibly also to position himself emphatically half-way between them and Adam's Embattled Britain prejudices.

"It is a mortification for a conscientious grammar-school pupil like me to have a son who was completely resistant to every attempt to educate him, in spite of the amount of money he accuses me of squandering on it. He really was the most impossible, undisciplined boy but for one thing: he never seemed troubled by sex. That's what makes his women-crazed stories the more incomprehensible."

"Well," I said, "why should he have trouble with sex? For an adolescent he was surely getting what he wanted, dancing and playing games with his adorable Mrs Shackleton — even if you count thrashing his pillow every night in the grip of hideous nightmares as not having trouble."

"Look at him! Gnädigen Frauen and all that pretentious rubbish, the swank," said Adam, "he'll be kissing hands next; one never knows if he means it sincerely or is he taking the piss? He can be so enigmatic, I saw him at the wedding with head inclined just so obliquely to Mrs Shackleton — I was deeply shocked at his behaviour with her, I had to look away; such unashamed eroticism was too disturbing for a father to observe... but who am I to judge? After he had done dancing he came with a bottle of champagne and sat down beside me in a daze of lovesick bemusement... for Hannah of all people, really, a nicer, more sensible woman you cannot imagine."

Clearly Adam hadn't taken proper note of the Philosophy of Kissing According to Nick. He scrutinised him across the room where he was examining the selection of cheeses with his nose, helping a couple of German ladies, who had followed him over, with their choice. Play-acting or not, when he was out to charm the ladies he could conjure up the most seductively sweet smile, one I never saw directed towards me.

"But what about me?" I said, near tears with annoyance — or, in spite of my denial, jealousy. "He swears I am the love of his life, yet it now appears he has quite a few others."

"Don't worry," said Adam. "Your marrying Gus was a smart move, Nick will never stop pursuing you now — you are something he wants and can't have, like Gus's house, something money can't buy. He has everything else."

As Nick came swanning back to us with his selection of cheeses, having created an appreciable commotion on the still waters of the dining room, Adam said, his tone changing from puzzled indignation to a note of vexation:

"It's all very well your boyhood wife wanting to advertise your burgeoning virility in high style, but now you are a mature man can't you get your tailor to cut your trousers so your genital display isn't quite so palpably obvious?"

Nick stopped short, holding his plate on high as he turned and looked at himself in the flaking mirror on the opposite wall. The fine dark charcoal alpaca he had put on for Gianni's funeral had been hung to steam in the shower and then out to air on the gallery — he was perfectly capable of looking after his things himself if Meg wasn't there to do it for him — and replaced by an old favourite that he kept in my wardrobe for emergencies. He stood buttoning his jacket and unbuttoning it, studying all angles, oblivious of interested stares.

"This is a suit I had made after my Afrikaner adventure, as soon as I escaped Eugenie's chicken soup and got to Savile Row," he said, "one of three: that's the amount of cloth and style choosing, measuring and fitting, and let's admit it, flattery, it took to restore my self-image after the physical and mental trauma associated with khaki shorts. I have been living on a less Spartan diet..."

He sat down and arranged his cheeses in a pleasing pattern on the plate and indicated to Adam that his wineglass was empty...

"... since I was measured for it so it may be a bit snug in the thighs — but you are exaggerating, it's a perfectly decent and, if I may say so, a rather attractive bulge — and you have to allow for the Sibylla Effect that is keeping it so obviously on the alert. My tailor, who doesn't know Sibylla, calls it the Gemini Effect: eleven percent of his customers have awkwardly up-front, symmetrical balls that don't dangle down conveniently to one side or the other, aggravated in my case by size and the general obstreperousness of my penis perched on top. It's a discussion I have with him every time I have a suit made: buttons or zip? We settle for zip as a concession to preserving a tighter, more elegant line. I assure you, dear Father, he wouldn't let me walk out his door in anything that wasn't a credit to his skill, so it is a tribute to him for keeping me decent while flattering my fuck potential."

"Dear Son, that doesn't need flattering."

Nick, demonstratively yawning, rested his chin on his hands and closed his eyes, the cheese uneaten in front of him.

"You made a fool of me," Adam said, refusing to let him rest. "Furzy came all the way to Abb's Head, when he was already at death's door, to check on your background. I had no intention of deceiving him — in fact he probably already knew more about you than I did."

Without opening his eyes Nick said, "All he wanted was to see what a decent, honest father I have. Did he tell you that his father started out in the family business as itinerant scrap merchant and went on to make his fortune breaking up ships? Ironic that he made considerably more money out of his scrap than you earned in your shipyard doing your patriotic duty."

"Yes, we got on fine. My rivets probably saved his life when he was torpedoed on the Arctic Convoy. I had suggested welding as quicker and easier but the bosses didn't agree and luckily the plates held long enough for him to get his crew off. I hope gratitude didn't deceive him into thinking Angelina would have an equally reliable husband."

Nick sat up as Clare came at long last proudly bearing a purple Murano glass dish of figs conserved in amaretto with the dreaded mascarpone on top.

"So I am. Angelina gets as much of me as she can take. I perform our ritual copulation just as often as necessary to maintain a pleasurable tension between us." He looked from the figs to Clare and back, frowning. "I never let her off the fundamental principle of marriage. She knows what's at stake."

He tasted a fig, spat it out and pushed the dish away without comment. Clare looked as if she would like to hit him over the head with it, but merely said, "Is there anything more I can do for you, Mr Deathridge? And don't make any lewd suggestions."

Nick's eyes sparkled as the gamut of possible lewd suggestions ran past them. He stood up and bowing, kissed her hand, just as Adam imagined he would with the German ladies: Nick demonstrating what he had recently described — the kiss as insult.

Clare responded with an equally insulting flick of her forefinger on his cheek. Nick shielded his face with his hand but it was only to hide his laughter and as Clare picked up her lovingly prepared sweet to take it away he said, "Don't waste your pearls on this swine, Good Woman of Edinburgh, take it to bed with you and feed it to your deserving husband."

"Eff off, you unspeakable Sassenach."

With that Clare made a dignified exit, solemnly not laughing.

Adam said: "Hannah Shackleton was right about your manners... but I can understand that with your disreputable past the instinct for secrecy is ingrained. It's your self-protective reflex."

"Obviously," said Nick, dismissively, as if he couldn't believe how long it had taken his father to grasp what was at stake. "Bolus was a true diplomat; he understood the real issue. He knew that in the arms business I don't give hostages to fortune. I know how to protect myself and my associates; no-one has come to any serious harm through working with me. There was an unfortunate incident near Dire Dawa where I had a rendezvous to refuel but while I can negotiate in Afrikaans, French or Italian, my Amharic is still rudimentary. And anyway, the gentlemen in question addressed me in Portuguese, another weak spot in my repertoire so I may have misunderstood their intentions — I didn't wait to find out but puddle-hopped to hell out of there."

I felt a certain satisfaction that I had avoided becoming an item in the trail of unfortunate incidents Nick invariably left behind him. Thank God for Gus Wittersworth!

"On consideration," said Adam, standing up, "maybe you should sacrifice the Deathridge bloody-minded aggressive non-conformity, your armed-to-the-teeth self-determination, to fix yourself a title. Angelina deserves some respect to compensate her for your maverick cock."

"Respected Parent," said Nick solemnly, hastening to open the door for him and giving him a squeeze on the shoulder as he went out, "very occasionally you hit the nail right on the head. Good night!"

"Sleep well," said Adam.

I doubted Adam would sleep well.

~

Corona
Especial

12

On our way to bed, pausing to admire the moonlit landscape below, Nick surprised me by grasping my head between his outspread fingers like a rugby ball and kissing me with the same intensity as that other time in his house when he was trying to persuade me to be the next, or supplementary, Mrs Deathridge. Obviously he had been stung by my earlier reproaches and was determined to prove me wrong.

"What are you laughing at?" he asked, letting go, ready to get offended again.

"You," I said. "I wonder what nonsense you are softening me up for this time."

Nick groaned. "The same as usual: to love me, to have my babies."

"I thought you just wanted your cock sucked."

"No, not that! That's too much like torture; it emasculates me, making me come to no good purpose."

"That's just an excuse not to keep your word and give me your impressive fortune. Remember you promised me, if I'd do it." I said it laughing, but I couldn't be sure it wasn't actually true, suspecting Nick's resourcefulness in wriggling out of rash promises. I had longed all evening to embrace him but not like this.

"My sweetheart, just shut up, how can I kiss you when you won't take me seriously?"

"Everything you do and say tells me what a fool I'd be to love you," I said.

"But you do!" he said.

I buried my face in his chest, refusing to let him see that his kisses too were a form of torture that had my emotions screaming with alarm, knowing how ephemeral this happiness was. A day or two, maybe a week, and he would be gone, leaving a non-presence so complete that when he turned up again, his tangible reality wouldn't fail to take me by surprise.

I understood Angelina's confidence in her rock-solid marriage. He had the same effect on me, even now, even after he had crammed into an evening's dinner talk tales of his exploits which were probably not only true but no more than half of what he could have recounted with equally cool aplomb for our entertainment. And it seemed that all the other women who populated his life could be equally sure of his constancy, justified or not.

Tomás announced his approach by the smell of the corona especial Nick had brought for him.

"I wish you relentless fuckers would confine yourselves to the area of my estate to which you are legally entitled," he said.

He sat down on the wall. Nick released me and sat down beside him, prepared to stay and talk another hour or two. Without a word Tomás passed his cigar over and Nick took a mouthful of smoke and slowly released it into the night air, earthy, humid, woody with a whiff of meadowsweet honey, then passed it back.

"*Muy espléndido!*" he said. "This is true contentment, to sit on a wall with one's friend and one's beloved... " he pulled me between his thighs to lean against him, "sensual and emotional bliss combined."

Tomás passed the cigar over again and Nick took it saying, "It smells enticingly of female pubes but what will it do for my kissability?"

Not that he was particularly concerned.

"Who better to try it out on than Sibylla?" said Tomás.

I took a deep breath of the drifting smoke, which made me splutter against Nick's shoulder; but though I couldn't detect the scent he described which was so pleasing to him, I could feel it's effect rubbing against my hip.

"I am such a slave to my balls," said Nick, regretfully handing Tomás his cigar back. "Rampant genes constantly demanding to be provided with a suitable receptacle, preferably Sibylla... that tobacco is damned good, let me have another go."

Tomás smiled at Nick's obvious pleasure in the spicy cloud he sucked from the smooth brown cylinder, singularly suited to wafting deliciously out over the dewy dark land below.

"I think Mrs Wittersworth would like to go to bed," Tomás said and I felt he would like to be rid of me so he and Nick could have the night to themselves.

"I'm past going to bed," said Nick but he wasn't letting me go either. "What about a midnight swim?"

"The piscina is damned cold at night," said Tomás.

"What pool?" I asked. "You can't go driving around in the dark after your good dinner."

"It's only the pozza where the men go for a dip to cool off before they go home, back of the rocky outcrop."

"In all the time I've been here," I said, "you never told me there's a bathing pool."

"Obviously not," said Tomás. "It's for the boys. For peace sake, they don't want to be embarrassed by you coming along to ogle them, taking your pick of the best pricks."

That silenced me. Since the midday when Nick humiliated me in front of the men I had avoided them, self-conscious of so many sparkling dark eyes collectively assessing the availability of my cunt, though when I happened across any one individual he would sidle past with the politest of *bon giorno, signora's.*

However, Nick wanted to go, so we crossed the yard and took a track along the side of the hill and there, out of sight behind a couple of boulders, was a small waterfall beneath which a series of pools cascaded down into the valley below. I felt cheated that such a lovely spot had been hidden from me until now that I was leaving.

Tomás threw the butt of his cigar in an arc into the dark and we watched it glow a long way down.

"Pity it's gone," said Nick.

"Why don't you keep your own Havanas? Why give them all to me?" asked Tomás,

"No, I like to keep my edge sharp, keep my balls a-twitch. Smoking would slow me down, make me too passive. Besides, Tsang insists I haven't fulfilled my breeding potential yet. A year to the good before I'm forty. I have time for another go with the Virgins, they are wonderfully prolific and Tsang's latest scheme is that he can make the twins have twins by encouraging the second ovary to release an egg even after the first one has been fertilised. He doesn't approve of anything that might spoil the liveliness of my sperm or affect my DNA."

Nick was taking his clothes off while he spoke and stood naked on the highest rock above the pitch-black pool.

"and Sibylla still owes me one," he added.

"Please don't jump," I said, terrified of the unknown depth below.

"If your heart stops from shock," said Tomás, "don't count on Sibylla and me to drag you out and resuscitate you."

Nick drew himself up, poised for a moment of sheer beauty, and dived straight down into the abyss.

"Oh, my God," I said and clutched Tomás's arm, peering into the darkness.

"This is where all the boys learn to dive," said Tomás, "Nick knows what he's doing; several of our lads have done well in competitions from watching his technique. He demonstrates how to control their wild tumbling — the damned conceited prick, he is such a showman, but the boys love it."

"Nick is wrong about how women experience sex, but having a cunt does exclude me from a lot of pleasure," I said, visualising how lovely it would have been to watch their sleek bodies in the sunlight and how annoying that even Gus hadn't told me such a delight existed.

Tomás sat down to wait until Nick climbed back up, and I sat beside him. Bats swerved around us on silent wings and in the distance an owl screeched. Nick's head reappeared where the moonlight struck the rocks.

"It's better than breaking the ice on the Hampstead ponds on Christmas Day," he said, and stood again at the launch position, his heels over the edge, and somersaulted backwards out of sight.

Tomás put his arm around me and I leant against him, so comfortable and reassuring, and we sat in silence listening for faint ripples of sound from down below until Nick, satisfied with his dip, clambered back into view and mopped himself dry with his shirt.

"Sibylla, for pity's sake, take this crazy man of yours to bed," said Tomás.

"If only I had Sibylla to take me to bed every night," said Nick. "I'm such a chronic insomniac"

"I know," said Tomás, giving me a hand to stand up. "Clare complains you keep me talking on the phone half the night and I presume you have other friends serving the same purpose."

The long solitary nights in Stratton Square came to mind, when Nick was getting over Dr Tsang's interference in our love life and I sat on the stairs listening to the sound of his voice below, the modulations rising and falling like waves on the shore, and loneliness had overwhelmed me because he didn't talk to me. Tomás calling him my man gave me the illusion that for this night at least he was truly mine, but nothing had changed. Monument-ally silhouetted against the moon, not even shivering with only his trousers on his cold body, I knew I could never possess him.

Nick put on his coat and said, "My cock is so chilled I can't feel it. It needs a warm burrow to recover in..."

... once again defining my value as accommodating cunt.

Cold and exhausted as he was, Nick's high spirits kept him fidgeting around while I and my cock-warmer sat in bed waiting for him to come in. The first time we slept together I was jealous that he got up to talk to his one-time wife — but maybe he was he telling her about me, teasing her that his uncircumcised cock had at last found its true home in a girl he had won with pure love: no bribes, no bargains, no gaming.

Dear Jesus, I prayed, how is it possible to be in love with a man who loves me, but who won't let me love him?

"When I was miserable after the gang-bang," I said in an attempt to focus his attention, "one of the stories Paul told me was of the Fisher King and the Holy Grail. Like Percival I was too stupid or ignorant to ask the right question."

"Yes," he said, "you and Percival have a lot in common, a charming gormlessness."

"That evening when Toby brought me home from the hunt..."

"... you mean, when he brought you back to me after fucking you into a drunken stupor..."

"You can hardly blame me after the way you terrified me, charging at me like that."

"I meant to. I scared the wits out of Frank too. He thought it would be me this time, not the horse, that I had met my match with Red Jasper and would finally get my come-uppance. Not yet, I said to him, that it would take more than him and a horse to get the better of me..."

"It's your vanity that frightens me," I said. "You looked like an Olympian but I cannot believe how reckless it is to dive into a black hole — and I can still see you standing in the firelight that hunt evening, in your shirt sleeves, your hair and face reflecting the red glow of the flames. Dear God, you had such a compelling, erotic charge and I was so furious with you. You held out a glass of champagne to celebrate something but I didn't understand what it was. It might well have been the Holy Grail you were holding out to me and I missed my chance to understand your meaning. I've been trying to find it ever since. All the stories you told us this evening only make you more of an enigma, the so-called explanations you gave to Adam leave me more confused than before. But even if I ask the right question, would you give me the right answer?"

Nick got into bed at last. "I thought I had already done that," he said. "How many times do I have to say that I give my life to you, and for you?"

"Infuriating man, that is not the question I am asking."

"This is the only answer you'll get," he said, "my cock will do the talking for me."

It did, eloquently.

Taking a pause he admitted, "That second jump into the icy depths was sheer hubris on my part. As Tomas said, I was inviting divine retribution."

"Kissing your cock back to life back was hard work," I said. "Even comatose with cold it's quite a mouthful."

"It was well worth it for such a marvellous fuck to follow, hot and cold, sweet and sour," he said, "revving up the motor, then zero to hundred in 60 seconds — wow, take off!"

"And I've earned a fortune doing it," I said. "Remember, you promised."

"You are a cunt in a million and you get me with all I possess — my money and I are inseparable. So, listen to the question I am asking you. Sibylla, for the last time, will you come to Hong Kong with me, to watch the typhoons sweep across the South China Sea, to live or die in each other's arms?"

Maybe he meant it, even though he already knew what I'd say.

"The answer is a definite no."

"But... I can't let Wittersworth get away with the pretentious simplicity of that Palladian casino. I will get you a sky-dwelling so fabulous it is beyond comparison and put myself at your mercy to make it the home I've been exiled from since childhood."

"You are such a fantasist, Nick, a romantic fool. I should have settled for Gianni; life would have been so much simpler."

"But less amusing," said Nick, not a bit put out, and went to sleep — at long last.

At breakfast the next morning Nick sat at the island of a table in the middle of our raftered kitchen, wearing the pyjama jacket he kept in my wardrobe, sober black with grey stripes, a single button at the waist so it barely concealed his genitals, humming with life after their plunge in the pool, with May and Augusta scrambling on the tiled floor at his bare legs, stealing the espadrilles he dangled on his toes and shuffling off in them, daring him to chase them. I paused from watching the toast to breathe in the happiness radiating from my loved ones.

"Precious Nick, you are the only lover I have left," I said in an outburst of tenderness.

Nick, distracted from his game with the children, looked at me in mock alarm and said: "Good grief, let's not go there again: don't ask me to find you another Gianni."

"There isn't another Gianni. If you hadn't paid him to fuck me I might have believed him when he said he loved me. Oh, God, I can't bear it, the mistakes, the misunderstandings. And you don't give a shit."

I burst into tears.

"For Christ's sake, don't burn the toast."

The children shrieked with delight as flames burst out from the grill and Nick took over from my snivelling fecklessness. He opened the window to chuck out the charred remains and let the smoke and smell disperse into the morning freshness. Then, after pulling on a pair of trousers, he tucked Augusta under his arm, her little legs kicking out behind, and took May by the hand.

"Come on," he said to them, "we'll go and see if Donna will give us a breakfast that's fit to eat," and to me as they went: "If Gianni's dust is out there among the stars he's damned lucky he escaped from the burden of loving you."

Once again I thanked my lucky stars I had Gus Wittersworth to save me from the madness of loving this man.

Pausing at the door, Nick said, "I picked up May's neat little Swiss-red passport when I was passing through our hometown. I'm taking her back with me."

~

Viennese Waltz

13

Regretfully I left my Alfa Romeo behind for Clare, and Adam rented a large Mercedes to take Augusta, Willie and me with our baggage to our new home. I hadn't yet seen what Nick derisively called my splendid villa yet but I could judge its worth from Nick's state of mind after Gus had taken him to see it.

"Grand-mamma is getting ready for us," Gus reported, "but really she wants to get out of the house before we move in. She is tired, she says, of carrying the weight of centuries and would like to pick up her pug, walk out and leave it all behind. It will mean that we are lumbered with an ancestral burden we'll just have to make the best of, living on a shoe-string," he warned, "until I am earning a decent living. It will be hard work for the first few years. It's fortunate Law Lords are fairly well paid."

"Except it may take you a long time to get so far."

"I aim to be the youngest ever — besides, honing my skills on Father William's less amiable clients I can earn plenty in the meantime."

"Nick says he and May are looking for a place for me in London so they can have me conveniently at hand. I remind him I am married to you but that doesn't seem to put him off."

"If Nick wants to park you in a penthouse on the river or something equally *nouveau* then let him; we can make good use of it as long as it's within walking distance of Westminster. It will be well worth an extra-marital fuck."

"Though he says it's for me I expect it will be just something he wants for himself so he can escape from the chaos he has created at home, and leave Angelina to deal with children, animals and Aunties. Stratton Square must be getting pretty crowded. He says May has taken up residence in his study. She has made a nest for herself on Napoleon's camp-bed with his Swiss Army blankets and a pile of pillows; it's her refuge from the Nickies and the bulldog — so he may be regretting the way he drove off with her in the Ferrari, the pair of them jubilant, untroubled that they were leaving me, Adam and Augusta bereft without them."

"When we have a place to live we'll get May back," said Gus, unperturbed.

～

Nick phoned Adam to report that the stripped bare garden room in Stratton Square was now ready to be converted into a studio.

"But I withdraw my over-generous offer to give you free run of my wine," he said. "It would be wasted on you after ruining your palette with Tomás's rotgut."

"I don't want to ruin my palette by developing a taste for *premier crus* that I can't afford," said Adam.

To me Nick said: "I've found a riverside apartment nearly as good as a mews with a live horse downstairs. I'm a lyre bird prancing in front of his bower, crest up in a state of high anxiety, hoping you'll like it enough to stay and mate with me, that leaning out over the balcony the river traffic below will distract you long enough for me get my cock up and fix you before you have time to say no."

He was still counting on getting me pregnant again.

It didn't quite work out as he anticipated.

I was feeling so ill when we arrived in England that we took Augusta and Willie straight to Gus in Marylebone where Evita took them in and sat them down on the horsehair sofa, now softened with rose-flowery cushions and woolly rugs. Then Adam, following Nick's directions, drove me to a high-rise apartment block called *'riverrun'*, identified by a bronze statue of a naked man and woman opposite the front door on the Embankment. Nick came down to meet us at the entrance.

"That's Eve and Adam," he said to Adam who was looking at it with interest. "Do you get the reference? Come on, you read books: '*river-run past Eve and Adams...*' Even I immediately made the connection with the most significant opening line in the English language, having heard it discussed at quite tedious length on the car radio. Academics do go on and on dissecting the bloody obvious. It's the first thing I noticed as I came cruising by; this Adam could be a portrait of me, even his fig leaf is a size too small, more like a barely adequate sun shade than a raincoat. If you look at him from underneath you can see he has balls fit to populate the world."

"Actually," I said, "that heroic figure is far more a Gianni than a lanky redhead like you."

"You're right," said Nick, reconsidering. "Adam was a shit, putting the blame on the woman. When I fucked my Eve I did it because my balls told me it was the right thing to do at that particular moment, while you gazed at me with irresistibly trusting eyes, leaving the decision up to me."

I'd lost count of how many ways he had of explaining how Nick Deathridge came to tip Sibylla d'Art sprawling heels over head onto the bed and force his well-tempered tool up her virgin cunt, but it was certainly one of his virtues that he had no trouble taking responsibility for doing it.

"I'm glad to see," said Adam, "that the artist was sensible enough not to follow the fashion for street level display but put them safely on a plinth..."

"High enough," Nick agreed, "not to be pissed on by passing dogs — this is a popular dog-walking stretch — or climbed on by small children. They can look up from below and see for themselves what it's good manners to hide."

He had my luggage put in the lift then came back to the car to say goodbye to Adam, whom he did not invite to come in.

"Angelina is waiting for you to come home," he said, "so off you go and do your grandfatherly duty."

"If I'm being called on to mind your children for you, you might have consulted me before you got so many."

"It's not so many, just Con and Jo, May, and only two Nickies so far. Angelina is quite capable though the Virgins are no help; they are far too busy entertaining the Chattering Mob of the Latest Renaissance, presiding over meetings from the grandeur of their bed, showing off their charmingly rotund tummies in bias cut silk negligées: damson is the flavour of the moment, and of course carefully made up: Cleopatra eyes and plummy lips. Meg thinks the world of them: Proper Ladies!"

As Adam prepared to drive off, Nick added, "Remember, no fucking. However flirtatious, in the interests of science the Virgins are strictly mine."

I noted he didn't include Angelina in his prohibition, but then Angelina was no flirt. But then, neither was Adam.

All the way up in the very fast, sick-making lift Nick held me close in his arms, enveloping me in his love. If anyone could cure me, he would.

I wept when I saw how Nick had ripped the heart out of his house in order to create this fantastically beautiful place to share with me: Grandfather Dumez's armchair, Bonne-Maman's piano and the intricate lattice and fantasy carvings from the garden room, without the mirrors. "They're *passé*," he said. "I chose Zoffany wall panels instead."

Not a trace of Biedermeier.

"It's a dream world," I said. "You are a magician, a conjurer of impossibilities, Nikolai Chudotvorets. And the Thames is infinitely more convenient than the South China Sea."

"I've given up on that; without you it makes no sense — besides it's too far for keeping an eye on the Nickies."

His priorities were shifting.

"But this will be of little use to me without you here," I protested. "You'll go away again and it will remain here empty as pie in the sky serving no purpose."

"Stay with me," he said, "and I'll stay with you."

The impossible dream: but at that moment I could have said yes.

My weeping went beyond my control. Nick gripped me by the shoulders and held me, as if by sheer willpower he could bring me back to life, until I was able to regain my voice.

"I am sorry," I said. "Dr Tsang is trying to find a cure for my sickness but nothing has worked so far."

"I'll talk to him," said Nick, and, leaving me to watch the sparkling river with its festive boats cruising up and down, he went to talk to Tsang. I could see him through the glass wall, talking, and imagined Dr Tsang's impassive patience at the other end, listening to Nick's furious condemnation that he was failing to do his job.

The balcony ran around two sides of the apartment at an angle to the river, jutting out like the prow of a ship, the view spanned by a perspective of bridges in both directions. Watching the river traffic could amuse one for idle hours but I had fallen asleep on one of the Titanic teak deck-chairs before Nick returned. When I woke up he was sitting in his familiar attitude with elbows on knees, gazing at me with the expression I presumed was the one Angelina interpreted as love-sick-for-a-goat: was it possible to distinguish between the objects of his affection? Maybe I thought of that because he was wearing the navy jersey Angelina said he had bought for milking the goat in, with loose pale linen trousers, fine as the pair he wore that day in Padua when he appeared across the piazza and the light shone through around his legs striding towards me, godlike in the sun.

"Rest," he said. "Tsang says rest until he can solve this problem."

"Did Dr Tsang tell you what he thinks the problem is?"

"Yes."

"Tsang Jun cheated me," I said in defence of my present predicament, "and it seems Gianni shot his final bolt that afternoon at Castello Guigno. Tsang isn't pleased but he is to blame. I bet he didn't tell the prelates at the Vatican about his vasectomy when they were so pleased with him at their conference, dear Dr Fertility."

"They wouldn't approve of your hit or miss method of getting pregnant either," remarked Nick. "Unrestrained multiple fucking with all and sundry is not quite *de rigueur*, I believe."

"Oh, Nick, who are you to pass remarks? Nobody fucks with more purpose than you do."

"Why can't I get you a baby then?"

I was silent.

Nick turned his attention to a pair of pigeons strutting along the rail, apparently house hunting.

"I'll ask Angelina to get me a sparrow-hawk," he said. "No unauthorised breeding on my patch."

Then after a pause, "I've spoken to Wittersworth and he agrees you should stay here. Tsang says it's a pity Gianni isn't here to provide the natural antidote to his alien proteins."

I didn't remind him that the solution with Augusta had been a diet of sperm.

"Tsang suggested we exhume the body to get a tissue sample; I had to convince him that is not a practical solution, seeing the clandestine nature of Gianni's burial; who knows what would come to light if we started digging him up again."

"Please leave Gianni in peace," I said, shocked at the Deathridge-Tsang Enterprises' take on practical solutions.

"If it were to save your life naturally I'd be prepared to do a bit of grave-robbing but even I am not willing to take that risk in a cause I consider a complete waste of time. Tsang will just have to try and find the right balance by trial and error. I'll send him a blood sample every few days so he can monitor how it's working. After all, he has Augusta's records to go on."

"Oh, Lord," I groaned. "I have no wish to be an interesting patient."

Notwithstanding my protest I was happy to drift from day to day in that dream world, moving from the daybed in the alcove to grandfather's arm-chair in the serene open space of the apartment. The riverside location gave a particular clarity to the light, sun and moon had equal value and we lived with little distinction between day and night. Nick was a constant presence, though if I'd given it any thought I'd have realised he retreated to the Chinese Chippendale to get some sleep though it wasn't obvious when. His house in Stratton Square, designed to be uncluttered, nevertheless had all the necessary paraphernalia for living with seven adults, five children and a large dog. Here very little was sufficient. The distance from the heart of

London to the solitude of Abb's Head was enormous, but except for the sounds of the city far below instead of the sea, it felt very much the same.

Two items of purely decorative value gained in significance from their isolation: the no. 15 jersey he had played Russian Roulette for and my palm leaf hat with the lifelike wreath of silken meadow flowers.

I was touched that he had my hat so significantly displayed on an otherwise blank wall. It hung there as if Nick had simply hammered in a large nail and hitched it up by the ribbon but I surmised it had been a very serious young interior designer who had drilled a neat hole after much judicious deliberation.

"Where on earth did that come from?" I asked.

"From on top of my safe where I kept it after you left me."

"So that's why Meg couldn't get it for my wedding when I asked her!"

"I was glad you had the sense not to go gallivanting downmarket to your puffed up pimp with a high-class milliner's hatbox in your baggage. When I chose it for you to play your part in my Russian farce, I was visualising how adorable you would look in it — and you did; that was one of the many occasions when I fell ever more hopelessly in love with you."

"You shamed me by kissing me in front of all those people. Luckily Paul was there to cover up my embarrassment. It was the first time two men fought over me, even if you were only playacting."

"I'd fight to the death for you, don't underestimate my determination — or my readiness to kill if necessary."

Nevertheless, when Gus came every few days to spend the evening, he and Nick got on perfectly amicably.

"Gianni had an optimistically useful little fund put aside for a grand wedding and a modest house." Nick said it as an off-hand announcement.

"How do you know?" Gus asked, mildly curious, while he considered the probabilities of what Nick meant to achieve by this remark.

"He told me when I offered to pay his expenses if he would mount a legal challenge against you over Augusta."

Gus smiled. "You think the money should be Augusta's?"

"If you need advice about investing it I'll be happy to oblige," said Nick.

"Watch out," I said to Gus. "He'll probably tell you to bet it on Rubstik at 24 to 1 and that will torment you because there is a good chance he'll be right so you'll curse yourself for not doing it — just like Clare last year."

"If I had any sense," said Nick, "I'd keep my ears stopped with wax rather than listen to you, you siren — but I'll chance a bet on your suggestion none the less."

"You should know better, Nick," said Gus. "The Sibyl is notorious for cryptic promises; it takes a wise man to make sense of her."

"Meaning you?"

"Yes... how is your cock taking the strain of her proximity?"

"Pretty well, thank you. On the whole my apparatus sits here in a squishy bunch, perfectly well-behaved, though ready enough to do its job if called upon. Quite contented really, at least it knows no one else is getting in there while it pines for a piece of the action."

Nick's cheek muscles twitched, suppressing his satisfaction that he was one up on Gus, and Gus smiled back at him with quizzical amusement. There was a truce for the moment between these two men who were my whole world. For the moment Nick was the one with the means and the place to give me the freedom from anxiety that I needed, while Evita, under Gus's supervision, looked after my babies. Cooperating over my sickness, my husband and my lover had reached a degree of understanding, even affection, for each other that bode well for my future happiness, however tiresome the present crisis.

Every few days Tsang phoned and he and Nick had long discussions though mostly Nick just listened with a tolerantly patient expression on his face until he had enough and cut it off.

"I'm a better druggist than he is," said Nick and administered his own cocktail of pills and potions to ease my misery and in my moments of distress supported me in a manner that was firm and gentle and completely unfussy. He tempted my sick appetite with delicate morsels of raw herring flown over from Amsterdam or chicken soup from Reuben's in Baker Street.

Since his African adventure he was a great believer in the restorative prop-
erties of chicken soup.

I was grateful that he was prepared to spend his days in comparative
idleness with me. He went out mid-morning dressed for his role as earth-
shaker and stayed away a few hours, presumably attending to his affairs
with fellow artful dodgers of equal elegance and gravitas, and for the rest
stayed at home in self-sustaining contentment, doing nothing much.

He offered to get Meg to come in but much as I'd have liked to see her I
hadn't the energy to face the distracting busyness of her presence. Nick
seemed perfectly happy to dispense with her attentions too, having
acquired a team of helpers he called the Gnomes and Fairies, who came in
like a swarm of worker bees and with great efficiency and good humour
attended to his needs, buzzing around bringing order to the place in a matter of minutes, which suited Nick just fine.

I was quite right: Nick said this place was for me, but he meant it was the
setting in which he wished to see me, just as the other house was the setting
he had created for Angelina. This was mine only to the extent he was willing
to share it with me, which would never amount to much given his force of
personality and dominance of the space around him.

I needn't have worried about Nick getting bored. He lifted the lid on the
piano and took up where he left off last November when he first revealed his
virtuosity by converting the dead princess into ragtime. He started again,
nothing from beginning to end but passages which I supposed had a logic of
their own, then drawing shapes in Indian ink on a large sketchpad, saying
deprecatingly that he was reverting to childhood.

"It's the shape of the music," he was polite enough to explain. I
remembered Toby saying how he bamboozled them by never explaining
what he was doing, so I took it as a kindness that he bothered to tell me.

"Gang Bang," I said. "That's what Toby said you called the one you did
at school."

"Toby is a gullible innocent. That's how I illustrated the expanding universe, beginning with Big Bang. I was trying to see it from the

centre out, with minor explosions where things collided, the origin of Chaos Theory."

"Really? With little green frogs and streams of frogspawn?"

"Life on Earth: the starting point from which Nick and Sibylla here in this room are the logical outcome."

"Now you sound just like Gus," I said.

"Gus fucks you in his way and I do it in mine," said Nick. "We have a lot in common besides you."

Drawing and playing the piano kept him busy for the rest of the time we were there. He even invited a French lady pianist from the South Bank to come along and play with him.

"I was passing and went looking for inspiration in the music shop and by my natural serendipity the lunchtime pianist sounded just like my grandmother playing *Gaspard de la Nuit*," he said "I asked her if she'd come and carry on Bonne-Maman's lessons."

"You hardly need lessons," I remarked.

"Who knows how good I might have been if Bonne-Maman hadn't been so foolhardy that she went down town in the middle of the V-2 bombing and got blown to bits, as if wearing her Schiaparelli coat and *Sacré Coeur* badge would work as talismans against loss — my loss. However, it was the friend she used to meet, who came from the Pas-de-Calais and provided information over the rocket launch site which proved useful in the D-Day landings, who brought me *L'isle Noir,* my manual for life. I never needed anything else. From it I learned how to be a proper boy with a fascination with small aircraft and fancy cars. So I can't complain."

"You don't have a little white dog."

"I have a little black one. He never leaves my side."

"Really?"

I could see that the Deathridge Chaos Theory might explain how the small matter of pheasants dropping on the kitchen table next to the mince pies led to Nick retiring early for a solitary night; the Virgin Aunties getting drunk and disorderly in his bed and three years later the birth of the

Nickies; his father-in-law Bott's distaste for Nick's grossly uncircumcised penis being the catalyst for the Virgins choosing the most fabulously chunky pink and yellow diamonds; leading to the Big Bang of Nick's financial implosion; expanding into a series of minor explosions: how Nick's desire to possess me against all reason, his envy of Gus's Palladian villa, the Sibyl's cloud dwelling, Bonne-Maman's piano giving way to make a boudoir for the Virgins, fused to bring us with the piano here, however temporarily, in these pure surroundings — the sound is amazing!

Chaos continues unfolding: there is no end in sight.

I was entertained by Nick's so-called lessons, not so much by the music they played, which sounded endlessly tedious to me until I got used to it, but because it amused me how his sessions with this severe Mademoiselle seemed to involve much arguing over what were to me completely indistinguishable passages, with constant repetitions, a lot of it noisily discordant: Nick expressing the love of anarchy that he kept hidden under his ironically polite exterior. He explained to me that Mademoiselle had very strict views on how the written score should be respected.

"I don't read music, which gives me freedom for spontaneous interpretation but Mademoiselle does her best to keep me on the straight and narrow of orthodoxy."

"What are you playing?" I asked. "It sounds vaguely familiar but all those wrong notes and changes of tempo make it very strange."

"Wrong notes? really! There aren't any wrong notes and you just have to keep the rhythm in your head while the music takes a detour before joining up with the dance again. It's a homage to Strauss, but also a satire on sentimentality — life is not a Viennese waltz; under the gaiety is anarchy, confusion, heartache."

Nick's interpretation of life, his life — but he wasn't looking for sympathy, continuing:

"I learned that as a child sitting on Bonne-Maman's lap. She played it as Ravel intended. That's when I let go of her because I got down and danced around the room and she played louder and faster to keep up with me until I fell down dizzy. It was our last game before she went off in a big bang — bits of her are probably still flying to the moon to the music of Ravel — but I had it played as I remembered it, by my delightfully intuitive wedding musicians; they were prepared to listen to me unlike this maddeningly self-opinionated Frenchwoman — it was too good an opportunity to miss."

"Angelina told me doing the waltz in her gorgeous gown was the romantic highlight of your wedding feast," I said.

The Balenciaga version of the wedding as opposed to the cuckoo-clock one.

"Angelina can ride on a crest of delusion until reality dumps her on the rocks," said Nick. "That's what she learned from our dance; I had her foot perfect — any fool can do a one-two-three one way and one-two-three the other way to Strauss. So when the tempo changed she had to trust me to keep us going.

"'All you have to do,' I told her, 'is to keep your feet moving and I'll keep you from falling — but I hope you're wearing sexy knickers just in case, or better still...' and the wedding guests demonstrated splendidly how it should be done: in bewilderment and dismay. Mother-in-law wanted to have someone in to make a film of Angelina's dance and costly dress — her quirkily handsome husband being a mere accessory, a clotheshorse in tails — but I am somewhat image-wary and wouldn't allow it. I'm sorry really; it was well worth recording. She wasn't too pleased either when I broadcast to the Furzy guests that my Swiss colleagues had pooled their winnings from our day at Royal Ascot to give my lovely musicians a generous fee for their brilliant performance — after subtracting their own reasonable profit, naturally — Hein was particularly pleased that he won nearly enough to cover the cost of the Fokker Friendship."

"It was pure devilment to say that," I said.

"It could have been worse," said Nick. "She told me not to interfere with the band, but of course I did; I wasn't going to spend the evening dancing with all those gorgeous girls, my sweethearts and wives past and present, to the Furzy choice of music. It really was pure devilment that I tried to have the Sex Pistols in, but they cancelled at the last minute —

a pity, it would have given the Swiss something to brag about when they got home to Heidiland."

"I must be a very superficial person," I said, "but I'd rather waltz to the real Strauss than your hideous noises."

"Divine Sibyl, my most blissful dance ever was your tango — the way your hips and thighs moved in and around mine, your witty little hesitations and deviations: to die for!"

"Oh, Nick, and I thought you were making fun of me! I just acted along with you not to let down your bella figura in front of all those fabulous people at the château."

"Good grief, I was too in love with you, my cock's delight, to be aware of anything but you and the music."

"The music? Those facile, hackneyed tunes on the squeezeboxes you hired from Marseilles? Really, Nick!"

"Listen to this then," he said, "this one is *Ondine*, a water nymph, seductive and menacing: my mermaid when you are in a good mood and my siren when you are tantalising me."

That was the first of his piano pieces I could distinguish, not exactly a tune but at least a reasonably recognisable sequence of notes if he played it straight through without the arguing.

"That is terribly clever," I said, "with all that rippling, sparkling water music, but the best part of it is your face when you are playing it: rapturously sentimental, quite out of character with your usual exasperating self."

"Sentimental!" said Nick, indignant, his expressive mouth snapping momentarily into its tight-lipped mode before relenting again just as fast as he challenged me with:

"What about this for sentimental?"

... and proceeded to reduce me to tears by singing in his husky Jacques Brel voice 'Ne Me Quitte Pas', a more pleading version than the original on our ride along the Westway from Heathrow, before the tape of *Nathalie* which he chucked out the window when I didn't know how he had lost his mother. Though I could see his ironic wit coming into play with exaggerated sobs and heartbreak, nevertheless with *'je ferai un domaine, où l'amour sera roi, où l'amour sera loi, où tu seras reine,'* I could feel that the satire merely served to defuse his sincerely felt emotion, rising, as Toby said, from a deep well of grief within him. Would I ever get to the bottom of it?

I watched his face and his hands as he scribbled, humming to himself, shapes on paper, the composition getting denser and denser as he built up layer on layer. I wondered if it would work as a musical score if one knew how to interpret it, or was it a picture of the inner workings of his brain.

"I have to imagine it as three-dimensional," he said, "since I haven't got the facilities here to construct it as I see it."

"You miss your workshop," I said.

"I miss the people working, the hum of activity, the rhythm of the machines. I was the conductor of a very complex orchestra. For myself all I need is a shed in a back yard like any of my workers who find themselves superannuated."

Nick looked impressed by his own modesty, but then realised he was talking nonsense and said, "Well maybe not. An aircraft hangar is more my scale."

Nick was actually talking to me quite sensibly. I thought it was because he wasn't being distracted by the surge in his testicles which he usually got looking at me, until he surprised me by saying, "I have the same feeling now as during the first months I was in love with you, my most successfully creative period; I was so high on testosterone, and fucking you was so easy... you lay there with big eyes and a shy smile and yielded with just the right amount of resistance to make me feel it working... the Sibylla Effect!"

"It's really quite considerate of you not to fuck on regardless."

"I don't need to. You are so exquisitely desirable that I can feel the pleasure I would get doing it. Knowing is enough."

"You astonish me, Nick," I said. "I never noticed that love meant anything to you but ramming it in, hard and fast, for as long and as often as possible."

"You are a singularly obtuse young woman, Mrs Wittersworth," said Nick and returned to his drawing with his pouty non-smile and deeply furrowed frown adding a scaffolding of receding arches under which a pair of frogs was locked together in a tangle of sprawling legs, weirdly penis-like wrinkly creatures — Toby's art class came to mind... I'd risk death in Nick's embrace making love to him right now but Nick went on with his construction of arches in ever more dizzying heights, leaving his frogs behind in their obscure corner...

"I was happy fucking my sweet Sibylla," he said half under his breath, as if the words were surfacing from his thoughts as he created his imaginary world. "It was damned Tsang who ruined it, that serpent, he took away my innocence."

I laughed with incredulity at Nick's interpretation of events.

"*Your* innocence?" I said.

But he seemed completely unaware of having said anything disingenuous.

~

Nick descended to the swimming pool in the basement every so often to work off his surplus energy. As I was feeling better — perhaps Tsang's remedies were working — I went down to watch him and was delighted that the beauty of the brimming pool with its wall of waterfall and wavy mosaics matching the elegance of our apartment fifteen floors up, an almost worthy setting for Nick's streamlined body gliding smoothly through the water with long unhurried strokes in tireless lengths, his bum encased in his neat black togs.

"Oh, wow," I thought when I felt the familiar delicious buzz, "I must really be getting better."

When Gus came that evening I told him what an unexpected pleasure it was to have such a lovely pool available, especially after my less than pleasant experiences at Gianni's sports club. Gus's response didn't surprise me, saying to Nick with his characteristic generosity of spirit:

"This place suits you so well, it could have been built with you in mind, and your friends are here — except for the mad Chinaman. You have so many talents to develop besides gallivanting around the world looking for trouble. Be content that you have a nice heap of gold under the Eiger — and no doubt equally satisfactory piles under the Mönch and Jungfrau, with their sturdy, hardworking trolls beavering away to mind them and keep them shiny. So just stay here where you belong."

"Only if you'll let me keep Sibylla," Nick replied.

"No chance," said Gus smiling. Their very rivalry had bound them together in a degree of intimacy which, though it might never reach the same maturity as between Nick and Toby, looked as if they were not far off it. Even the way they talked to each other began to sound the same. It exemplified the triumph of logic and tolerance over the unbridled sentiment that had destroyed the Grati. Or in Dr Tsang's words: the brain is a higher authority than the testicles.

If Angelina thought that Nick didn't have any real friends, I wondered how she defined friendship; it seemed to me he had a remarkable talent for loyal and generous camaraderie. What more could one wish for?

Gus said to me as he was leaving, "Angelina has an appointment with Father in his chambers tomorrow midday; would you care to be there too?"

He said it quite casually but I knew he wouldn't suggest it unless he wanted me to come.

Nick looked from Gus to me, calculating the risk.

"Is she looking for a divorce?" he asked.

"Is that your worst fear?" asked Gus.

"Yes," said Nick, unequivocally.

"You'd better come and find out then," said Gus. And he departed, enjoying the opportunity to disconcert Nick.

That night after Gus went home I left my sickbed and got in beside Nick in the Chinese Chippendale.

"I think Tsang has found the right formula at last," I said.

"You look better," said Nick, noncommittally, caressing my head against his shoulder.

I felt his crotch: firm but not hard.

"I'm feeling like it again," I said.

"I may have a fuck-ready penis but it's squeamish; it doesn't get turned on

274

by a woman who is likely to miscarry at any moment — especially not when it's some other man's doing."

I was so shocked I froze. Nick however went on, apparently unaware or else indifferent to the effect of his words: "Tsang is doing his best to save it, but I can't see the point. We disagree. I say you are resilient, let it abort and we can start again."

"You wouldn't want to lose it if it were yours."

"Don't be ridiculous! If it were mine you wouldn't be sick; it was your indiscriminate fucking that got you into this mess."

I got out of the bed and went back to my alcove in the living-room. It hadn't struck me as odd that I hadn't been invited into the bed in which I had already given birth to May and Willie, but now I could see that Nick wanted to protect his precious nest from any bloody disasters of an unpredictable nature. The daybed would do well enough for me with the temporary inconvenience of a Grati baby in the offing.

Early in the morning Nick came, decently clad in his traditional blue-striped pyjamas, schoolboy vintage, with cups of tea, and got under the covers to sit beside me.

"If you think Gianni's baby is worth saving, you'd better come with me to Tsang's," he said. "Tsang wants you to; he, of course, is interested in how far science can go in correcting nature's mistakes."

"No," I said. "Gus is taking me to his Grandmother's as soon as I feel like travelling. I'll tell him I'm ready to go now."

Nick sat silently cradling his teacup in his hands with an expression of such contempt on his face it chilled my soul.

"Oh, Nick, have a heart!" I cried. "Dear, handsome Gianni, I have to give him his last chance. It is so unbearably sad and the worst of it is that now I wish I had said yes to you, but you were so utterly infuriating — it pains me in my cunt to remember how you came out of the water, the Mediterranean streaming off your body, Poseidon rising up off the seabed, quite amazingly beautiful — and still I said no. Truly I am sorry."

Nick sat in silence but his look was highly sceptical. He didn't believe in apology by hindsight.

"Tsang cheated me over his vasectomy," I said, " as you knew very well. Why didn't you just tell me instead of teasing me, hiding your insider knowledge? So now I'll allow Nature to take it's course, not Tsang — or you."

"Nature? The coward's excuse for passive ineptness... go back to your philosopher husband and let him deal with your silliness."

"Do you still love me?"

"If I didn't I wouldn't be here. Surely you understand that, beloved goose!"

Oh, Nick!

~

I had never been to Father William's office before; it was just like a rather grander version of his room in Marylebone: the same jumble of books and papers, the same Fortnum & Mason's biscuit tins, coffee and boxes of teabags to sustain him through his long hours of pondering on philosophical conflicts between law and justice, a study which later sustained him through his long years of retirement.

Angelina was there when Gus and I came in, looking lovelier than ever. She was pleased to see me. It struck me how unfailingly gracious Angelina had been throughout the varying stages of my relationship with her: as Pinkerton nanny, as Nick's fuck-ready cunt in the basement, now as the honourable Mrs Wittersworth. It also struck me how cordial Father William was to her; Gus had already said how Father William admired her equanimity in the face of Nick's financial debacle; surviving Nick's trials seemed to have given her inner strength and maturity.

"I'm glad you came," she said to me. "I want to assure you that May seems happy with us, but I am certain she should be with her mother. It's all very well when Nick has time for her but he's away too much and when he does come home there is the question of the Nickies. He walks around with them perched on his arm, talking nonsense to them, totally infatuated."

Angelina sounded no more than mildly exasperated but I felt quite irrationally jealous. As Nancy said: all men have to do is produce the gunk; it was my choice that I didn't have an armful of Nickies. I found myself wondering if Dr Tsang could make twins for me too, while Angelina continued:

"I do believe that it's just to tease me that he proposes impossible names for them, so I keep saying no to Vladimir and Illyich, Yuri and Pyotr, Ottokar and Ludovic, while Rose and Violet just go on calling them both Nickie — 'open your mouth, Nickie Baby,' and in pops a soft-boiled quail's egg which one or other Nickie Baby heroically struggles to swallow with his little dimpled mouth and startled eyes. They are the most endearing babies: the Renaissance Women, Mother, the monks at Great-Uncle Harold's, all adore them, and Connie and Jo-jo follow on like a pair of altar boys, I can just imagine that Uncle Harold would have them in attendance swinging incense burners."

"Bodyguards to the holy infants," I suggested, "like the weird and wonderful collection of Baby Jesuses in the Uffizi with their attendant boy angels."

"But May doesn't have to lose her own good home to share one with the sacred Nickies. She sleeps in Nick's study where he does his business on the phone for half the night, but then there is the occasional session with Rose and Violet across the hall and though the boudoir is well muffled with drapes and heaps of eiderdowns, the murmuring and giggling goes on for hours, punctuated by occasional ladylike shrieks..."

"Did you not mind losing your drawing-room to your Aunties?" I asked.

Angelina waved away such an inconsequential objection. "When the choice was giving up the best room or losing the whole house it wasn't difficult. And of course Nick is quite right, it makes no difference to me at all; the Women spend as much time there as they ever did and enjoy it more now they have Rose and Violet in exotic *déshabille* to entertain them."

"Nevertheless," said Father William, "You are perfectly justified in demanding that your husband find some accommodation for the Misses Furzy and his illegitimate children other than in your house."

"It's when Nick wants a quiet night alone that hell really breaks loose," Angelina went on. "When he retreats to our blissfully peaceful bed one knows that it's a huge surrender to fatigue, whether caused by sexual heroism or jet-lag, and once he goes under he can sleep for twelve hours at a stretch. But the Aunties foolishly creep up to our room and one can hear him shouting at them to bloody well confine themselves to their fucking stable — and worse: the language! Tears and pleading, followed by tremendous thwacks as he chases them downstairs flourishing his riding stock, one can only guess what goes on in there. They make a great fuss that their bottoms are too sore to sit on, 'Nickie is so cruel, he beats us,' they complain, but with such naughty looks I supposed it was largely an act until Dolly said they showed the Women that their 'cute little bums' do have actual red marks across them and there is an occasional bruise on their legs where presumably he failed to miss."

I concluded this must be a rather rough game Nick played to the Aunties' delight. No matter how provocative I was I knew he could never hit me. Whenever I felt he was being hard-handed with me it was unintentional, as I realised when I met real violence at the hands of Todd and Gino. And Angelina too understood that, whatever he did with his poppets, his attitude to her was nothing less than tender loving respect.

"They are utterly maddening" she said, "and honestly I don't care what he does to them, it's the proliferation of little Nickies I dread. When the Aunties came to live with us I said I hoped they were being careful, that one set of Nickies is quite enough. Rose said, 'don't worry, dear, Nick just likes to have his darling cocksie tickled,' but now Violet says that when they have more Nickies they will be getting a chateau in Normandy and a small airplane to fly around in. This is probably pure fantasy but Nick says they can have anything they want from him."

I simply could not imagine Nick having his cocksie tickled, considering how touchy he was about any interference with it. The one time I dared to make love to it led to the downward spiral of his rain-dance and abrupt departure. Adam said he had gone to fight for the release of his working capital from its sterling straight-jacket but that came about only coincidentally on top of his shame at allowing me to manipulate him. But then, he had no shame with the Foolish Virgins.

"What about you while this is going on?" I asked Angelina.

"Goodness, I go down to Adam in the studio and stay well out of it. Adam is the perfect father-in-law; he lets me cry on his shoulder when the tomfoolery gets too distressing. Connie and Jo-jo demand pancakes with syrup for breakfast because Daddy and the Aunties were playing giddy-up all night again — they know that I'll make it for them and it makes a nice change from a boiled egg. When Daddy objects that I'm giving them rubbish food, Connie asks him who won last night. That child is getting far too cute; he knows perfectly well that Daddy has the whip hand and always wins."

"Nick only gets away with it because you let him," said Gus.

"I know," said Angelina, sighing. "I can't even feel cross with him. He carries it off with such élan, quite unselfconsciously and without apologies. When their high jinks spill over and they start running around the house he hounds them back to cuckoo-clock-land — thankfully Paul dismantled the mechanism so we no longer have to endure Nestor's preposterous clock playing the overture to William Tell on the hour all through the night."

While I sympathised with Angelina I had to avoid catching Gus's eye not to get a fit of giggles. Even Father William looked unnaturally solemn.

"Paul says I act the Patient Griselda beyond the call of duty," Angelina went on. "When Nick closed the factory he turned down a lucrative publishing deal on business ethics and etiquette saying he can't write and he couldn't risk the lies a ghost-writer would put in his mouth, that all he can do is talk. I was mortified but it was just Nick being clever. Now even more than before he is sought after as speaker and he won't accept unless it's wives and decorations on the menu so he obliges me to go with him for an evening of looking beautiful and mind-boggling boredom and he can be ostentatiously undecorated — this silly claim to Swissness! The whole farcical ritual of the evening extends to coming home and going to bed together. He says if I won't sleep with him I'll have to divorce him, and that would be a betrayal of everything our marriage means to him, but the truth is, he comes home in such a good mood from the attention and flattery he gets, and embraces me with such warmth, how could I refuse? He says to listen out for the blackbird's love-song in the darkness before dawn, that's how much he wants my love. I think he must have specially trained melodious blackbirds let loose in Stratton Square for the occasion because I am seduced by it every time."

"A good bargaining point," said Father William, already working on his brief in his head.

"A preliminary signal to a night of conjugal love is a salmon, London smoked, landing on the doorstep the morning before — when it's delivered Connie and Jo-jo say 'Goody, Daddy is going to sleep with Mummy to-night: he'll give us a decent breakfast.'

I fixed my eyes on Gus and tried to ignore the waves of jealousy brought on by Angelina's affectionate tolerance of her husband's eccentricities. I had to believe Nick when he said I was the love of his life; when he sat beside me in bed with a cup of tea, his refusal to make love to my ailing body was in itself a demonstration of pure love. Gus shook his head at me: I could almost hear him say 'chalk and cheese: jealousy doesn't come into it.'

"The salmon has to be a whole side so Nick can slice out the middle bit. I used to think it so wasteful, but the boys hang around like a pair of scav-engers to pick up his leftovers. Nick makes the whole performance such fun for them, sharpening the salmon knife, crushing peppercorns in the mortar, squeezing out a lemon in his fist. He found the perfect Irish soda bread at Bentley's and has them deliver a loaf early in the morning. He eats bread because you have to have something to put the butter on — only Nick would find a cow in central London so he can have it freshly churned, extra salty. It's one of the few occasions when we sit down as a family for a meal in the dining room and Meg acts as a proper maid for once. The Aunties stay in bed — they tend to go into a huff when Nick sleeps with me, there is no fun and games about that, and they know he means it when he tells them to stay out of his way. Connie and Jo-jo get the Nickies from the nursery and teach them how to crawl backwards down the stairs — it's the most exercise they get, the little darlings, they are carried everywhere — and have fun feeding them scraps of smoked salmon. Nick — and I — encourage them to see them as little brothers, not just odd little creatures belonging to the Aunties. They are so sweet and we love them so much it almost makes me wish I'd let Nick have his way to give me more babies myself. Nick enjoys it hugely, brimming over with love and enthusiasm; he has the knack of creating precious moments of happiness for us all."

"One has to presume that you actually enjoy being his wife," said Gus.

"I love my husband," said Angelina with dignity.

"Loving your husband is an abstract concept," said Gus. "Having to put up with Nick misbehaving and creating pandemonium around the house all night is quite something else."

"Mrs Deathridge needs to establish firm boundaries to what is acceptable," said Father William, tapping his pen as if impatient to draw up the necessary agreement for Nick's squiggly endorsement.

"A few weeks ago Nick came home from supplying optics for an eye clinic in Djakarta and brought a Javan woman with him — well not quite with him, she travelled at the back while he went First and after he saw her through immigration he put her in a taxi; he said he didn't want batik bundles in the Jaguar. Her name is Wilhelmina. She's exceedingly polite and sleeps on a mat in the Virgins' dressing room. She says she's a midwife but Nick says she's a goena-goena and her witchcraft will keep the Aunties calm; she tranquillises them with coconut belly rubs — that's his solution to my complaints, but as usual it only makes matters worse. She spends hours concocting her weird brews in the kitchen to Meg's utter disgust and if anything the Aunties are sillier than ever — I ask you! It's a madhouse."

Nick had said he'd make a successful bigamist if only I'd cooperate; it was a mystery to me how he kept all his balls spinning in air at the same time. It was time I left.

"And May?" asked Gus. "Where is she in all this?"

"She doesn't come out of her room much, only when Madge takes her out to ride the pony or to help Connie toss mice for the peregrine."

"Deathridge's contention that he should have custody of May on the grounds of Sibylla's immoral life hardly stands up to scrutiny," said Father William.

"I'm not going to fight him on moral grounds," I said. "In fact, I'm not fighting him at all. Knowing Nick, it would have exactly the contrary effect."

"We're not asking you to," said Father William. "We don't anticipate having to go to court; all we want is enough to put pressure on him to settle. What Mrs Deathridge needs is to get her name on the title deeds of her house... she has no control over the situation as it is."

"The house Nick smuggled diamonds to pay for?" I said. "Shot two men and dumped the bodies in the Drakensberg— or was that Mozambique? — my geography is vague — and unknown others in the course of his embargo-breaking gun-running enterprise? He fought too hard to win that house; he'll never let control of it go."

The Wittersworths were looking at me with such blank faces that I realised they didn't know what I was talking about. Nick as raconteur teasing Adam and me was so cryptic he hadn't actually admitted anything — only that conversation with Leon Bolus was more explicit, but Leon was dead.

"I shouldn't have said that," I said. "I am only guessing. You can't use that against him."

Father and son said nothing but nodded to each other, satisfied cryptic was enough.

Knowing how Nick sought confrontation, I was surprised he hadn't taken up Gus's challenge and come to circumvent whatever was going on behind his back in Father William's chambers. But of course he was only holding back to make a more dramatic entry, which he did by coming in with May by the hand. I jumped up to hug her but Nick held her firmly behind him while he kissed my cheek, then sat down beside me, across the table from Angelina and Father William. May leaned against his knee, her lips pressed together. Clearly she was under instructions to play along in his game with Mamma. He wasn't letting her go before he got what he wanted.

"How nice to see you here, Mrs Deathridge," he said to his wife. "I see you have my highly esteemed legal team at your side."

"My dear Mr and Mrs Deathridge, I hope I may give you both the benefit of my advice," said Father William, ready to launch into his tactful arguments.

But Nick put his hand in his inside breast pocket and took out a small leather pouch, which he slid across the table to Angelina. "Happy anniversary!" he said. "And many more of them."

"It's not my birthday," Angelina protested, suddenly dismayed.

"Seven years," he said. "Don't you remember how disappointed you were with my wedding present to you, seven years ago?"

The sugar heart!

Angelina's eyes filled with tears as she picked up the pouch.

"I'm sorry, Nick. I didn't pay attention to the date, I've been so busy and distracted."

Inside was a blown glass heart with embedded in it a tangle of hairs, strands of blond, red gold and copper.

"From Con, Joe and me," he said. "Even if you don't appreciate what's on offer, this time at least read the message before you throw it away."

"*Today — and the rest of my life.*" Angelina recited with tears in her eyes, flattening out the screwed up bit of paper that had Nick's completely illegible spiky black ink squiggles on it.

"Oh, Nick!" she cried and blinked her brimming blue eyes. "You are pitiless. You made our wedding day the most distressing day of my life — that rowdy gang in the church, that dreadful dance, you making love to everyone but me; I have never lived it down; my friends still laugh about it, pretending it was a big joke; so much money wasted on a complete farce!"

"Yes," said Nick, "and it completely formed your character. You were such a girlish prig and that's when you belatedly started to grow up. You had to, to deal with me."

"I had practised some idiotically sentimental little phrase to murmur to you when I reached your side at the altar," said Angelina, "But when I saw you standing there — you, who always came courting conspicuously under-stated in grey flannel and an oversized mackintosh — you looked quite startlingly splendid, as if I were seeing you for the first time, I couldn't speak for fear of making a fool of myself — but a fool is what you proceeded to make of me for the rest of the day."

"I hired an open-top red bus as your bridal coach, complete with Swiss Guard, cruising by scenic route all the way to London, fanfares at the round-abouts, being cheered by passers-by and motorists honking their horns. The Swiss said you were like the Queen on her wedding day waving to the crowd. Sitting with you in the prow on the top deck with iceboxes of champagne and Alpine mountain beer, oysters and Bockwüstli, was the high point of our wedding, our epiphany!"

"It was a calculated act of sabotage," said Angelina, "to upset Mother by not arriving at her carefully planned reception."

"A fitting transition into our future," said Nick, "I took you into my future, not the one Mother Furzy planned for us. I was entitled to be happy in my own way, with my arm around my bride, surrounded by comrades who show me the kind of affection and understanding I get from no one else."

"Not one of them was on the guest list..."

"I don't do lists."

At last Angelina began to see it from Nick's perspective.

"I should have trusted you," she said. "Thank you, Nick. A long overdue thank you for being such a brilliant bridegroom and a generous husband."

"And look at you now," said Nick, "a woman of substance, ruling the roost. You have my heart in your hand. If you don't want it you can smash it."

~

That afternoon Gus took me with the children to inspect our prospect-ive home. May came with us. Nick told her she had better go and see what she was missing — I concluded that having made his point he was prepared to let me have her back.

"You haven't got a bulldog," said May, nevertheless taking my hand in a firm grip.

"No," I said, "and we haven't got a Madge either."

"I'll get one when I'm grown up," said May. "Madge says a good bulldog costs hundreds of pounds so I'll work in my Daddy's office in the Kügelgassli and people can pay me a lot of money. I know how, he showed me when we made a bunny-hop landing into his cockpit on the way here."

The office of which Leon Bolus so emphatically denied any knowledge.

"The Deathrage Menace is getting trickier by the minute," said Gus, driving us in his newly acquired second-hand family-sized Volvo, "he says he has nothing to do but improvise on the piano — as if! His workers have come off with adequate pensions while unemployment hangs as a threat over everyone else; he made a very smart move getting them out when he did..."

Chess or war games, outwitting the planning office, the treasury or the trade union, all added up to Nick's Selbstbestimmung, himself and his little band of brothers against the world! May, with or without bulldog, would no doubt fit in very well.

"He invited me," said Gus, both flattered and slightly horrified, "to the farewell party he threw for them in May when Arsenal won the cup; I thought better of it, I haven't got his knack for dealing with the plebs in merry mood, but I hear it was a fantastic success. Father says he encourages rowdiness by handing out cash to cover the damage but Nick says he simply calculates it in along with the cost of drink, the band and the buses and it was well within reasonable limits. No one was hurt. He has even made money out of his dozen apprentices. With Hein's help he sold them on to firms in Europe — you'd think they were prize footballers — he didn't want them hanging around here gossiping about him and his activities. By the time they've learned German or whatever they'll have other things on their minds."

"He's lucky they agreed to go abroad," I said. "I wouldn't have expected it of London boys."

"Luck?" Gus laughed at me. "You know yourself — chosen and trained by Nick, is it probable that they wouldn't? He has even taken a couple of likely lads to spread the gospel according to Deathridge in Hong Kong — I wish he'd quit this nonsense in Hong Kong. He's needed at home — and as for the multiplication of Nickies!"

"Is it true he's hoping to get more?"

"Father complains that Angelina is as much a victim of his emotional blackmail as you were when you turned down his offer to get a handsome settlement for you, before I rescued you from his clutches. We could have got Angelina anything she wanted on the evidence, but that goddamn fucker can beguile the pants off any woman, even his wife... even my wife come to that."

I was so used to hearing Nick's ingenuity condemned as trickery that I was hardly listening, but I protested, "Not Mrs Shackleton's. Nor your sister Amanda."

"Yet!" said Gus.

Nick's description of his visit to Gus's Grand-mamma had prepared me a little for what was coming, but in reality the sheer unlikeliness startled me.

"I expected something unusual, but my imagination didn't stretch to this."

The villa looked as if it had been transported by angels from the Italian countryside — like the holy house of Loretto — I imagined their wings twirling like mad with the effort, celestial helicopters, and it even had the slightly dilapidated look of the castello where the pinkish stucco was flaking away at the corners to reveal the terracotta bricks underneath. The roof had a high peak over the square ground plan with spire-like finials at the corners. Pairs of pillars supported the projecting porch over the double flight of steps up to the massive front door that had impressed Nick. His childhood fortress, his grandfather's Hampstead Lutyens, didn't achieve quite the same monumentality: this front door would scarcely tremble under the onslaughts of a seven-year-old's football.

"I can see why Nick has his opportunity at last to break the tenth commandment — this really is something money can't buy," I said.

"Built on the cheap for those days; the really rich built their Palladian villas in stone," said Gus apologetically. "At School the boys with grander titles and proper mansions used to laugh at the pathetic shack of the lowly Wittersworths. We love it. As children we used the ground floor doorway into the kitchens, but I think Grand-mamma will expect us to make an entry in style, so come on up to the *piano nobile*."

The most notable feature of the house was its great central hall where the scantily clad Virtues, who so amused Nick, dominated the space with their overbearing presence.

"You can see it was designed in a warm climate," said Gus. "You need a fur coat to cross the hall when the wind from Siberia comes whistling through."

"I have the poodley jacket Nick bought for me in New York," I said. "It will come in useful at last. Maybe I should have said yes to the nice long sable he offered me when he wanted to outsmart Amanda."

Gus herded us across to the drawing room on the left where his Grand-mamma was sitting on a pile of boxes smoking a cheroot with an air of detachment from the chaos around her. She was wearing an Hermès scarf around her wispy grey hair, and high suede boots.

"So this is the divinely inspired Delphic Sibyl," she said when she saw me. "Yes, I can see William didn't exaggerate. Thank God you're here at last," she said. "I hadn't planned to abandon ship so quickly but when Gussie proposed bringing his bride here I saw it was the only sensible thing to do and now it's the sooner the better."

"Where are you going?" I asked,

"For the moment my camper van to move around in, when I get too decrepit for that I'll cast anchor somewhere — but I'm not worrying about that yet."

"You can always cast anchor back here," said Gus, "you could park your-self in the paddock and we would bring you hot soup on cold days."

"God help me," she said, "I was thinking of something a little more five star than that. I can always join the Ancient of Days in his tower, provided I get deaf enough not to have to listen to his ranting — though I could put on earphones and listen to Wagner instead."

"All this clutter has got to go," said Gus, "so don't come back here in six months time looking for a pair of slippers you left behind."

"Do you think if I took the van to Paris I'd be able to park somewhere convenient?"

"Well, not in the rue St Honoré," answered Gus, and took me on a tour of the house. May and Augusta came hand in hand after us, happily reunited.

We left Willie with his great-grandmother.

"I like her," I said, "does she really not mind leaving?"

"Everything has its pros and cons. She'll feel like an old Hindu setting off into the sunset with her begging bowl, or the English county equivalent. She has friends and relations in all the remoter parts of the country; it will take her years to get around visiting them all. She may even go hunting the Loch Ness Monster with her Scottish sister-in-law, two old bats having a lark."

I wandered over the house visualising how we would live here. The main floor was soberly and sparsely furnished in the classical tradition but the upper floor contained a profusion of furniture and objects, including rows of portraits of quaintly eccentric Wittersworths going back hundreds of years. It was the antithesis of the stylish London dwelling of the Deathridges so perhaps Nick was right in thinking it was more suitable for the Grati daughters and Willie than for May with her ambition already fixed on being a worthy citizen of a medieval Swiss city.

Why did I think Gianni's final fling would produce another girl? I could see her already growing up here with her mop of black hair and heart-stopping smile. Would Willie suffer as much as his father from a surfeit of sisters? Well, it had not done Wee any harm.

"I'm glad I'll have Meg to help me," I said, taking in the work involved.

When I left Nick at 'riverrun' he had demonstrated his sincerity with his parting gift: the offer of Meg's services.

"You'll need a capable pair of hands living in that museum," he said. "Meg is indefatigable."

"What about Angelina?" I asked. "How can she manage without Meg?"

"It has nothing to do with Angelina," he said with his usual brusqueness. "Meg is my woman. What I appreciate about her is she does her work without comment or conversation, no redundant remarks about the weather, the traffic or anyone's state of health. The perfect servant..."

I had to laugh at that: Meg, who had kept up a running commentary on everything that happened in the house! No wonder she missed me when I left: no one to listen to her.

"Yes, she had your interests at heart," I said, "though not without protest. She used to watch out for your fuck sessions; you weren't exactly discreet about it. I suppose she got a thrill out of it by proxy the more shockingly reckless you were. Her worst — or maybe better than best — moment was your carry-on behind your study door with Mrs Hein at your wedding party, which was going a bit far in improper behaviour, even for you."

Nick showed a rare flash of embarrassment. It amused me that Meg's good opinion was the only one he truly seemed to value. "As I can't protect her from the Javan witch, dead mice and half a dozen little Nikolayeviches," he continued, choosing to take no notice of that dig, "what better use could I have for her than looking after you in a way that I can't?"

So now I was greatly relieved that I would have hard-working Meg with her practical common-sense to help me through the task of living in this daunting house. Besides, I thought, trained by Nick as the perfect gentleman's servant, Gus would have the benefit of her sending him off to work impeccably turned out, though, clad as he was in tradition, without her previous master's assertive sophistication.

We stood in Grand-mamma's bedroom, which seemed an impertinence.

"I'm not sure how I feel about sleeping with my wife in the bed my father was born in," said Gus.

"They are all rather grand. We could let Willie have this one."

Gus dismissed that. "It's the view, really."

The three windows above the entrance porch certainly had a commanding view of the processional approach up the avenue with its ancient lime trees. Gus was almost visibly growing in stature to match his setting, filling out his father's suits and the ancestral hall.

Wandering on, Gus said, "We'll have to give a party for all the people we didn't invite to the wedding."

"We'll put on a show to impress our absent mothers," I agreed.

When we went down again we found Willie had been abandoned to find his way crawling around the expanse of the vaulted kitchen with Grand-mamma's pug snuffling noisily at his behind. I washed him off in the kitchen sink, an act that brought home the idea that this place could actually become my home.

"As soon as Nick saw the black pug," said Gus, "he picked him up and kept him under his arm or on his lap all the time he was here, talking to him — in French, an undercurrent of chatter he kept up while he was acting perfectly normally with us. Weird! He hardly seemed aware he was doing it but I had to prise him loose when it was time to go home. It was very odd, normally Pug sticks close to Grand-mamma but he was quite prepared to be adopted by Nick, listening to him as if he understood what Nick was saying to him."

"Coco the Clown and Little Nickie," I said. "The little black dog he had as a child. That was a French bulldog, quite similar. I suspect Nick has delusions of revenants. When he sits for hours in a state of abstraction I fancy he is in communication with his spirits, his familiars — and the nightmares, where do they come from? Leon Bolus asked him if he didn't have nightmares, but I suppose Leon was thinking of the heavies whose bodies Nick left for the vultures, while in fact Toby says he was already suffering from them at school."

Grand-mamma stood facing the wall presses filled to overflowing with glass and china.

"I suggest you sell all this," she said. "My mother-in-law had a mania for china and I never had the drive to sort it all out."

"I expect that will conflict with Gus's instinct to preserve what he thinks of as the archive," I said, though I could see I would have to reduce the quantity of stuff to manageable proportions.

"Within reason," Gus agreed as he made the tea. "One has to protect the evidence from contamination, that's all. I'll get Cats to come and help me set the library up as our family archive. He's a civil servant; he's used to tedious tasks."

"Who is Cats?" I asked, mystified at a friend or colleague I hadn't heard mentioned before.

"You know — Catullus."

"Oh, no," I protested, alarmed.

Grand-mamma asked. "Do I know him?"

"I suppose so. He's the terribly decent chap who used to bugger me at School," said Gus.

"You mean that charming boy of the Melroses who came to dinner in his pyjamas? I thought he'd end up in a whorehouse in Alexandria — so he's a Whitehall boffin, is he? How disappointing!"

"Don't look jealous, Sibylla," said Gus, "he's not going to do it in the library. He's always having tragic love affairs with would-be pop stars who treat him badly — all terribly boring but he's judicious and a meticulous archivist. I can use his expertise."

"I'll make sure there are no cucumbers in the house if he comes here," I said.

~

Grand-mamma did as she said she would, driving off in her Volkswagen camper with Pug in his basket and the barest essentials she needed to survive. Gus had relented and agreed to store her spare shoes and old ball gowns, knowing perfectly well she would never need them but they would do nicely for May and Augusta to dress up in.

"It's going to be wonderful living here," I said to Gus, "It's everything I could wish for; I'm just so sorry I'm not fit enough to enjoy it more. I am thankful that I have this life of my own with you and the children and our fantastic house, but when I should be more than happy I feel just miserable."

I couldn't ask Mary or Julie to visit me. They would be no help, I could just imagine them standing in the hall surrounded by the semi-clad bossy Virtues, telling me what a damn fool I was. They would blame me for my own misery. Gus — and Nick — had allowed me the fantasy of a China baby, but not one of them understood my regret over the betrayal of the Ranelagh Road version of my life, which had resulted in Gianni's baby instead. And just when Gus had provided the promised hobbit-home for me and our children, Nick with his Adam and Eve dream-time refuge in the sky had proved himself once more to be the perfect solution to my real need.

Besides, none of them had ever been pregnant.

"Amanda is out of a job," said Gus. "Now she's not swanning around embassies any more I'll get her to come here and lend a hand."

So Amanda came to help Gus in restoring order to the jumble left behind by their grandmother. Rather to his dismay his sister Jane came too. Jane, home disillusioned from a love affair with a natural history specimen hunter-gatherer in the Mata Atlântica, was closest to Gus in age and the worst of the Harpies but he was quietly pleased with the role reversal now he was master of the house after a lifetime of being bullied by his sisters.

"My happiness came to a sad end when I was four," said Jane. "That's when this little brother came along and everyone lost interest in me."

"Life seems to turn so inexplicably on trivial things," Amanda remarked. "Like Baby Gussie ending up with this fine house just because he came out of the womb equipped with a willie."

"He puts it to good use," I said, determined not to feel guilty about my fortuitous good fortune while his sisters had to find their own solutions.

"The Deathrage Menace is back," Gus announced when he came home on Friday evening. "I rang his secretary to tell her to get him to pay up the prince's ransom he owes Father in fees and to my surprise she handed the phone straight over to him to answer for himself. I asked him if he is in back in Basel to do the devil's work, he said yes, and happily it is very profitable."

I wondered if he had abandoned Tsang to return to the safe haven of Hein and Bott where he could practise the medieval arts of alchemy and weapons with impunity.

But if I needed him, it appeared he needed me as much.

"He says he's on his way over," said Gus, "and asked me to lend him you, Sibylla, that he needs you to keep his fuck apparatus in tune with the music of the spheres so he can make the violin sing. I refused to get drawn into a philosophical discussion about the harmony of Nick's balls with the move-ments of the planets; I told him to go fuck his gollywog."

""What a highly improper thing to say, Gussie," said Jane, but Gus was long past caring what his sister thought of him and went on:

"As usual he was moaning about my treachery in stealing you from him; I said it wasn't a question of stealing, you are free to choose whom you want, when you want. So he said to ask you to choose him."

"Oh, Gus, you are a sweetheart."

I understood that this was Gus's way of saying I was free to escape the upheaval and drudgery that surrounded me, though it did seem a contradiction that I should hope to find peace with that master of mayhem, Nick Deathridge.

"You're a lunatic, Gus," said Jane. "I danced once with that foxy guy and he literally swept me off my feet. I certainly wouldn't trust him with my wife if I were you — is he still married to dim-wit Angelina?"

"What do you know about happy marriages?" said Gus. "You might actu-ally learn something about true husbands from Nick and me."

So, leaving the Wittersworths to quarrel amongst themselves, I went back to Nick, the truly honourable Gussie dropping me off at the bulgy fig-leaf before going on to his office.

I appreciated more than ever the clarity of space Nick maintained around him. Even his drawings from the previous occasion had gone; prob-ably filed away by Toby for future reference, leftover paper and ink disposed of by the Fairies.

"Look," said Nick as soon as I walked in and, hiding his discomfiture under even more than usually twitchy brows, he held up a violin.

"Who gave in to you at last?"

"I did," said Nick.

He explained that, bored with Tsang, he had been only too happy to respond to a phone call from his steep-alley-cat-in-the-window crony.

"When I answered the phone Mug didn't say a word, I just heard this amazing long chord in B Minor asking me a question; I shouted Yes. He had found exactly the right tone of voice for me at last, a Guarneri, an intimate whisper of a voice that penetrates the soul, not bright and frivolous like the last Stradivari he offered me — I'm not performing for the multitude. If Mug auctioned it collectors everywhere would have been chasing it, Americans and Japs outbidding one another, so I offered him a sensible amount to keep it where it belongs and got straight on a plane home."

He could speed-dial Swiss Air, get a flight number and be on his way in less than an hour. So I was right. Basel was still his anchorage. He had served his apprenticeship there, in love as in work, and acquired his chosen identity — not that his modest veneer of Swissness could ever quite suppress the Deathrage maverick lurking under the cloak of the mild-mannered law-abiding citizen.

Nick had finally got over his umbrage that no one loved him enough to give him a violin. Only a *Guarneri del Jesu* was rare and satisfactorily expensive enough to justify him actually paying for it himself. I didn't dare insult him by asking how much, but guessed it would be a price beyond my comprehension.

"Well," I said, "that's more dignified than trying to coax it out of some woman with your cock."

"It's not really. I'd rather have fucked for it, especially Mrs Shackleton."

"She couldn't possibly afford to buy you at the price you demanded."

"She chose not to when I was appealingly young and adorable and comparatively inexpensive. Make sure I'm not buried in the earth — I don't want to take to the grave the bitterness that I didn't fuck her father's old violin out of her."

"Now you are just being difficult," I said.

"My price kept going up every time she refused me but I swear I'll sweet-talk my way up that K2 cunt before I die."

I felt I was back where I belonged, in the air-conditioned, soundproof serenity of *'riverrun'* and this time I was allowed to spend the nights in the magician's bed whose delicate lattice-work had been bleached to harmonise with the light up in the sky. Nick had no respect for the patina of antiquity.

The odd thing, I thought to myself but didn't say, is that now I was used to living with Gus in our own home as husband and wife, my feeling about being with Nick had changed too, as if I now accepted him on his own terms, fucking his passionate heart out for me, his Sibylla. No need to be his second (or third) Mrs Deathridge.

Besides which, he could no longer say 'thank you, Miss d'Art!' in that tone that hovered between über-polite and insulting.

During the day I was entertained as before, this time when Nick engaged what he said was the most expensive teacher available — 'she only took me on to save the Guarneri from abuse' — and practised for hours a day, filling in for lost time between phone calls and lunches in the city, which unusually for the time of year was nicely humming, keeping a close eye on the way the money markets were moving under the new government and the radical change of policy which was letting loose some wild speculation.

Nick complained that I was the only one who would listen to his music, an audience of one. It was hardly surprising. What he called the right tone of voice went from painfully slow and exquisitely drawn out sharps to a deep throated moaning that was positively torture to the ears and brain. Eugenie's refusal to be married to such suffering was perfectly valid; it was an instrument that brought out the most, or worst, of Nick's obsessive and self-absorbed moodiness. For me however, more than the sound, I loved watching him: his expression, his stance; I thought, even if I were deaf, from deep in the embrace of the Dumez armchair it would still be enthralling just to observe him. He made music as if he were making love. Often I drifted away, still listening, spellbound. Ever after, the sound of a solo violin, sadly melodious, lovingly beseeching, would bring me back to the blessed peace of those evenings with Nick up in the sky with the city lights below competing with the stars and the winking lights of airliners passing by on silent wings.

As important to him as his music teacher and an entertaining part of his preparation to play was how he stripped naked and submitted his body to a sternly efficient young Swedish masseur who came to knead, flex and stretch not only his hands, shoulders and back but all the way down to his toes, as if he were an athlete in training for the fight.

"Play naked," I begged him. "I want to see the way your whole body is tuned to the music, pointy prick doing counterpoint."

"You do have the most indecent ideas behind those limpid Botticelli eyes, Mrs Wittersworth," he said, pulling on a black jersey for his performance.

"I'm the one needing a massage," I said. "It's hard work fucking for two."

"I feel pregnant," said Nick, "waiting for this damned interloper of yours to get out of the way."

"It will get worse before it gets better," I said. "Four more months to go."

"Gino cheated me out of Gianni," said Nick. "I left it too late to beat him up and throw him in the river. I would have done it that morning he challenged me outside the house, but the Death Row building proposal was up for discussion and I had to meet a delegation from the council at the site. I couldn't arrive late looking disreputably dishevelled and I didn't want the bother of having to load the body on to his bike, getting rid of it and going back to change my shirt."

It didn't seem to occur to Nick that fighting Gianni might have caused him more damage than a crumpled suit or bloodstained shirt. Toby said that as a schoolboy he went around more or less continuously cut and bruised; maybe going to a meeting where his financial future was at stake in a less than perfect shirt would undermine his confidence more than a swollen lip or black eye.

Lazily having breakfast in the shade on the terrace, I felt suspended in time, not wanting this perfect summer ever to end, living in this *Land of Cockaigne*, delicious food laid out before me, balmy breeze up here above the heat of the city below, only Nick's music to introduce a deliberately discordant note. Nevertheless I was aware that with September coming I really ought to go home. This was after all only a dream, a web that Nick spun around me to hold me in his enchantment.

"*Sweet Jesus*," I prayed, Great-Aunt Kathleen's voice in my head, "*give me strength!*"

I didn't specify what for.

Nick came up fresh from his swim and sat alongside me, leaning back with his eyes closed.

"You are looking quite blissfully pleased with yourself," I said, envious of his strength, his highly functional, lean body at the service of his indomitable will.

"I have every reason to be," he said. "Except for you and your hapless bastard — you are the one stinging hornet in the sweet honey of my life... Tsang is on his way, he's hoping to see his most ambitious experiment come to fruition."

I sat up. "I'll take a taxi to Waterloo," I said. "After the way he betrayed me I couldn't stand Dr Tsang tut-tutting over me, interfering with my baby to satisfy his scientific curiosity."

Nick didn't stir or open his eyes.

I went in and packed my bag, expecting he would come to help me and drive me to the station, or preferably all the way home, but when I went back to say good-bye he was still in his deckchair, his normally fidgety fingers clasped firmly on the armrests, the familiar pout indicating an obstinate sulk. I watched him for a minute through the glass and then, thoroughly mystified and very annoyed, I left him and his Guarneri del Jesú in his looking-glass world and went back to mine.

~

"Good," said Gus when he saw me. "It's time my sisters took themselves off about their own business. I was getting worried I might have swapped a perfectly satisfactory wife for a pair of Harpies."

The Harpies had however done a good job on the house, which was now cleared of the accumulated clutter of generations and all I had to do was use their help to arrange the rooms as I wanted them. A day or two after I got home Meg phoned to say she was ready to move to La Malcontenta. The departure of Grand-mamma's housekeeper had left the lodge free for her to live in. I suggested her father might like to come too but he was resistant to change.

"He'll come around to it in the end," said Meg, "when he realises what it's like without me to slave for him."

He did move his pigeons into the dovecot over the stable since demolition work encroaching on his house in Kentish Town was too disturbing for them. So it was only a matter of time.

Meg was happy with her new home.

"That Javan woman was the last straw," she said. "The Missus with her mice was bad enough and the Misses Furzy cavorting around in their underwear to show off their bellies swelling up like balloons; they'd have gone floating off out the window if they weren't tethered to the bed. Then the Chinese doctor came back and the Javan locked the door and wouldn't let him near the ladies, so he was on the outside and the ladies inside with the witch, wailing and moaning that the wicked things Sir did to them hurt them dreadfully and now they were going to die — again."

Meg's remarks revealed that I was right to leave London when I did, ignoring Nick's reproachful silence, showing him the impossibility of keeping me spinning in air as one of many dumbbells in his juggling act of a life while he attended to his other interests: his model family; his imminent new Nickies; his tightrope walk over the abyss of finance and politics.

"Sir and the Missus left the doctor and the witch to fight it out and went out for the evening to some South American ambassador's do all dolled up to the nines, Himself in what he calls his fancy dinner jacket — the other is his serious one — the Missus in her latest spangly Bruce Oldfield, bright red — what was she thinking of with her apple blossom complexion? though her figure is sensational in it — she and Sir are a right pair of stunners together, Fred and Ginger only he's the ginger one."

I smiled at that, seeing Angelina as part of his wardrobe, the wife he put on with his fancy dinner jacket.

"I ought to have gone home to the Ancient," said Meg, "but I couldn't bear to leave before I knew the outcome. When Sir and the Missus came home about midnight the row was terrific, screaming and hammering on the door, with the little devils Connie and Jo-jo squatting on the stairs watching everything as if it were a Punch and Judy show and the big Nickies crawling around — Connie brought them down from the nursery to join in the excitement. The Missus picked them up and took them to her room out of the way while He dealt with the turmoil. He made the Doctor sit on a chair in the hall with the door open so he could see what was going on inside without getting in the way. He got the Misses to shut up their screeching with laughing gas and they lay there giggling and yelping while the witch did her stuff, dosing them with her hideous brews.

"Madge came down and caught hold of Jo-jo, but Connie escaped and stood on the Doctor's knee so he could see better and the Doctor gave him a running commentary, he said it was a lesson in biology but it sounded more like a football match, the two of them mad with impatience that they weren't allowed any nearer. I got Sir's jacket off him before he got blood on it, and all those pearly studs and the cufflinks, but the shirt itself is a goner; even if I get the stains out and bleach it he'll never think it's good enough to wear again — as soon as the babies started arriving the whole thing got out of hand. The Chinese got in there, arguing with the Javan in whatever gibberish they talk over the hysterically shrieking ladies and I swear I saw Connie kneeling right on bed cheering the little heads as they came out. Laid out in a row they were like a litter of piglets; Connie and Sir were laughing their heads off over them, swapping and comparing babies—they were all high on the laughing gas — Connie tried to run off with one of the babies but Sir hauled him back, telling him he couldn't have it for keeps until it's a bit bigger — what that child will grow up into I can't imagine, the things Sir says to him! Scandalous! I wouldn't have missed it for the world. But I spent the best years of my life keeping that house perfect for Sir and now it's a shambles: crazy women and babies everywhere. I quit."

I clutched my tummy and was glad Nick had nothing to do with mine.

Angelina came out to see the house I had so unfairly come into in spite of my immoral life — or maybe because of it.

"Nick said the house is impressive," Angelina said looking around at the Virtues with an expression that suggested she didn't quite agree with him. It was not her idea of a comfortable home. "I've never known Nick to express such approval, and goodness knows we've stayed in plenty of splendid houses — it's so handy when friends' houses are on the map, easy to find."

That surprised me as to me Nick had been nothing but disparaging, laughing at the Wittersworths, but on second thoughts he might have been teasing me and actually he'd really like to have a Palladian casino himself. And he never read maps — though I doubted he could find houses navigating by the stars. Too shifty, unlike the star of Bethlehem.

"Of course this would be too out-of-the-way for the likes of Nick and me," Angelina went on. "There's nowhere to go; we like to walk, St James's and the theatres, and Dolly and I do enjoy a healthy stroll across the park to Harvey Nicks and Harrods."

Dismissing the Virtues, she glanced through the arched doorways in the angles that led into the four main reception rooms beyond.

"I'm glad you have a lovely place of your own at last, Sibylla, but you look ill; you must be very tired, this is no time for you to be moving into a house like this."

"I know," I said.

Angelina came with me down to the kitchen and joined Amanda and Jane in their final sorting out of the colossal jumble of china, shifting stacks from the presses to the long table, and back again while I sat and said yes or no to their suggestions.

I hadn't felt well since I had so hastily departed out of Nick's Land of Cockaigne.

"Nick soothed me with sonatas on his prodigious violin," I said, more to Amanda than directly to Angelina as I didn't like to confront her with the fact that Nick had spent August making love and music to me, for the first time in twenty years not dutifully training with his troops in the Alps, keeping William Tell up-to-date.

"He said he felt a fraud travelling with its case sitting on a First Class seat beside him..."

"... because it had a violin inside and not a gun?" said Amanda, laughing at the idea of Nick acting the gangster.

"No, because he's going to have to work terribly hard to be worthy of owning it," I said. "He's slightly embarrassed that he has it only because one simple idea passing randomly through his mind in an idle moment made enough money to buy it."

"He's being politely modest," said Amanda. "It isn't as random as he says, ideas don't come drifting by on the wind, and it takes drive and concentration, organisation and production know-how to turn them into money."

"As I should know, seeing him go out the door every morning at 7:45 without fail." I was ashamed of my facile acceptance of Nick's self-denigrating remarks, the humour with which he masked his industry.

Angelina looked slightly bemused. She took her hard-working, high-earning husband so for granted that our comments puzzled her.

"He plays with such tender sensuality," I said, reclaiming my advantage. "I simply adore the way he expresses his emotion with the finest of bows. I offered to play with him on the piano if he got me the music but he said he prefers just to hear it in his head and not have me distracting him. "Oh, I said, then the rest of us will just have to fill in the gaps as best we can."

"I'd no idea," said Angelina. "I've never heard him except for teaching Connie songs of the Frère Jacques variety and heaven knows what else, I can only hope they are not too rude. Nick and I have a perfectly happy marriage but I accept that there is much I don't know about him."

Nothing Angelina said suggested she was aware of Nick's refuge in the riverside apartment where he could retreat to play the violin when the explosion of Nickies got too much for him. Angelina survived as wife by not knowing.

"You remember, Jane," she said, "that you and I used to meet a lot at weddings and parties, and I was so proud of having Nick beside me, so soberly articulate, no silly jokes, a first-class husband and provider. Even though all he did was produce some inexplicable bits of things in those dilapidated sheds — not that I ever saw them, but that's what people said, as if laughing at him — I never knew quite what to say when I was asked what he really did — it's so much easier to have a proper profession that doesn't need explaining — but when I said to him that not knowing what to say made people think it was something embarrassing like lavatory pans he thought that quite amusing and told me to tell that to anyone rude enough to ask — really he has the strangest sense of humour — but as he is seriously well-connected and successful, he makes our social life easy."

Success in Angelina's vocabulary meant she wore important jewellery and couture dresses.

"If I remark that he bought something more than usually extravagant he says something improbable like he'd sold his great-grandfather's Russian railway bonds at an astronomical profit — even I know that can't be true! He's such a fantasist."

Jane laughed with more than a touch of the Wittersworth mischievousness.

"None of us knew anything about Nick Deathridge until you let him loose on us innocent maidens with a big bang at your wedding. I was seventeen so I felt a bit silly that my little brother's school friend invited me to be his girl at his sister's wedding but I wasn't going to miss such a big do. I was invited to sit with Paul at the top table and your mother was sweet to me, such a lovely lady — our mother is a frightful harridan, I never knew if it was me or the pony she was whipping, I can't tell you how dire it is to be the fourth girl in a family that needs a boy — My first encounter with Nick was when he said to Paul, 'well done, *hermanito*, I couldn't have chosen a better pair of legs for you myself!' I was totally spellbound from that moment. He scarcely noticed me again but I couldn't take my eyes off him — that waltz you did after dinner was amazing, simply brilliant, and you both looked gorgeous, the way he held you and looked at you so adoringly, you were the most divine couple I'd ever seen."

Angelina was gratified at such extravagant praise from an unexpected quarter. After the glass heart incident she was beginning to show a glimmer of appreciation for his wit, nevertheless she said: "Nick is diabolical; he lays traps for people."

"Paul told me to hold on," said Jane, "so I was half prepared for what was coming."

I was interested in what an independent observer like young Jane would say about the incident of the Wedding Waltz.

"He had these girl musicians fronting the band," she went on. "They started off quietly while people were getting into position and twirling around nicely but they turned up the amplifiers and it was getting more and more cacophonous and discordant so people started tripping over their feet and giving up."

"But Nick kept to the beat," said Angelina, "remorselessly faster and slower, and he made me follow him with a grip of iron every time I faltered so in the end we were the only couple left on the floor, with Nick making me spin and turn in an ever more maniacal frenzy while the music got wilder and wilder— it was a nightmare but somehow I stuck it out to the end. When that final crashing chord came there was dead silence. Then the guests gathered their wits and cheered — probably out of sheer relief that it was over."

"Nick did it in memory of his grandmother and her career as interpreter of Ravel, mourning her untimely loss," I said. "But he is even worse now he has the violin. The grief he wrings out of that... it's sheer agony..."

But they weren't taking in what I was trying to say to them and I felt too ill to make the effort to point out that one couldn't explain Nick's behaviour as bizarre or infuriating, or even funny, without acknowledging the underlying burden of tragedy he carried around in his heart.

"One couldn't not be impressed," said Jane "I couldn't stop watching his feet, spinning on the spot or with long strides eating up the floor: what a mover! I would have tried too but Paul knew we had to leave Nick to enjoy his triumphant finale alone."

"You should have seen him, Amanda," said Angelina, laughing now she had Jane to share her embarrassment. "His hair slicked back like a matinee idol…"

"He had to retreat to the gents beforehand to fix himself after that Voortrekker woman wrestled him to the ground and ruffled his feathers…"

"She wasn't the only one who had a go at him…" said Angelina with a grimace.

"… but Nick was unfazed," said Jane "That's when he stood out for me as a distinguished individual, standing in the middle of the floor making his speech. He thanked everyone who joined in, without the least hint that doing an impossible piece of Ravel was anything out of the ordinary by way of bridal dance."

"I was afraid everyone was laughing at us," said Angelina, "… well so they were… all that was demonstrated was that in spite of sounding like a waltz it was quite impossible to dance to and made everyone feel silly for even trying. But I suppose that was Nick's point. Of course I had to say I enjoyed it and he kissed me and everyone said how charming. Nick stood chatting with his two musicians — he handed them ostentatiously fat brown envelopes, presumably their honorarium in one pound notes — so I sat down to hide my embarrassment in a glass of champagne knowing everyone must consider him quite mad."

"I was so hoping Nick would dance with me," said Jane, "every time he glanced in my direction I couldn't stop myself blushing. Wow! I thought, lucky bride! Fancy going to bed with that!"

"That's what they all said," said Angelina, a bit wearily.

"I asked Paul to ask him for me, but Paul said Nick has no interest in little girls — how insulting was that! — so I was quite surprised when he unexpectedly caught hold of me and swung me around shoulder high, goodness, he is strong! My legs went flying. I never thought I'd jive with a 30-year-old in tails and not feel perfectly ridiculous, but with those tip-toey feet he's nimble and poised as a matador. But he was away again just as quickly, back to spooning with that slick Swiss dolly-bird he was so hot for."

"The notorious Mrs Hein," I remarked. I did not say 'the First

Mrs Deathridge' though it was on the tip of my tongue. I realised this was the Jane who had passed on to Paul Nick's kissing technique...!

"Nick loves being the centre of attention," said Angelina, "and in that shimmering emerald dress she was certainly eye-catching."

Was it the dress that did it? Angelina didn't mention the disaster of the Balenciaga that he didn't like.

"Where is he at the moment?" asked Amanda, sparing Angelina any more distress from Jane's indiscretions.

"At home, but honestly, most of the time I don't know," said Angelina. "I leave messages for him with his secretary — all I have is her phone number — she's still the best means of communicating with him. Sometimes, as if by magic she can connect me through to him. Other times I have to wait for days for him to answer from I don't know where."

Gladys and Meg, Nick's Fifth Column: they were our best hope of knowing what was going on.

"I'm sorry now that stupid Furzy business made him close the factory," Angelina said. "It has left him very foot-loose. I had to get out of the house to-day because of the kid. I couldn't stand it any longer — even Adam was no help, he and Nick are in this one together."

Apparently the first time the goat had a kid for the sake of the milk supply it was a female and one of the Renaissance Women adopted it, but the last one was a billy and when Nick came home a few days earlier he decided it was big enough to eat.

"For Goodness sake, Nick," Angelina had begged him, "get the butcher to collect it and, if you must, have it delivered back in neat packages."

But Nick refused to hand his billy over to die at the hands of a stranger and banged it on the head himself.

"The awful thing is," said Angelina, still shocked, "that Connie and Jo-jo stood watching and they thought it was great the way he knocked it out with one brisk wham. Nick and Adam with the boys cut it up and Nick is going to barbecue it for dinner. Rose and Violet are running around — in the batik kaftans Wilhelmina wraps them in with tight sashes to hold in their tummies; she makes them exercise and massages them back into shape —in tears over the kid and tripping over the Nickies let loose to crawl around and get in the way. I just don't want to be there."

Angelina shuddered. "Connie wants the skin made into a hairy bag for his secret dispatches. He claims he can read and write better than Nick already —'You poor little bugger,' says Nick, 'bad luck having such a dunce for daddy,' — 'Never mind, Dear Duncy Daddy,' says Connie, 'you have me to do it for you.' So Nick dictates cryptic messages to him, which Connie posts off to some mysterious destination. He won't let me see, saying it's a secret; Nick is a truly dreadful father and Connie being the eldest gets the worst of it. Connie can't reach the slit of the pillar-box so he lifts Jo-jo up to post it. Or they lurk waiting for the postman to come collecting and hand it to him with elaborate instructions."

Nick's own boy!

"We used to have magnificent feasts down here," said Amanda, indicating the long table under the arched ceiling of the kitchen. "When you've had the baby we must organise a proper party for the family. You didn't invite us to your wedding so you owe it to us."

"Gus says so too," I said. "He wants to introduce me to all his associates."

I didn't know if Gus's sisters knew the baby wasn't his. My regret for Nick's sake was something between him and me but I was ashamed for Gus's sake. My parallel lives were no longer my private affair. Being La Malcontenta imposed a different responsibility.

"For our wedding Nick wanted a midnight feast," said Angelina, "where he would have had the house all lit up and the garden, and musicians, and we could have gone to bed under our own roof with our friends celebrating around us. I can see now what a romantic vision that was but Mother was shocked at the idea and I was too timid. I see now what a difference it would have made to our love life. He is so maddeningly always right."

"We'll get Nick to serve us sucking piglets so he can have the wedding feast Mrs Furzy denied him," I said, thinking how lovely it was having these women to gather around me and gossip. Mary was so disapproved of me for not marrying Gianni she hadn't spoken to me since she flounced out on Gus and me, dragging Bobby away from his professional interest in Nick acting suicidal in the foreground, and when Julie told her about my splendid house it aggravated her so much that she and the Pinkerton girls met, it seemed, for the sole purpose of discussing how it was possible that a prim pussy like Sibylla d'Art could so unscrupulously ditch her faithful fiancé for the sake of becoming mistress of La Malcontenta.

Bad cess to them anyway!

Amanda smiled. "That reminds me how provocatively he tried to stir me up at Castello Giugno with the lambs' testicles," she said.

"You should have told me who you were," I reproached her for my embarrassment.

"Leon and I thought we'd see what Gus's wife was like while we were passing," Amanda explained apologetically, "and if we liked the look of you we'd introduce ourselves, but as soon as I walked into the dining room I recognised your flaming lover-boy from meeting him briefly as a teenager, at the strangest funeral I've ever been to. So I wanted to see if I could find out what that was all about, what really happened between him and Joey Madigan. That dinner became a duel between Nick and me as he did his best to distract me from his own iniquities by telling me that you enticed my father to fuck you on a bed of law books — he has such a quaint way of putting things!"

"That was simply unforgivable of him," I said. "I still cringe with shame that he told you that."

"Did you really...?" asked Jane. "You and Our-Father-Which-Art? Golly!"

Jane was so staggered by this she sat in silence, no doubt trying to imagine me and her father – not having a romantic encounter over tea and cakes in Fortnums, but as Nick said, frolicking with bare arses amid the trappings of the legal profession.

"Yes," I said, rallying, not to be put down by them: "Sweet Father William! I am so acutely shy with men that it's as if it's only through sex that I can relate to them. I can't remember how often we did it, not more than three or four times. Apart from the gang-bang. The best time was when he paid me a visit and offered to rescue me out of Nick's clutches. I followed Meg's advise and repaid his kindness on your drawing room carpet, Angelina. I let him feed me lovely Beluga, and with a bottle of Nick's very best champagne we spent a blissful afternoon. I'm glad he found Evita to rescue shortly after; she's a much more worthy cause and far more useful to him, in bed and out of it."

"Really, Sibylla, you are just as incorrigible a liar as Nick," said Angelina, simply disbelieving me. The Wittersworth sisters looked doubtful as their imaginations failed to conjure up their august father getting it up for the young Mrs Wittersworth-to-be. Maybe they hadn't given due consideration to his real relationship with Evita either. Angelina however seemed pleased that my affair with Father William acted as a counter-irritant to the sting of the sisters embarrassing her with their stories about Nick.

"Nick made it awkward for us to tell you who we were," Amanda went on. "But if he thought he'd shock me with the testicles — I told him that I'd had something similar when I went to see my old school friend at Witwatersrand; she researches indigenous African food and likes to serve up such strange items as baked aardvark, snout and all. He had to know her because she talked to him at that funeral — but I never did find out the story behind his extraordinary carry-on because he wouldn't admit that he'd even been there."

"No, but that evening at the castello he was mad for you," I said, still jealous of the flush and the spark in his eye in the firelight, mindful how visibly his lip quivers with desire. "If I had invited Leon for a stroll in the moonlight you could have extracted all the confessions you wanted from Nick on the hearthrug."

I kissed Nick's grandmother's ring, my talisman. He could spend his fantastic earnings on Angelina but he had given me his one possession that was beyond price.

Angelina looked up from the stacks of Wedgwood black basalt teacups on the table, brushed the hair back from hiding her face, and touched the ring on my hand with a faint smile. She no longer seemed to resent it. It occurred to me that she was opening up to a greater sensitivity of feeling.

Perhaps after Nick pointed out to her what his token of a sugar heart represented, a ring was no longer so important to her.

"This is a valuable service," she said, "and there's lots of it. You could sell
this quite profitably."

"No," I said, and to tease her, "It's the one Nick likes to drink his tea from.
It suits his black humour."

"At home he won't have anything but the plain white..."

"It's the Wittersworth Effect, like fancying Amanda by firelight."

"I know," said Amanda. "But he was only trying to get me to make a
fool of myself, knowing perfectly well how fatally irresistible he is. He has
matured well, but he was utterly enchanting as a youth."

"The way Toby and Frank describe him is rather less flattering..."

"That time at Joey's funeral the schoolboys came as a group in their black
suits but he turned up quite unabashed in a greeny-blue Harris tweed and
superbly flattering pale trousers on his lanky leggy legs, if you know what I
mean; tangle of dark red hair; pallid, scarred face; looking aggrieved and
sulky; not a bit remorseful. Everyone was talking about him; it did him no
harm at all to be in disgrace and dangerous."

Like ginger in the Stratton Square marmalade, less sugar and more edge,
still delicious.

"Maddie did her best to talk to him — she asked if it were true he'd made a
century at Taunton on Saturday and would he rather play for Somerset
or Hampshire — but he scowled furiously and told her to shut up, he was
listening in case Joey was banging to get out, making sly comments about
Finnegans Wake, saying if only we had a bottle of ginger beer to break on
the coffin Joey was bound to wake up. We girls were shocked, but at the
same time we were trying not to giggle so Mrs Madigan wouldn't be hurt.
Maddie said it was a pity he didn't think of bringing a few bottles then we
could have had a proper wake."

Joe, mavourneen, why did you have to die?

I imagined the funeral under the colourful carved roof of the abbey with
Nick and Joey, as Toby described them, jiving riotously around the coffin,

their spins and lifts as usual ending in a brawl...

"Maddie seemed to take it as the most ordinary thing in the world," Amanda went on, "that Nick and Joey were playing Russian Roulette with a live bullet. She asked him where they got it from but Nick acted dumb. Mrs Madigan kissed him and said all Joey's letters home had been full of the fun they had together and she thanked him for his friendship, saying when he came their way he was to be sure to visit them. He said that there was no point in going back to school now Joey wasn't there..."

... as if he had any choice in the matter...

"... and so he proposed accompanying Joey home and, as he didn't fancy going down the Limpopo without him, he'd row the coffin down the river to sink it at sea. But even Mrs Madigan thought that not quite feasible and of course Mrs Shackleton and Mr Dyer said absolutely not. So, he said, he'd have to think of something else to do with his life."

Perhaps he was still searching for that something else, the reason he walked out of one successful career after another.

Amanda and Jane carried coffee out to the kitchen garden terrace and Angelina took my arm going down the step, supporting me but, I thought, also to reassure herself. If anything, she saw me as a steadying influence on Nick, an anchor against his wilder excesses. The Wittersworth sisters telling tales were a greater threat to her peace of mind than I in my present condition.

Amanda sat down with her coffee cup to continue with the sport of teasing out the tangles of Nick's affairs, to Angelina's continued chagrin. "It was of course quite typical that nearly ten years after Mrs Madigan's invitation he had the nerve to drop in on Maddie literally out of the blue. She said this delightful bright red and yellow aircraft, all struts with a four bladed propeller, shiny nose cone, high wings and cocky tail, bounced to a halt on the dirt track that leads to her research centre and out jumped Nick Deathridge, rather the worse for wear but even sexier than she remembered him as a youngster."

I could just picture Nick's expression, I'd seen it so often when he arrived on my doorstep, polite reserve failing to conceal his total self-confidence. How could she not be delighted to welcome him?

"So that's who the Voortrekker woman at the wedding was," said Jane. "Big bony blond with a skinny black man trailing behind her."

"That woman?" said Angelina, indignant. "Nick had been terribly quiet during the dinner, barely responding to Frank's and Nestor's efforts to distract him; he looked tired, as if his mind were elsewhere..."

— having been seen by Meg not so long beforehand with Mrs Hein's legs clenched around his waist and her red knickers on the floor —

"... but he came down to earth when this bronze amazon came swanning in with her bodyguard as she called him, causing a disgraceful fuss... and then swanking out again leaving a flabbergasted silence behind."

"She left Nick in such disarray that Nestor took him away to pull himself together. The whole disruption she caused was such a distraction the dinner came to an inconclusive end and we forgot about the wedding cake."

"It would have been a pity to cut it," said Jane, "and spoil the snowy layers of frothy sugar piled up in peaks, most unusual and lovely: a flock of snow buntings in marzipan, dozens of them, some in the snow and more flying down suspended on icicles of spun sugar, a work of art on a side table."

"Nick's sole contribution," said Angelina. "When he offered to get the cake Mother thought it was one thing he could safely be trusted to do right, Mother not being able to envisage the possibility of a cake that is not round and in a standard number of tiers. Mother tried to divide it up later to send it around by post; she said the mountainous confection wasn't really cake at all, it was all icing and marzipan which collapsed into a pile of rubble as soon as the knife went into it. She had to buy a cake to cut up and put in a piece of the decoration with each box. It took her days. So it would have been another monumental embarrassment if we had posed for the guests with the knife and had it crumble to nothing before their eyes. Nick's excuse was that no one was ever actually going to eat the thing — but what an escape!"

We returned to the china presses, stacking the services in some kind of logical order, though in the effort to fit everything in it wasn't always possible to keep the relevant pieces together. The black basalt service went safely back in the cupboard and Angelina picked up another cup and saucer and said:

"... Nice Minton tea set; if you are selling any of this I'll have it for Rose and Violet, just the kind of thing they love, little pansies and wavy gold rims."

"Maddie says Nick comes to visit her every now and then," said Amanda, returning to the enjoyable scandal of Nick's love life. "At first I assumed it was a rather bizarre love affair — but she curses every time his name is mentioned — *verrekte klootzak*, whatever that means — she is so furious with him for not staying and being her partner, in her research centre as well as in bed. He is so good at her kind of thing she can't bear it that he chooses to live in London with his model English wife."

"I understand that Nick may well have had love affairs before meeting me," Angelina said, "but I was only twenty and right under my nose this lioness was actually attempting to undo my husband's fly buttons... and he was laughing so much he wasn't trying too hard to stop her — I'd never seen him actually laugh like that before — or since!"

"Dear Angelina," said Jane, "she was only teasing him and all the girls were curious about Nick's potential — it's sheer snobbery to have a buttoned fly, especially Nick, he doesn't need any bulking up in the fly department — admittedly none of the others went quite that far. If I'd known she is a friend of yours, Amanda, I'd have talked to her, but she came in with such determination and left again so abruptly it might have been for the sole purpose of getting her hand inside Nick's pants..."

"... that tiresome Nestor was to blame," said Angelina, stopping Jane from expanding any further on that, "setting up his competition to get the girls chasing Nick for kisses, with his stupid cuckoo clocks. The annoying thing about him was he thought he had to tell me all about Nick as if Nick were a complicated new car that came with an elaborate instruction manual. And you will not credit this," Angelina was still horror-struck at the memory, "but Nick had proposed taking this Nestor with us on our honeymoon! In the very boat his mother fell off and drowned! How ghoulish is that? Not to mention the embarrassment of spending one's honeymoon being seasick in close proximity to a foreigner... well you know what I mean. So when I met him at the wedding with his cuckoo-clock jokes I was even more relieved he wasn't coming with us. Actually he is the man I danced with the most — he was really terribly nice to me, saying I was a graceful swan in my ivory dress surrounded by birds of paradise; it was true the Swiss wore bright, strong colours, nothing too subtly understated about them in their party clothes — I was glad someone seemed to appreciate mine, considering what it cost. But maybe he, and Frank, were only doing their duty as best men to keep me distracted, letting Nick off the hook to carry on flirting with everyone else."

It seemed to me more than flirting. The occasion seemed to have unleashed in Nick a wild unspecific desire, displaying himself as all-encompassing love personified, joyfully surrendering himself to the love of all women.... I wondered — if I had been there, would he have heeded all the others?

"Nestor is a really nice man," said Angelina, a little wistfully. "Though he was slightly boring about their endless cross-country skiing expeditions and how he tried to trick Nick into getting lost but never succeeded, Nick swearing that though one damn snowy peak might look much the same as another he had spent too many unpaid hours and days piloting Hein around them being lectured on the principles of navigation — I could have flirted a bit with Nestor myself only he was far too circumspect. Mother seemed to think I was doing Nick a favour by marrying him — as if he were the lucky one! Now I know better."

"Think what it would have done for your self-esteem if you'd realised that all those other women chasing him were your defeated rivals, that you were the winner."

Angelina looked at Jane in surprise. Such a glorious thought had never occurred to her — but then Amanda rather spoilt the effect by saying:

"Maddie has a cuckoo-clock."

"Maddie?"

"When I saw it I thought it was just an oddball piece of gear belonging to a screwball lady. She keeps it in her office at Wits, on the wall behind her desk. She says she uses it as a test of character for her students. She judges them on how they react to it when she's interviewing them. Terribly distracting I should say, it's big and incredibly complicated with a little man frantically waving a Swiss flag to mark the seconds and a brass band that bursts into a fanfare every hour and three couples dancing across a balcony and if you're really quick you can see that in the blink of an eye the last little man, chasing the woman in front of him, drops his trousers and shows his bare bum just as he disappears off stage. She said Nick brought it for her in a crate with some other pieces of equipment, she didn't say what —"

Guns, I thought but didn't say.

"If it were a kissing competition she must have won it with him under the table."

"I refuse to believe Nick was doing anything improper," said Angelina. "That woman was dragging him down."

"You must be right," I pointed out, "you say he came up from their struggle laughing and you know it is easy to tell, he has a distinctive fucking expression on his face and he absolutely never laughs when he's doing it."

"Honestly, Sibylla, I wouldn't know," said Angelina. "When his face comes that close to mine I keep my eyes tightly closed not to embarrass myself."

Maybe if she kept them open next time she'd see the sincerity behind his love mask.

"He stayed about ten days while he assembled the pieces and got the mechanics of it working. You can't have been married very long at the time, did you know he was making trips to South Africa?"

"Probably," said Angelina noncommittally. "That was his work. If something specially complicated or expensive was being delivered to a client he went to check it had been set up properly and see it working. He loves nothing better than fiddling and solving problems. But I didn't know that included cuckoo clocks."

"Maddie didn't attach any importance to the clock; she saw it merely as a piece of Nickish eccentricity to fill in the evenings between scouring

314

the veldt for scarcely edible animals by day and fucking half the night —
sorry, Angelina!"

Angelina shrugged. Seven years on it hardly mattered. She had accepted
his glass heart.

"Another one," she said, "as if the Aunties' weren't bad enough!"

I was reminded of the trouble caused in the Shackleton household and
Toby's indignation that his mother received her outrageous gift of a clock.

Angelina continued: "I can understand that with the excitement, the
dancing and all, he might enjoy teasing all those girls a little, but I couldn't
grasp why he was embracing that older woman like that. Toby's mother is
not in the least glamorous, an earnest 'Committee for the Protection of
Everything' lady: girls, butterflies, ancient dovecots..."

"He's quite romantically devoted to her,' I said, "— or so he says."

"I thought she was stunningly glamorous," said Jane unexpectedly. "What
a dame! She was superb. It was after midnight and we were talking about
taxis and who had a car across the road in the car park and I was wondering
what on earth had happened to the girlie top I'd cast aside in the heat of the
moment when Nick kissed me — he made fun of it, saying the frills were an
invitation to a bit of bodice-ripping, but how was I going to go home with the
Furzys half naked in my slip without it — expecting the night to come to an
end with a rousing finale..."

"Mother was getting worried about overtime, it was supposed to be all
over by midnight," said Angelina.

"...in the middle of the dance floor Nick and this Junoesque lady in grey
appeared out of nowhere to the tune of *Moonlight Serenade*, looking incredibly elegant, just the two of them drifting in the dimmed light to this slow,
really cool swing number, very quiet — you could see the band leader was
loving it, stroking it with his baton, giving it real style."

It delighted me that Jane could appreciate Nick's grateful love for his
mistress-of-the-lobster, which was troubling to Angelina and laughed at by
everyone else.

"People thought it was just Nick's little demonstration of how to do

old-fashioned," said Angelina, excusing her bridegroom's folly, "a compliment to this mature lady who had been sitting all evening with his father —
very few people realised that the unobtrusive, handsome man in the background was Nick's father, I hardly knew him —"

The Heini girls all knew and took turns dancing with him, being nice to
dear Nicki's Dadi.

"and stopped shuffling their belongings together to watch with sleepily
indulgent smiles."

"None of us knew who she was," said Jane, "and after Nick's earlier extravagances it was a pleasure to see how he slowed down, moving with cool
restraint. They did it beautifully, dreamily smiling at each other, just silently
in a close hold, her velvet dress swaying and his tails swinging, occasional
breaks and twirls, they knew what they were doing all right. But it went on
and on, that steady relentless beat, the band swinging seamlessly from one
tune into the next without a pause — *String of Pearls, Moonlight Becomes
You*. It was a lesson in grown-up style."

Jane was still enthralled by her youthful hero-worship.

"It was getting well into the small hours by now and Mother was desperate to end it," said Angelina, "and I was simply exhausted, but the music was
so attractive people stopped sneaking off home but came back to join in, so
as long as the cock of the walk kept it going it was impossible to break up.
Eventually Nick and this lady came to a pause at the side so Mother charged
in with the Gay Gordons."

"Yes, Paul and I were going to join in too when Paul held me back, grin-
ning with mischief," said Jane, "and, there to the side of all the hearty back
and forth and Highland flinging, was the real interest for those who were
watching: the time-keeping, calculating Swiss, Mr Shackleton in his wheelchair, the elder Mr Deathridge... was Nick with his grey lady..."

"He loved the silvery velvet of her dress," I said. "He never misses the
opportunity to say how her dove-like bosom sends him into an ecstasy of
love, he's not shy about it..."

"... busy earning her cuckoo-clock with the most shameless display of love-making outside the cinema," said Angelina, still mortified.

"That was Nick, not the lady... though she went along with his humping, while the rout of the highlands was going on around them," said Jane. "Maybe at seventeen I was utterly romanced by this man who had kissed me, but to me it was beautiful. It was Paul who came between them: he left me standing and dashed off to get a bottle of champagne which he trust in Nick's hands and jigged the lady away into the mêlée..."

"You jigged away with the bug man and didn't come home for two years," Amanda remarked.

"He lent me his coat and said he'd give me a lift to the ends of the earth — I admit it was because I couldn't bear the thought of having to go home to Mother that I let a nameless stranger pop my cherry in an underground car park — it counted for something that he was a fellow guest at a posh party — anyway... I could see Paul felt he had to do something to rescue Nick from looking witless... of course I understand for the white-faced bride dying to go to bed it looked different."

"Yes," said Angelina, "Nick had a wonderful time until he was completely spent and just sleepwalked up to our suite barely conscious enough to take off his jacket and shirt and lie down on the bed. I sat for hours in my bridal nightgown unable to sleep beside Nick lying there out cold in his evening trousers with his braces undone and his chest bare. I was disenchanted with how my wedding night was turning out; the one thing I did that made me feel like a wife was that I unbuttoned his waistband so he could sleep more comfortably. The tiniest step towards the bonding we should have had and which nearly never happened because he flirted with everyone but me."

Angelina, Paul, Nick: they all had their varying accounts of the wedding games, different versions of the same thing — Nick himself getting quite frighteningly angry when I questioned him about it — but it was Amanda who put it in perspective.

"Delayed bonding perhaps, but once it happened it was obviously successful," she said. "You do have two very happy children. And it takes more than a good dance partner to make a good marriage."

"... in fact," said Angelina, "I'd better hurry home; he'll be in the mood for it after devouring the billy-goat..."

Leaving us somewhat bemused, she went, taking the Minton tea set in a box for her darling Aunties.

~

Boar
Hunt

14

Angelina's departure to reclaim possession of her errant husband, closely followed by Amanda and Jane to seek another purpose in their lives, left me properly with the title of *La Malcontenta*. If only I hadn't brought this burden of pregnancy with me the transition from being ecstatically cherished by Nick's love back to hardworking, responsible wife and mother would have been less painful.

"I hope this child is either divinely beautiful or amazingly clever to be worth all this discomfort," I said to Gus. "It seems interminable."

"Well one thing is for sure," said Gus, "it's not interminable."

But however sick and tired I felt, when I thought of the catatonic days of boredom I suffered waiting for the first Grati baby, I appreciated how happy I was with my children in my beautiful house and Gus's cheerful company to see me through it. I wondered if Gus's composure was due to his naturally phlegmatic character or if he was relieving his tensions with the help of Evita's affectionate courtesies, but I could never ask. I began to be more sympathetic towards Angelina for not knowing Nick's affairs, in bed or out of it.

I had forgotten all about Tomas's great boar hunt until Gus reported that Nick had phoned him to tell me to be ready when he came for me.

"What should I do?" I asked in a panic.

"I had hoped we'd done with the Mad Fucker for the time being," said Gus, as usual leaving me to make up my own mind.

"I feel so useless as a wife I might as well go and be useless to Nick instead."

Nick was crazy to think it was a promise I had to keep when I was so unwell, but I couldn't refuse him. He was set on shooting something, anything, and he would be safe with Tomás. Otherwise he might go to his African friends with a supply of elephant guns or a crate of assault rifles to protect their King Solomon's Mines and be lost to us, maybe forever. In my apprehension for his safety I felt I had to keep him in my sight.

When Nick came to collect me from La Malcontenta Adam came too to take May with him for a trip to Abb's Head where he proposed putting her in a wetsuit and teaching her to sail a small dinghy.

"And we'll go fossil hunting," said Adam. "Any left-handed illiterate can shoot a dumb boar; but fossils, now that's interesting. A dinosaur egg would be really worthwhile."

"Take her to see Mrs Shackleton," said Nick. "Show her what a great little girl she missed out on when she wouldn't let me fuck her."

"No, I have no wish to discuss you and your children with the Shackletons," said Adam, "you are the one subject we avoid mentioning. I have been telling Nick," he said to me, "that he really doesn't need you; he can perfectly well spend a week with Tomas without dragging you along. A seven month pregnant woman can't be the sexiest of companions on a hunting trip, however much he says he can't be happy without you."

"You interfering old codger, what do you know about the mysteries of the heart in love?" Nick made his ritual protest at Adam's concern.

"It's not as if you could use Sibylla as bait for a boar," said Gus. "Tiger hunt now, I could understand, she'd make a tasty decoy goat, tethered to a tree — there's a bit of the William Tell in you, putting your beloved in danger so you can demonstrate your marksmanship with vainglorious panache."

"You can trust me," Nick said. "I'll be so cocked up by bedtime I'll need a body with more bounce and resilience than my pillow to roll over and hump, and Sibylla in her present size and shape invites lustful penetration like a lady manatee on heat: I'll set out at dawn in the best possible state of mind and come back in the evening to the perfect welcome. I shan't be taking her out on the trail of any wild animals."

"The most dangerous wild animal is you," said Gus.

"I'll guard her with my life. If anything goes wrong with my sweetheart I'll feel justified in shooting myself."

"That won't do much good," said Adam. "We can do without you; Sibylla is more indispensable."

"Have you ever shot a boar?" asked Gus.

"No, though I had to shoot a rather intrusive aardvark once — actually, when I felt it chewing on my foot I thought it was something more dangerous. I had fallen asleep rather unwisely but by good fortune with my boots on. I sat up and shot without waiting to make sure — I might have shot myself in the foot, that would have been ironic."

"You do tell the unlikeliest stories, Nick," said Adam.

"I took it to Maddie Madigan. She was delighted with the hog, just what she needed for her experimental cuisine. She had it pit-baked by her students with the usual mealy munchies. Then she gave me a lesson in how to fuck tough in Afrikaans —ever since we met at Finnegan's Wake she'd been itching to get her hands on me. She then attempted to poison me with puff adder stew and when that didn't have the desired effect sent me off with a supply of jellied zebu cock cut in quarter inch segments but still barely edible, and for variety, dried ostrich and kudu, very compact and light-weight, to fuel my flight home. She said I would be able to live on it for a month. Even with the hazards of the journey it didn't take me that long to get from Johannesburg to Zurich though I'm not sure if it's what kept me alive or nearly killed me — or which was her intention."

"Obviously a woman after your own heart," said Gus.

"She tries to get a grip on me whenever I venture into her territory: a praying mantis of a woman, it's fuck fast and get out alive."

"She must be irresistible," said Gus.

"Another of your improbable loves?" said Adam.

Having heard Amanda defending her friend Maddie Madigan's invasion of the wedding party against Angelina's complaints, I was curious to hear Nick's side of the fly button story, but he didn't oblige, saying:

"Gino Grati is the boar I'm out to get," miming the action of peering along the barrel of a gun, eyes wide and fixed on the Virtue of Prudence across the hall, daring us to disbelieve him.

~

The members of the shooting party, who were paying Tomás prodigious sums for the privilege of bagging a boar, were accommodated in the central block of the castello. Mostly men, there were also a few women, all there, it seemed, for the pleasure of displaying their beautiful guns, dressing the part and tramping through the woods, sophisticates getting in touch with their primitive natures. With my primal belly I didn't feel too out of place amongst them. Nick introduced me to everyone as the sublimely inspired but thoroughly unreliable Sibyl so I felt I was elevated to the status of presiding goddess of the hunt; even more so when we gathered in the upstairs state dining room and I was seated in the middle of the long table, with in front of me the Scottish silver pheasants that in leisure moments I used to help Donna to polish, gossiping under the walnut tree. I was pleased to see them in action. During Clare's lavish feast I sat saying nothing, eating little, looking as wan as any Renaissance beauty. Since my hair had grown long again Donna completed the picture by plaiting Nick's pearls through it in loopy strands. Posing like the stylishly prancing pheasants as centre-piece, I got a feeling for Angelina's life of dining out with Nick. Happily as the talk was all in German I didn't have to even pretend to share his enthusiasm for gun palaver and competitive killing. Nick's aardvark story would be taken seriously here, however ludicrous he made it sound in banter with Adam and Gus.

Clare had her grandest state bedroom reserved for Nick and me but I was quite grateful to Nick that, after a night in princely comfort, in spite of Clare's protests that it wasn't suitable for me, he had us moved to Tomás's cabin up the mountain near the hunting area. We would camp there in idyllic isolation and Nick could stay in contact with the daily progress of the hunt by radio and be picked up at some meeting place on the way.

He unpacked a surprisingly utilitarian pair of boots for hiking over the hills. "My Light Walking Boots" he called them, of the same vintage as his SIG 510. I wondered what heavy boots were like if these were called light.

"If I lose these I lose my life," he said. "My boots and my pistol were the two pieces of equipment I took home with me out of Africa; nothing else survived the rigours or the barter. I ended up barely decent in shorts and a shirt but with my body and my booty intact, thanks to these two essential items — and my Swiss passport — all I need to survive."

There was a sprinkling of early snow around the cabin and the countryside looked beautiful. The weather forecast was clear and bright and Nick's humour matched it.

We had never lived so intimately together as there in that one room cabin. At last I had the opportunity to observe the great shaving ceremonial Toby had described, but Nick's usually lengthy ablutions were reduced to that single basin of hot water in the evening before getting into bed. I lay and watched, entertained as usual by Nick's act as genial mime artist, squatting on a stool over the basin with his eyes closed, performing by touch, stroking the back of his hand over his skin to locate a missed hair.

"You've found even smarter underpants," I remarked. "You've been back to Bloomingdales recently?"

"Eugenie says the Bloomingdales are like body armour," he said. "She likes to see more mobility up front and these she got for me at home frame my enticing bum with more subtlety — her words, not mine."

"My God, Nick, you are letting your ex-wife choose your underwear for you?"

"My Number One wife," he said, taking them off. He must have been doing that fairly recently for Eugenie too. Presumably it was part of going 'home' to Basel; this was confirmed when he said, "Don't look so miffed, sweetheart, it's what husbands do, part of the job — and even after twenty years, fucking that vixen gives me the illusion I'm getting the better of Papi Bott, foreskin and all."

He didn't fall asleep as usual taking up most of the bed, half on top of me but, with pillows and his body as buttress, he made love with an intensely brooding tenderness, wrapping himself around me in an octopus embrace. Though I was used to the intensity of his passion; this loving selflessness went beyond physical desire. Caring for me at *'riverrun,'* for all his gentleness, he had still maintained his edge of acerbic humour at my expense, but even that was gone.

"How do you do it?" I said to him, "How is it possible that you fucked me through four pregnancies and you can still surprise me? If this were all there was to life I would spend the rest of it here with you."

"So, your choice is between living in Palladian simplicity with Wittersworth or in the real thing with me, a shack with an outdoor bog? That puts me in my place!"

"Gus expects me to behave like a responsible adult; with you I can happily do nothing and let you carry the burden for both of us."

"I take that as a compliment, Mrs Wittersworth."

The primitive lavatory was out in the shed. Nick used it but he put a bucket in a corner for me saying "I don't want to have to escort you out in the middle of the night for every little wee."

"The only intimacy you have denied me now is to see the expression on your face when you shit," I said.

"You are welcome. A good shit is one of life's most simple and satisfactory pleasures," he said, 'and one I perform with ease. Getting my bowels functioning again was the greatest benefit from Genie's kosher chicken soup after the dehydration caused by Maddie's biltong."

"Ever since I came here I'm having rather loose motions with cramps," I complained. "It's getting really tiresome."

"Stick to the fresh meat I bring you and spring water," said Nick. "Clare has this nonsense about eating greens, terribly dangerous, especially as her workers probably crap in the cabbage patch."

Bivouacking on a mountain was a familiar setting for Nick and he was happy. After shaving, the rest of him received no more than a cursory wipe with the damp towel and within twenty-four hours he was looking rougher and tougher than I had ever seen him and smelling stronger too, getting deeper, richer, and interestingly more spicy, while his mood settled into one of blissful tranquillity. His rifle lived in its sling on his back; he didn't set foot outside the door without it. He went off at daybreak in his old boots and khaki fatigues topped by the red crocodile which, by now weathered to a more subdued hue, in this context didn't look too outlandish though the Germans wore stylish hunting-green outfits.

"They irritate me," Nick complained. "They play the part of the correct huntsman in all earnestness, though not as stupidly as the Italians who bang away at anything that moves, blasting tiny birds out of the sky, a complete waste of wild-life and ammunition — good grief, for a country so recently at war you'd think they'd appreciate the value of bullets."

They were a good excuse for Nick to wear his red jacket, aware as he was of the danger of being shot in the back, a hangover from feeling his hackles rise as the two Africans behind him on his epic flight quietly plotted how to dispose of him, they little realising he was ahead of them with his plan for getting rid of them, his advantage being that they couldn't afford to knock the pilot out in mid-flight.

Clare came up to see me, ostensibly to bring fresh supplies of the vegetables Nick so despised, but really to find out the current state of my love life.

"In spite of being sick most of the time I've never had such an interesting pregnancy," I said. "Gus and I have a house of our own at last and Nick has been quite exceptionally good to me — since he sang about the crucified Christ at Gianni's funeral, Gianni making love to me in Nick's mother's old Chinoiserie bed while he looked out of his window upstairs doesn't trouble him any more; I think he may even be reconciled to Gianni's baby."

"Really, Sibylla, you have a husband and children at home, with your lover out here in the hills, and your belly with a baby that comes from neither of them!"

"There is room in my life for them all. Nick grumbles but really it suits him to have his freedom and it stops him getting complacent. Gus tolerates my absences; it's not in his nature to be jealous. The irony is that Gianni slipped in and got me pregnant in what would have been our last encounter even if he hadn't tumbled over your wall. Nick is annoyed he let Gianni slip through his fingers. Let's hope Gino stays well away — Nick is looking forward to showing off the long-range sniping accuracy of his Swiss rifle."

"Let's hope he gets to kill a boar instead," said Clare, not really taking my words seriously.

I remarked to Nick how calm he was, not a bit excited or even exhilarated by the hunting. He said: "That's what shooting does. It requires a cool head. I could never commit a *crime passionnelle*; you can be sure that when I finish off the Grati I am doing it in cold blood — not that I'll go out of my way, but if Gino crosses my path I won't hesitate."

Idyllic as it was to be on the mountain with Nick-in-a-good-mood, I didn't tell him that the hours I spent alone while he was out with the guns were anxious ones. Just as when walking around New York at midnight, I felt his vulnerability in a way to which he was quite indifferent. I also felt nervous for myself. I had never been so isolated, always in a house with people around me, even at Abb's Head Adam was usually nearby, only in the loneliness of Stratton Square before Paul came to keep me company, when Nick and Angelina went out in their evening outfits leaving me with the baby and the radio. But Stratton Square didn't give me the sense of uneasiness as did being on this lonely mountain.

For the few hours that the sun lit up the hillside I'd potter around outside for a bit, but by three it set behind the ridge in the winter afternoon and I'd sit dozing in the rocking chair Tomás had brought up for me. Any sound outside the cabin had me peering out the window expecting to see a boar or some other wild creature. I passed the time feeding pine cones on top of the slow-burning logs in the stove to keep it crackling, thinking I must remember to unbolt the door before Nick was due back, for fear he would say I was being silly locking myself in.

But my fears seemed justified when I looked up and saw a man peering through the little window.

I couldn't be sure that is was Gino.

I watched and listened until I was sure it was Nick stamping the dirt off his feet outside, then shot the bolt back as quietly as I could.

"We're going out earlier tomorrow," said Nick putting a solitary hare on the table. "The Germans are taking the afternoon off to go to the *enoteca* in Siena. I'll take you for a walk instead. You're not getting enough exercise."

"I've got you to exercise me in bed, thanks, that's quite vigorous enough."

"Thank you, Mrs Wittersworth, my cock is wholly dedicated to your service."

Nick left next morning in the dark so I bolted the door after him, left the shutters across the window and went back to bed. I slept so soundly that I woke up with a start with the sound of a very loud bang echoing in my head. I sat up and waited but nothing more happened, no sound. I crept out of bed and opened the shutters.

Outside was the boar. It came snuffling around the cabin and I watched it through the window, fascinated, until it trotted off. I went back to sit and wait.

I didn't notice that Nick had returned from the morning's shoot until I looked out again for the boar and saw Nick washing his hands and face at the pump. He didn't seem to care that the scarecrow raincoat he had on was getting wet too, not to mention his boots where the water gushed onto the stoney ground before flowing down the hill. I watched this unusual performance with curiosity. Eventually he came in carrying a pair of partridges and hung them up by the necks to deal with later and his coat near the stove to dry out.

I said, "I had no idea boar were so big. Scary."

"It's unusual to see one like that out in daylight. Is that all you saw?" he asked, dismissively, as if the boar was of little importance.

He cooked lunch with eggs and pancetta, even, as a concession to health, threw in a handful of Clare's frozen spinach reduced to a puree with a large pat of butter. He took his plate to eat sitting on the bench outside the door: morose but perfectly contented. I knew him well enough not to intrude in his solitary musings.

Even when Nick was doing nothing he never gave the impression that it was time spent without a definite purpose, so when he stood up and said we'd go now, it was clearly time to go, even for something as casual as a stroll on a mountain path.

We walked around the shoulder of the hill, the ground undulating gently, neither gaining nor losing height, rocky ground with scattered trees. Nick held my arm, encouraging me to keep up, not allowing me to lag behind. Though we could hear a distant noise, shouts and an engine revving, he showed no curiosity but proceeded steadily on his rather wet Light Walking Boots. I smiled; they seemed to dictate a certain pace — an inculcated discipline; if he broke into a run it would fit into the syncopated footfalls of his troop around him, the echo of many similar pairs of boots, yet each individual marking his own time.

When we got to a break in the trees where the ground dropped steeply away into the valley below we could see what the commotion was. Much lower down where the path looped back on itself, a small van had left the road and was now being hoisted up by a farm truck, with a saloon car in attendance nearby.

"What a lovely fandango!" said Nick standing stock-still to watch the drama below. When eventually the van was righted and the driver, limp and unconscious — or dead? — was taken away in the car, Nick in his red crocodile stepped to the edge as on a stage, raised his voice and sang after it as it wound its slow way down the track: *non più andrai farfallone amoroso*, Figaro's mocking dismissal of the philanderer, very loud, resonating across the natural amphitheatre of the valley. The remaining men standing around the farm truck looked up, spellbound. I recognised Tomás amongst the faces turned up towards us and a number of the others: the very men in front of whom Nick had humiliated me at their working lunch. When Nick finished with a triumphant *a la gloria militar* they cheered and waved, giving him their thumbs up like the crowd in the coliseum, and he waved back and held out his arms to embrace his audience and the world beyond: a grandiloquent gesture in keeping with the music. I thought it odd that Italians could be so opera-mad they would applaud a fine performance on a hillside in such strange circumstances.

Men! Incomprehensible.

Back in the cabin Nick reported by radio to Tomás that he wouldn't go out to meet them the following day, that I was feeling unwell. It was a good excuse, he said, for doing a bit of stalking independently of the group. That was how it came about that simultaneous things of consequence happened:

Nick shot the boar;

I heard the gunshot — the same menacing snap of a rifle that had woken me up the previous day —

and I ran up the hill to find him standing astraddle the bristly twitching creature with — I had forgotten he had it — his pistol ready to finish it off, but it wasn't necessary as it stopped twitching and lay still;

I screamed and clutched my belly with an amazingly awful pain;

Nick caught me as I fell in a faint, bleeding heavily;

it started to snow.

What happened after remained a blur. It was so dreadful I hardly remember. I could hear myself screaming in a faraway remote kind of way as if it weren't me. Nick was there with his hunter's knife to detach the tiny body. He laid it beside the boar and his rifle and covered them all up as best he could with the scarecrow waterproof he had again put on over the red crocodile as camouflage on his solitary hike.

All I remembered afterwards of how he carried me down to the cabin was his face close to mine, the dirt streaked with blood, mine and the boar's, and sweat, snowflakes settling and melting on it; his nose and mouth so close I could feel the whole strength of his body, muscles and bones, heart and lungs in the measured, controlled breath on my face, and I was thinking: if I die now this brave, generous mouth is the last thing I'll see; it's the last thing I want to see. Nothing matters any more.

Notwithstanding the pain and the strain of carrying me he was reassuringly steady, digging his boots into the snow at every step. Even with my feeling of imminent death I was stupidly thinking: going downhill in the snow must be easier than carrying me up six flights of stairs the way he did after the gang-bang, but his face was carved with the same lines of grim suffering.

I lay on the bed and waited to die. Nick rummaged in his case for his bottles and syringes, his drugs and painkillers, a front-line medic who proceeded with ruthless efficiency to clean up the mess — as if it weren't over yet, as if I hadn't known from the minute I saw his killer eyes fixed on mine, coming up the stairs that first night, that this was how it was bound to end.

"Trust me," he said. I didn't feel the needle in my thigh.

"I love you beyond reason..." I hadn't the strength to say more, but there was nothing more to say.

"I know" he said and kept on talking to me, seriously calm, while I dissolved into nothingness.

The End.

I was surprised to open my eyes again to find I wasn't dead and Nick beside me sitting on the stool, his head in his hands and humming quietly to himself, quite unperturbed. I recognised the tune but couldn't think what it was. Something French.

"You're going to be all right," he said. "You've got me, your life-line, your living blood bank if necessary."

I had to believe him though I felt remote from the reality of my situation.

"The snow has stopped," he said, "I'm going back up the hill to have a look."

He took the shovel from the hearth, coiled a length of rope over his shoulder and set off. I dozed an hour or maybe two, feeling better now the bleeding had eased off and Nick's drugs were taking effect.

He came back looking extremely cheerful considering he was covered in dirt and exhausted, with bloodied hands having dragged the boar down the hill to the woodshed to save it from potential scavengers.

"*Mamma mia*, it's a magnificent beast," he said. "What a bag! What a fantastic hunting trip!"

I wanted to say, what about my baby? But I couldn't.

Nick was putting some wrapped up packages in the freezer compartment of the butane gas refrigerator. I didn't ask him what, but incongruously I was thinking of Angelina's complaint that he didn't have the butcher deliver the billy kid in neat packages for the fridge but knocked it on the head himself. Why did I have this vision of Nick with his hand raised for the killer blow? Or for that matter, raising his gun and aiming down the valley. Gus would put it down to one of my Sibyl moments.

Nick got on the radio and contacted Tomás.

Tomás's voice came over before Nick said a word: "Good God, Nick, what are you up to now?"

"It's only the boar," I heard Nick say in an appeasing tone of voice. "It's hanging in the shed but I can't do more without help so come up to bring it down. And bring a litter and some men, Sibylla isn't well and can't walk."

When I opened my eyes again I was in bed in strangely familiar surroundings and Dr Tsang's was the face close to mine, keeping watch, smiling benignly. I wasn't in the least surprised to see him, only this time he had been caught out and missed the baby.

It took me a while to realise I was in the cottage where I used to visit Adam. I'd been in this bed before. Nothing was said until Nick came in triumphantly holding up a length of tubing and out of his pocket he produced a couple of needles wrapped in his handkerchief.

"Don't worry," he said to Tsang, "I put them through the steriliser."

He had been to the local hospital with one of the maids whose sister worked there and acquired, however furtively, some large bore needles and the attachments.

"I've set up a dozens of centres with blood transfusion equipment," he said with amusement, "and look, this is all you really need. If humans were all as compatible as Sibylla and I, I'd be reduced to small beer instead of Château Margaux."

When Tsang tied up Nick's arm and stuck one needle into it and another into mine and the blood was flowing from him to me I said to him, "I feel like a vampire reversed, being force-fed your blood so you can take permanent possession of me."

"How many times have I said I would die for you? that you would have my heart's blood? Well, this is the next best thing. This is so we can both live."

Though I could see it was more painful for him than for me, Nick was prepared to go on clenching his fist to keep pumping his life into me until Tsang said it was enough.

"... *si vous disiez que mon sang,*

est plus à moi qu'à vous, ma Dame,

je blêmirais dessous le blâme

et je mourrais, vous bénissant...

"I've been waiting most of my life to make that song come true," said Nick, "only I don't have to die to save you with my blood, thanks to chatting up my fifth form science mistress."

"And that's your Don Quichotte song again, the one you practised your growing-up voice on," I said, remembering Toby's stories. "You are truly a Don Quichotte, an heroic mad knight."

"With plenty of *piété* and *pudeur* though the *pureté* and *chasteté* may be a bit lacking, and my lady is truly beautiful and unconditionally worth dying for," Nick concluded, pressing his thumb on his vein to stop the bleeding. His face looked pale and damp with sweat and, surprisingly, tears, gazing at me with a compassion that belied the tone of derision in his voice.

As always, I thought, he's unable to express the painful sincerity of his emotion without mocking it.

I spent the next few days in Adam's one-time cottage with Nick and Tsang in attendance. Tsang was grateful that Nick had cut most of the essential organs out of the dead infant for him to analyse, but complained he had left the brain behind. He wanted to go back up the mountain and dig up the remains, but Nick refused to show him where it was.

Nevertheless I felt, as I lay there feeling empty and disorientated, that both Nick and Tsang were perfectly in their element and positively enjoying themselves, turning the living-room into a laboratory with whatever pieces of equipment Nick could gather or borrow or tinker together, as well as the supplies Tsang had brought with him. I stopped myself from thinking: that's bits of Gianni's baby you've got there under the microscope, as if that would tell you what a beautiful person Gianni was and what a tragedy it was that Nick paid him to fall in love with me instead of leaving him for some nice Italian girl who would have been kind and faithful and given him healthy babies.

Once Tsang got over the disappointment of losing the baby he was thrilled with what he saw on his slides from frozen bits of liver and lungs and blood, counting antibodies and clicking his tongue.

"It wasn't too bad, I might have saved it."

His regret was heartfelt.

"What for?" asked Nick. "A seven month foetus? Just because you can doesn't mean you have to."

He had said before I should abort it and start again. I wasn't sure if he said it out of concern for my health or jealousy that it wasn't his.

"You should have listened to me," Dr Tsang said to me. "But then you never did. You are the most obstinate, heedless female I ever met. If only you had come to me your baby would have been safe. What's the point of having the world's fertility expert at your service if you won't take my advice? I could have saved it..." and so on... and on...

"If you can let nature take its course for the sake of evolution and the survival of the fittest, so can I," I told him. "You cheated, you deceived me, you used me. If you had given me your baby when I was ready for it I wouldn't have had Gianni's by mistake."

"I told you at the time your husband is the one. You didn't listen to me. Maybe you will now."

"I was hoping for a China baby. But when it was Gianni's it seemed such poetic justice — even you thought so, Jun."

"Poetic justice maybe," said Dr Tsang, "but I warned you it was likely to turn out badly. Augusta can have her immune system boosted with regular inoculations, but after the first the odds against were likely to be overwhelming. I was curious if the sex of the embryo and at what stage of development the differentiation in the hormones would make a difference, if any."

As Nick didn't believe in pain he kept coming to stick needles in me lest

I suffer the least twinge of discomfort, somewhat to Dr Tsang's disapproval. Floating tranquilly on a narcotic cloud I could hear them arguing, but I could tell from the quiet satisfaction in their voices that Nick and Tsang were enthusiastic about what they were doing: a pair of mavericks who recognised no limits to their own capabilities or restrictions on their power to do whatever they saw fit. Nick had caught the ball and was running with it. No Frank to shout at him to stick to the rules of the game.

"You are a pair of witch doctors," I said. "I feel better already."

And the truth was, I did. Indeed, for months after, the couple of pints of Nick's hormone and mineral rich blood had me brimming with confidence and courage and I wondered if this echoed Nick's usual state of being. If so it would explain much. It faded eventually, but ever since, whenever I have an unexpected burst of energy and sense of euphoria, I call it the Don Quichotte Effect.

I felt so much stronger that I announced, "I'm sending word to Gus to come and take me home. I'm not staying here any longer to provide you two with material for your tests and theories."

"No, please wait," said Nick, "Now I've done my damnedest here I'll take you back to your husband. Just let me have the St Hubert's feast with the boar, then I'll be ready to go."

That was almost an admission of some kind.

"I've done all I can," said Dr Tsang. "I'm getting out of here in the morning."

It was unlike him to seem impatient. Now the worst had happened I was disappointed he was going away so soon. I wanted to lie at ease and listen to more stories about the revolution and hardship in the time of Chairman Mao, and young Jun's adventures before turning himself into Dr Tsang, as well as his recent explorations into the vast and varied regions of his land. He had so much to tell: there was never enough time to hear it all. And I was hurt that now he had his samples I was of no further interest to him.

Tomás came to the cottage to take Dr Tsang to the airport. Nick stood at the door to see him out and asked, as a last-minute afterthought: "Any positive reactions yet to your Virgin Births? You are being a bit slow about getting your research papers out. I was looking forward to organising a press presentation to explain to the world how to get such beautiful babies. Think of the publicity you are missing out on."

"You mean the publicity for Deathridge Instruments. After all, your profits depend on it too."

"You old Chinese charlatan," said Nick, laughing at him, "I've finished with the Virgins and I've already sold the sperm selector patents to the Indians for quite an absurd amount of money. What do I care now if they make a profit or not? Are you not going to London to see how your investment is paying off? Or don't you think you'll get past the *komodo waran*, their Javan dragon?"

"Thank you for inviting me, dear Colleague," said Dr Tsang, "to this present demonstration of your exceptional skills — on all fronts: lover, life-saver, killer; an impressive display of your mastery over death as well as life."

"Yes," Nick agreed, smiling just as cryptically as the Chinese. "I've got the balls to destroy as easily as I create. My God-awful father-in-law Böttli used to quote his bible at me — *revenge is mine, sayeth the Lord* — that's what he said after he failed to drown me and paid me off with a Porsche instead, relying on my recklessness to do what Yahweh was failing to do for him — not that I wish to do God's work for Him."

When the door closed behind Tsang I said to Nick:

"That was a bit harsh. Surely you should be thanking him for his help."

"I didn't need any help from Tsang. Don't trouble your head over his feelings; that exchange was a muted bit of mutual blackmail. He was twisting my arm over what he observed here, thinking he can use it to offload the multitude of Nickie Babies onto their Nickie Papi, but I was just reminding him that if either of us speaks out of turn, his loss will be greater than mine. I have the babies and the money: his medical career is at stake."

As usual I understood only half of what was going on.

I watched Nick cleaning the dried blood off his red crocodile with a damp cloth. He was wrinkling his forehead and pursing his dimply lips over the task but inside he was happy enough.

"Those marks will never come out," I said. "I remember how shocked Meg was when you told her to throw away your lovely heather tweed jacket when it got muddy at the fox-hunt. There was nothing wrong the cleaners couldn't fix; you were just angry because of me skiving off with Toby to pass the day in his bed."

"Not angry," said Nick. "Just grief stricken that I was losing my one true love. But don't worry, I won't be throwing this away, these stains are precious to me. They add real value to an worthlessly ostentatious piece of animal skin."

Clare came to discuss the evening's feast with Nick, asking if he had any special wishes about the boar.

"Yes," said Nick. "I'll have the loin cut up raw in strips and marinated in grappa, garlic and chilli to kill the trichinella.'"

"That won't penetrate enough in a few hours," said Clare. "You'd better leave it to Donna. She has generations of boar cooking behind her."

To me she said, "I'll send some nice thin slices of boar ham in a ciabatta down for you."

"Good," I said. "I'm starting to feel hungry again."

When Tomás got back from seeing Tsang to the airport he stopped by to talk to Nick.

"I presume that radio message I got about an accident came from you," he said. "You have only to breathe down the mike to be recognised."

Nick looked mildly amused but didn't answer.

"The surgeon was puzzled that in spite of quite tragic injuries the patient was so passive. He phoned me this morning to say that he had to conclude that someone must have given him a stiff morphine injection before we picked him up. But the patient himself isn't speaking about what happened. I suppose he is still in shock."

"A rather humiliating position for any man to find himself in — naturally he won't talk."

"And neither will you."

"It is sufficient that your men know I got the boar. I am exonerated."

"You made sure of that — you have a sexy voice, give us il catalogo of your love affairs this evening and your reputation is assured across Europe."

"Not likely," said Nick. "My modest half dozen isn't going to impress anyone."

Nick went off to shave properly — even for the virile St Hubert he wouldn't go to a party with a twenty-four hour stubble — and Tomás made a move to go, but I detained him.

"I know the music," I said "but what is that song really about that the men cheered him so triumphantly for it?"

"It's a farewell to the folly of love, and to the glory of *maschilismo* — guns and all that, big boots tramping over mountains — it's meant ironically. Mozart and Nick have a lot in common, including their feeling for the absurd."

"Do you know where Nick buried the baby?" I asked.

Tomás shook his head. Obviously not something he wanted to talk about.

"It doesn't matter," I said, "anywhere in the forest is all right, dust to dust, earth to earth and all that. I was just curious why he didn't want Dr Tsang to see it."

"Nick has his own peculiar sensitivities, especially around death. He is quite shaken by this; he feels responsible."

"I don't think so. I heard him and Tsang arguing while they were working together. Dr Tsang was troubled that Nick let it happen like this, kept asking him questions, but Nick wasn't a bit guilty about it."

"I said responsible, not guilty."

"Oh," I said, feeling foolish. Why was I still so bad at picking up such nuances? After all these years with Nick I should be able to listen more attentively.

The maid brought me my supper while Nick went to the feast to revel in the glory of being the one who had single-handedly located and shot the prize animal. When I was alone in the cottage I realised the eve-ning was likely to be a long one. Feeling dizzy I went to look in Nick's bag for any of his drugs that might steady me but they had such cryptic names in Nick's upside-down, wrong-way-round handwriting I didn't dare take any, but the meticulous labels made nonsense of Nick's claim to be illiterate. Unless of course the formulae were pure fantasy, his own secret code.

It was well after midnight when he came back, escorted by Tomás, Tomás laughing and Nick groaning and complaining.

"Never again," he said, holding his head. "After that appalling fire-water they toasted me with I feel brain-dead."

"Nick appeals to the German sense of humour," said Tomás, "they got great entertainment out of baiting him."

"How I detest them," said Nick, "All this enforced *Gemütlichkeit* fills me with atavistic distaste."

But his secret smile and the gleam in his eye betrayed how he had derived an equal pleasure from the encounter, "and the *Hubertus Verein* with feathers in their hats and loden coats — in my Armee fatigues I would have spoilt the stylishly heroic picture when they lined up with their guns around the boar, only I obscured myself behind the fat dentist from Hamburg; when it's developed I won't be there — how they despised me toting an unpretentiously functional service rifle instead of the fancy sporting guns they favour."

"Well you know they are demonstratively anti-military," said Tomas.

— contrary to Nick who was aggressively protective of what Paul called his *aidos*, Gus his *Selbstbestimmung*.

"Their moral superiority was somewhat deflated when I pointed out that some of their best guns came from my workshop."

"They were really quite annoyed with Nick," Tomás explained to me, "for not telling them sooner that he's a gunsmith by trade. Not a banker."

"They suspected me of bluffing to impress but my handiwork is signed by my talented engraver with an *ND & Deaths-head*. My catgut friend Mug channels them for me to a couple of exclusive outlets so I don't often have the opportunity to discuss my work with the people who pay the equivalent of an equally well-engineered automobile so they can swank on the shoot with guns so uniquely beautiful. I had them in a cleft stick; they couldn't do anything but admire my genius or else show themselves up for undiscriminating fools. But they can go home now and boast that they know who the elusive Totenkopf is."

The elusive Totenkopf! Another of Nick's cryptic personas. They all had a different story to tell.

"They got their jovial revenge," said Tomás, "by obliging him to eat the *suites*, the boar's cock and balls."

"I was happy to comply," said Nick. "The best bits of boar cooked to perfection by Donna — better than Maddie's zebu cock and salted grubs which kept me alive on my way back to chicken feet soup and matzo balls. I wanted Donna to include the brain; traditionally those are the parts of the defeated enemy one eats but Clare reminded me in time that hogs as well as men have parasites unpleasantly fatal to humans."

I was extremely sorry I had missed seeing that: Nick with his deft hands cutting up and with his discriminating nose relishing such indecent delicacies. And since his apprentice days he was well able to hold his own in German bawdy.

"Tomás's jovial huntsmen took to singing, urging me on to contribute what Tomás promised was my great musical talent to the general merriment but all I could think of was Joey's homesick song..."

"*The Rivers of Babylon*," said Tomás with a wry smile.

"Why is it that it comes into my head at the most inopportune moments? Joey and I silenced Mrs Dyer's 40th birthday party by singing it — I didn't mean to mimic Joey's 16-year-old voice but sometimes he just takes over — the Krauts didn't react other than with sympathetic applause but didn't hide the fact they consider me a spoilsport, quite apart from shooting the trophy animal in solitary glory instead of sharing him with the band of brothers..."

"It's comradeship the bankers from Frankfurt come here to enjoy," said Tomás.

"The only satisfaction in hunting is the thump of the bullet going into solid flesh," Nick concluded. "And it is so much more satisfactory to hit a man than a dumb beast — and I could have had what was left of his balls for breakfast too."

"Every human has to fulfil his own destiny," said Tomás, "It's not for you to interfere in the course of history."

339

"I will if I can," said Nick, unrepentant.

Tomás and Nick were prepared to discuss the morality of killing one's enemies, and indeed, how to define enemy, into the small hours of the morning, so I withdrew and went to have a bath in preparation for our journey home tomorrow. As I stood watching the water gush out of the tap I felt dizzy again; the water seemed to be making waves in the tub.

"Nick, Nick," I shouted, thinking I was about to faint.

There was no answer and I staggered across to the door. Neither he nor Tomás was there but there was a tremendous rumbling sound and the ground was shaking.

"I'm dying," I thought and for once Nick wasn't there when I needed him, so I sat down and waited for the worst. Almost immediately however the noise diminished and the earth stopped shaking. Not long after Nick came in, covered in dust but glowing with exhilaration.

"A great spectacle," he said, "I wouldn't have missed it for the world. At last Tomás got what was coming to him, the incompetent sod. Exactly what I said would happen, a little earthquake and half the crumbling mass comes down around his ears."

I went out on Nick's arm to join the crowd that had gathered to see the damage. The courtyard was covered in debris with fallen masonry and roof tiles strewn around, but actually it didn't look too bad. I thought, that would tidy up quite nicely. But when Nick took me to the chapel door where Tomás and Clare stood in stunned silence I could see the reason for his excitement: the floor piled high with heaps of rubble and broken furniture topped by ceiling beams like toppled matchsticks. If my new mattress were there, it was buried.

"Why aren't you digging with your bare hands," said Nick giving Tomás a shove with his bundling-into-touch shoulder. "That could be Sibylla under there."

"We haven't had anyone staying here since she left," said Tomás, stepping back out of Nick's way. It was not a wise thing to say.

"No, you wouldn't risk a German life there; you'd be sued out of existence.

Don't dare talk to me again about not taking revenge; any harm to Sibylla and I'd cut your heart out."

He was eager to dig in and get his hands dirty but luckily no one was hurt, so the Germans had an exciting addition to their hunting tales when they got home without having grounds to sue Tomás for damages.

Trembling, I hung on to Nick for support, but also to restrain the aggression the sight of such destruction aroused in him, the culmination of days of bloodshed and killing.

Contrary to his violent words however, after seeing me to bed, he spent the night helping Tomás establish the extent of the damage, together with one of the Germans, an engineer who incidentally had bought one of Nick's costly rifles from a dealer in Düsseldorf. After the boar suites and the *Rivers of Babylon* he was happy to be added to Nick's circle of conversationalists to talk him through his insomnia with matters of stress and resistance and how best to undermine the burden of the masses and build escape hatches for the spirit.

After all their consultations over Tomás's financial worries, Nick, to his annoyance, hadn't come up with any quicker solution than the one Gino had already been working on, the improvement of the wine so it could be classified as one of the better Chiantis and sold on the international market, rather than relying on his visitors and passing trade to take a few cases home. Nick had however found a Lloyd's insurer reckless enough to take a gamble on Tomás's quasi-Giotto frescos as works of art and this now paid off handsomely; Tomás actually made enough money out of their loss to pay for the repairs to the main courtyard of the castello, new mattresses for all the beds and something put aside for Marco's education, which was all they ever wanted. As Nick said right at the start of the discussion, what they needed was an earthquake; Nick had provided the solution.

Nikolai Chudotvorets: Wonderworker; Earth-shaker!

～

I travelled home cradled in the front passenger seat beside Nick who drove steadily on, taking only a short break when necessary to refuel. He never spoke much while driving but beneath his silence I felt deep reserves of emotion beyond the inexpressible erotic longing that united us, the spiritual desire to be one forever, in life or in death.

In a lucid moment in my semi-comatose, dreamlike state, remembering his promise to Gus and Adam, I said:

"I think you would have been perfectly happy for us to die together there on that mountain."

"That's the misfortune of being a Gemini," he said. "I defeat myself."

"*Liebestod* postponed," I said, "... again! I am very grateful because no matter how magic it is on the mountain with you, I have a duty to my husband and children."

"I'll give you magic mountains," Nick snapped back and abruptly veered off the autostrada, following his compass due north towards the implacable barrier of the Alps. No more tango along the Riviera, sexy rhythms that would never be recaptured. Instead, heights of thickening snow and dizzying views of sunless lakes deep below added to my illusion of existing out of time and space, helplessly in love with a man whose love had nearly killed me, beyond the laws of civic society. I held tight at every loop in the road remembering his earlier death-wish going over the edge in his high-speed Porsche...

But then, as if to demonstrate how he was equally in command at whatever level of civilisation he found himself, he wound his way back down to earth, to where the range of snowy peaks we had just transversed receded into a backdrop for factories and warehouses seemingly randomly scattered throughout a crisscross of roads and rail, the sky a cobweb of electric lines; heft-trucks and cranes busily at work amid high stacked piles of metal and concrete. I thought of Angelina complaining about the, in her eyes unnecessary, work done to her house, protesting how Nick couldn't leave well alone, his Swissy busyness, never satisfied that it couldn't be made better,.

"Bern," said Nick, crossing a bridge over a deep green river, "is a city like no other," and added after a moment's silence, "I need to do some shopping."

I surmised he had only just thought of that as an excuse for stopping, and in eager anticipation he drove the Jaguar into the heart of the old town. There he parked me at a cafe table with hot chocolate to keep me happy while he hurried to join the stream of people moving up and down in the busy arcades.

At my little table I was part of the pantomime of city life but I was dismayed at being abandoned in an utterly foreign place where I didn't understand a word of the language being spoken around me. Nick presumably had enough faith in the efficacy of his drugs to trust I wouldn't panic and run away. Besides, where would I go?

The nanny in me approved of the unfussy orderliness, the uniformity of sandstone houses sheltering a motley of cafes, shops and people under their buttresses, but — Why was I here? I felt lost in a place where I was nothing but a passing drinker of hot chocolate, a microscopic blip in their thriving economy.

Yet I had to smile as I recognised how Nick was displaying his usual skill, as when moving through the Renaissance Women, or the Germans at the castello, not allowing himself be deviated from his purpose by the required social exchanges, pausing only to shake hands in solemn greeting with people he met on the way until he was lost to sight amongst his fellow citizens, substantial men with the same unpretentious self-assured demeanour.

"*What's new on the Rialto, Antonio?*" Merchants of Venice came to mind, exchanging news, doing their business on the nod.

Waiting uneasily for Nick to return I listened to the rush of melting snow, out of sight in its underground channel down the middle of the street, aware of my emptiness but too drugged to feel the pain, distracted by trolleybuses passing every few minutes close in front of me, which, attached to their umbilical power lines, swerved up and down avoiding obstacles — such as the illegally parked Jaguar — but with no apparent regard for the pedestrians who sauntered across between them at their own pace, equally in possession of the cobbled street, a kind of orderly chaos.

They're all Nicks, I thought, all free spirits. This is his spiritual home, where he reached maturity and found his independence, cut loose from Hein and Bott.

I had finished the chocolate and was nearly through a large mocha ice-cream with a mountain of whipped cream on top which had appeared in front of me, presumably on Nick's instructions, when Nick re-emerged through the screen of grüezi's and air kisses, and opened the car door for me to get in.

"Are they all friends of yours?" I asked as he drove off.

Nick's gesture dismissed the question. He didn't do friends any more than he did lists.

"I lived out my bachelor solitude up there," he said.

Somewhere up there behind the window boxes and the flags... above the quietly busy cafes, and shops selling precious handcrafted goods, clothes, shoes, jewellery, untroubled by the weather... above the cellars where he played the piano, not dancing, his libido transferred to his Porsche, filling in the gap between the First Mrs Deathridge and me... guns too, the gun shop window display in the arcade suggested Nick's atelier above that Leon vehemently denied having any knowledge of — where May intended earning enough money to buy a bulldog — Leon Bolus knew he had been outmanoeuvred here but couldn't spot the deception.

Usually Nick played tediously repeating tapes of violin concertos, to dissect and gut them, he said, of their musical ideas, but now it appeared his cisalpine adventure had produced the need for something more heroic and he came back from his foray through the Bernese arcades with a selection of Wagnerian tapes — mercifully all orchestral so I didn't have to endure grandiose German voices keeping me awake all the way home. Nick kept up his long silences but he was nonetheless elated. The boar hunt had given him all the success and satisfaction he could have wished for. It would have been tactless of him to say so, but he had achieved everything he set out to do.

"My mad Quichotte," I said, putting my hand on his on the steering wheel, "in spite of everything, I do love you with my whole soul."

He dipped his head in acknowledgement and paused long enough in Boulogne-sur-Mer to feed me mussels and frites amid cries of encore du Muscadet.

A Nickish moment of inexplicable happiness!

~

When Nick delivered me home Gus expressed his opinion of us with a rueful shake of the head.

"You let this man take you boar hunting, seven months pregnant. You are both quite mad."

"He saved my life."

"That was the least he could do."

Nick said: "If Sibylla had miscarried here she would have gone into hospital; they would have tried to keep alive a baby nature rejected as unfit, and she might well have died of an infection. It was going to happen anyway so she was better off with me to deal with it efficiently and without anthropomorphic sentimentality."

"I'll update my thesis with a footnote on the Deathrage philosophy," said Gus. He smiled as he said it but he was beginning to see how the Deathrage might become more than a mere footnote to his own thought.

"Nevertheless," I said, lest in their philosophical arguments they overlooked my ordeal, "it was truly horrible, lying in the snow beside a dead boar, with the most dreadfully painful contractions. Nick is amazingly resourceful; his notion of a first aid kit doesn't stop at sticking plaster and a bottle of disinfectant."

"In my line of business I need to be self-reliant," Nick remarked off-hand, as if dismissing any praise, but pleased to have his skills appreciated. "The only thing that caught me a little off-guard was the loss of blood; but even so I knew I could cope, I knew from Tsang's interest in rare types it was safe to give you mine. Otherwise it could have been a risk too far."

"And to think that the night I met you," I said, unable to resist mocking

his self-assurance, "you backed off from the sight of Angelina having a normal birth in a clean bed, and your unwashed infant nearly made you sick."

"I'd never been in on a birth before; I had a crisis of conscience that my
wilfulness had forced such suffering on my lovely Angelina."

"So you fucked me regardless of how you'd make me suffer too."

"Yes, my Fabulous Cunt, and it was the best thing I ever did; our contract
is signed in blood."

"My blood..."

"I had reached a point of perfect equilibrium in my life when you came
along and sent me into a spin from which I've never recovered — not that
I've ever regretted it."

"You have come a long way since then."

"So have you," said Gus, indicating to Nick it was time for him to go.

It was only when I was safely in bed with Gus that I could face the full
horror of what I had been through.

"When I heard the shot," I told him, "I was sure it was Nick who had been
killed. I ran up the path and I could clearly see him lying dead with a hole in
his head, and do you know? I thought of how he used to worry about how to
shoot himself without spoiling his looks... of course I was hallucinating
because when I got to the top he was standing beside the dead boar... I was
utterly confused. I could hardly move and called his name and when he
turned around to look at me with the gun in his hand I felt the pain and fell
as if he'd shot me. It has been my recurring nightmare ever since he didn't
do it at our wedding."

"I'm afraid," said Gus with his arms around me, "that being a Sibyl is a
curse, not a blessing."

"Now I feel terrible about how often I've misjudged him. He is truly
awe-inspiring, a real hero. I just wanted to die, only Nick kept telling me to
have courage, with his blood and morphine he wouldn't let me die."

"All that matters to me is that he brought you back — that you came back."

"Dr Tsang was remarkably practical about the whole thing, he was pleased
it was a Grati boy baby he had bits of, it gives him an extra dimension to

work on. How lucky he was there so quickly, knowing how difficult it is to get hold of him. He could just as well have been tied up dealing with some film star in Hollywood."

"The unholy alliance of Tsang and Deathridge would have made arrangements beforehand how to handle the situation — should the eventuality arise."

"You think Nick was prepared for it to happen like that?"

"Obviously. In my profession I have to consider every practical and likely possibility, taking the characters and motives of the people involved into account."

I felt sick, as if my heart had been cut up and put under the microscope.

Having, intentionally or not, successfully eliminated the rival Grati, Nick took himself off about his business, checking by telephone on my mental and physical wellbeing, I presumed not to miss the next window of opportunity in my breeding schedule. It took me a while to realise that I had been converted into one of Nick's midnight friends until I found myself looking forward to his phone call and when it came settling down contentedly to that familiar voice so intimately in my ear, as if he were lying beside me, though I knew from watching him when I was curled up in his grandfather's chair wrapped in my camel robe and May in my belly kicking with impatience to get out, that he was probably sitting, leaning back with his feet against the edge of the table, the phone propped against his ear and his hands fiddling with something, a length of copper wire and pliers perhaps; or even, God help us, sitting up with a greasy rag or emery paper and a dismantled gun spread out in front of him. Nevertheless, the catches in the breath, the huskiness, the little grunts that punctuated his flow of words were so close that I could feel his body, his movements, capture his smell. When Gus complained from his side of the bed "do you realise you've been listening to that man for nearly two hours — could you tell him to kindly shut up?" that I understood Clare's protests to Tomás. Did Mr Hein make the same complaints to Eugenie?

I fell in love all over again, responding to the seductive flow of vibrations transmitted via the airwaves. From the instant our eyes met I had been held by his magnetism, but this was absurd. What Nick was actually doing remained a mystery. When asked where he was, his disembodied voice gave ridiculous answers such as "up the Orinoco, studying the drumbeats of the jungle."

"Oh, no, Nick, what are you really doing?"

"Do I ever lie to you? Trust me."

"Did you kill my baby?"

"If you mean murder, no. I may have mercifully shortened its pathetic little life."

Tsang too reported that he was becoming more difficult to keep track of, according to Tsang because, having made enough money out of their collaboration, he was now evading any further obligations.

Gus said: "The Tsang-Deathridge partnership it is coming unstuck. Tsang isn't Zen enough to cope with Nick saying he has done enough to help evolution along and withdrawing a couple of million from their research fund to pay for a violin instead."

"Nick lost faith in Tsang when he gave him an itchy penis," I said. "He is very unforgiving. It's really quite funny that he took the Guarneri in payment for giving his genetically superior sperm to Tsang's test-tubes; he was forever complaining that none of the women he so diligently spunked up loved him enough in return to buy him the violin he wanted."

"He does have a finely tuned sense of equivalencies," said Gus, quite impressed by the value Nick put on his balls.

I didn't mention the mutual threats exchanged over my miscarriage. If Tsang had identified any possible interference with nature — it might have been something as simple as cascara in the coffee — Nick clearly felt he had the upper hand, especially when he mockingly referred to the miracle of the multiple Nickies and Tsang's lack of progress in publicising it.

The transfusion of Nick's blood worked its miracle in me for months after. I was full of enthusiasm for my new life, and strangely light-hearted after the loss of my baby, as if a great burden had been lifted from me. The last vestiges of regret for Gianni were well and truly buried in the Tuscan woods.

"It's a terrible thing to say," I said to Gus, "but I feel free at last make a new start and enjoy our splendid house with our family and my utterly admirable husband. Nick doesn't believe in luck, but I do. How else did I get you? That was sheer fantastic good fortune."

"Of course it wasn't luck," said Gus. "Watching your fuck-artistry with Paul showed me that a girl like you would be highly satisfactory to do it with, so I got over regret for the somewhat painful pleasure of having Cats the Eagle do his thing ..."

"You horrible queer..."

"... until he dropped me and took a chubby-cheeked young bum under his wing — when I saw you I saw the future and all the mysteries of life unfold before my eyes. Admittedly it took patience to get you to see it too, but it wasn't luck."

'Predestination then."

"Now the Menace has done his damnedest let's hope he leaves us in peace for a while."

In defiance of Mary's disapproval, Julie came to see if the rumours of Mrs Wittersworth's place in the world lived up to the promise of the wedding in St James's. She arrived in her smart new Mazda sports car dressed to kill — me, if no one else — and told me that Biba hadn't come because she and Luigi had gone to Italy to see if they couldn't effect a reconciliation with Gino.

"The fact is," Julie said, "that they need him. Papa says that without Gianni and Gino it's hardly worth him carrying on the business, he might as well go and work in a restaurant and let someone else do the worrying. So they've gone to find out what can be done about him."

She stood admiring the view from the balustrade that demarcated the formal sweep of drive from the extensive well-kept lawns below. I remarked we were finding it difficult to get the boy who gardened for us to do anything but sit buzzing around on the lawnmower. Luckily the layout didn't require much else. To stretch his legs he'd occasionally walk about spraying weed-killer on the gravel.

"Is Gino still married to Guilietta?" I asked.

"As far as we know. We've heard nothing from him since... you know; it was Guilietta who wrote to say Gino had a serious accident that has left him with a bad limp and some other problems, and very depressed, but otherwise he is getting over it. But Gianni isn't going to get over it; Gino had better not come to England or I'll see he gets what he deserves. You ought to move that clump of trees higher up the hill."

My heart gave a thump. "An accident?... The trees are where Capability Brown left them."

"Well maybe your posh husband should look around for a better class of gardener to improve the view... Tomás said it was a fairly typical Italian accident. They don't go shooting in organised groups like here, but wander loose around the countryside with a gun and a dog. Mistakes happen."

"Yes, Nick says it is easy to fake a shooting accident. So you can stop fretting; Gino is already serving his sentence," I said. "I heard the shot shortly before I had my miscarriage. Nick congratulates himself that we both got what we deserved."

"That shark! But oh, Sibylla, why did it have to happen?"

She tiptoed to save her stiletto heels across the gravel until she reached the security of the stone steps where she paused to take a photo of me against the background of the loggia.

"Baggy jeans may be the fashion out here in the backwoods, Sibylla," she said severely, "but they don't disguise the fact you are very thin. This house is too big, too much hard work."

"I've got Meg and a girl for the work," I said. "I'm naturally thin when I'm not pregnant. Dr Tsang is watching my weight; he'll tell me when to fatten up again, the old bossy-boots, as if I do it to his orders."

I had to resist the impulse to ask Julie how Gianni was. Somehow, in my mind I still saw him living on in a shadowy nightclub existence amongst the women who would have done anything to gratify his desires, whom he had rejected for the sake of a hopeless and ultimately fatal love. I could never forget him singing that he would never forget me to the tune of *La Cumparsita* in that deserted ballroom where we didn't get married. The Malcontenta would be haunted by the ghost of the child who never was.

I led Julie in through the presiding Virtues to entertain her in keeping with the high style of her taking-tea-in-the country outfit — oatmeal jacket and skirt with a turquoise satin blouse. Pausing in front of Justitia she said: "Now your legal husband has stolen Augusta from us, what do you intend to tell her about her father?"

"Whenever the function of penises arises in conversation," I said, "— and it hasn't yet — I'm prepared to name the one that did that particular job for each of my children. It's just a sperm. The name makes no difference to their lives, for better or worse."

And I took her in to the drawing room.

"What a beautiful room!" she said. "So robustly functional. I had expected it to be full of swank."

"The architecture speaks for itself," I said. "Just like Gussie."

"But there is still room for aunties?"

"This family is blessed with a wealth of aunties."

By the time Julie left she'd have plenty to tell Mary and the rest of the Pinkertons about La Malcontenta. I had no hope of reconciling her to the loss of Gianni's baby, her loss was so much greater than mine. I had Gus and three children and might have more. Julie had nothing but regret. I was glad she had come; I needed her sharp tongue to keep me up to the mark and her sense of style was impeccable even if she hadn't a clue about gardens.

But I was sorry I'd lost Mama Biba.

"Paul dropped in to see me in chambers," said Gus. "He's just back from Greece where he met up with Nick — visiting his friends in prison before it's too late, says Paul, he is so indiscreet — and they went to Epidaurus together. Paul got Nick to sit up on the top row while he stood on the stage and gave a one-man enactment of his play; he says it's in homage to the spirit of

Aristophanes, a satirically updated *Iphegenia in Aulis*, child sacrifice for the sake of the great enterprise."

"Paul has so much love and respect for Nick, he'd do his best to make sense out of Nick's actions, however taboo," I said.

"Yes, he did it to show Nick that he can put his amoral deeds in a different context, give it mythological significance. He presented it somewhat in trepidation but I could have told him that he needn't worry, Nick would be deeply gratified to see his heroics immortalised in the cradle of civilisation, he'd think it fitting. And I was right: Nick promises to back him to put it on if Paul can get a production organised."

"Very Greek, " I said, "except it isn't clear to me which of his great enterprises Nick has in mind, hardly the killing of a boar. Or was it the final act of the Grati Circus?"

Why did I feel that between them I had been assigned the part of tethered goat, innocent participant in the drama of *maschilismo* played out between the Grati and Nick, with a troop of bawdy vineyard workers as chorus commenting on the action, cheering the victor? I thought of Tomás's men giving Nick the thumbs up when he sang them Figaro's mocking farewell, triumphant as Gino was carried away to the applause of the men who had been interested observers throughout.

"They won't be making horns at you any more either," I said to Gus. "Nick fixed him for good."

"I'll refer the morals of the issue to Father William," said Gus. "Law and justice is his thing; I'm too biased in this case to make a judgement."

It was reassuring to hear from Paul that Nick hadn't evaporated into thin air leaving just a voice on the phone as his presence on earth, but even his phone calls became less frequent and as the months went by I felt I was losing him, his absence creeping up on me as a distressing emptiness. At odd moments such as driving home from dropping May off at the village school I'd feel suddenly anxious that something was missing, that perhaps I'd forgotten something important, and that teasing glimmer of a smile would pass before my eyes, mocking me.

"I hate to admit it," I said to Gus, "but I miss him: not just the push-me-pull-you battles with his cock but the farcical wealth of incident and dramatic tension he creates around him; even, God help me, his whole peculiar approach to the business of life — and death."

"I'll check on where the liveliest revolutions are happening," said Gus "so you can send your Sibyllic signals out to bring him home."

"If he got his money out of the Greeks on their way to the gallows he's probably at the back of beyond fucking his African Queens... either or both of them, black and white."

"In that case it's a combination of all his main interests," said Gus.

It was Adam who winged him and brought him, along with Connie, out to visit us. I saw them from an upstairs window crossing the gravel and from that distance and angle Nick was obviously in his role as linchpin of his family, between father and son. Nothing to do with me. He came in, his spare lean physique radiating energy, one expected to see sparks flying — maybe he really had been up the Orinoco.

I ran downstairs to meet them. Up close Nick had an air of maturity about him that was quite impressively breath-taking.

"That's my wife you are embracing with somewhat excessive enthusiasm," said Gus.

"I need to reassure myself I didn't lose her on that Tuscan hillside."

"Ha!" said Gus. "So you admit you nearly did."

"I didn't think so at the time," said Nick with a flicker of acknowledgment, "but my nightmares tell me otherwise — as if I don't already have the Un-Dead in sufficient numbers stalking me... now you have imprisoned her in the image of La Malcontenta I'm suffering terrible deprivation."

He took me down with him onto the sofa in a parody of intercourse. I rubbed my cheek against his sleeve, recognising the suit from his formal nanny-fucking days in the basement, one of many. One I loved.

"Oh, come on, Nick, there are other women in your life," said Gus.

"Sibylla is the only one for whom I wake in the night howling in anguish — and I had her first, you double-dealing cheat."

"I don't suppose your cock has been totally inactive these last few months."

"I do my duty by my wives," said Nick, primly virtuous, sitting up but keeping me in a tight grip.

"How do you identify them as wives, Mr Deathridge?" said Gus in his best Regency manner.

"The ones I act as stud to, of course," said Nick. "Call it half a dozen. I've given up on Tsang and the Virgins and I don't quite include Maddie Madigan though she'd like me to; I would have included Mrs Shackleton if only she had let me — she was younger than the Virgins when I first fell in love with her. I must ask Tsang if he can't work his magic on a fine figure of a sixty-year-old; it would be a challenge for him to reactivate any residual eggs lurking in the last chance saloon. If he could achieve that for me I'd quit him of the Nickies and he might even forgive me for fucking up with the Virgins."

"The cuckoo clock was scandal enough for the Shackletons," Adam said, as usual driven to comment after doing his best to ignore Nick's nonsense. "You're not proposing to plant a cuckoo's egg in their nest as well?"

"If only," said Nick.

Connie was treating May and Augusta to Great-Uncle Harold's ginger-bread Baby Jesuses in the dolls' corner under the virtue of Verity when a row broke out, which reached a climax when May kicked Connie.

Connie came to appeal to Nick for permission to kick her back.

"Certainly not," said Nick. "You have to understand that women are allowed a greater leeway for physical violence than men. You'll have to find a different way of dealing with her."

"I was only telling her how you made the real live Baby Jesuses," said Connie. "She says I can show her when I have a big enough dickie. I said I'd rather do it with Augusta; she's prettier and she doesn't kick."

"Boy, you were asking for trouble there," said Nick shaking his head solemnly. "You'd better go and make it up with a kiss and a walk in the park. I blame it on that stupid Verity. Who wants to hear that kind of truth?"

I smiled as I wondered what theory Connie had passed on to May about the origin of the Nickies and looked forward to hearing it. I struggled free to sit beside Nick in a dignified manner. It wouldn't do to initiate another gang-bang under the reproachful eye of Chastity.

Adam said, "What is this strange notion Connie has? He has been acting mysteriously since you brought him back from your ski holiday, going around saying you are not his Dad. Angelina is getting embarrassed. She regrets she let you take him. It's like having a changeling in the house."

Connie, still resentful at being kicked, had remained skulking behind the sofa.

"Who am I, Con?" Nick asked, amused that Connie thought being out of sight was enough to deceive his father.

"You're Smiley," said Connie, sticking his head up over the parapet.

"And who is Smiley?" asked Nick.

"That's a secret," said Connie. "Nobody knows."

He dropped down out of sight again.

"What's this Smiley business?" said Adam. "You haven't been reading him le Carré? Isn't he a bit young?"

"You know that *Tintin* is the limit of my literary achievements, in balloons with pictures. No, Roger is the le Carré enthusiast. Since last year he has been running a spy ring in Gstaad — rather as I fought Waterloo on Cranborne Chase — and he allows me join in when I go to visit him. He was quite cooperative about recruiting a Junior Nikolayevich into the Service. Connie seems to like me in the role of Smiley."

"Fair enough," said Adam, "considering the kind of Dad you are. But where does Roger come in? I presume he is another of your bastards — of which there seems to be an increasing number."

"Not quite. After all his mother and I were married for five blissful years..."

"When you let slip the not uninteresting fact that the very attractive Mrs Hein once shared your bed as your lawfully wedded wife, you never mentioned the little complication of a child."

"... so there was nothing improper about us fucking for a child, admittedly some five years after the fact. As long as Eugenie had me she had no desire for a child as well."

"Hardly surprising," I said, "when you were little more than a boy yourself."

"By the time I was twenty-four I was man enough, I wanted a child, to recreate my perfect childhood for one of my own..."

"Perfect?" said Adam, "hardly that, surrounded as you were by violence and grief."

"Ideal in a Nietzschean sense," said Gus.

"Yes, blissfully perfect," said Nick, as usual indifferent to Adam's concerns, "I enjoyed every minute of it. Having sons is also a longing to recover the child who was lost when I lost my home."

Adam groaned. "Let's not have that all over again. There was a war on. The entire nation was losing their loved ones and homes. You were only one of many unlucky ones, and it was not too bad. You had a very substantial roof over your head, someone to take care of you, you never went hungry..."

Nick sighed in mock resignation at Adam's intransigence.

"Only my respect for the Fourth Commandment..." he said.

"Do not invoke the Fourth Commandment to me again," said Adam.

"... prevented me kicking back at Papi Bott when he blamed my uncircumcised cock for my failure to get him grandchildren. I proved him wrong with Roger."

"Hardly a valid reason for getting a child!"

"Perhaps not, but it certainly added to my satisfaction. After I decided that being suicidal over Eugenie was a waste of my life, I left my safe career behind and returned to the point where everything went wrong, when my grandfather shot himself. He had told me I'd have to make my own future so I started again where he left off. My life as Conrad Dumez's grandson is the one where Angelina is my ideal wife and Con and Joe are my boys, Sibylla my cunt-to-die-for..."

His grandfather's presumed approval of a cunt-to-die-for must have been an added dimension to fucking in his armchair...

"So, meeting Eugenie again on neutral ground in Geneva, the city of reconciliations, I finally mended my broken heart and gave her my all as dutiful ex-husband..."

I thought of Dolly's description of Nick, red-faced from sun and wind on the lake, wandering off with some Swiss acquaintance while Angelina's girl-friends tried to persuade her that before she agreed to marry him she was an idiot not to find out if his po-faced lack of humour was compensated for by a lively enough cock.

"... and I delayed her as long as possible over coffee arguing about who was to blame that we weren't still married — simply to give my buggers a chance to swim upstream before she changed her mind again. So that's how, foreskin and all and with the aid of a sick-making quantity of coconut-cream meringues, I got Roger."

"Did you get me with meringues?" a hopeful small voice asked from behind the sofa.

"No, son, I got you straight, with love, no nonsense. Happily for us your mother is not a tricky witchity but the loveliest lady in the whole world."

"But your Roger is a boy with brains?" I asked, laughing at his satisfaction at having the best of both worlds.

"Of course, first class."

Connie popped his head up again at this.

"Have I got brains?"

"Come here," said Nick, and when Connie came around to stand in front of him, Nick felt his head between his two hands.

"Well," he said, "it's either a lot of brain or else it's a very thick skull. We'll have to wait and see."

"I'm Mrs Wittersworth's little boyfriend, you know," said Connie, edging closer. For once Nick didn't tell him to scamper so he climbed up over us to drape himself full length on the sofa-back behind our shoulders.

"Magnificent Eugenie," said Nick, shrugging Connie into a more comfortable position, "she was a brilliant wife for a young man but now that she has Roger she has more respect for me as father of her son than she ever had when I was her goy-boy husband. But I am terribly unfortunate with women. I fuck my heart out for all of you and you all treat me badly: Mrs Shackleton wouldn't allow me in further than the elastic of her marvellously generous knickers would stretch however much passion I put into pleading with her to give just a little bit more; as soon as I grew up and got serious Eugenie told me to fuck off; Maddie tries to poison me — she may yet succeed; Sibylla snared me into her shameful gang-bang…"

"That was a long time ago; you are very unforgiving…"

"Why should I forgive? You wouldn't hesitate to do it again if the fancy took you — and I'd fall for it all over again."

Mind-reader.

"Your story gets more and more unlikely," said Adam. "I don't know how you can complain about women treating you badly when so many are willing to let you… you know what I mean." He stopped out of consideration for Connie pretending to be a lion cub asleep dangling along the limb of a tree with pricked ears.

"Eugenie caught me by my stiff willie when I was eighteen and now she realises that it's a fountain of pure gold she can't let go."

"If Hein is the wronged husband," said Adam, "he seemed surprisingly affable about your performance with Mrs Hein at the piano —love songs is one thing but the uncompromisingly sexy rhythm of *Burning Love* is something else —but he seemed to find it quite amusing."

"He would, after all he thought stealing my wife from me quite a joke too, positively hilarious. So after I planted my red-poll cuckoo in his well-feathered nest, and his discreetly blameless attempt to eliminate me was a failure — imagine his dismayed giggles when I made it back across the deserts of Africa, bolder, feistier and randy-dandier than ever — we consider ourselves quits."

"This casts a new light on your fantastic story. I can't help thinking you are maligning the good man," said Adam.

"No," said Nick, "I trust his judgement — I used to consult him on manufacturing problems and, bearing in mind how successfully he exploited me, on labour relations. Now he wants me back on his board so he can pick my brains but I tell him to piss off. *Genug schon* — enough already!"

"It's quite nice to know I'm not the only man you fuck," said Gus.

May came looking for Connie and was indignant to see him enthroned in a place of privilege on top of his father and her mother but he succeeded in repelling her attempt to join him.

"If you and your sons are running a spy ring in the high Alps, don't you think you should include May?" I said.

"Only if you are prepared to risk it," Nick said. "I can't guarantee she won't go hurtling over a precipice or get swept away by an avalanche. Boys are expendable but it would be a pity to lose a promising young female."

His off-hand disregard for life never ceased to trouble me.

"Nothing like that ever happened to me," said Connie.

"I can see why Angelina says you're a dreadful father," I said.

"Boys have to learn how to handle the hazards of the natural world not to be useless as men. Sure there are going to be losses in the process but that's nature's way of weeding out the incompetent..."

"Or the unlucky," I said.

"Same thing."

"Another footnote to the Deathrage School of Philosophy," said Gus.

"Well I suppose," said Adam, "if you are going to take such a cavalier attitude to losing the odd son or two it makes sense of why you have so many."

"Are you expecting any more?" asked Gus.

"Sibylla may yet oblige," said Nick with calculated mischievousness, "and the Virgins should have been good for a few more but for Wilhelmina performing *goena-goena* in the background. No luxuriating in the afterglow of a good fuck with the witch around and the Virgins in a duet of weeping and wailing and love-mad sobs begging for mercy."

Nick's squeaky falsetto mimicked the pretence of maidenly dismay, fading to heartbroken whimpers and moans of surrender — "They're having fun, really," Connie whispered in my ear.

"It's too much trouble. You know how long it takes me to ejaculate," Nick went on deploring the cruelty of women. " Tsang says it's a psychological resistance to letting go, a consequence of wallowing in mother-fucking nightmares; but so what? it prolongs the ecstasy as well as the agony."

"We've loads of babies in our house," Connie confided to May who had succeeded in climbing up from behind. "The Aunties grow them for us in their tummies..."

... love-apples in a greenhouse...

"I saw them coming out, all slimy and pinkie with tiny little willies. You can have one when they're bigger. Dad says we'd be getting more only he'd have to get the better of Willymina — she's evil. She made us eat bits of billy-goat on a stick with coconut and peanuts, gooey and gorgeous. Golly, she can't half cook! Our mum is useless."

"Anyway, the clairvoyant on St Barths said I'd have ten and that's approximately what I've got — you and May had better go for a walk now. Ask the Ancient about the birds and bees." Nick stood up, dislodging Connie and grimacing as he slithered down with a well-aimed knee as he went.

May was more interested in beehives than babies but Connie followed her reluctantly, knowing he would be missing more gems of paternal wisdom.

"Your Connie is a surprisingly well-behaved little boy in spite of what he sees of your unruly carry-on," said Gus, "Why haven't you given Angelina back the peace of her own home yet? Father is terribly disappointed that she wouldn't go through with legal proceedings against you, Nicolai Pasha."

"Happily my boys have my intelligence," said Nick. "They can see that correct behaviour is a question of what's appropriate to the occasion. Their mother behaves with perfect dignity and I treat her with respect. Auntie Rose and Auntie Violet make a game out of their skittishness and I do whatever gives them pleasure. Their pottiness knows no bounds; Con and Joe find them highly entertaining — so do I."

Oh, Nick!

He wandered over to the window to watch Connie and May race down the drive. Augusta stayed behind under Prudence feeding her dolls and Willie the leftover gingerbread Jesuses.

"Our outing with the goat to get her mated was great theatre," said Nick, coming back to sit with Adam and Gus. His dry-humping act had been a bit of theatre too, to assert his sexual and moral authority.

"What we need," said Gus, "is a small flock of nice curly sheep as lawn mowers instead of that lazy boy. I'm sure Meg's Ancient would be a good shepherd."

"Jacob Bott would take delight in identifying my sons as Cain and Able." Nick was not interested in lawnmowers. "Joe hopes the kid is a girl so he can keep her for himself to milk, Con wants a billy he can kill and eat: the eternal conflict between husbandry and hunting. Every time I visit Bott we end up having the same futile argument; he interprets the story in his patriarchal way and refuses to see that it's really about the unstoppable progression in which the land-grabbing Cain kills the wildlife-conservationist Able. Able has lost the fight nearly everywhere though it's still being fought out on a large scale in Africa: elephants or cassava; on the Pampas: beef or soya beans. When my boys are older I'll send them to Maddie, she'll sort out their priorities."

"This Maddie you talk about," said Adam, "I didn't realise she is that blond Amazon you were fucking under the table at your wedding. Talk about inappropriate behaviour, I suppose you think it was appropriate that you were rolling on the floor as if she were your..."

He stopped short, avoiding Nick's forbidding ice-cold eye.

"I am so maligned," said Nick. "The ridiculous slander that circulates about me!"

His face was turning red with annoyance that this story simply wouldn't go away.

"You mean it wasn't true? What we saw with our own eyes?" said Adam, also annoyed that he had become embroiled again in this ever-recurring argument.

The fly-button story: at last I might hear what that was really about and Gus too looked from Adam to Nick... he already had a collection of witness accounts of Nick's wedding in his Book of Evidence, but this promised to add a new twist.

"If only I'd had the time!" Nick sighed with regret. "But I'm too slow a fucker to bring that off. All that happened was, Maddie had perched herself on my knee — remember how tight the chairs were due to parsimonious Mother Furzy not allowing enough room for all the Switzers so they had to crowd in — why go to the Dorchester if one has to count the cost? Maddie, in her tactless Boerish way, said to Angelina that she tried to marry me herself only it was like trying to chain a bull elephant; she hoped Angelina's success would last a little longer and she'd get more out of me than a couple of murderous fucks. Sweet Angelina, who had already had an emotional day, was dreadfully upset so I tipped Maddie out of my crotch and she slid between my legs under the table."

"and you dropped down on top of her," said Adam.

"She had me by the short and curlies but I should have known better; I laid myself open to a singularly diabolical attack. Angelina was hanging on to the tablecloth for fear we'd drag it and all the china with us onto the floor."

Not Angelina's somewhat censored version of what happened!

"One of the many times when being your father has been deeply shaming. And I was sitting across from you beside Mrs Rigby, the Headmaster's wife! She's rather deaf and demanded loudly to know what the commotion was while my only thought was how to evade trying to explain this embarrassing imbroglio."

"Maddie came determined to wreck my marriage but it was only another round in the hilarious sport of catch-Nick-with-his-trousers-down — the Deathridge Wedding Games: she wasn't the only one to challenge me that day."

Adam looked discomfited. He was having to admit that, outrageous as Nick's behaviour was, he had also been on the receiving end of a relentless onslaught of baiting from his compeers, both male and female.

"Still, the sight of that black man dragging you out by the heels was quite impressive," he said. "You were lucky to get away with nothing worse than a shaking."

"Even my own father slanders me," complained Nick, exasperated. "Broer Joep didn't shake me. He rescued me from the clutches of an aggressively jealous woman."

"And buttoned up your fly for you..."

"With dignity and discretion," said Nick. "A pity really; imagine what a climactic end to a dull dinner — a Lewis Carroll moment: Maddie and me fucking to the death amid the clatter of cutlery and all the guests jumping up in a flap like a pack of playing cards tossed in the air! I must tell Maddie the next time I see her what fun we could have had if only she hadn't... well, done what she did... at the time my only thought was how to get out alive and with my tackle intact."

Nick took a moment to contemplate his alternative scenario then added, "Maddie Madigan thinks that she is entitled to torment me — did she think I wouldn't dare fuck her — even at my wedding? She made the same mistake that was fatal for Joey. When have I ever backed down before a Madigan?"

At last! I looked to see if Gus was paying attention when at last Nick might make some admission about his part in the Russian Roulette.

"They never identified the source of the bullet... or found the gun," said Adam. He too was quick to take advantage of Nick's defensiveness concerning the Madigans.

Nick moved restlessly around the room, stopping at the tall looking-glass between the windows to frown at himself reflected there with the three of us, watching and listening, behind him.

Reflections are so transient, I wished Gus could capture this moment with his Leica, but Gus respected Nick's taboo.

"Grandfather used to have a large framed photo in his room," said Nick, catching my reflection and bouncing it back at me. "I loved it because it seemed to be the essence of me, very formally posed, a sulky cherub on Bonne-Maman's lap... I can still visualise it clearly: Bonne-Maman restraining my left hand in a characteristic gesture, evidence that she had just popped the thumb out of my mouth like the pop of a champagne cork causing the pout, while my right fist is already on the way up to replace it."

"The baby I never knew," said Adam.

"My heart melts with love for the child I was and for Bonne-Maman who defined my place in the world: the lap I sat on and the hands that held me. I was all there already: the little feet with the wriggly toes that made the perfect no.15, running and kicking with equal power from either side of the field; the piano playing hands; left hand for finesse with the knife, right hand trigger finger...."

"They didn't send me photos," said Adam. "They wanted to keep you for themselves."

"When Bonne-Maman didn't come home, Grandfather burnt her albums full of photos: her with Maman, with me, himself as a young man at the height of his power; we all went up in flames. I watched us curl up and die in his fireplace. Joan of Arc on the scaffold couldn't have suffered more or her child, if she'd had one, watching her than I."

I took a devious route to approach him from the side, avoiding the reflection, and took his arm to guide him back to the sofa. He continued talking as if he hadn't noticed the move even though he held me tight, his consolation and talisman against misfortune.

"When I played cowboys Grandfather took my Great-grandfather Yussupov's Nagant M1895 out of his drawer for me to shout bang with; it was heavy and I couldn't pull the trigger but it was beautiful. I wanted to sleep with it under my pillow but he wouldn't let it out of his room... he left it on his desk for me to find — he used the other one to shoot himself with — so I took it before anyone came. I emptied his document case into his desk drawer, and then I went to the bathroom and got the razor, so I had the two best things safely stowed in the only strong case with a key I could carry as a child. I sat in the kitchen eating raw carrots for my eyesight until someone came and found him. I forgot about the Highbury tickets until it was too late that's why I had to climb in the window to rescue them."

I could see the questions on Adam's lips, but we were too mesmerised listening to Nick's careful explanation of what happened to speak, thinking of this little boy already showing the resourcefulness in a crisis that saw him scale mountains and fly solo across continents.

"It's a pity you lost the Dumez-Yussupov's hoard of obsolete currency," he said, adding to his grievances against his father. "The gold and silver would have set Roger up for life in the gnomic world of banking."

"I had more urgent things than Conrad's junk to worry about at the time — it's probably somewhere in a bank vault, all that's lost is the key."

"What is junk to you is treasure to me," said Nick, "but no lack of judgement on your part surprises me... The case had C D stamped on the leather so I got a needle red hot on the stove and burnt and scratched to change the C into a D and added an N in front so it became N D D the way he taught me — you see I'm not completely analphabetic. I kept it under my bed at school."

The case even Toby wasn't allowed to see inside.

"I was trying to get Joey to accept my Chaos Theory and we were arguing about chance and how it works, that's when I showed him the Nagant. I told him that officers always kept the seventh cartridge in the barrel in case they needed it for themselves and when they were retreating from the Reds they turned it into a game of chance to prove how brave they were in spite of losing their country. Obviously my Great-Grandfather survived, so the bullet had to be still in the gun."

"Your grandfather would hardly have let you play with it if it was loaded," said Adam. "Even Conrad wasn't that mad."

"I felt it would be cheating fate to look. Joey dared me to put it to my head and see if it worked. I said I would if he would."

"You took the first shot?" wagered Gus.

"Of course. Toby was supposed to be acting as referee but he's pretty clueless when it comes to abstract concepts, that's why he's still dealing with small matters of boundaries and title deeds. He should have taken the pistol from me, spun the barrel and passed it over to Joey. But he was dithering so Joey grabbed it off me himself."

Nick was so phlegmatic about it I wondered if even now he felt the full horror of what he'd done.

"Chaos Theory was working for me, that a group of birdwatchers on the far side of the lake swore they saw us three taking turns and the splash when Joey dropped it and it fell in the water above the weir. Of course the divers never found it because what the boys saw splash was a stone I kicked in. I was thrilled when I discovered that the same cartridges as the SIG P210 fit the Nagant so I can use it myself when I need to. It's the one I took to your wedding, not the neater, flatter SIG: a purely romantic, one might say historically significant decision. Your father, Gus, kept me talking."

"I know," said Gus. "Paul told us you'd spent the night before polishing it."

Complete silence followed this.

I had a picture of myself nursing my baby, talking to Mary and Julie, and Mary remarking how Nick was white-faced in his morning suit personifying Death, while Gus and Paul staged a mock fight on the lawn between him and me.

Adam and Gus withdrew from this conversation and as Gus closed the door behind them Adam was saying:

"That dauntless spirit is both better and worse than I realised."

Their footsteps faded in the direction of the archive. The children's voices were no longer in the hall. I lay against Nick listening to his heartbeat. His hand on my hip asked a question and my answer was a yes.

It was already dark when Nick said: "I'm rubbish at killing myself."

"Surely you realise, Nick my sweetheart, that if you shoot yourself it won't be like in *Taxi Driver*; you won't see blood dripping artistically down the walls in muted Kodachrome."

"It may well be exactly as in *Taxi Driver*: I may have, for a few dying minutes, the illusion of perfect happiness, thinking that everyone, even you, loves and admires me."

∼

La
Malcontenta

15

O n the 31st May 1980 we were finally ready to hold our grand inaugural party for La Malcontenta. The house had been built exactly two hundred and twenty-five years ago, and after the years of austerity and neglect it was now entering a new era of glory with Gus at the helm.

It was a gathering not only of our friends and relations but Gus's associates, and Father William brought his colleagues along to help launch Gus on his meteoric career in the legal profession and, with Father William holding forth under the Virtue of Justice in the hall, the setting was wholly appropriate.

Gus had sent a splendidly crested and gilded letter by special courier to his grandfather. "Actually," he said, "it will be his hundredth birthday and he's still going strong. Poor Mother! But of course he won't come. It looks as if I'm going to be the lowly Hon. Gussie for nearly ever, so Paul can go on gloating that I'll be abolished before I get a chance to voice my reactionary opinions in the House."

It didn't seem to worry Gus unduly. He had a good enough forum for voicing his opinions as it was.

I sent my mother a letter to which she responded with a postcard saying: thank you for your invitation. I'm sure it will be lovely.

This wasn't very enlightening but I supposed it meant she was coming. I sent one back saying: "If you let us know when and how you are travelling we will meet you. Otherwise take a train from Waterloo."

We heard nothing more and I didn't really expect her.

As Meg helped me address envelopes I told her I was sending an invitation to Mrs Deathridge alone, not Nick.

"Though I know perfectly well," I said, "that even if Nick has to come by yak from Outer Mongolia he won't fail to turn up — Mrs Shackleton's bad penny — but with our wedding party in mind I'll be quite relieved if he doesn't."

"He's not in Outer Mongolia," said Meg.

"How do you know?" I asked, taken aback by her confident denial, not that I meant my remark to taken seriously.

"Gladys says Sir made a serious pile of dollars selling his stash of Bobuto silver to the mad Yanks and is in Rhodesia buying up all the platinum he can get hold of while the going is good, he says, nothing else is worth the bother otherwise he might just as well walk to the Claraplatz and buy gold over the counter but there's not much profit — or excitement — in that..."

"Really, Meg! You know all along where he is and you never tell me..."

"You never ask me."

Why was I surprised? Meg had always known him better than I did. Nevertheless I was annoyed that while I was anxious and heartsick over him it never occurred to her to put me out of my misery. Perhaps like Tomás she considered it only proper that I should suffer for love.

"Well maybe you'll tell Gladys to tell him I don't want him here making mischief. I'll have enough to occupy me just with being Mrs Wittersworth."

Nevertheless, getting ready, I dressed for our grand reception in my most beautiful mermaid frock, the one I chose to please Nick at the château, the one I was wearing when he demonstrated to me that his erotically charged tango movements were not just dancing's equivalent to sex, but a sublime experience of a complementary nature, transcendently absolute in its own right.

My Armani, with its slinky pleats like little sea-green waves, happily adapted to the ever-changing line of my breasts, belly and buttocks, at present in perfect equilibrium. I was grateful that Clare had persuaded me not to throw it in the bin after our Mystical Itinerary when again Nick had left me feeling naked, bereft of the meaning he attached to my appearance.

Putting it on again, in my room upstairs, in spite of all that had happened in the intervening years, I relived that orgasmic dance moment with Nick's thighs, the provocatively satirical turn of his lips poised tantalisingly close as a challenge to how one should respond to his advances. He was hardly less of an enigma to me now, with his unexplained absences and the uncertainty of his presence, his sporadic intrusions into my life leaving me all the more blessedly thankful for my life with Gus. Only in moments of domestic crisis when the hot water failed to flow or I couldn't find where Willie had hidden my car keys did I think momentarily of our empty refuge-on-the-Thames and wished he'd come back and unlock the door for me.

I took Gus's arm and paused nervously at the top of the staircase to look down on the guests assembling in the hall below.

"You could just pose here looking beautiful," said Gus, eager to get on. Grown to his full Wittersworth stature, with his Palladian villa and his classical intelligence, nothing could shake the self-assurance that came along with such a birthright.

"Honestly, Gus, sometimes I think you regard me as much part of this house as one of those Virtues on the wall."

"My Sibyl, you are," he said, "only more so: you are La Malcontenta herself. The Wittersworth who built this house must have had you in mind, knowing that you were bound to turn up, all in good time. I knew it the minute I saw you that you were destined to stand here on this spot, on this day, and be my wife."

"Good grief, Gus, that's a bit of wildly speculative philosophy, coming from you. I don't think you wrote anything like that in your thesis."

"I did really; read it again and see if you can spot it. It's just a matter of interpretation."

"It sounds more like Nick's Chaos Theory,"

"Same thing."

The Hon. Henrietta arrived with Amanda and the two little Bolus girls — at the end of the day she would have to go home in the Bentley with Father William and Evita.

"Poor Mother," said Gus, "she finds it easier to tolerate Father having Evita in bed with him than not having a chauffeur for the motor; then the seating arrangement with Evita in front would be more obviously correct."

However, going home with a Bolus granddaughter to sit on either side of her on the broad back seat would take away the ambiguity of her position. Amanda would have other plans, come the evening. Jane had gone back to the Mata Atlântica to lead wildlife expeditions, Diana was still sailing around the world in easy stages and Polly sent word from Mullingar that her best bloodline mare was about to foal. Gus was quite relieved at the lack of sisters to cramp his style.

Paul came with Madge and Adam. He was still, thanks to Nick's encouragement, in thespian mode in a flashy striped blazer though Madge was determined to see he made himself known to any figures of political influence.

Adam wandered around looking at the Virtues with professional interest in the heroic interpretation of female anatomy. When he was identified as an artist he was taken in tow by the Hon. Henrietta and marched around the motley collection of the house's art works and made to give his not-very-expert opinion of them all.

"All those weird Wittersworth men," she said, pointing out the portraits, "no wonder William and Gussie are lewd as coots, not to mention the Ancient of Days sitting on his throne, an embarrassment to us all."

The Ancient of Days's existence remained a mystery to me though Gus tried every so often to arrange an audience for us. Gus had moved the portrait by Watts to a place of honour over the drawing-room mantelpiece as it was nicely allegorical, showing his ancestor as a young man between the two globes, the originals at present in the archive, turning his back on the terrestrial and reaching for the constellations. The Hon. Henrietta hated it.

"If only my dear father-in-law had paid more attention to his position in the Empire instead of star-gazing, William wouldn't be so penniless now," she complained, which seemed unfair when Father William earned a good living by his own efforts. Hardly penniless, even if he drove his own Bentley.

"Let me add to the circle of your admirers," Father William said as he took my hand and tucked my arm under his elbow. With Willie dangling energetically on my other hand, we circulated amongst the groups of his friends, being introduced as 'Gus's wife and the youngest Wittersworth'.

Nick's dress gave me confidence, and it was also an advantage that I had had the pleasure of Father William's flatteringly fervent love-making; it made it possible to see all these genial older men as so many potential lovers rather than elders I need be overawed by. Out of exuberant gratitude I kissed him.

"Mrs Wittersworth," he said, "I am your humble, devoted servant; please don't incite me to any more acts of folly because I couldn't possibly say no."

Angelina came in Dolly Miller's latest Cadillac, the rear section of which had been converted into a spacious play area for Nickies One and Two, with their guardians Connie and Jo-jo. In fact Dolly called it the Nickiemobile as she had installed two independently swivelling and tilting little thrones, which gave them the maximum freedom of movement.

"My goodness," said Amanda when she saw Angelina coming in with a Nickie on either arm, looking very much as if they were her own cherished darlings. "Lucky you, that your husband provides you with such pretty baby dolls."

I was disappointed they weren't wearing their seal pup hats, but the 31st May was a warm day. Their sweet round faces with pouty pink lips and little pointy chins were almost totally obscured by wide brimmed linen hats from Samaritaine where the Virgins went shopping when they wanted to impress Nick with how sensible they were and prudent with money.

"The Renaissance Women have taken the Virgins to Sanibel Island," said Dolly, "to give them a holiday and get fit for if there is to be another set of Nickies. We are all supporting them and the Doctor to the end, only it's a pity they wouldn't agree to let the Doctor do it the way he wants, by artificial insemination, but they say they won't bother if they can't have the fun of getting Nick to chase them with his dick... personally I think he overdoes it, he chases a bit all too enthusiastically."

"The Women are studying the egrets," said Angelina, "and the Aunties went along hoping they'll pick up a few feathers for their hats. Nick says he has a bundle of dollars handy for if he has to go and bail them out of a Florida jail and a small jet standing by for emergencies — he'll be terribly disappointed if nothing happens, he is such a romancer."

Angelina parked the Nickies with Evita who immediately recognised their status as budding wonder-workers and took Polaroids of them to send home to Manila. Dr Tsang joined her on the sofa and together they plotted a possible world tour with the precious babies: a far-fetched compromise between anthropology, genetic engineering and religious mania.

Dr Tsang had come with Elsa, whom I hadn't seen since she went to Hong Kong on my ticket, and Julie with Xin. The Grati sisters instantly raised the tone of beauty and stylishness with their presence. Seeing Xin playing with Augusta I felt a pang of regret that relations with Biba and Luigi had broken down since they had gone to Italy. I had been taken aback by the ruthlessness with which Gus and Tsang, in the politest possible way, used Gus's accumulated evidence, not only his photographic record but his samples of Gianni's blood on the sand and other items of interest, to gain possession of the children: Augusta officially a Wittersworth, and Tsang had his Xin as planned, with Elsa to care for her, relieving Biba of her Chinese incubus. Dr Tsang's Buddha smile was as sweet as ever but I thought he looked aged. He had got himself more than he bargained for with Elsa knowing her own mind on one hand and Nick keeping a firm grip on the private lives of the Virgins on the other.

"Dear Sibylla," he said, "I am happy to see you looking so well but it breaks my heart to see what a beautiful woman I might have had if only you had said yes to me. I loved you for your lightness, your playfulness but your frivolity took away my peace of mind. Life without you is nothing but work and worry."

"Oh, you do talk nonsense, Tsang Jun. The only person who upset your Buddha repose was the devil Deathridge. I'm surprised your Zen couldn't deal with him."

Talking of the devil, Nick came in accompanied by Toby, Toby complaining that the new Jaguar was scarcely more comfortable for a well-built man than the old one. Toby was looking good in quite a smart suit. Nick must have vetted him before allowing him to join the party — Nick himself was brilliant as a summer's day.

Nick went straight over to Angelina and kissed her.

Damn him, I thought, he wasn't invited so now he's ignoring me, the hostess. Dr Tsang had the grace at least to act as if he still loved me.

"My dearest Mrs Deathridge," Nick said, "every time I see you I am bowled over with love just like the first time at the Royal Exchange. It is a privilege to call you my wife."

Angelina looked doubtful. What meaning could one attach to anything Nick said?

"Are you coming home this evening?" she asked.

To-morrow, 1st June, would be Nick's birthday so her question was putting him to the test.

"I have a previous engagement, my beloved," said Nick.

From that I gathered he hadn't been home recently.

"How are my precious little Nickies?" he asked.

"Did you have to come here to find out?" Angelina said. "I have Alexi and Boris sleeping with me for company, but there's still room in the bed for you if you care to join us. Wilhelmina has the little ones up in the nursery, sleeping on the floor beside her on mats. I leave that for you to deal with."

They looked each other in the eye, at first challenging, then wryly, quizzically smiling.

I was reminded of the way they faced each other across the table at Father William's. Until then, in all the years I had known them, there had been an air of remotely beautiful emotional coolness between them; but at the very moment when their perfect marriage seemed under threat they had never appeared more intimate. Now I felt it again, an emotion so deep, an understanding so great it surpassed the physical desire of a lover. For all the fire in his genitals and the sobbing in his heart with which he declared his love for me, this was the exemplary union of husband and wife. Truly their ideal marriage.

I looked away; my familiarity with them both made my gaze an intrusion.

I was thankful I had run away with Gino when I had the chance. Gino was the catalyst. I hadn't gone to Gianni, only away from Nick. It was of little consequence to Angelina to know that her husband was fucking the nanny in the basement. The only thing she ever begrudged me was Bonne-Maman's ring. I was never a rival Mrs Deathridge, any more so than Maddie Madigan with her jellied zebu cock.

I turned to Father William with tears in my eyes, seeking his reassurance, and heard Nick remark to Amanda, "Do you believe me now? Look at them. Can't you just imagine them in an amorous embrace getting merry on my Dom Pérignon. Ask your father if he enjoyed it."

"Deathridge keeps a good cellar," was Father William's comeback. "I hope he is equally enjoying the Wittersworth hospitality."

With that he returned to his duties with Gus's interests at heart, mingling with his colleagues and cronies under Prudence in the hall.

How long would Nick hold out against me, as if he didn't see me? I remained frozen in the middle, surrounded by the people who made up my world but in my head I was still coming down off those snow-high mountains and reliving the anxiety of seeing him disappear into his other world, moving slowly through the friendly non-friends who closed ranks around him. I had lost something of my Nick in that moment when he was lost to sight amongst the grüezi's.

That day I had waited for him, sipping hot chocolate with my eyes fixed on the spot where he was abruptly not there, but he had reappeared unexpectedly from behind a moving trolleybus turning a corner, startling me as if he were a stranger in his dark coat and neat chestnutty head. He said he'd been to see his barber for a proper haircut and shave not to go back to London looking like a savage and when I protested, admitted he really went to hear at source what was the latest news around town. I was upset that he'd left me alone while he went gossiping, but unperturbed he pointed out that there is no such thing as gossip in Switzerland. Which maybe explained why it was difficult to have any easy small talk with Nick though he could worry any topic of substance to death, a bloodhound digging up the bones of truth.

I came down off my magic mountain in time to hear Amanda's response to his remark about her father: "You iniquitous man, telling me all those risqué stories, pretending you didn't remember me. I certainly knew you from the time you had us all gathered around for Joey's Wake, knocking on the coffin to get him to wake up. It was quite uniquely outrageous."

"Do you remember I was there too?" said Toby. "Probably not, I was only one of those insignificantly black-suited schoolboys..."

"Of course she remembers you," said Nick, "the nice boy sitting beside me with your magnificent mother who held my hand trying to stop me making a fool of myself... she didn't succeed... on the contrary, I went one better when I wheedled my way into her bed... did she tell you...?"

"Oh, go away, Deathrage," said Toby. "Go and find someone else to embarrass with your ridiculous stories."

Toby seemed to be getting on fine with Amanda, and Nick left to give him scope for a high-speed courtship of my sister-in-law. I watched him go to rescue Adam from his menial post as art advisor to Lady Wittersworth. The Bolus girls spun a lively fandango around him to accompany him as he went. He let the pink tutus and satin pumps twirl him around the hall before two-stepping them in quick time to attach them to their grandfather instead, then he went with Adam out on the loggia to talk. Just as at Castello Giugno, the confrontations that they avoided at home they could risk on the neutral territory of La Malcontenta.

"Angelina is lucky," Dolly said. "Considering Adam's pictures caused her so much distress, the man himself has turned out to be a great moral support."

What Dolly, Queen of Un-tact, seemed to overlook was that it was Adam's paintings of my naked body that distressed Angelina, and Nick's use of them. Angelina however quickly moved on:

"When Nick is at home he and Adam spend hours together thrashing out world affairs in the minutest detail; Connie and Jo-jo join in; it's the

Deathridge men's club down in Adam's studio. They miss him terribly when he's away."

Dolly looked sceptical, taking in the adversarial stance of the two men on the loggia.

"Obviously you can't miss him too much nowadays," she said to me, her sarcastic glance taking in my entourage of family and friends, no doubt including the remarkable house.

"No, I don't miss him," I said.

My sense that Nick was slipping away from me was not something I was going to confide to Dolly Miller even though it was a topic the Renaissance Women would happily spend an afternoon debating over tea and carrot cake in the Virgins' boudoir. Elusive Nick, no one was going to admit how much or how little they shared his time and attention.

Skirting around each other on the edge of desire, we went on keeping our distance. I knew him so well I didn't have to feel his heartbeat to know the fidgetiness of his dick, and his sidelong sardonic glance was equally aware of me.

Adam and Nick's conversation, leaning against the balustrade, didn't look anything too serious though I knew Nick's explanation of the Russian Roulette incident the last time they were here together had left Adam quite disconcerted. He had assumed, as had everyone with the exception of Mrs Shackleton, that Nick set up the Russian Roulette as a recklessly ruthless gambling game in which Joey Madigan was the unlucky looser.

One had to shift the viewpoint only a little for a different perspective to emerge: Nick's developing Chaos Theory, from its earliest beginnings on the rugby field, demonstrated by the bounce of an oval ball, unpredictable but nevertheless constrained by the rules of physics; to two elephant folios taped to the wall, his drawing of the expanding universe misinterpreted by the boys as an allegorical Gang Bang, which was taken to Cambridge whither he had not followed it due to his need to evade the law; to the Russian officers' idea of death as the ultimate gamble, which in turn initiated the experiment with the Nagant. Its seven chambers and one bullet he explained in terms of the mathematical problem: how to calculate the odds, depending on whether one wants to die immediately in the face of shameful defeat or to keep alive the possibility of a future. Seventeen-year-old boys do wildly reckless things, but in the context of the game Nick was using his cool intelligence and did his best to make the risk strictly equal. Taking first shot Nick had a six to one chance of survival. If Joey had spun the barrel he would have had an equal chance. But Joey was impatient and pulled the trigger with reduced odds: the death option.

Possibly Joey assumed that Nick was bluffing and there was no bullet at all.

No wonder the Deathrage School of Philosophy stated that the so-called unlucky deserve what they get. Nick had spent his life ever since giving fate the chance to get even with him for Joey's sake, but the concept of luck didn't come into it. I was curious about these conflicting interpretations of the apparently obvious; maybe there were versions of other events that Adam needed to review.

As they stood silhouetted against the sunlit sky, I couldn't be sure if Nick's eyes met mine, but I was transfixed by his shining light: with all his quirks and foibles, his wit and acerbic humour, his sense of fun, his sulks and temper, all the little things that added up to this awesome man.

I wasn't the only one who felt it. Paul, leaving Madge the task of promoting his career among the convention of crows, came to join Angelina, Dolly and me and remarked:

"Nick has his clown's mask and Casanova suit on."

"That's his tea at the Ritz suit," I said. "It seduced Elsa and Biba against their better judgment."

"I wonder which of the ladies present he anticipates seducing before the afternoon is over," said Paul.

"That is a banally Furzy statement," I said, correcting Paul's flippancy, determined to hold my nerve in the face of Nick's evasiveness. "Nick has a very strict sense of propriety; there's nothing inconsequential about his affairs."

"Maybe not," conceded Paul, "certainly when he took me to the brothel with his Cossacks he made sure they had a good time but he didn't do any-thing to compromise himself..."

"You must admit," said Dolly, "There is something terribly decadent about a guardian taking a boy to a brothel as a form of education."

"No worse than inoculating a child with cowpox," said Paul, seizing on the chance to tease Dolly. "Like the time he took me to Madrid for the bull-fights to toughen me up to the idea of death... and he kept the girls at arms length there too."

"And," I said, facing up to my own demon of jealousy, "he engaged that prostitute in Gustavia because he wanted the whole experience of having a pro; he enjoyed the bargaining process and the frilly condoms as much as the actual sex..."

I shut up, seeing Angelina's look of bewilderment.

"It's the way he goes about his love affairs," said Paul, unheeding of my blunder, "that makes them pure farce. But of course if the captivating cock is dressed to please anything but his own vanity, it is obviously you, Sibylla. You are the really good dare. He looks ready to set in motion the explosive climax of his raging death-wish. Unzipping himself to fuck La Malcontenta before the grand assembly of the Wittersworths is too good an opportunity to resist."

"La Malcontenta is perfectly well able to deal with the Master of Chaos," I said, catching Boccaccio by the coat-tails.

"Oh really, Paul," said Angelina, "you and Sibylla do talk nonsense. Of course Nick wouldn't do anything to spoil Sibylla and Gus's housewarming party. Nick is the most socially adept person I've ever met."

"Oh, no?" said Paul. "Have you ever known Nick not to spoil a party?"

"What about the time he left us eating ice-cream by the lake to go..." said Dolly.

A-fucking behind the palm court?

"Well there was the wedding..." admitted Angelina.

"And the Christmas pheasants..." I reminded them.

"That was pure devilment," said Paul, "Poor Mother, she expected trouble with Nick and she got it — about ten times worse than she could ever imagine. But she misses him terribly now he doesn't come to annoy her any more. She loves living in the cottage; she can sit at the window and see the people letting their dogs out on the village green and complain about it to the parish council when they don't scoop-a-poop. She is a one-woman neighbourhood watch but without Nick to keep her on her toes the real spice has gone out of her life. He may have been a big thorn in her side but, whatever about the money, she should appreciate how well he took on the responsibility of hounding me through School and keeping me out of trouble — not that she need agree with his methods."

"He's simply wonderful with the children," said Angelina, finding a virtue with which to defend her husband in the face of our laughter, forgetting her earlier grievance that he was dreadfully irresponsible.

"Quite remarkable," said Dolly "considering his own difficult childhood — a war baby, bombs, food shortages and all that."

The war baby himself came in from the loggia to face us. In his Ritzy suit he was swaggering along a fine line between belligerent and debonair, and well aware of his appeal.

I smiled, thinking how Nick's own assessment of his childhood happiness was at odds with the opinion of outsiders.

He gave Dolly a frosty glare.

"Wandering over Hampstead Heath at dawn," he said, explaining the facts of life according to Deathrage to the silly girl he met beside the lake in Geneva, "with a catapult shooting pigeons for the pot wasn't a bad way to learn to be resourceful when ma chère Maman could no longer bring home the bacon from her wartime adventures — especially with a grandfather who read from Escoffier to tell me how to cook them. What more could any boy want? Not corn flakes from a cardboard box."

Dolly Miller raised her brows in scepticism. "There were no doubt compensations for ration books and the loss of one's family."

I thought this last a cruel remark though Dolly must have seen enough of Nick over the years to know how he was well able to deflect anything she could throw at him.

"I'm making up for the loss now," said Nick, looking around him. "From here I can see five of my children and…"

"And a kennelful of Nickie puppies you still haven't found a home for…" said Dolly, saying what Angelina was too tolerant of her dear husband to mention.

"Connie is enthusiastic about the wonderful time you had skiing in Gstaad," said Angelina in a vain attempt to change the subject. "He says the breakfasts were the best of it — he's getting as fussy as you over food — he and the boy he made friends with had toasted cheese topped with crispy bacon bits, and flaky apple pie with quark. And as much hot chocolate as they could possibly drink. But your floppy scrambled eggs with caviar and sour cream was disgusting, according to Connie. All that surprises me is that you rounded up only one other child for Connie to ski with; it would be more like you to muster a half dozen to boss around."

"I didn't succeed in getting more than one, his mother wouldn't co-operate," said Nick with a gentle smile, teasing Angelina; she obviously didn't realise that the other boy was Nick's eldest son who had proved to Papi Bott the validity of an uncircumcised cock.

"The most pleasant breakfast I've had in recent months," Nick went on, "was croissants and raspberry jam on Boulevard St Germaine, nice coffee too, and entertaining traffic. The skill and daring of Parisians parking their cars to jump out for an espresso and a newspaper on the wing makes me want to join in and share the ego boosting thrill of it. Not having ever read a newspaper I'd ask the next table for the headline news just to see how long I could keep them talking before they got nervous, though I never saw a traffic warden there, not like London where they pop up out of the ground as soon as I've moved three steps away — I think they lie in wait for me."

"You must have had a charming companion to make croissants and raspberry jam palatable to you," said Paul.

"Given the right female company it's extraordinary what lengths one will go to, to accommodate their desires at the expense of one's own,' said Nick.

"It's not every man who takes his wife's aunties to buy them French knickers and diamanté cocktail slippers in the rue Cambon."

With that he ambled off again to see where he could spread a little more discord. Diabolical Nick! Paul was right, a Wittersworth party presented him with a happy hunting ground for mischief.

While Gus was furthering his career in the Palladian hall, the conversations and exchanges went on, in varying configurations like a dance of intricate steps and subtle manoeuvres: scagliola pillars and sienna marble floor formed the parade ground where the congress of hooded crows assembled in festive mood, amongst whom Gus blended with characteristic ease. Father William teamed up with Nick talking to the elder statesmen, and in such company Nick looked just as soberly distinguished. The chameleon at work. I wondered if Nick were still angling for a title with Father William's backing, or had his egalitarian virtue won the day? It was only since I'd seen him embraced by the sturdy citizens of Bern that I appreciated the reality of his Swissness. And no traffic warden had come there either to harass the inconveniently parked Jaguar.

Tsang, however, like the London variety, was waiting across the room and caught him as he passed. Whatever their conversation was about, it was amusing to watch it as shadow boxing; all it needed was Chinese lanterns and gongs to emphasise the points scored, Tsang politely pushing for answers, Nick evasive but secretly laughing as he foiled Tsang's efforts to pin down the truth.

"Diamanté slippers indeed!" said Paul. "You only have to look at his face, you can tell he is getting it in the neck for bringing Tsang's miracle babies into disrepute."

"Nick was making fun of us," I said. "It's all a big tease and he has found the perfect accomplices in his poppets."

Elsa came to join in the chorus of protest.

I said: "According to Nick's Chaos Theory, the logical sequence to his invitation to the sex guru to come from Hong Kong to teach me the Zen Art of Fucking is the Nickies now throning it over there — even Meg has deserted her gentlemen clients for the little Chudovorets."

"You do realise," said Elsa, "that I am slaving away to support those little cuckoos. I simply cannot understand on what grounds the Misses Furzy are given such enormous maintenance costs just because they agreed to undergo fertility treatment — the only fertility treatment that pair of in-nothing-but-name Virgins needed was getting the Deathridge cock up their cunts, which it seems, is exactly what they got — or why Tsang Jun ever got involved in such a senseless project in the first place."

"How I wish I were a fly on the wall during that session," said Paul. "The Aunties had for years giddily accused Nick of luring them into his bed and doing naughty things to them, so I suppose Tsang's experiment put him in the position that he could ethically give in and do what they'd teased him for so persistently."

"It's so unfair," said Elsa. "Jun is getting nothing but opprobrium from his medical peer reviewers. Yet Jun is supporting them and Nick gets off scot-free. The injustice of it!"

"Nick has better lawyers," I said, indicating Father William, Gus and Toby.

"What's more, I do all his contracts out east and successfully negotiated this sperm selection thing, but while the Renaissance Women — backed up by a gang of thugs from Hong Kong — have been protecting the darling froggies in the swamp, it is now revealed that it's really about the rafts of mushrooms Nick is harvesting there, and he sneakily had his Gladys fix it with his fellow sharks in Basel to extract the alkaloids — really, Nick! They'll probably find it's a miracle cure for some rare disease or a dire poison..."

"What about a truth serum?" I suggested, thinking how useful that would be.

Protesting how she had been cheated, Elsa went up to Nick who was modestly hanging his head under Tsang's reproaches.

"I suppose you take no responsibility for so maliciously introducing Jun to the most expensive pair of virgins on earth," she said.

"Not nearly so malicious as Tsang stealing my surplus buggers in a mis-guided attempt to create a tribe of redheaded Chinese," said Nick. "Don't pursue this any further, Madam Tsang, just shut up and pay up."

"Did you shoot Gino?" asked Elsa.

Nick gave her his deadliest glare.

"I saved his life," he said. "I was on the trail of the boar and saw Gino's encounter with him down in the valley. He staggered into his van; it swerved off the road; I radioed for help."

No shot, no mention of the morphine injection. And Nick in his scarecrow raincoat spent quite a while washing at the pump.

"You're such a liar, Nick."

Nick smiled.

"I never shot a man who wasn't double-crossing me. But Gino wasn't crooked; he was just a boar who skewered my sweetheart. I didn't leave him for the vultures but he can sing his Monteverdi now in genuine castrato."

I hardly dared go near the Nickie Babies as it was clear that they did somehow exert a curious fascination over people, yet I was interested to know if it was the Nick effect or something else which made them the centre of an almost idolatrous circle of admirers. They seemed to babble quite fluently if incomprehensibly to each other but though they were exactly the same age as Willie they seemed far less mobile, making no effort to get down and run around on what Nick, with exaggeratedly tender love, called their tumptytumtoes, at the moment encased in white kid blue beaded moccasins tied on with ribbons around their ankles.

Before I could commit myself to the magic circle, Adam came hurrying over to me and said, "Your mother is here."

He seemed anxious. I was by now, with my house, my husband, my three beautiful children, established among friends and family as an iconic figure and none of my admirers wanted my mythic status as reigning Aphrodite to be undermined by the appearance out of nowhere of a probably terribly ordinary mother.

Father William was seeing out an important guest at the door when the station taxi found its way through the parked cars and deposited a thin, modest woman in black with a headscarf, a large handbag and a small suitcase at the bottom of the grand steps to the portico, so he was in position to come to her rescue with cash for the driver, since she had taken the taxi as an act of faith, having no idea of the distance involved nor what it might cost. At first sight her appearance did nothing to dispel any trepidation the Wittersworths felt about her integration into the family. Beyond what was known about her, that she lived a religious life devoted to good works in Belgium, itself a land of such bourgeois eccentricity that she was quite unremarkable there, they had no idea what to expect.

Affable as ever, Father William escorted her into the house, to the drawing room where I hastily entrenched myself with May, Augusta and Willie lined up in front of me as a protective barrier. Following in her wake, drawn by curiosity, the men followed. I looked at her in amazement, feeling as if I were seeing her for the first time; she was both smaller and paler than I remembered from waving good-bye to her outside Pinkerton's several years ago.

"Oh," her first words were, "So many grandchildren! Where did they all come from?"

This struck everyone as a hilarious comment on the diversity of fathers, so unintentionally she was an instant success and all listened for what she would say next. Her headscarf and coat removed, she sat down with a prim cup of tea, in her white blouse and grey skirt, with her tranquil, unlined face and limpid grey eyes, smiling her approval.

"Yes," she said, "you were always a good girl, you've done very well, just as I expected."

It was clear that her approval took in Gus and the children rather than the house and the splendid formality of the occasion.

"I brought you a present," she said opening her capacious holdall of rat her horrid flowery stuff. I thought: I'll have to give her one of the Bottega Venetas Nick bought for me in Florence, already choosing in my mind the black buffalo-hide rather than the brown intricata but then pulled myself up, to respect her choice and not to behave with Deathridge condescension.

Out of the bag she took a book with green cloth binding: Poems of W. B. Yeats illustrated by his brother Jack.

"But that is mine," I protested.

"You didn't have a home of your own before and I thought it would be a pity if you lost such a pretty book, all those nice pictures," she said.

"Well, thank you very much," I said, barely suppressing my sarcasm. "I am very pleased to see it again, and I assure you I am not likely to lose it even in this decrepit hovel."

I glanced at the flyleaf — possibly I had never opened it before — in elegant script:

"*To my Sibylla,*
"*That you may remain forever virtuous, wise and beautiful,*
　With a blessing from your —　　　　*Felix Barrington S J...*
the dash with a long curly flourish.

Hmmm! I thought. Who does he think he is? Another mortal man, as Nick said, even with a dog-collar on. I had never thought of him as a man until Nick made his typically cynical comment that Jesuits are ballsier as well as brainier than most celibates. I never understood Aunt Kathleen's antagonism as the Jay couldn't have been nicer and always applauded with suitable enthusiasm her *Ave Maria* — or was the annual *Ave Maria* a form of torture she inflicted on him, the way having to play it for her on the piano tortured me? I didn't even remember his name though I must have known it when I went to see him about my baptism certificate. He had introduced me to a whole flock of Jays who looked at me with such curiosity it made me cringe with embarrassment; though some were friendly others had appeared severely disapproving of this little girl in their midst. My Jay seemed amused by the effect my presence had on them and I was only too glad to escape, armed with the written evidence that I was his spiritual child. It signified that he had known me from birth, hence this farewell gift when I left for England. I had been surprised, after all the Ave Marias he had endured in the Christmas spirit, at how upset he seemed at Aunt Kathleen's funeral — something like the look of mute despair I recognised in Nick when his mind was elsewhere.

I handed the book to Gus saying: "You'd better put that in the archive and make a note of its provenance for future generations of Wittersworths to puzzle over."

Gus took the book and said, "I'll give a place of honour to the unknown donor."

"I'm sure your mother-in-law will be delighted to give you chapter and verse," I said. But Rita D'Art had already turned away to greet Dr Tsang, no longer interested in Felix Barrington, S J, and of course Tsang was captivated by a pure spirit in an uncorrupted body; it filled him on sight with intense longing to know, explore, understand and possess. He didn't leave her side, to all practical purposes, ever again.

"Hers must have been the real virgin birth," Paul could be heard murmuring to Adam.

"I don't know about that," said Adam, "more like Bernini's St Theresa."

Paul and Adam continued extending this discussion on and off for the rest of the afternoon, comparing the ecstasy of religious fervour with the soul-shattering transports of orgasm, which had brought about the birth of the Child Sibyl.

"Your mother is a genuine beauty," said Gus, not concealing his relief.

"Meaning I'm a fake compared with her?" I said.

"Meaning to see her is to understand where you came from, how you came to be who you are. Mothers are so extraordinarily revealing."

"Like the Hon. Henrietta?"

"Well, maybe," conceded Gus, laughing.

We were joined by Toby who came ambling in carrying a bottle of whisky which he had grabbed in passing from one of the catering staff, afraid they were not circulating fast enough to keep him topped up.

"I hope you don't mind, Gus," he said, "I asked your sister to show me something of the house and we dallied for a while in what I presume is your princely bedroom. I just have to steady my nerves as it seems I have committed myself for life to a rather high-born lady."

I had to laugh. "Don't tell me, Toby, that someone has called your bluff at last, and actually said yes to your chivalrous post-coital offer of marriage?"

"You are welcome," said Gus, "by all means have a session in the ancestral bed. Many a Wittersworth has been conceived and born there. I daresay Amanda was aware of what she was doing."

"And it seems she has two children already. Could you please point them out to me so I know what I've let myself in for."

Amanda's girls, nine and ten years old, were sitting side-by-side in their pink tutus, arms draped self-consciously over each other's shoulders, knees and feet sharply plié-ed, disdaining the childish inanities of the younger children.

"Lucky Amanda," I said, "with Father William and now Toby, she has cornered the two nicest men in the world. But the dog won't be too happy to be booted out of the bed."

"Poor old Bark, it's time she was retired to the happy hunting ground in the sky. It is high time I got someone else to sleep with. I did honestly try to warn Amanda off. I gave her my credentials: Tobias Shackleton, Quaker, votes Liberal, pacifist in principle if not always in practice, and I believe in mercy killing'. She said she'd be delighted to be Mrs Shackleton. The only drawback to being your brother, Gus, is that I shall feel obliged to stop fucking your wife."

"That might have been a pity, Toby," I said, "but you've long been relegated to the league of ex-lovers."

"Even if I have to have you as a brother," said Gus, "don't think I'll let you get away with any tricks on behalf of Nick Deathridge."

"Strictly professionally," said Toby, "don't think I'll not do my best to outwit you."

Amanda reappeared, hair brushed and eyes sparkling, and called the Bolus girls to come and meet their prospective stepfather. They posed mutely in front of him in gracefully exaggerated attitudes, all pointy toes and cocked bottoms, dropped their curtsies to the floor, then ran away again giggling. They looked like children who imagined they performed their lives to a background of rapturous applause. I could see Toby would have his hands full.

Ma, the ex-Montessori teacher, attracted the numerous children around her and Tsang: Tsang, the Pied Piper, found himself happily reinforced by another of the same ilk. Even the Nickies got down off the sofa, quite skilfully evading Evita, and marched with determination, if slightly unsteadily on their toddler legs, hand-in-hand over to Mother Rita, climbed on to her lap and perched eyeing her solemnly, left and right thumb in a mouth like mirror images of each other. It occurred to me that a good way to distinguish them would be if one were left-handed. Of course, being Nick's, they were probably both ambidextrous, to make it even more confusing. How would Tsang explain his relationship to them other than that they were the product of his failed experiment so they were nothing more than an embarrassment and a huge expense to him? I wondered if my birth, twenty-four years ago, would disqualify my mother from a trial into the effectiveness of Tsang's unfrozen sperm.

Julie seemed to be following the same line of thought.

"It looks as if my illustrious brother-in-law has found a better project to work on than Deathridge's pre-fucked-virgins."

"Or Mama Biba," I said, offended that she was being sarcastic at the expense of my beautiful, saintly mother, though I rather liked her description of the Misses Furzy — I must remember that to tell Gus. "The Grati don't seem to be very lucky in love."

"Elsa wouldn't have married a sex technician if she had been in the least interested in love," said Julie.

"Has he offered you any course of treatment?" I asked. "I'm sure he could hypnotise you out of Todd just as disastrously as he 'cured' me of Gino. It certainly proved the effectiveness of Tsang's control — why else did I have to let Gino fuck me again in the van, and go on doing it, even going out looking for him, inciting him to come on and make me suffer again and again?"

"I don't need that kind of treatment," said Julie. "My heart is in the grave with Gianni and I'm quite content to let it stay there."

"I'm embarrassed by my Mother's assumption that three children, a husband and a fine house constitute a virtuous life," I said. "No wonder people smile at her innocence."

I could see myself over her head in the mirror and saw the same grace, the same clear-eyed lucid look; no matter what I did people still read my looks as evidence of a pure, unsullied character.

"Your rosebud dress, Julie, was a masterpiece of cynicism," I said, "and Gino demolished that image completely when he ripped it off me. In retrospect he was quite justified in doing it. It was a cruel deception. I really am a complete fake," I said.

"The dress was a gift from me," said Julie. "It was how I wanted to see you, you dim-wit. I wanted to love you pure and simple and not have to know about all those lewd, lecherous fat dongs spewing their venom up your cunt. My God, seeing my own hairy Papa groping between your lovely legs was utterly vile. When I got to Mama's and saw all those people waiting to congratulate you and Gianni, the beautiful couple with your lovely baby, I had to go and be sick."

Julie gave me a fierce hug, then went back to where Xin and Augusta were listening to Mother Rita, leaving me thunderstruck.

Adam too was scrutinising Rita d'Art.

"Are you planning how to draw my Mother?" I asked him, focusing my mind back on the present scene.

Adam shook his head. "Oh, no, there's nothing there to pass judgment on. I've never seen such an untroubled face."

"I've just had an unexpectedly shocking revelation of how my face affects people. I always think it something of a mystery how men fall in love with me; I can't see why they should kill or castrate one another over the right to fuck me, it's quite beyond my control. But Julie?"

"Aphrodite doesn't have to justify her beauty," Adam said. "It is a gift of the Gods."

"Have you given up lewd art?"

"Not quite, but I need to make money and the portraits pay rather well. People don't seem to mind being portrayed critically severe; it makes them look important. I was just telling Nick I see at last how I could work his uniquely distinguished features up as a kind of archetypical Dick Whittington — he says it will be convenient to have it ready to present to the National Portrait Gallery if he ever does become Lord Mayor of London or otherwise achieves the necessary notoriety. I can't tell if he's mocking me or himself, or if he really means it."

Adam was looking at Nick as if the question of how to portray him for the nation was going to be interestingly tricky. As I saw it, the superficial man with his serious straight face, the ice-cold eyes and sardonic mouth was not a problem, but how to stop the mischief creeping in, the mayhem peeping around the corner, the flamboyance getting out of hand? I was reminded of the Reynolds portrait of my ancestor, now in the National Gallery, with all the excessive trappings of fame and fortune, but the little black coot lurking under his pink velvet cloak was a reminder of the real person out of which this phantasmagoria of splendour arose.

"He improves with age," sad Adam, "positively handsome on a good day."

"It's your perception that's improving with age," I said. "To me he is unreservedly dazzling."

"I'm not in love. I have to keep my critical faculties sharp."

Too sharp, perhaps.

I could tell that Nick and Toby were discussing my mother, observing her from the far side of the room, and from their expressions and gestures I could almost read their lips. Toby was chortling with glee and Nick was looking disconcerted, as if fate had outwitted him and, being needled even further — perhaps the way his Nickies were captivated by the saint added to his dismay — he turned away. Toby gave him a consoling pat on the back, which was instantly converted into a gigantic man hug, Nick with his face buried in Toby's sturdy shoulder, shaking with laughter or sobs, or both.

Big-hearted Toby is the one, I thought, who gives Nick this kind of affectionate reassurance. Adam as father is far too anxious, too critical, too apprehensive for Nick's sake.

Toby left him to go and join the legal coterie. I went over and put my hand on his arm. "What do you think of Mother d'Art?" I asked.

"She worries me. Toby says I'd better make the most of the time I have left before you turn into Mother Rita."

He still had his eyes fixed on the saint with her accumulation of children when Angelina and Amanda came to join us. Amanda kissed Nick on each cheek.

"I'm going to marry Toby," she said, "so if you want to be invited to our wedding you will have to be nice to me for a change."

"My dear Amanda," said Nick with a flourish, kissing her uncompromisingly on the mouth, "you are the most beautiful, most charming, most attractive and intelligent of all the women I've never had the pleasure of fucking. I congratulate Toby on having captured such a prize. A great improvement on a large hairy dog."

With that he escaped us and went to rescue his numinous Nickies from being mesmerised into taking part in the wrong mystery play.

"Oh," said Amanda, her hand to her lips, looking after him with amusement. "Is he like that with all your friends, Angelina?"

"He gets worse — or maybe I just notice it more," said Angelina.

Nick stood in front of my mother and put out his hands for the Nickies. My mother, raising her eyes from her immediate admirers, met his. Another crossing of swords, one could almost hear the clash and see the sparks fly.

The mother in her recognises him as the Wrong Man, the one she warned me against: the saint recognises the sinner.

There was a moment when the two opposing magnetic fields pulled them, then the Nickies grasped their father by the hands and were lifted away, dangling and clinging to him like a pair of monkeys.

I thought: he too has the fanaticism to be a saint if he hadn't chosen to be a sinner. At what point could one suppose a choice had been made? Maybe the day of his grandfather's funeral when he infuriated his mother into calling him a demon child by relentlessly, persistently, fanatically rattling the house with the thuds of his eight glorious goals against the hall door.

Seven is the age of reason. That was his defiance in the face of misfortune, his rebellion against betrayal; maybe the turning point that precipitated all that was to follow.

He walked away with his Nickies hanging around his neck. Connie and Jo-jo ran to join the group, Jo-jo shinning up Nick's leg into position on his right arm and Connie holding on to one of the four little Nickie feet: the quiver of arrows with which Nick had embarrassed Great-Uncle Harold by claiming the biblically sanctioned right to fuck for ad lib.

Dolly Miller, who had been making friends with Julie, came over to Angelina.

"Don't let Nick get away with the babies," she said. "We'll need them soon for going home."

"With those silly hats I still haven't seen them properly,' I said. "Do they resemble him? Can you tell that he's their father?"

"No," said Dolly. "They have cute little round faces like their mothers."

"Oh, but they do," said Angelina, "solemn pouts like Nick, and his eyes; but the mystery is this amazing charisma."

"Well, look at him," I said, "an icon of fertility with his boys stuck to his body like chippings to a magnet. That's charisma. That's what May misses out on."

I suppressed my jealousy on May's behalf. And his little Switzer, who got to know what kind of person his father was only when they went skiing once a year, but I said nothing. Angelina had enough to contend with without me stirring up trouble.

But Dolly in her rambling way said, "Do you remember that woman by the lake...?" consciously or not making the association in her mind.

"That was Mrs Hein," I said, conveying to Amanda a nodded agreement not to tell Angelina she wasn't the one and only Mrs Deathridge — it wasn't just that Angelina avoided knowing the truth: the truth was what no one would tell her,

"I thought it rude of him to leave us like that to go and talk to her," said Dolly. "But then, with that poker-face and cool manner he never struck us as a satisfactory fiancé."

Apparently not realising the poker-face hid a hoaxer of quite epic magnitude... so I didn't tell her that Mrs Hein invited Nick to start his family where it rightfully belonged, with his first wife, a dare he couldn't refuse even as Angelina was waiting for him, the Bartered Bride surrounded by her girl friends.

"You were always jealous of him, Dolly," Angelina said, for once giving vent to her chagrin. "He was so strikingly handsome coming off the water in his über-cool Porsche aviators and wind-cheater, and he spoke such elegant French to those people crowding around at the bar and then German to some women — goodness knows what they wanted, he knows all sorts of people. You, Dolly — and the other girls went along with you — were saying money wouldn't make up for a lifetime of boredom with someone so unamusing, but how right I was not to listen to you, it's you who married that boring old pedant Jack Miller who wouldn't say boo to a goose. Nick is the most interesting man alive. He is absolutely the best."

It was a revelation to hear Angelina appreciate 'interesting' as a virtue in her husband. She had come around to putting a value on qualities other than the river of liquidity that kept her afloat in her little world of frocks, rocks and tea-parties.

"I'm perfectly happy with a quiet husband," said Dolly. "I get all the entertainment I need from observing yours."

"Mrs Hein in her shiny white Lamborghini with her red-head cuckoo on the back seat," said Amanda, "inviting us to Nick's wedding! Oh, if only I'd known... won't Maddie be furious when I tell her!"

"That dreadful woman," said Angelina, "I still can't believe my own eyes what I saw her doing."

"It was all because of the dares," I said, trying to defuse this fresh attack on Angelina's composure. "From all the stories I've heard about them, he and Joey were always in trouble over ridiculous dares. Ask Toby, he was the peacekeeper."

"How much is Toby involved?" asked Amanda.

"Toby knows everything. How else can he keep Nick out of trouble?

Would anyone have believed how Joey came to shoot himself if Toby hadn't been there to back up Nick's explanation about the Russian Roulette? And it was Leon Bolus who was manoeuvred into giving him the diplomatic stamp of approval when he was doing his dodgy arms dealing and diamond smuggling. Didn't you know? It's what he and Leon were talking about at dinner in the castello."

Amanda laughed with surprised delight.

"Oh, dearest Sibylla! Any more bombshells to blow us away with? No, of course I never suspected Leon would do anything so risky, it is totally out of character."

"I understand that Leon filled out some forms to help Nick with the paper work and then found he had done more than he bargained for – Nick's sleight of hand as when he got Adam to agree to a marriage he knew nothing about. Or possibly it was just a bit of excitement on a dull day. Even Gus says the adrenaline rush of breaking the law could become addictive."

"So diamond smuggling is what his visits to Maddie were really about," said Amanda. "With the sex as by-product."

"And guns," I said. "Leon seemed a bit dismayed when Nick so casually revealed his flying in the face of the embargo."

"I suppose Nick knew he was risking Leon's career." Amanda was calculating the cost of succumbing to Nick's charisma.

"There can't have been any risk," said Angelina, rallying to Nick's defence. "Nick leaves nothing to chance."

"Well, I don't know," said Amanda. "How can you say that about someone who can play Russian Roulette with his best friend knowing one of them might be killed?"

"We don't know the rules of the game," I said, "and Nick won't talk about it."

"When I heard you were engaged to Nick Deathridge," said Amanda, "I thought you too were letting yourself in for a lifetime of Russian Roulette. I wondered why a nice girl like you was contemplating marrying the likes of him — Maddie Madigan now I could have understood. I could easily imagine her driving a Land Rover across the veldt with Nick and his elephant gun perched up beside her, culling wildlife and chasing poachers, though I don't suppose it would matter to Nick which side of the law he was operating on as long as he got to pop a few shots."

"Jane said they didn't understand if Maddie and Nick were fighting under the table or having fun because it was in some odd language," I remarked.

"One of Nick's many peculiarities is his ability to speak weird languages like Swiss and Afrikaans," Angelina said.

"Toby blames it on the mind-boggling hours they had to endure at school listening to the Classics teacher expounding on the fundamentals of grammar and philology. Nick did his best to make life difficult for him, asking questions in Zulu saying: explain that! Nick was learning it from Joey."

"Oh, dear Nick," said Amanda, sighing. "He and Joey were plotting a life of crime together — one doesn't know whether to be sorry that it didn't come off, or not. That little turboprop he had such fun with when he arrived at Maddie's — she said he was like a boy with a Meccano set taking it to pieces and screwing it back together again. She wouldn't go up with him, it seemed likely the bits would fall off in midair. And how right I was, that time when he took Leon for a spin up into the Berner Oberland they skidded and bumped downhill for about half a mile over a glacier before he took off again practically vertically just as the glacier broke up and dropped into a crevasse; Leon never found out if this was a deliberate scary manoeuvre to prove Nick's skill, the plane's amazing airworthiness, or was it a near accident?"

All three, I supposed. With Nick there was a very narrow margin for error.

"Come on, Angelina," said Dolly, reasserting her bossiness. "People are starting to go. Get the children and we'll make a move."

Nick came out with his armful of babies and unloaded them onto Angelina telling her it was time she got her driver to take them home.

"Yes, dear," said Angelina, "Dolly is ready to take us now."

"I'm staying with my Daddy," said Connie, dodging behind Nick and refusing to be herded along.

"Good," said Nick. "Run down to my car and get a large brown envelope you'll see in the side pocket."

Connie scampered off. Nick called after him: 'Handle it with care, it might go bang — and guard it with your life!"

"Yes, Sir," Connie called back, wiping the smile off his face and trying to look worthy of the responsibility.

Gus, backed by Father William and the Hon. Henrietta, was seeing the guests off down the steps.

"I must just say a word to your mother," the Hon. Henrietta said to me so I went with her to where Dr Tsang, the Grati and Rita d'Art were also gathering to take flight.

"It has been lovely meeting you, Mrs d'Art," said the Hon. Henrietta graciously, though in fact they hadn't spoken all afternoon. "Dear Gussie seems very happy with your lovely daughter."

"Yes," said Mother Rita, "He's a nice young man. But I knew Sibylla would have no trouble in finding a good husband. She was a little angel from birth. Her father and I counted ourselves uniquely blessed to have her."

At that she turned back to Dr Tsang and he took her arm.

"Good-bye," she said and departed out of my life, flying off to Hong Kong having decided to abandon Jesus for Confucius, leaving me speechless.

Gus hurried to escort her out. Nick stood watching Angelina go down across the drive, with Jo-jo behind her kicking up the gravel in protest as he followed. I noted how cool Angelina looked in her light grey outfit in spite of carrying two sleepy Nickies. Out of nowhere came the vision of what a dignified widow Angelina would make, exquisitely sad but no hysterics. Of course, having a clutch of lovely sons and Nick's Death Row fortune would ease the pain.

Dear Jesus, another Sibylline doom scenario to torment me!

Meg's Ancient Parent, who had finally given in to being sanitised out of existence by the gentrification of Camden Town, was keeping an eye on the traffic, making sure no one was upsetting his pigeons or his bees. Nick went to say something to him and for a dreadful moment I thought he too would drive away, leaving me with nothing more than his reproach that I was too like my mother. If Gus thought that a point in my favour, clearly Nick didn't.

Maybe the Saint had saved me from the Wrong Man at last.

I went out through the gap in the balustrade that led to the meadow. To my heart-thumping joy Nick followed.

"Take me for a walk," he said when he caught up with me.

Oh, Good God, my life turns on a circuitous wheel of repetitions.

"I've a mind to give the Wittersworths a repeat of my performance at the gang-bang and fuck you right here in full view of everyone," said Nick, turning to face the house with the air of an actor taking a bow. "I'll show them and their allies who fucked you first — and last."

As if to set aside his exaggerated sense of decorum he took off his jacket and unknotted his tie to carry out his threat but I took his arm and said, "Don't push your luck, my beloved; use a little discretion so you may live to fuck another day."

I waved to the procession of cars moving slowly away down the drive, thinking it a pity really that Nick couldn't have the pleasure of defying my mother, the Hon. Henrietta, Dolly Miller, Julie, Elsa, and impressing all other passing witnesses with his prowess as recklessly as the original Casanova.

"How annoying," I said, "the Nickiemobile has gone and I haven't had a chance to see your miraculous babies close up. What is it about them that's so special?"

"Tsang puts it down to hitting on the right formula for his sperm selection. He's going to recoup his professional loss of face by touring the world with them to show what brilliant children one can create by following his advice."

"Oh, no, Nick, you can't allow it. You can't let him use your children to perpetuate a hoax."

"Dolly has her Nickiemobile all set to go on the round of their adoring public with its photosynthetic sunroof to provide maximum exposure and a video camera to monitor their safety and broadcast their worshipful presence. It's the kind of silliness the Virgins would love: Dr Tsang the snake oil merchant! Evita selling blessings and holy pictures! But Angelina is their guardian. I consulted that grim old prophet, Jacob Bott, and he advised, based on the Wisdom of Solomon, that I sit back and let the women fight it out, he says the true mother instinct will prevail. I'm backing Angelina to win."

"Why do they have to wear the ridiculous hats?"

"To suppress the halos, of course. They are beautiful enough as it is without people being blinded by their shining light."

I was tempted to thump him the way Toby did when he was too exasperating, but found myself laughing and hugging him instead.

"Just like you that day in Padua," I said. "You walked towards me with the sun behind you and I could have sworn you had a fiery halo; you were utterly godlike and I've worshiped you ever since in spite of the fact that you are the most annoying, bloody useless lover a woman ever had."

"I did save your life."

"After doing your best to terminate it along with my baby, you murderer! But you were kind enough not to shoot me at my wedding even though you were dressed to kill."

Nick spread out his hands in front of me.

"Haven't you noticed anything?"

No death's head ring.

"Not terribly observant," he said. "I haven't worn it since. I was rather expecting you'd offer to replace it. After all, I gave you a wedding ring: am I not entitled to one in return?"

"If I can find something suitably awful, I will."

"I gave the Deathrage ring to Roger as I can't give him my name. I told him it is a coded message he has to guard with his life, that when his hand is big enough to wear it without slipping he'll understand what it signifies."

"But suppose the poor child does defend it with his life? You know your record for creating unfortunate incidents."

"I hope my son is not a fool; I'd be bitterly disappointed but it's a risk one has to take."

Nick paused to reconsider the competing interests of loyalty and common sense, then dismissed it saying, "He's Swiss," as if there was nothing more to add to the fact that entrenched in the Alps with the world at his feet, his moral choices depended on achieving the achievable.

Or as Nick would put it: "I will if I can!"

I took my shoes off to stroll through the damp daisy-studded grass. Nick didn't mind the wet either, his feet bare in the sooty soft suede shoes Elsa so admired. We reached the ramshackle remains of a misplaced Gothick tea-house, half obscured by the drooping, dripping branches of an equally incongruous monkey-puzzle tree, and there Nick stripped naked, defiantly, like a gladiator preparing to take on all comers, confident of being the last man standing. Not that anyone of the present company was likely to come exploring this way though no doubt in a more romantic past of crinolines and knee britches it had served often enough for lovers' trysts. Nick's Casanova suit, the one that Elsa had described with such enthusiasm after their tea at the Ritz, with his tie of pink and gold spermatozoa swimming in a deep blue sea, he draped carefully over the veranda rail to keep it out of the damp garden debris littering the floor. I as carefully removed my misty dream of a dress and hung it up on a nail so I could put it on again later without it looking crushed and soiled; equally the decorum due as Gus's wife and mistress of La Malcontenta was having its influence on how I conducted my affairs. Mr Deathridge and Mrs Witterworth: the balance steady at last.

Nick fingered the necklace on my breast, the one he had given me to stop me crying when he was so brutally callous about Gianni's baby: a chain of pearls, mostly white with an occasional black one interspersed along with the odd teardrop sparkle of diamond.

"I wear it when I want to remind myself that you do love me — sometimes," I said.

"I'm not callous," said Nick, "On the contrary I'm a sentimental bloody fool, and I went looking for the most delicate, lovely thing I could lay my hands on in a hurry before you upped and left me yet again. I went wandering along Bond Street in a state of emotional distress and saw exactly the fitting response in Jensen's 'window: perles de pluie, venue de pays où il ne pleut pas. Good grief, how I torment myself over you! But you needed a ruth-less maverick like me to help you to the logical solution. I saved you from the potentially fatal mess you had created for yourself. Admit I was right.”

“The annoying thing about you is that you always are.”

I looked down at Nick stretched out on the rush floor, leaning on his elbow.

“Nick Deathridge, what are you like! Lying there on the bare ground as vain as a pasha with your cock *en garde* — how ridiculous to lie down in discomfort in the late afternoon of a party when really we both have more urgent social obligations to attend to.”

“*Carpe diem*, Mistress Wittersworth,” he said. “It is the eve of my thirty-ninth birthday; the endgame commences: after tomorrow I maybe not be here.”

I knelt down beside him and leaned over to kiss him. A large part of Nick’s erotic appeal was how his kiss, his hair, his body diffused a scent both sweet and sensuous, spiced with unadulterated male animal. Dizzy-making! Like his red crocodile jacket: shocking, amazing, irresistible.

“Gus Wittersworth may be your husband, but I am your mate.”

I smiled at his obsession with his role, his function, his status.

The quintessential male!

“All right,” I said, “I surrender, so go on, fuck me to kingdom come.”

Nick responded to my invitation with an explosion of overwhelming gusto, then he rolled off and lay on his back in the unswept fragments of dead leaves, eyes closed, his breath slow and measured, his penis barely less than upright in its tangle of wiry copper hair on the taut stretch of his belly.

“You are such a stud,” I said. “How do you keep it up?”

I kissed its tip: tender pink, silky soft, a rosebud.

“Sweet Sibylla! You are such an honest lover, I surrender myself totally, fearlessly to you. Until I met you I had my emotions and my nightmares under control; I certainly had no romantic notions about falling in love — my sex life has been a battle from the start — until I lost my head over you: the silliest and best thing I ever did.”

"I never wanted to be 'a good girl' like my mother says, it's just an assumption people make based on my looks. Your reputation too is based on how you look, so severe, so supercilious, and that constant striving for perfection."

"No matter what diabolical intentions you and my Dad and now your Mother attribute to me, Wittersworth and his distinguished friends take me for what I am, a perfectly honourable man."

"Apart from: smuggling diamonds...?"

"Swiss francs are of equal value..."

"selling guns...?"

"my trade is gunsmith."

"killing...?"

"when necessary, in awkward situations. My *Vol de Nuit!* it would fill a separate novel to tell that whole story."

"Then what about fucking the innocent young nanny?"

"My only weakness — and look where that has put me! on the floor of a garden hut with cobwebs in my hair — you'd think I'd have more sense."

"You didn't have to do it. The expert Tsang says the brain is a higher level of command than the testicles."

"Of course he's right; don't I prove that every day of my life? Are you pregnant?"

"That can't possibly matter to you," I said. "Your have a hive full of honey and a pair of queen bees whose whole existence turns around filling it for you with little Nickie grubs; God help the world when they mature and fly..."

"That can't possibly matter to you, Mrs Wittersworth. Please, Sibylla, don't deny my love. Just say yes."

"Oh, Nick! Why on earth do I let you make such a fool of me?"

"Come on, Cunt. One last gamble before I die."

I lay on my side looking into his face, trying to get the meaning of what he was trying to convey with such sudden brutality.

It's his despair, I thought. Because his deep well of grief will never run dry and because for all my Sibylline insights, Nick's eyes could penetrate further into the fog of the future — and he was afraid.

Nick's Garden of Gethsemane.

He had finally given me all he had to give.

He stood up and delicately removed a spider from his trousers before putting them back on.

"What a ridiculous situation I find myself in for the sake of capturing your chimerical love! Why do I bother?"

Out under the spiky branches of the tree I saw Connie running away across the lawn.

"I bet he came to spy on Smiley," I said. "The folly of encouraging your children in devious ways!"

Nick shrugged, re-arranging his tie in a studiously complicated knot, a Windsor to suit the shape of his collar; getting into his jacket.

"Thank you, gracious lady, for a quite remarkably successful fuck," he said.

I smiled at how he adjusted his custom-cut, well-shaped trousers with a congratulatory caress to its precious payload for having splendidly fulfilled its proper purpose. I had to admit that he was quite right: sublimely transcendent as this coupling of our two bodies was, without the penetrating force of his fucking tool this miracle of love couldn't happen.

"Thank you, Sir Cock, I appreciate your exertions on my behalf. May I invite you to stay to dinner?"

"I was counting on nothing less."

We walked slowly back in our party clothes like any hostess and valued guest enjoying the last of the sunshine and polite conversation. Pure happiness caught by the tail in just such moments as these!

Yet echoes of that other time with Gianni when he and I escaped the wedding party to wander across the fields came back to haunt me. I remembered the closing day when we climbed back towards his self-willed death, the pale montgolfière so still and remote in the fading light, leaving no trace of its existence behind except this image in the mind and memory, an image of unbearable sadness.

I would have held on to Nick but he was walking too loosely and freely to be grasped. He too felt the post-coital melancholy of the late afternoon.

"That time I made an emergency landing in the Drakensberg, I spotted a stretch of bare earth though drifts of mist," he said, in his imagination far from an artfully landscaped expanse of Kentish parkland, "timely mist as it happened as I had a couple of bodies to dispose of. I had to make a few passes first to scare off the wildlife, it was a bit bumpy — nothing to one used to the Alps. At first I was too busy patching up bullet holes, reattaching loose cables, tightening screws and so on, to have any existential angst about death, but the mist didn't clear and it began to feel as if I were stranded on the mountains of the moon, lost in time and space, quite a pleasant sensation of loneliness, waiting for the stars to reappear so I could find my way to Maddie's. I thought, this is how it is being dead: alone on a mountain with my familiars, the spirits of the long lost to keep me company. We sang to pass the time; it kept the demons at bay. Joey sang the *Rivers of Babylon* again, homesick for the tobacco farm beyond on the Limpopo, on the other side. We never made it there."

I pictured Nick busying around his Pilatus Porter, its jaunty red and yellow dimmed in the mist, singing to himself, and quite without thought or intention I hummed what came into my head and sang:

Whack Fol-De-Da, *now dance your partner*,
welt the floor, your trotters shake.
Wasn't it the truth I told you,
lots of fun at Finnegan's Wake.

Nick stopped in his stride and his face creased up, frozen with distress.

"Joey!" he shouted, tears on his face. "*Schei uit, verdomde lul*. Leave me in peace."

He turned and walked away from me, muttering incomprehensibly, paused, then came back and said, "Every so often I have to deal with him; he is very persistent."

"What does he want?" I asked, taking him seriously.

"He's lonely. He misses me as much as I miss him, sometimes unbearably, but he doesn't understand that when I've just been fucking my sweetheart I'm in no mood to talk nonsense with him. He's only seventeen."

Though Nick spoke matter-of-factly the furrows in his cheeks were wet.
I wondered if tears were what caused them. I wondered if Joey had put that
silly tune in my head. But for the regrettable incident of the loaded gun
Nick's solo flight with his illicit cargo and the ruthless disposal of some
unwelcome passengers wouldn't have been quite so lonely an undertaking.

"I tumbled the bodies of my would-be assassins down the escarpment
and when at last I spotted a lammergeyer circling above I was glad it wasn't
my corpse it was waiting for this time — not that I'll begrudge it when the
time comes."

The holy Mothers at school told us to pray for a Good Death. Nick's
obsession with the manner of his death probably wasn't quite what they had
in mind.

"On moral grounds I couldn't refuse to eat the puff adder hotpot Maddie
put in front of me. I told her she could lay me out for the vultures — unless
she planned to convert me into one of her ethnic menus – *Nick au poivre*.
She said out of consideration for her students she couldn't; I'd probably be
more poisonous than the snake."

"Did you really think she might poison you?" I asked.

"One spoonful of chilli she loves me, two she hates me." Nick's lips took
their sardonic downturn. "The odds are much shorter than at Russian Roulette, and fucking her has all the fascination of mating with a black widow
spider. Every so often I get a craving for that hot chill of fear only she can
inspire in me after her attempt to wreck my wedding night — unnecessary as
it happened; I am quite capable of my own damnation — by squirting a tube-
ful of her chilli paste — one of her diabolical concoctions, supposed to make
a mess of beans more digestible; all it does is make the inevitable thunderous
farts extremely painful — into my pants to paralyse my fuck apparatus."

"So that's what was going on under the table! I must tell Angelina and
Adam, they are still mystified and arguing about it — Angelina giving you
the benefit of the doubt and Adam believing the worst."

"Maddie thought she could disable me but I said I'd fuck her on the spot
so she'd suffer just as much as me — worse because it is quicker to hold a

burning cock under a tap of cold water than it would be to hose out a cunt. It was a typical Madigan manoeuvre to annoy me — though on the whole Joey doesn't interfere in my sex life. He's not interested."

So I was right when I said Maddie's cuckoo-clock was for the dare, not for the sex.

"By way of appeasement I financed Maddie's ethnic foods to go into commercial production —the enterprise consists of some barns identifiable from the air by flocks of guinea fowl scratching around in the scrub and ostriches legging it around the perimeter. The roof space is useful to me for storing odd jobs."

"Such as guns?"

"What do you think? Bullets among the beans; gunpowder among the spices? No need; Maddie has the law on her side."

Meg's report of how he had wandered singing through his splendid newly acquired house, cock-a-hoop after surviving his epic flight, by skill and wits succeeding in his risky trade, negotiating, bartering and shooting his way over his long and devious route from Maddie Madigan's grub pies and baked bush baby back into Eugenie's bed to be spoon-fed her kosher chicken soup. Home at last, after turning up in Zurich in sweat stained shorts, his colour high with the flush of exhilaration on his cheek bones and triumph in his translucent grey eyes, his body whittled down to pure muscular strength as lean and functional as the machine he had flown over ten thousand miles, man and machine fragile as butterflies that cross continents on odysseys of incredible endurance: Meg reported that that was when he was truly happy.

Fucked out, what hope could I have of holding him?

Connie was sitting on the balustrade above us waiting for Nick to come up, too polite to interrupt grown-ups in conversation.

"You seem to have your sons well under control."

"My sons, yes, but not my women: after my mother's unenthusiastic effort at child-bearing — I have my grandfather to thank that I wasn't aborted at first wriggle — I clung like a limpet to my Bonne-Maman for the next four years until she too escaped me, setting me down to stand momentarily on my own two feet and never returning to pick me up again; I am still hopefully pursuing Mrs Shackleton but I don't suppose she will ever take me seriously, and you, my most precious sweetheart, you are my greatest failure, a constant fugitive from my love: my nemesis."

As he was mine!

At the top of the steps he paused to sweep Connie up off his perch and together they looked back at the sinking sun, large and bloody with a dusky halo around it.

"That's Mount St Helen's exploding," Nick pointed out to him. "*Polvo del planeta*, dust of the dead — you can see why I'm against cremation. When I'm dead dump me naked in the sea for the lobsters — don't forget to tie a weight to my ankle or I'll come floating back to you like disgustingly rotten bread upon the waters."

"I've been waiting ages," said Connie. "Guarding with my life."

He handed Nick the brown envelope he had been sent to fetch nearly two hours before.

"I saw you going into the hut with May's Mama so I kept watch until you had done your stuff."

"That's my boy," said Nick. "Come on, we'll give it to Mr Wittersworth. It's a present for him to say thank you for his hospitality."

"Is there one for Mrs Wittersworth?" asked Connie.

"She has had her thank you already."

"In the hut?"

"Yes."

"May I give you a kiss too, Mistress Wittersworth?"

I crouched down to Con level and received a lippy fat kiss on the lips. Nick's boy, all right.

The library, across the central hall from the drawing room, was already the home of the Wittersworth archive, as yet just begun with plenty of space cleared on the shelves and in presses for all that was yet to come, where Gus would sort, catalogue, rearrange the facts and fantasies of our lives, shuffling and re-shuffling to see how many variants on the same story one could devise, saying: the truth doesn't change but its appearance does. But there on this 31st May 1980, Gus with Nick and Paul, friends and rivals, put their heads together to plot their next career moves while Adam pointed out to Madge the significance of wildflower meadows in the context of villa horticulture and Toby beamed happily on everyone.

"It's a housewarming present for Gus," Nick explained as we went in." Dad will never get around to my portrait, it troubles him too much to look me in the eye, so it has to be a photo."

"What I don't understand," I said, "is that with all the functions you attend why has it taken so long to get a photo?"

"I'm not in politics," said Nick, shocked at the very idea. "The people I mix with keep their faces out of the papers. Who wants to be a target for extortionists and madmen? The worst thing that can happen to the likes of me is to commit an indiscretion and get one's face in the public eye."

"Oh," I said, not laughing. "May Jesus preserve you from ever committing an indiscretion! What about you jumping off the top of the bus in your top hat? Surely that must have been photo-worthy."

"Yes, Nestor shat that one out: Bridegroom Arrives in Style! Not what Mrs Furzy had in mind for the society pages; what do you imagine happened to all the others?"

Nick indicated Toby, his accomplice, who smiled back at him. He was standing by the window watching out for Amanda who was seeing her father and mother off, the last to go. The seating arrangement in the Bentley was finally settled with the Hon. Henrietta sitting in front so she could argue with Father William all the way home about the propriety of their eldest daughter remarrying so soon, a provincial solicitor at that, and Evita sitting in the back whispering and giggling with the Bolus girls.

"There you are," said Nick, handing the well guarded envelope to Gus, "for the Wittersworth archive, for what it's worth: N. D. Deathridge as he would like to be remembered."

No one questioned that the proper place for the long-awaited portrait of Nick was in Gus's custody.

"I met the famous Korzennick in the bookshop at the United Nations in New York of all unlikely places: I went to meet someone who thought that would be a good place for us to find each other; he was late or maybe never turned up for all I know as I had second thoughts about why he wanted me there — acting decoy for the CIA probably — so I latched discreetly on to Korzennick and we went off for a chat over coffee. When I heard he was on his way to Mexico I invited myself along — I handed my ticket JFK to Heathrow to a backpacker on the way; I hope he got home safely — and headed south instead. Our trip covered several thousand miles. Eventually we parted company in Cape Town where Korzennick lives when he's at home. When he turned his camera lens on me I felt I'd been set up before a firing squad but I'm an irredeemable sucker; being the focus of the Great Eye is such flattery, I submitted to being shot."

"Uhmm," said Adam coming to look. "My sitters, even dressed in their finery, often remark they feel they are being stripped bare by the artist's eye..." he studied Nick's to see if he could detect the same effect.

Nick's eye, however, was the one that did the stripping, the photographer was the one exposed to scrutiny, and beyond him, all of us, to Nick standing in a completely empty, scrubby field, head tilted, chin up, clear, colourless eyes gauging the distance, wearing a dark, double-breasted suit with widely spaced chalk stripes, but casually, the coat loosely fastened by a single button and his hands scrunched in the pockets, the tension in his shoulders indicating a cold wind.

How on earth did Nick get himself photographed in a bare field with nothing but a few dim pylons on the flattened, unfocussed horizon against which he stood out sharply, so sharp that one could distinguish the pattern on the horn buttons on his chest and the thread with which they were stitched, his face sharply sculptural in repose, slight blur of windblown hair?

Nick in a crowd at the races maybe; Nick in double-breasted chalk stripes at a gathering of bankers more likely; Nick holding forth at the bar of the Opera House, yes! But alone on a vast empty plain that could be anywhere: Patagonia, Southern Africa, even Outer Mongolia?

"An unusual setting for you, Nick," said Gus, struck by the eerie vibes coming from the black and white print, or rather, monochrome with a strange absence of colour.

"You look like the stag in '*The Monarch of All He Surveys*'," I said. "Or even better, '*The Man Who Would Be King*.'"

"Good grief," said Nick, "I'm not a maniac of quite such hubristic pretensions. It is merely land I bought, a small patch of the earth's surface where I may build a new factory, an airport, a wind farm — or maybe not. It shows how low the sun was in the afternoon, how tall I am and the length of my shadow."

"Well, I'm sure that's very significant," said Gus, "but the important thing is that it is an excellent portrait; I'm positively jealous of the photographer, it is so much better than any I could have done."

"You do very well with your handy Leica," said Nick, "but this is a contact print from an 8 x 10 plate taken with a mahogany and brass Deardorff field camera, 24 inch long lens — Korzennick was so far away I couldn't hear what he was shouting at me in the wind so I just stood there without moving knowing what a slow lens it is in that light, and fine grained film too — the print selenium toned on Seagull paper for maximum archival quality. Timeless and indestructible — like me."

Gus, Toby and I all groaned in chorus. The vanity of the man!

One could just picture him standing aloof in his bare field in the middle of nowhere while some wild-eyed, bushy-haired troll fiddled with light meter; bellows with tilt and swing adjustments; balancing his tripod, dark cloth flapping with the wind whipping over that forlorn steppe, or maybe acres of abandoned potato fields, possibly even deserted pampa or the veldt, no clue to wherever it might be. No wonder his face had that interested, analytical, mildly amused expression that was Nick relaxed and in a good mood. Nothing gratified him more than having someone make a tremendous fuss over him in difficult circumstances: so a windblown steppe was clearly just right to produce a good portrait.

Adam studied it. "I was just beginning to clarify my own mental picture of how I would do you, now I feel pre-empted."

I saw what Adam saw, that he didn't need to bother capturing on canvas what the photographer had caught to perfection: every line and crease of the subject's face, the quizzical expression, the dignity and power of his stance, the disregarding stylishness of his self-presentation. Not to mention the eerie emptiness of the chosen background. Nick dominated simply by being there.

"I'd have enjoyed sitting for you, Dad," said Nick, "we could have carried on our late-night conversations for months or even years, for as long as it took to reach a conclusion — but there's no time left for that. I entrust myself to Gus's archive, Korzennick showing me at the zenith of my career, just before the earth-movers begin the dance of death: my *memento mori*."

"What is going to cause me nightmares," said Toby "is that you will go off again on some illicit venture and not come back. You will simply disappear and I'll spend the rest of my life trying to round up your affairs, searching for a final settlement."

"I turned up all right the last time — like a bad penny as your mother said. Draw up a will for me so that that if you don't hear from me for another ten years you can divide my assets between my children."

"You'd better give me a definitive list of your children so far," said Toby. "I'll update it as necessary."

"I think half a dozen is enough. Let Tsang pay for the rest. And definitely not the Heini cuckoo. He'll remember me as Smiley, the other intrepid red-head, he's my spiritual legacy."

Toby grumbled, "I can foresee years of litigation..."

"I rather like the idea that you may never know what happened to me. That way you'll never be rid of me. My remains may lie rotting in some swamp being eaten by lampreys or my bones broken by lammergeyers but you will go on expecting me to come back to annoy and embarrass you. It would be as if I were living forever, just to be a nuisance."

"Oh, do stop, Nick, you can't inflict such misery on your friends," I said.

"I'll frame it," said Gus, studying the photo. "No need for a name, just *Memento Mori* on a brass plate, a warning to us all — why a man as outrageous as you should have so many friends ridiculously in love with you is beyond reason."

"He's really my Dad," Connie told Gus in confidence, reappearing from under the library steps. "Sometimes."

"I am to-day," said Nick. "Go along now; see if you can find May."

"I'm having a fight with her," said Connie, pulling a face.

"Go and finish it," said Nick "Get it over with before bedtime. Take Toby with you. Quakers make great referees."

With that he gave Toby a mockingly hard-handed little shove out the door. Another joke I didn't quite see the point of — unless it was his failure at Russian Roulette.

Nick, who had not been invited to our party, had come prepared to stage a midnight birthday feast for himself, his uncompromising memory at work, holding us to our word. I went with him to collect supplies from the treasure chest that was the boot of the Jaguar — mainly because I didn't trust him not to have a change of heart and drive away into the darkness. My happiness was too fragile to lose again so soon.

The sweep of the drive looked forlorn now the only cars left were Nick's, Paul's and Amanda's, stranded at odd angles emphasising the emptiness.

"Toby will be thrilled with Leon's old Humber," said Nick, "It has just the kind of sick-making soft springs and fat-arse seats to suit him. Amanda had better let him drive it, the bloody great tank, not at all suitable for an exquisite woman like her."

"Oh Lord, Nick, go and fuck her for heaven's sake and get over it. She might do it for a pretty little Porsche, I don't suppose Leon left her all that well off."

"I doubt she would have me," he said. "I daren't ask, she'd make a mockery of me and I'd never hear the end of it. She is Gussie's sister after all; it would be the revenge of the Wittersworths."

Infuriating man! But, like Angelina, I couldn't even feel cross with him.

The kitchen in La Malcontenta had a colossal old range even bigger than Mama Biba's and, with a certain amount of grumbling and Meg's help, Nick got it stoked up hot enough to start cooking the contents of the crate Paul had already stored in the larder: half a dozen piglets to the utter fascination of Connie and May who wanted to know if one could eat the tails and the ears; a saddle of wether for a more grown-up taste; and a half dozen lobsters that escaped their creel and crawled clickety-clacking around the kitchen floor. When Connie went to catch one Nick shouted urgently at him to leave them.

"Oh," I said. "You're not so callous about accidents as you pretend."

"It's one thing to get killed out of carelessness or stupidity, but losing one's fingers to a lobster just leaves one miserably handicapped for life and an inconvenience to everyone else."

"Suppose he broke his neck in a skiing accident and was paralysed? That would be an even greater inconvenience."

"Mercy killing is the answer," said Nick. "Shove him down a ravine, he'd quickly and quietly freeze and no-one would be any the wiser."

"Oh, really Nick! How can you say that in front of the child?"

"Look out, Con," said Nick, "you know what's coming if you don't keep your wits about you."

Connie grabbed Nick by the leg and said "I'll hold on tight so if I fall you'll fall too."

"So we'll both be going nowhere. That's not much fun. You'd better just chance it."

"Are you and May's Mama making a new baby?"

"I'm doing my best," said Nick. "I don't know how much cooperation I'm getting from Mrs Wittersworth."

"Try harder," said Connie gleefully. Obviously something Nick frequently said to him.

Nick swept him up and held him by the ankles so he could stand on his father's shoulders, somewhat precariously balanced.

"There you are, on top of the world: a pigmy on the shoulders of a giant."

"Look out, I'm coming down," shouted Connie as he slid down into Nick's arms and hugged him, kissing him passionately, then dropped onto the ground and ran off catching May by the hand on the way.

"You'd better go to bed for a bit," said Nick. "You can get up again when the pigs are ready to eat."

"Come on," Connie said to May, "I'll show you how they do it."

"Good lord," I said, "do you think he can? He's not your son for nothing."

"Don't worry," said Nick, "I'll give him a serious talking to before he's able to do too much damage."

Nevertheless I went after them to supervise an orderly going to bed of the children while Meg and Paul rounded up the lobsters and Madge helped Nick get the animals into the oven.

When I came down again I found Nick with Toby on the loggia in the long twilight, much as Nick and Tomás used to lean on the wall at the castello. All that was missing was the aroma of Tomás's cigar. The fiery glow from the volcano had disappeared behind the clouds and a sudden squally shower passing over the lawn left it smelling of fresh cut grass with a sparkle of roses and irises.

Though they were talking with their usual air of friendly combativeness I sensed a certain standoff between them.

"Amanda is threatening not to invite me to your wedding," Nick complained. "But it doesn't matter anyway, if you are going to have a grand affair in Salisbury Cathedral with hymn singing and a thundering organ I won't want to go."

"Don't worry, we'll sit quietly at the Friends' Meeting House and you'll be allowed in as a witness," said Toby. "Since the one useful thing your grandfather taught you was how to write your name you may even sign the book, however incorrectly. Mother will instruct you on how to behave. She is going to be ecstatic; she had almost given up hope that I'd ever have serious intentions."

"Ask your mother: if I come the night before, will she let me sleep with her."

"Are you out of your mind, Nick? Of course I can't ask Mother that."

"Ever since I saw Ken Russell's film about Tchaikovsky I've wanted to sleep with your mother like he does — not that I have Tchaikovsky's problem, quite the contrary, and I can't promise it will be totally pure and sexless, but I'd lie beside her like a knight *en pudeur et chasteté*. It will be the nearest I'll get to a religious experience."

"I'll tell her you asked, just to give her something to laugh about," said Toby. "It won't even surprise her since she has put up with your bizarre carry-on ever since you were a cocky adolescent."

"It won't surprise her because she knows how I love her, my turtle dove, mi paloma triste. She fed me and chastised me and I showed her how to make her violin sing."

"Well, since poor Father is confined to his wheelchair you can be her escort and sit beside her at the meeting but for pity sake don't feel inspired to say anything. You were an embarrassment enough at your own wedding, I don't want you making a farce of mine."

"I had a splendid wedding day," said Nick, quick to defend his behaviour, however bizarre. "May you have it as good!"

Angelina used to say that too, but in retrospect she had come to a more realistic assessment. Nick on the other hand was ever more exultant about what he perceived as his successes, which improved on every re-telling.

"And night," he added, thinking it over. "I surfaced every now and then in a state of rapture, light-headed from champagne, my cock glowing and gloriously at peace with itself, my highly efficient liver doing its job so when I finally woke up next day I felt great. It was only when I saw beautiful Angelina across the breakfast table dressed and ready for going away that I realised I had probably done nothing for her though I couldn't be sure about that at first. In my state of erotic satiety I might have just forgotten how that particular episode had worked out, but her rather aggrieved expression suggested that she wasn't exactly the happy blushing bride. If only my cock had woken up I could still have fixed her before we left but he was blissfully content to just sit there smiling away to himself, saying leave me alone. So I thought, I'll deal with my lovely Angelina later, time enough, a whole lifetime in fact. It was a pleasure just to look at her and know she was my wife. It still is."

That must have been the moment I stopped being quite so jealously in love with him. I had already received as much as he had to give and it would last me my lifetime, happiness and grief in equal measure.

"I was slightly mystified," he said, "why I felt so exceptionally good. I'd had the fun of a good fight with Maddie Madigan over her attempt at a passing castration, I'd had a thrillingly fast fuck with my Eugenie. But they were both teasing me, more intent on preventing me giving it to Angelina than on giving me pleasure themselves — that bitch Eugenie did it to get me worked up, then danced with me throughout the evening, reminding me how happily we used to pass the time when we were married, but much as I enjoy dancing I have to be in love with a woman to get the ultimate pleasure out of it, from that point of view it was fun dancing with the Aunties, the first steps on the road to the Nickies..."

"Paul said you embarrassed the Furzys doing a pretty dramatic *paso doble* with him." I remarked.

"Yes. I regret that Joey and I didn't discover the *paso doble* in our dancing days. He'd have made a feisty little bull. Paul was quite a foxy little tease too but he never made up for Joey."

Toby looked like a man with a long-sought-after truth within his grasp.

"Mr Dyer tried to control you and Joey dancing. It disturbed him; not just the way you held each other by the back of the neck or around the waist but your expressions were so shamelessly sexy," he said.

"Naturally, one can't dance and not feel sexy, that's the whole point. Joey and I had a very physical bond, as you know perfectly well. Fighting too gets the balls raging; my cock was forever insurgent. For heaven's sake, we were two very ballsy boys, how else could we express ourselves?"

"The others used to make pretty crude jokes about you. Was there any truth in... it?"

"If you mean, did we bugger, the answer is no, of course not; it wasn't like that. We didn't talk sex either. We were comrades; we didn't embarrass each other with emotions. He's still the most significant person in my life."

"Then how could you...?

"... and of course at the heel of the hunt I danced with Mrs Shackleton," said Nick, cutting short Toby's bewilderment.

"I'm only too glad," said Toby, "that I went strolling in the park with my lady-for-the-night before you and Mother got going. From what I heard later I would have been mortified. My father ranted for a week on the misogyny inherent in devotion to the Virgin Mary so I knew this had to be the fall-out from some very disturbing form of sexual jealousy..."

Nick's sex life was a mystery even to his best friend and Toby was still hoping for a clarification that would explain the disconcerting incident of the cuckoo-clock. Nick however remained blissfully indifferent to Toby's concern and continued:

"When I danced with your mother to her Joe Loss 78's — she accused me of destroying them by playing them so much they were reduced to scratchy wrecks, but it was your fault for being so engrossed in *King Solomon's Mines*, She or some such rubbish that you forgot to change the needle – a slow one, I kept begging you but you didn't know the difference so it was a matter of luck when I, a randy sixteen-year-old on fire for the thrill of getting my arms around her, got the right tune. I longed to bury my face in that divine bosom but she'd say: 'Posture, Nick! head up, tight waist, pull up through the breast-bone.'

"In gratitude, my plan was to end the wedding ball with a swing and it's such infectious music everyone was having a good time, all the usual stuff until they started on *Tuxedo Junction*, the fuckingest piece of music on earth; I couldn't stop my arse from moving into rhythm, exactly right for a slow fucker like me with the trumpet giving it a terrific blast to jolt me on — 'I love you, Nick,' Mrs Shackleton said, 'but even on your wedding day this is going too far.' That was such a dare! I had to show her how much further I could go. The lights went up —Mrs Furzy throwing a wet blanket on proceedings! — but I was too far gone to care and anyway I thought we'd be lost in the rowdiness of the Gay Gordons stomping around us. Apparently not. Eugenie of course knew just by the look on my face, wave after wave of glorious release — in spite of Maddie's chilli cock dressing, or maybe enhanced by it — she can sell it as a less lethal substitute for Spanish fly — and she alerted the Heini crowd to what was going on. That is how your mother got the cuckoo-clock. So it was that a Quaker lady with a soft spot for a wayward boy who delivered the *coup de grace* and sent me to bed in a state of bliss that propelled my shirt into the air as a rampantly heraldic beast on a battle banner, swimming all night in a tide of sperm."

I leaned against the balustrade, shaking with suppressed laughter — as Paul said, Nick's love life was pure farce. Nevertheless I utterly adored him, world without end, amen!

Toby was looking at Nick with an air of disbelief, all the more dismayed by Nick's insouciance, his lack of perception that what he said might be offensive to his friend.

"I know, Nick, that I told you, you have to tell me the truth about all your crimes, quarrels and risky undertakings, but I wish you hadn't told me this," Toby said. "It shows you up as a blasted mother-fucker, and it's my mother."

"But, Toby, my comrade, my ally, my alibi, I've always been a mother-fucker. You knew that from the time you stole the coroner's report into my mother's death and read it out for me. And your mother is not a faceless, disintegrating corpse: she cured me of that nightmare. She forgives me my demons and accepts my love. So, please..."

Nick stopped short and turned away, screwing up his eyes against the distance where the passing midsummer raincloud was shrouding the far-away hills, a pathetic fallacy of Nick's grief.

Oh, dear God, I prayed, don't let him cry! That would be too humiliating.

Toby paused a moment, drew himself up then stepped up behind him and gave him a fierce downward thump on the shoulder blade.

"You blasted, goddamn, mother-fucking fool," he said. "I've compromised my conscience and subverted all my principles to keep you out of trouble, you made me your accomplice in murder and now you've reduced me to swearing at you."

As if the swearing were the worst.

"I saw you," said Toby. "I was standing beside you when Joey put the gun to his head — but he couldn't do it. He couldn't pull the trigger so you did, telling him not to be a contemptible little cheat."

"You were the referee," said Nick in a low voice, keeping his back obstinately turned. "It was your job to see he kept his half of the bargain. I took my chance and survived. I couldn't let Joey get away with being a pitiful chicken — so I did it for him."

Toby took him by the shoulders and shook him, which Nick resisted merely by hunching up and hanging his head, protecting his face with his hands.

"Look at me," said Toby, ready to punch him again.

Slowly Nick turned around and raised his head. He was laughing.

"Dine with the devil and you'll get burnt fingers," he said. "Bloody Quaker!"

"Lay a finger on my mother again and I'll go to the newspapers and tell all," said Toby, relaxing his stance. "That will put an end to any hope of a visit to the Queen."

"It will take more than you and the Queen to stop me," said Nick, "Next time I fuck your mother I'll get her knickers all the way down — I'll bring along some of Angelina's lubricant when I visit, just in case..."

Having uttered his defiance of Toby, Nick took my arm and went to lead me down the steps to see how the piglets were getting on in the kitchen, but halfway he turned back.

"By the way, Toby, thank you for stealing the coroner's report for me," he said, looking up to where Toby was still standing immobile at the balustrade. Toby waited for an explanation, knowing Nick wasn't much inclined to random expressions of gratitude.

"It did after all tell me what I wanted to know, that my mother loved me."

"I don't see how the scant remains of flesh and bones could tell you that," said Toby with for him unusual bluntness. He was still smarting from the way Nick had annexed his mother; he was still cross about the lobster, still devastated by their friend lying dead between them with a hole in his head, and Nick calmly walking away with the gun hot in his pants.

"That's all that was needed: the long bones are what show the signs of syphilis."

"And?"

"So, she left pox-ridden London to find a cure with a healer who claimed to have the secret of the Amerindians, but because it was hopeless she stayed away so I wouldn't have to suffer with her while she died, and when it got too bad she jumped. People in St. Barths knew that, the healer and the fortune-teller amongst others. They helped her on her way. If my dimwit father had agreed for us to go and fetch the boat ourselves as I begged him to, I'd have asked questions and had the answer sooner. He could have spared me the worst of my grief — for a child to be abandoned and unloved — how was I to know it was not my wicked bad dreams that made her leave me? Dad had been obsessed with building that damned boat, that's all he was thinking of; it blinded him to Nathalie's silent agony and my desperate efforts to make her laugh and love me. Not that I hold it against him; he did the best he could; they were both belated victims of the war. I try to tell him but the truth is still too much for him to hear. Maybe if you pass it on to your father, he can mention it to mine."

Toby looked truly stricken.

"I'm sorry, Nick," he said. "I'm a complete failure as a Friend, a friend and a lawyer. I believe in principle and try in practice to give people the benefit of the doubt, to weigh the evidence without bias or malice and not to use my fists in anger. Failed on all counts. I read the report and didn't ask the simplest, most obvious question: the source of the infection and when?"

"I blame that General I didn't like," said Nick, "the one in the back of the Daimler with the big cap he put on my head. He smelt peculiar. I find it disgusting that he fucked my mother. I hope you don't feel the same about me kissing yours, Toby. After my 1001 nights of unfulfilled mother-love, when yours came along my cock woke up and crowed for joy. Truly, she is the first woman I loved and I still do."

"I know you do," said Toby, smiling again. "It was bloody obvious that you were flaunting your cock at her from the minute she told you to wash your hands and comb your hair, aged fourteen. You invariably turned up at our house in a state of carefully cultivated grime just to shock her into cleaning you up. As an adolescent I would have died of embarrassment to let my mother see my penis but you were cock-proud and shameless. Well, good luck to you! You've been a source of high entertainment to her for the last twenty-five years, long may it continue."

So the prelude to Nick finally settling the Mrs Shackleton affair was at La Malcontenta, with Nick and me poised on the steps and Toby on the loggia, hands on the balustrade, regarding his friend with an air of affectionate compassion.

~

Gus and Amanda had spent the evening in the archive in a businesslike discussion of Amanda's coming marriage and they now emerged ready for some entertainment.

"As it's Nick's birthday we'll play games that he can bamboozle his way to winning…" said Gus.

"It's up to you to stop me," said Nick. "I'll take you on, Gus, at chess and we will do our best to cheat. Neither can protest, but we'll have a team of spotters to back us. The winner is he who gets away with the most false moves. I'll take Sibylla on my side as she is clueless and I'll have Amanda and Madge as well. Gus can have Dad and Paul. Toby will be referee as he's a complete failure at that job so once again I can get away with murder."

A singularly defiant statement following on the revelation that he had shot his best friend — just to prove that his Chaos Theory is no abstract concept!

The arguments that arose out of this game set-up went on until midnight when Meg came up to remind Nick he'd better have a look at the pigs.

As if by instinct as soon as the food was on the table May and Connie came staggering downstairs still more than half asleep but they woke up enough to enjoy Nick showing them how to suck out the heads of the lobsters. Though they were delighted when he demonstrated with a flourish how a properly baked *tostón* could be chopped up using the edge of a plate — the black basalt I put out for his birthday— when it came to eating the piglets they rejected the crispy ears Nick sliced up for them in favour of ribs with Meg's messy plum chutney.

Adam sat beside Meg at the far end and the whole meal long was deep in conversation with her, getting up to keep her supplied with food rather than the other way around.

Look out, Angelina, I thought, you may be losing your moral support, your Nick substitute.

Tsang had gone off with my mother under his wing.

Toby hadn't lost a minute pinning Amanda down.

Was this a third match to be made by La Malcontenta?

Meg produced her traditional trifle knowing the birthday boy himself probably wouldn't touch it, but he had May on his knee and helped her eat hers as she was really too full of lobster and pork to face sponge cake soaked in eau de vie de framboise with raspberry coulis and lashings of cream, a potent mixture even for the strongest of stomachs.

May whispered something in Nick's ear at which Connie burst into tears and attacked her with his fists. Nick stood up with a child on each arm and said, "It's time to say good-night. Say: thank you all for a lovely party and we'll see you in the morning."

Off he went with his children still punching each other, presumably all three of them to sleep in a heap in May's bed. Our proper guest room was offered up to Amanda and Toby while Paul and Madge decided to drive straight home in the early hours of the morning. Adam declined travelling home with them but stayed behind to help Meg do a thorough sorting out of the left-over food ready for Sunday lunch, then sat the rest of the night drinking tea with her in the ship-shape kitchen.

The 1st June was a continuation of our house party of the day before. When Gus and I woke up we were surprised how late it was but found the reason for our peaceful Sunday morning was that Nick had all the children in the kitchen and with Adam's help was feeding them lobster with mayonnaise on toast for breakfast. Meg had gone home to the lodge to get ready for the day ahead.

Adam and Nick went out for a stroll in the meadow, neither of them having had much sleep. After Nick's apparently off-hand rejection of Adam's projected portrait, which would extend their intimacy into too uncertain a future, they didn't seem to have anything left to say but Nick had his hand on Adam's shoulder, perhaps a peace-making gesture, an unspoken apology for causing so much anxiety and frustration even if, inherent in his personality, it was and would remain inevitable. It also struck me how similar they were at that distance, same height and build, Nick relaxed in a mimic of Adam's non-assertive demeanour.

Meg's Ancient Parent came out and joined Nick in contemplating the activity of the bees around the late spring flowers and for the next hour gave him the essence of Maurice Maeterlinck's *The Life of the Bee* with additional personal observations, so Nick increased his store of knowledge and wisdom in his usual way, while Adam went inside to establish a precedent for future week-ends in the bee-keeper's cottage.

Nick came back to the house in a prickly argumentative mood, spurning any attempt to wish him a happy birthday.

"I liked being thirty-eight," he complained, "it's a dignified age, mature but not dull. There is something panic-stricken about thirty-nine."

Reluctantly he came with Gus and me in search of a birthday present. The junk of centuries, accumulated by generations of Wittersworths, broke down his resistance and he delved into the many drawers of curios, and cupboards overflowing with once treasured possessions now orphaned, which reminded me how much work I had before me to make room for the future. With May and Connie reconciled as his assistants, Nick helped in the clearance by organising a treasure hunt with abundant prizes for everyone. Nick himself was tempted by an old leather football but after pumping it up and kicking it up and down the upstairs landing with Connie, he sent it spinning down into the hall and out the front door with the children whooping after it. Nick sat down on May's bed with a 1920's reading primer.

"Teaching yourself to read at last?" I asked.

"Dad's art is a liberation for him from the obsessional accuracy of detail in naval architecture. It's now about the bare bones, the essential minimum as he sees it. But look here how meaning has been reduced to even less: M-A-N; G-U-N; D-O-G."

"That's the whole point of the alphabet," I said.

"I prefer Chinese," he said and threw the book at the wall, breaking its spine.

I had found a ridiculously appropriate present for him among the more valuable items in the archive. It was an ivory netsuke in the form of a tiny, beautifully carved death's head, wormy eye sockets gruesomely realistic enough for Nick.

"Attach it to your waistcoat pocket and the next time you feel like shooting yourself take it out and think of me, May and Connie, Jo-jo and the Nickies, and all your friends who love you and would be desolated to lose you."

"Oh, I do," he said. "Every time. But if I don't succeed in gambling away my life I'll live too long, a miserable old struldbrug shrivelling up like a mummy until I disintegrate into dust at well over a hundred. It doesn't bear thinking of."

"God knows you are recklessly infuriating enough, so it shouldn't be difficult to get yourself shot if that's what you want. There was really no need for you to come to my wedding elegantly equipped with a gun under your coat. Besides, it would have been in shockingly bad taste, really showing off, to shoot yourself in front of the wedding guests — or was it me you were aiming for?"

"I can't answer that question," he said. "I played Russian Roulette with Joey. I lost. Every time I try to steal a second go, Joey reminds me that he won — even though I had to pull the trigger for him — he would have been mortified that he let a momentary loss of nerve make him lose his self-respect — now he won't let me die. Every time I try he tells me that I too have to stick to the rules of the game."

"Toby says you never did; you were a notorious cheat."

"Toby is simple-minded; I don't need to cheat: I outwit them. As for rules; who makes them? Moses up some mountain trying to figure out a way to control the mob: I'd have done the same."

"You fancy yourself as Moses?"

"I led my band of cadets through the wilderness back to their beds, I taught my apprentices to shoot the besiegers and how to survive a famine. From my years of *Eidgenoessische-feldschiessen* and guerrilla tactics I'm equipped to organise the Resistance or lead a revolution should the need arise— we used to argue about it all night in Madrid, me and those South Americans; they all had their plans. Mi compadrito from Santiago didn't survive: so heroic but so wrong. Ever since then one of my better nightmares is that I'm facing a firing squad. I don't mind — it would be a dignified way to go, the ceremonial lining up of four good marksmen, it will be over in minutes."

"If you knew you were going to be shot it wouldn't be over in minutes," I said, too shocked by such calculated pessimism to think of anything more relevant to say. "You'd be awake all the night before thinking about it."

"Yes, think how alive one would feel in those last hours before death; I would look at my hands and summon up memories of all they have done..." he held out his hands and looked at the prominent veins, spreading out his strong slender fingers, turning them over with an air of wonder. "I'd marvel at human frailty; at a thing so delicate and yet so enduring..."

"You have beautiful hands," I said.

"My best feature," he said, "my most valuable asset.
Miro en el alba mis manos,
miro en las manos las venas;
con extrañeza las miro
como si fueran ajenas. (Borges)

"It used to give me the most delicious creeps when Joey sang '*may my hands wither and my mouth freeze... if I forget you...*' he didn't have a great voice and a curious accent, an unlikely combination of Strabane and Afrikaans, but he could send a cold shiver down one's spine. I played the piano and hummed along for him to sing it for Mrs Dyer at the 40th birthday party Frank organised for her. Everyone was dumbfounded; they'd heard me practising terrific glisses all week and expected us to rock them with *Great Balls of Fire* but with that psalm of exile we put a blight on the party. It reminded the boys of how homesick they were underneath all the bravado, except chumps like Toby of course who actually liked school. Mrs Dyer wept and tried to persuade us to do it again for the school concert, not bloody likely — actually I'd shot Joey by then and left. I don't think Joey's hands will ever wither; I'm thankful they didn't cremate him. They took him home to the Limpopo. I'd have gone with him only Dad needed me to help him sail the *Espérance* to Monte Carlo."

Nick studied his own hands again carefully. "I don't think mine will wither either."

"Nikita Deathwish," I said, rapidly changing the subject before he could elaborate any further nightmare scenarios, "will you please stop it. You fuck with the declared intention of seeing me get a huge belly with your child inside..."

"and tender pink tits — I can't wait..."

"so," I said, "having had your wicked way with me you'll have to stick around and be a father to it... oh, no, Nick, not now, not again..."

"It's my birthday..."

"not on May's bed..."

"Call her in and it will be a lesson in biology; a practical demonstration... do you want to know what May said last night that so upset Con? She said he wanted to show her how to make a baby but they couldn't get it to work. Of course it didn't work, I told her. You are both far too small. May said, it's not me, it's Connie; he can't do it."

My heart sank. "I hope you didn't show her yours," I said, knowing full well that he would feel no need to resist such a challenge.

"I impressed on her that she too will have to be quite a bit bigger and wiser before she can engage with the rigours of sex. Connie of course hangs over the banisters to cheer me on when the Virgins escape the confines of decency and I have to chase them, so he knows what my dick is like in full flight but it somehow didn't occur to him that such a dramatic discrepancy in size might make a difference to what he can do with his. I'm grateful that you and Angelina show how to fuck with style and good manners; I'd hate Con and Jo to think all women carry on like prudish nymphomaniacs."

"I think you can safely leave May's education to me..." I said severely.

"They were both pretty subdued but snuggled up quite happily beside me. I was happy too on a very basic level, sheltering my little ones with my body — May is a little porcupine — you were a lovely girl, my mermaid, and now, three babies later, you are fantastic."

"As good as Mrs Shackleton?"

After a pause, during which he took time to test my abundant tits against his memory of the peerless mamelons-to-die-for which, being the first he'd got his hands on, set the standard, he said: "You know about child development; is May due to fall in love with me yet?"

"Absolutely, spot on."

"It's a pity that I nodded off. After being thumped by Toby for daring to be in love with his mother, I was dreaming that she was tantalisingly saying yes to me, inviting me in, so I woke up with a wishful erection. I felt two reproachful pairs of eyes staring at me and had to wriggle out of that as gracefully as I could, somewhat deflated."

"Oh, really, Nick! You are an embarrassment to everyone but yourself. What is this nonsense with Toby's mother? Do you seriously want to sleep with her?"

"I will too," he said. "I've no more time to waste; now that I've worked the Sibylline cunt to the limit it's my last chance to prove myself as mother-fucker before I go."

He pocketed the netsuke and went down to see about Sunday's midday meal.

"Come in here," Gus called me from Willie's room, "Willie has a very strict sense of protocol, apparently you know the right order in which to button up his shirt."

"We'll do it together," I said. "I think Nick has just said good-bye to me."

"As in, 'It's been a pleasure to know you, Mrs Wittersworth, and farewell!?"

"Not quite so politely."

Meg and Adam reappeared in time for lunch with a bunch of mint, which Adam chopped up for Meg's sauce to go with the cold lamb. Then Nick ruined it for most people's taste by the quantity of garlic and salt he ground to a paste in a mortar and stirred in. He, bravely imitated by Connie with smarting eyes, ate most of it.

"I'm surprised you eat mint," I said.

"The sauce works as a digestive and vermifuge, not a bad idea with cold meat, and it's slightly less awful than Maddie's chilli paste — not that I've tried rubbing it on my cock. I must tell her to add it to her range of ghastlinesses."

After the treasure hunt Toby and Amanda departed westward for Amanda to meet Mr and Mrs Shackleton Senior with a pair of Meißen pugs from Grand-mamma's vast collection of pug memorabilia, to put on Toby's mantelpiece, flanking the portrait of Bark in her prime.

Nick presented May with a penis tassel from the Ancient of Days's moth-eaten, weevil infested collection of tribal art, telling her that when she figured out what it was she would have unravelled the mystery of life.

Nick's prize was a cannon ball from Waterloo but he stood at the loggia balustrade tossing it from hand to hand and then bowled it over-arm into the long grass of the meadow and drove off unburdened and alone in the Jaguar, flushed with the success of his birthday party but also feeling resentful and embarrassed that the love and overwhelming good-will of his friends put an obligation on him he was resolutely not going to honour.

His departure was watched by Adam and Connie, clutching their carefully chosen treasures, a camera obscura and a magnifying glass, holding hands to bridge the gap their son and father was leaving in their lives.

May held my hand and said with a scornful downturn of her Deathridge mouth, "he's way too big for his pants."

"Exit the Deathrage Menace," said Gus. "I don't suppose he'll be back any time soon."

~

End
Game

16

On the 1st March 1981 my baby appeared on the scene with all the attributes one expects from a Deathridge.

"Oh, Lord," said Gus, "I thought we'd done for good with the Fuck Master."

"That's not so easy," I said, "I'm afraid Nick's off-spring are impossible to disguise."

"Angelina managed to have blonds." Gus grumbled. "Why couldn't this one take after you?"

"Dr Tsang says that when Nick's recessive genes and mine get together they've a three in four chance of producing red. It's Mendel, you know."

"Well, no doubt Tsang will be fascinated to have his theories demonstrated so graphically," Gus grumbled.

"Of course, it may be Nick's Chaos Theory in practice, based on the bounce of an oval ball."

"Never mind which," said Gus, "it's the luck of the draw, and the only one who'll object to Nick's contribution to the genetic diversity of the Wittersworths is Mother, but I'll tell her a banshee like you is perfectly capable of producing a redhead all by yourself."

"You are such a Doctor of Philosophy, Gussie," I said. "Thank you for being so tolerant of an adulterous wife."

"I never doubted your loyalty," he said. "In the end it was between Nick and me and now it looks as if Nick's self-destruct button may have sprung already — I had hoped it would be later rather than sooner. He is such a ballsy bastard I miss him when he's not in the offing challenging mine."

Since Nick drove away alone and empty-handed from the love and warm-hearted generosity of his birthday party at la Malcontenta, he had ceased to exist in our lives. During a brief appearance at Toby and Amanda's wedding he maintained his not-here, noli me tangere attitude throughout the Friends' meeting in the Barn, and Gus and I tried to guess from his demeanour how successful his proposed vigil with Mrs Shackleton might have been.

"He is staying glued to her side with his dopily love-sick-for-a-goat expression..." I whispered to Gus.

"So he has either had his way with her or he is still hoping to," said Gus.

"I can imagine him lying on his back like an effigy in marble, staring at the ceiling," I said. "He fancies himself as Don Quichotte."

"It is easier to picture him on top of her..." Gus said, "... like a limpet clinging to a whale."

"Cajoling kisses..." I said.

"and pumping his buttocks..." said Gus.

"Begging her..." I said.

"'Let me in'," Gus imitated Nick doing his high squeak.

"He knows how to jiggle it on the hot spot," I said, suppressing inappropriate giggles. "Hard, fast and for as long as it takes."

"Well, if anyone can do something as bizarre as fuck his best friend's mother while addressing her as Maman, it has to be Nick," said Gus. "God-damn him, the gormless mother-fucker!"

I shook my head at him and said, "It's respect; he addresses the Queen as Ma'am."

Gus's wicked smile betrayed his irreverent response to this comparison.

I wore Nick's *perles de pluie* looped around my neck but Nick's turtledove was fingering a rather nice string of Quakerish grey pearls with somewhat embarrassed amusement at Nick's chivalry as he acted his part as her groom.

"I'm beyond jealousy," I said.

Gus, seeking to provoke a reaction that would give him a clue to satisfy his curiosity, remarked to Mr Shackleton that Nick had done nothing obvious to disrupt Toby's wedding — apart from monopolising Toby's mother.

"I really don't know," said Gus, "how Nick resisted the temptation to say something outrageous at the Friends' meeting; it seemed a unique opportunity to make mischief with impunity."

"Nick is a remarkably loyal and generous friend," was Mr Shackleton's surprising response. "And as son he is exemplary."

Gus held his tongue, curious if any explanation would follow.

"Both our sons, Nick and Toby, have put Adam and me to shame in our narrow-minded blindness but it is a redemption for Adam that at last he is able to face the truth that he failed his wife in her sickness and death. And that unfortunate boy — at least my wife gave him her full support and some consolation, and to his credit, Nick has never failed to respond with sincerest gratitude. Of course he flirts disgracefully but he makes her smile and his nobility of spirit and his courage win my total admiration."

"I thought it strange Adam was wearing a black tie to a wedding," said Gus. "So now we know."

Since then, nothing.

"It's disturbingly peaceful," said Gus. "No more midnight calls so he can moan for hours at a stretch how he is lusting after you."

"What worries me," I said, "is that even Meg doesn't know where he is and if Gladys does, she's not saying."

Toby came to consult with Gus, me and the baby.

"I am supposed to keep the tally of Nick's off-spring," Toby said, "so I'd better check this one out. He conveniently makes up the half dozen Nick said he is prepared to acknowledge, together with Alexi and Boris now Angelina has adopted them as proper little Deathridges."

"Evita wants to take them to Manila," said Gus, "It seems they have quite a following there thanks to her uncle broadcasting daily bulletins on local radio. Father absolutely forbids it. He has appointed himself guardian to support Angelina in her fight for sanity. Nick himself would probably think it terrific sport to have his little Chudovorets worshipped by the credulous mob."

"Wittersworth is right," said Toby, "the important thing is to protect the children from exploitation and they should be given a normal education. They can't all be illiterate polymaths like Nick. Keeping track of the Little Nickies is quite perplexing too. The Virgins are coy about admitting how many there actually are — they come in multiples of four — but that is Tsang's problem."

"Angelina says they are overrunning the place like rabbits," said Gus, "pesky little Nickies underfoot everywhere. She has Evita's two young nieces living in to cope with the work but the girls are nearly as much trouble in their own way so she'll be pleased to see the Virgins take the whole circus off to France..."

Toby shook his head over the problem of satisfying the Virgins.

"Tsang declines paying for the château Nick took them to see before he left — they fell in love with its elegant high walls with stone greyhounds prancing along the top and pointy turrets, some comte's hunting folly — I have the Misses Furzy weeping all over me that Nick would buy it for them if Tsang won't. And I draw the line at the small plane they say Nick promised them for flying around in; I tell them they'll have to wait for Nick to come home to see to that. In the meantime I've agreed to buy them a suitable house but after that Tsang has to foot the bills. I earmarked a couple of nice places and they've gone sightseeing to choose from them. That will have stop them nagging me for more of Nick's money."

"Don't be too optimistic about that," said Gus. "Nick registered the surname as Nikolayevich as he didn't want his children known as Furzys, so they'll never stop tugging at his coat-tails."

"As soon as I can fix the exodus into Normandy they can invade the village school in smocks and white socks and get a perfectly adequate French education," said Toby. "Even Nick wouldn't object to that."

"You are assuming Nick hasn't his own plans for them," I said, annoyed at how easily everyone seemed to be writing him out of any active role in our lives.

"Apart from the confusion over the Nickies, he left detailed instructions covering everything from the goat in Angelina's back garden to his Friggin' in the Riggin' pub on Death-row... he says you are to put his piano in the centre of the hall surrounded by the Virtues and play hymns on it..."

"No," I said, "I'll practise sonatas so when he comes home I can accompany his violin..."

"So, let's see the youngest and last recruit to the Deathrage army," said Toby.

"He's not," Gus said. "He is Felix Wittersworth. If Nick wants him he'll have to come and fight me for him."

"Felix! That's an optimistic name," said Toby, still gloomy.

"We've given him the name," said Gus, "of the donor of the green book. It seemed appropriate since we learned his name on the day Felix was conceived."

I held Felix on my arm, a scarcely more than embryonic little red-poll cuckoo, so like the photo Meg showed me of Nick on his great-grandmother's deathbed, same pointy chin and lippy pout, my talisman to bring Nick home. Nevertheless I was deeply anxious that all the messages I'd left on the phone would never reach his ears, the whirrings and beeps that came from the machine would crop my words off into space unanswered, chopping them off the tape to make room for other, random, less urgent voices.

"My mother has the totally unrealistic idea that it's her duty to go looking for Nick the way she went to rescue him when he disappeared after Joey's funeral," said Toby. "Father says it's because of the whippet. Such a strange gift to send as a thank you for her hospitality."

"Not really so odd if he spent the night beside her *en pudeur et chastite*. A faithful whippet to lie at her feet seems a wholly appropriate gesture after a night of love."

Toby couldn't deny the possibility that Nick might at last have breached the defence put up by sturdy Quakerish knickers.

"Except that it's Father who has the benefit of her company; she sits on his wheelchair, leaping off every so often to go chasing rabbits."

"Besides, when your mother went looking for him the first time she had a phone number," said Gus, "and found the darling boy securely embedded in the safest place on earth. Now, how would she know even where to start?"

"She got this postcard from him a few days ago," Toby said, taking it out of his pocket.

I found myself giggling uncontrollably. A postcard from Nick? Of all the unlikely things!

It was a picture, from a watercolour original, of a gaucho with wild red hair on horseback. On the reverse it was signed recognisably "Nick", but the address was in a neat loopy hand, and a multitude of small blurry postage stamps filled up the space around it, evidence of rampant inflation with which the post office couldn't keep up. No message. No return address.

Frustratingly useless.

"I'm not sure it's as useless as you think," said Gus. "Correos Uruguay is a starting point and if it becomes really necessary we can trace it by the — admittedly illegible — postmarks. I could take it to my friend in forensics to have it analysed; you'd be surprised what they can deduce from next to nothing."

"At least we can deduce he's still alive," I said, daring to admit my worst fear.

"It looks worn," said Gus, turning it over and over. "Who knows how long it has taken to get here."

"Well, it's not exactly a ransom note," said Toby, almost as if he wished it were.

His words struck a chill in my heart.

"I think I'm going to faint," I said. "Do you think he's in trouble? Is it an appeal for help?"

"Hardly that," said Gus. "He probably thinks the gaucho looks like him: Nick in fancy dress. Paul said he fancied himself in bombachas; he bought a pair in alpaca to wear tucked into his Hemingway boots but couldn't stand the itch on his inner thighs, nearly as bad, he said, as the itch he got from Tsang's cock-booster."

I see Nick standing alone on the platform of a deserted railway station, in his double-breasted chalk-stripe, hands in pockets. He turns his head to look at me with slightly raised eyebrows and furrowed forehead, his expression of being tolerantly amused by the strivings of mere mortals. A train is not expected any time soon.

A Sibyl moment.

What worries me is that he is wearing the wrong suit.

"He's going too far away," I said, dragging my mind back from the question: was there ever a train called the Patagonian Express or was that too a figment of my imagination...

Gus held the postcard to the light.

"Don't rub it," said Toby. "You'll damage the surface and wipe off the fingerprints."

"I doubt fingerprints will mean much after handling by an unknown number of postal workers," said Gus. "Blood, now, that would be interesting. One could infer something from whether it were B Negative or some other." He poked at the corner of a stamp where it was glued down. "That looks like the tail of an ampersand — I think it's actually addressed to Mr & Mrs Shackleton only the Mr is obscured under a stamp."

"Mother won't be pleased with the suggestion it is not exclusively hers. That will alter her perception of its significance."

It altered mine too. It made it less of a love token to his turtledove, though if he were going to send postcards, why not Mr & Mrs Wittersworth. Gus would shift heaven and earth for his friend and was not confined to a wheelchair.

Toby examined the postcard again, as if it might reveal something new, but it kept its secret.

Paul came back from a trip to Harvard and remarked quite casually that he'd been talking to Nick on the phone a few weeks before, he couldn't remember exactly when or even if Nick was in Buenos Aires or Montevideo, or maybe Nick hadn't told him exactly. Paul had other things on his mind than his brother-in-law's vagaries.

That accorded with Mrs Shackleton's postcard.

I was quite unreasonably angry that my torment of anxiety was unfounded and that Paul attached no importance to it.

"He said he was having a good time dropping in on political meetings in cellars, or playing polo and hunting nandu (emu to you and me) across the pampas wildly swinging his bolas to the hilarity of the experts, though when he brought down several and demonstrated his ruthlessness with the knife their sniggers were silenced. He says it's eating beef, drinking vile wine, talking guns with one side or at some estancia eating beef, drinking marginally better wine, talking money with the other. He crosses the river when the police get interested in him."

Maybe my anxiety was not so uncalled for after all.

"He places too much reliance on his Swiss passport," said Gus. "It's not going to stop a bullet."

"He says he has gone native," said Paul, "but he must look conspicuously eccentric swanning around in his red crocodile, his too chic chinos from Hermès, his britches from Huntsman. But he said he found a jolly laundress to keep his twenty Budd shirts washed and ironed and his Zimmerli underpants bleach nicely in the sun."

The pants Eugenie bought in Basel to enhance the liveliness of his frisky cock.

"He met her in a bar in Palermo drinking whisky and she offered to do him a hutch rabbit with baked squash in her back yard while his clothes were drying, so he was willing to be lured behind the scenes to see how she did that — he regards himself as the rabbit expert and he'd never had a Patagonian..."

"We'd better not tell Nancy," I said, "she'll be furious that he went without her."

"... he admitted a certain resemblance this Mirta has to Mrs Shackleton, fading honey curls, probably fake in this case, might have been what tempted him to drop his guard..."

"and, one presumes, his trousers as well..." said Gus.

"... if it's any consolation to you, Sibylla," said Paul, "he complains bitterly that being in love with a Strumpety Cunt condemns him to pass his nights under the Southern Cross embracing his pillow, howling with frustration..."

I took this with a pinch of salt knowing Nick's proclivity for poetic exaggeration. It was all too easy to picture him passing the midday in the shade of a backyard fig tree naked with his Patagonian while his clothes hung to dry in the sun — liberated from the straightjacket of prudery by years of intercourse with this Strumpety Cunt.

There was consolation for me as well as him in that scenario. I could only pray it was true.

But when I phoned Toby to tell him what Paul reported he said, exasperated:

"Nick and women! I'll tell Mother she can stop feeling guilty now he has found a whisky drinking, tango dancing alternative Maman to fuck instead of her. Why doesn't he just phone me so I can talk sense into him? If he ends up in an Argentine jail it won't be lust that is agitating his balls, a cattle prod more likely."

"How can you sit on your backside and say that?" I said, feeling sick again. "If you think he's in danger, go and do something about it. He would for you."

"I'm a small-town solicitor. If Nick is in trouble he got himself there. You can't expect me to travel to the other side of the world to some dire prison to ask if Nick Deathridge happens to be among the *desaparecidos*. My job is to look after the home front — and that includes you and this latest infant."

"I've got Gus for that," I said.

As I talked to Toby on the phone Gus was standing at the window with Felix on his arm and Willie beside him. Outside we could see May and Augusta in their beekeeping veils and gloves helping Meg's Ancient Parent and Adam move the beehives back on to the meadow again in preparation for the spring flowers. A few years ago Nick said that Adam had no business worrying about him; he'd find out soon enough if he were dead. Now Adam was taking him at his word, only this time there was a complication. He was as impatient as anyone for Nick to come home as he didn't like to get married while Nick was away, not that he needed Nick's approval, he just wanted to show how much his troublesome son meant to him, in spite of their differences.

"It's one of Nick's virtues that he had the courage to go and find the unhappy truth behind the apparent facts of his mother's disappearance," Gus remarked. "Though it is only a matter of interpretation, it altered Nick's self-perception — no longer left alone to fend for himself but a child who was after all truly loved by his mother dying slowly, in despair that she was losing her mind."

"... though Nick using his quest for the truth as an excuse to frequent go-go bars with prostitutes on his honeymoon remains indefensible," I said.

"I tell Adam not to wait; I don't see the point of giving Nick the opportunity to cause him more mortification," said Gus.

"Adam is right to wait," I said. "When Nick comes home he'll make it a great party. He'll roast an ox in the yard and get in fiddlers and Northumbrian bagpipes for his Dad's wedding. Mr Shackleton is right, his generosity goes way beyond cuckoo clocks and whippets."

~

The 1ˢᵗ June 1981 was, or would have been, Nick's fortieth birthday. Paul and Madge with the bulldog came to spend Sunday 31ˢᵗ May at La Malcontenta. I was disappointed they didn't bring Connie, thinking how desperately he must be missing his Daddy but Angelina had taken him to join the rollerblading kids in Regent's Park.

No one mentioned last year's party. Only that it was the hundred and first birthday of the Ancient of Days elicited some ribald comment.

"Grand-mamma says she can't think why she gave up our lovely casino only to have to go and hold the Baron's hand while he tells her for the thousandth time that he experienced a total eclipse of the sun at Delphi, the silence, even the rock buntings ceasing to twitter."

"Poor Gus," said Paul, "The Old Man of the Mountain still making a nuisance of himself at that age, how does he keep going!"

"I bet Nick will be just the same, an embarrassment to family and friends *in perpetuum*," said Gus.

"Yes," said Paul, "it's either that or he's at the bottom of the River Plate feeding the fishes."

Paul had just returned from a flying visit to Buenos Aires where he had been on a secret mission backed by a government agency to find out if there were any truth in the Malvinas rumours, on the grounds that his brother-in-law was there and from his dealings — in syringes, dollars or guns wasn't specified — would know exactly what was going on. This rather gave the lie to the Foreign Office claim later that the invasion took them by surprise. Paul hadn't mentioned to his bosses that said brother-in-law had disappeared and he took the job solely for the opportunity it gave him to make confidential enquiries about Nick, but fortuitously it was the start of his career as negotiator in tricky situations, which extended in later years to the delicate matter of hostages.

"So it's all Nick's fault," Paul said. "Just because he knows all these outlandish characters and how to deal with them without losing one's nerve, I'm stuck with his reputation for the rest of my days. It puts an end to my hopes of being the British Aristophanes, though I don't suppose there's a future any more in trying to promote the eternal verities as an art form."

Madge fetched Adam from the lodge in spite of his determination to stay out of Nick's affairs, but Gus and Paul were equally determined to make him listen. They weren't allowing him get away with a repetition of his Nathalie fiasco.

"Nick has denounced me often enough for a Useless Old Man," he came in protesting, "so why not leave me enjoy my uselessness in peace. I don't need to know the latest Dumez scandal that has my name attached to it. I wish his mother were alive so she could take responsibility for her brilliantly awful son. If only I had met a woman like Meg sooner I wouldn't have been duped into marrying a high-class whore like Natalie. I should have fucked and gone on my way and left her to deal with the consequence. If I hadn't been there to be press-ganged into a respectable marriage she'd have done away with her accidental brat and this whole house of cards would never have existed."

"Dearest Adam, you know that Nick is very attached to Meg," I said, falsely-sweet, incensed at Adam's persistent denial of his son's existential despair. "They worked together all those years without any emotional demands on each other, in what Nick called symbiosis — I don't know what Meg calls it: a fucking great nuisance probably. Think of her devoutly picking up a million splinters of glass after he shattered his cheval mirror with a magnum of Taittinger — which was the moment when he lost control of his carefully constructed life."

"Because Gianni's motorbike parked all night under his window shattered Nick's emotional carapace," said Paul, remembering his own agony of jealous disappointment, walking through the night with Gus.

"Or indeed," I said, withstanding this implied condemnation of the Lorelei role wished upon me by Nick himself, "that Meg's most profound sexual experience was probably Nick teaching her how to uncork a bottle of Krug with finesse and no vulgar fizzing. Perhaps, Adam, you are getting the benefit of that lesson in sensitivity."

"So, Paul, tell us, what did you find out in South America?" said Gus, intervening before I got too explicit telling tales: Meg seeing Nick in action, fucking his first wife on his second wedding day, or her loyal keeping watch over his love for the nanny in the cellar as well as monitoring of the fluctuating state of the bed he shared with Angelina.

"Oh yes, the damned Argies will go to war all right," Paul replied. "They are calling up youngsters from all corners of the land, shoving a load of cheap rifles in their hands — not Nick's SIGs of course, only the police get those — and with a crucifix around the neck send them off to die for the flag."

It seemed Paul was reluctant to say more.

"But any news of Nick?" Gus insisted.

"I don't think he's there any longer."

"Come on, Paul," said Gus, "Give us the gossip. Don't spare us."

"I can't be sure that this has anything to do with Nick," said Paul. "I dropped in on Jörg Mosiman, his bank's representative in Buenos Aires — obviously one way to find out where he is has to be where the money is going.

Of course Mosiman wouldn't admit to knowing anything about that, but told me that some weeks previously a man claiming to be a Swiss citizen was rumoured to be in police custody. He sent someone to enquire, as their duty would be either to see this person alive or, if not, to repatriate the body, but they were told that the suspect was already free and had left. No names were mentioned — the usual Swissery! Mosiman said he had doubts about the truth of the story, the circumstantial details were ambiguous. The person in question had been brought in for interrogation over contacts with known *furtivos* but he'd held out that he had no personal knowledge beyond what he had picked up in a bar. He was kept overnight in a cell with a suspected KGB agent arrested coming in from Cuba. To prove there was nothing to hide, Mosiman was allowed to hear the recording from the bug in the cell. The two men spoke in English and at first the guards listening in thought they were getting useful information, stories about a Russian, a Pole and a German, but when the translators came they started to laugh. They said it was just a recital of bawdy stories and disgracefully indecent, sacrilegious and slanderous jokes. The English voice also had a nice range of porteño swear words in which he cursed his discomfort, and they sang sad songs: lugubrious Russian ones and an impassioned lament about the death of a bullfighter — the guards were quite entertained listening in."

"Well," I said, "the guards may have thought it quite a joke..."

"It's what persuaded me it might well be Nick," said Paul. "I've heard him sing that song before. But then Mosiman said something really disturbing. He said that in the midst of all the larking about, it was as if this person knew where the microphone was concealed and under cover of Pushkin's passionate *Farewell to Georgia* he heard a distinct undertone of Basler deutsch. He wouldn't say what was said but they took it seriously enough to warn Geneva that the reports of torture and murder were not a purely Argentine affair but done with the skilled cooperation of a so-called friendly power, sustaining the global dictatorship of greed."

It can't be Nick, he's far too prudent to get himself into a position where torture and murder were on the menu... it must be Nick — I recognised the

tone of his jeremiads in my ear, untold nights trembling through the airwaves to tell me he loved me...

"Anyway, in the morning instructions came from *Extranjeros* to let the
two go — Mosiman didn't say but I guessed it was the little red passport at
work — and the jokers walked away together, arm in arm, still singing like a
pair of drunks and were never seen again."

"It certainly sounds like Nick," said Gus. "But it seems unlikely they'd be
allowed to disappear of their own free will."

"It appears that there were several shootings in the city that day
which kept the police busy, but Mosiman too had doubts; he said he found
no evidence they had ever walked out of that hell-hole alive."

"Bawdy jokes and sad songs," I said. "It's the way Nick would choose
to spend his last night on earth. Wailing in flamenco would do for lack of a
violin to express pain. I wonder if Joey was there to sing along with him."

My voice was trying to talk sense while inside I was numb with distress.

"Yes," agreed Gus. "Typical Deathrage, he'd sing a long-drawn-out complaint about the ghastliness of life, ending in rage."

Oh, dear Jesus on the cross, please may Nick not end his life in a rage.

I prayed impotently in the hope that there was a power somewhere
which could change the course of history at my request; a cultural difference between Nick and me: Nick took life as it came, cursed his enemies and
used his wits to save himself.

"He learned Flamenco in the bars around the bull ring in Madrid," said
Paul, torn between the happy memory of Nick having a good time and
remembering the frisson of anticipation Nick had had of his own death in
the slaughterhouse. "*Que buen torero estaba!*" That describes Nick all
right, dicing with death, bleeding his life away in the sand. He really fancied
himself as a torero. He loved the way they bend their backs with their arses
tucked in so the horn skims along behind them. Shouting *olé*, it sent him
wild with excitement."

"Nick was always fancying himself dead," I said, bitterly frustrated that
a man so full of life could be so obsessed with how he looked in death.

Sheathed in a skin-tight black and gold *traje de luces* surrounded by a cheering, weeping crowd would appeal to his love of farce, the clown!

But not chained and broken...

Adam, who stood throughout as if he would walk away at any moment, leaned against the window, his forehead on his arm, looking out down the drive to the lodge he shared with Meg.

"You'd think they could spot the red crocodile," said Madge going to stand beside him.

"Well, that's not quite all," Paul added after a hesitation. "Since Nick had mentioned playing polo, I went to Palermo to ask if he'd been there lately. Someone thought he'd been seen on the Aliscafo crossing over to Colonia, the Swiss colony on the River Plate, apparently with a woman, but it was uncertain when. Then there was a report that a body was fished out of the river in an unusual red leather jacket, but it was a *moreno*, no red hair."

"Even if he got knifed and dropped overboard for the sake of the most expensive piece of tawdry ever invented, no-one would expect to get away with it, walking around in that coat," said Gus.

We exchanged glances behind Adam's back.

I said, "Nevertheless, there is something reassuring about Nick exchanging tall tales with a Russian spy, even if the circumstances were grim."

Infuriating Nick, I thought. Locked up in a foreign jail, when all he need do was live out his life on a celestial level, high above his native Thames, making music — and love.

"Look," said Paul, "he was seen crossing the water, so if he's in the clutches of the Tupamaros we'd have had a ransom demand; if he's dead there's no point in worrying; if he's roaming around somewhere, he can talk the hind leg off a donkey in any language, so he'll find his own way back when he feels like it."

"You've done your bit, Paul," said Adam. "Go and get on with your own life, you've more important things to keep you busy than trying to save a man so hell-bent on taking risks that it amounts to suicide."

He turned to go, but paused at the door.

"Meg and I will stick to our decision to wait until Nick gets home."

I watched him take a shortcut across the lawn back to the lodge, but half way he stopped and stood with his head in his hands, shaking it. He probably realised he had made a rash vow. As likely as not there'd be no fatted calf or fiddlers for his wedding.

I'd persuade Meg to drag him to the registry office, with Gus pushing from behind if necessary — even if the ensuing feast of roast pig and Château Petrus from Nick's cellar made it more of a wake.

Whack fal-de-ral-de, grab your partners,
Thump the floor, your trotters shake
isn't it the truth I told you
lots of fun at Finnegan's wake!

Gus and Paul spent the rest of the day discussing their own more imme-diate concerns while Madge took the children for a run, accompanied by the surprisingly agile lumbering of the bulldog.

I sat alone in the hall with the Virtues, listening to the tapes Nick had bought under the arcades in Bern and played loudly all the way down the Rhine to where the melted ice-water of the Bernese Oberland lost itself in the boundless North Sea netherlands: a song of exquisite yearning, my undying belief that against all the odds my impossible brave Lohengrin would come back to me... that first time I heard it was in a narcotic dream, with Nick in his ineffable reality beside me...

I could still see him and feel him; he was totally present in the music.

By the time the tapes were worn out I would be able play the themes modestly, without embellishments, on Bonne-Maman's piano. Following Nick's example with his violin, the hall would be peopled with a vast orchestra of ghosts playing their parts in support, calling him back.

"Well you know," said Paul as they were about to leave, "Nick always ima-gined himself as the last man standing against the Hunnic hordes, holding the Gothard to the last bullet."

"He's a long way from the Gothard now," I cried. "He fucked for sons; he said I was his biggest failure. I want to tell him that Felix is the success he was asking for."

"Can you imagine him trying to make an international call from a public phone booth in whatever hole he's hiding in?" said Paul.

"No," I agreed, "he relies more on telepathy."

"How old is the baby? Three months? Well, obviously your cunt is itching for the master cock to come and strut his stuff again."

"Oh, fuck off," I said.

Nevertheless, around midnight Nick phoned.

"My One and Only Sibyl, I am dying without you."

It was clear what he meant — he had saved my life, now it was my turn. Yet his voice was coming to me from far, far away with a sighing in the background, maybe the airwaves, or the wind in trees, or perhaps, with rhythmic recurrence, waves rolling softly on a sandy shore.

In a desperate effort to reach him I whispered, not to wake Gus:

"Where are you?"

"When I was incarcerated in the dark I was crying out for you."

I had always been ready to answer his call, prepared to sacrifice everything for him, but now he had landed himself in one of his so-called awkward situations and this one wasn't so easy to get out of.

I lay in the dark with his voice in my ear, a little husky, with quickened breath as if his body were thrusting itself against mine, eager to make love.

Please come home! I tried to speak but I was so choked with tears I couldn't.

But he continued quietly, unhurried, having all the time in the world to tell another of his tall tales. I followed his words in my imagination.

"You wouldn't want to know where I've been," he said. "I saw the slaughterhouse. I bluffed my way out of the hands of the CIA-clones without much permanent damage. They were careful not to leave any visible scars. Mirta took me under her skirts and guided me across the water to where she has a summer cabin on the Solis Chico."

Yes, we had a reported sighting on the boat. He was recognised by the red crocodile.

"That was probably the last time he was seen alive," he said. "Butchered. Apparently I wasn't in it at the time."

They said the body fished out of the river wasn't Nick.

"I exchanged it during the crossing for a not very stylish poncho like the one on the postcard Mirta sent to Mr Shackleton."

Mr Shackleton?

"The stamps are hiding an address where you could have found me, had you wanted to badly enough."

Stamps for the philatelist!

"Obviously you don't need me."

He meant: if we needed him, not that he might need us.

I tried to speak, to protest that we wanted more than anything on earth to find him, but my throat was so tight my voice made no sound.

"I was a bit shaken up but Mirta looked after me. Imagine a Latino Queen Mother with the added attraction of a pair of smoothly sculptural thighs so well articulated at the hips that when she lies back they open up like the gates of heaven to let me in.'

Oh, Nick! He had no trouble finding a hiding-place for his cock.

"We console each other through long afternoons of uncanny quiet. The only thing we disagree about is, whenever itinerants set up stall under the trees selling a few scrawny chickens, is how to cook them — long, strong yellow claws from foraging around in the scrub, Mirta's chicken soup is nearly as good as Mami Bott's. But she wrecks my shirts; she can't understand the difference between cloth one washes in a stone trough with a scrubbing brush, and Swiss cotton from Jermyn Street. She goes to Mass on Sundays and crawls up the aisle to the communion rail on her bare knees to demonstrate to the locals that even though she's a *sin vergüenza* from Buenos Aires they can't outdo her in penitence and piety."

Meg's worst nightmare, the ruin of shirts she had kept in lovingly graded rows, immaculate cuffs meticulously aligned.

"I spend quite pleasant evenings working for a chap whose modest arsenal I found hidden behind Mirta's shack, not very artfully disguised under a heap of empty wine bottles. I was using the bottles for target prac-tice when he came creeping up on me. I persuaded him I'd be more use as gunsmith than dead. He isn't voluntarily a killer, he'd prefer to fight for justice with words but he said he wasn't achieving anything sitting at his table writing poetry. Nevertheless he recites them to me while I tinker with his   little collection of FAL's and Brownings. I listen and suggest better words; he tells me to shut up and stick to my greasy rag. His poems will last longer and eventually have more influence than his bullets and dynamite. Occasion-ally others come to join us; we talk all night the way I did in Madrid with the chaps from Santiago and Bogotá: these guys talk a great revolution — I have to restrain myself from telling them, after my years of training on Europe's watershed, how a Swiss officer would go about the fight against dispropor-tionate odds. What do I know? It isn't my quarrel; all I do is fix the guns. We disagree most over whether killing a kidnapped US agent was a triumph or tactically a colossal blunder. It's the reason they are hiding in a deserted seaside watering-hole instead of negotiating from positions of strength in the city."

I close my eyes, drifting along with his voice getting quieter and quieter, caressing my cheek, until I am straining to hear, panic stricken that I am losing him.

"I am strangely happy," he says, but with a sharp intake of breath, a change of pace, then continues, "It's a little lost paradise: hummingbirds and herons. Every morning I wake up to the miracle of sunrise, I walk for miles in a forest of pine and mimosa and emerge from the trees to slip across the dunes and swim in the calm water of the River Plate while out yonder the South Atlantic pounds away. I swim out to join the dolphins. I am temp-ted to stay with them forever but they will have none of it, they're in league with Joey and escort me back to where I belong. Like it or lump it, I can't escape my human fate, no short cuts, no easy way out.

"It is something of a shock to step out of the water and find my comrade dead at my feet, being rolled back and forth by the surf, his face washed clean of wet sand by each successive wave. I feel extraordinarily naked, but with a show of indifference I pull my trousers on and retrace his footsteps and mine, walking slowly back through the dunes towards the trees, knowing every step can be my last. As far as I can tell there is no one on the strand behind me so I am walking towards my killers and I feel strong, daring them — they are retreating before me..."

His voice continued without pause, an endless cycle: *end here; us then; on again; Finn again; along the riverrun past eve and adam's, from swerve of shore to bend of bay, brings us back...* ; repeating dolphins and death over and over while I listen in sheer terror, lying in the dark without moving or making a sound, seeing him washed clean and walking, with his trousers on, to die with dignity, bleeding into the sand.

Gus leaned across me and loosened the telephone from my grip. He listened to the hum a moment before putting it back in its cradle.

"Wake up," he said. "You're having a Sibyl moment."

I couldn't speak, but I knew it was Nick's voice all right, clear and unmistakable.

~

The Rush
on the
Ultimate

17

So on Monday, 1st June 1981, I stood alone in the drawing room before Watts's portrait of the Ancient of Days. I opened a bottle of Taitinger rosé and drank a toast to his memory. He had died at three o'clock in the afternoon of his hundred and first birthday. I was now Lady Wittersworth. Angelina, eat your heart out!

I propped the Korzennick photograph of Nick as he wanted to be remembered, on his barren windswept steppe/veldt/pampa on the mantelpiece partly obscuring the Watts. I studied the photograph he claimed represented himself at the height of his power, taken when he was thirty-eight, the best age in his opinion.

"It's Himself," Meg's voice announced.

I thought she was commenting on the likeness in the photo, but when I turned around it was Nick Himself standing at the door looking at me.

I was awestruck.

He had such presence: thin, austere, sober suited, as ever empty handed, fingers relaxed. He had never appeared more imposing.

Having survived the thirty-ninth, his year of panic, his face with deeper furrows and more permanent lines, his body whittled to an ever more minimal structure of bone and muscular strength, tough and purely functional, surely now was the point of equilibrium: if he continued on this course he would destroy himself; but if, as he predicted, at forty his balls quietened down, it might be possible to love him without too much anguish. I was quite prepared to listen to the disturbing intensity of his violin if only he would stay at home and not distress me by his unpredictable absences, his game of hide-and-seek with death.

That smile!

The glass I had been clutching with numb fingers fell and shattered on the stone hearth: shards of crystal and gold in a pool of pink fizz.

"My offering to *Fortuna*," I said, hoping he wouldn't see the dread his spectral reappearance gave me.

But Nick shaped his destiny with his own hands.

While I poured two glasses full he walked over to stand beside his photo, facing me across the hearth.

"Happy birthday," I said. "I knew you'd come."

The Divine Malcontenta, he used to call me. I was artfully backlit by the tall drawing room window, ample with motherhood; I knew he was loving me more than ever — the Look, such expressive eyes, his face taut with desire.

"Where have you been so long?" I said. "You look as if you must have been living on raw beef and red wine for maximum adrenaline and sperm production, focused on this moment."

I had left so many messages for him, an excessive number. He was coming anyway; he didn't need a thousand reminders. Such urgency, he would think I must be dying.

"If I had needed your Don Quichotte blood I'd have been dead by now," I said.

He stood holding his glass but not drinking, keeping his distance, and though we spoke there was an unbridgeable gulf of silence between us.

His life was already beyond my reach. I could no longer hurt him for all the hurt he had ever inflicted on me, or drag him back from the self-destructive path he had chosen regardless of me and our children, his many beautiful children. He had sold his workplace, all his bright ideas, walked out on a life so rich in friends, to lose it by a chance shot, because he had shot his friend Joey — by mischance.

His lip trembled though he hid his anguish behind the off-hand gesture with which he dismissed all of life's little misadventures.

"If you are thinking of a quick fuck and tomorrow to be gone again — well, think again; postpone your heroics a bit longer," I said furiously. "Wait here."

I ran down the stairs to fetch Felix from his pram in the June sun and carried him up, smiling at his startled ice-blue eyes. He looked at me as if wondering what momentous event was about to disrupt his placid routine.

"This is your big moment, baby," I said. "You're about to meet the other most important person in the whole world."

There was no one in the room, only shards of crystal and gold in a pool of pink fizz on the empty hearth.

And an unfathomable well of grief.

~

CHARACTERS

Sibylla d'Art	Nanny to the Deathridge family, later married to Gus Wittersworth
Nick Deathridge	Supplier of medical equipment to laboratories, with a number of sidelines
Angelina	Nick's wife, mother of Connie (Conrad) and Jo-Jo
Meg & Gladys	Housekeeper and secretary respectively
Toby, Frank, Nestor	school friends of Nick's
Paul Furzy	Angelina's younger brother, friend of Gus Wittersworth
The rest of the Furzy family	Aunties Rose and Violet also known as the Virgins and Great-uncle Harold, medieval music expert
Mary and the Pinkerton girls	Sibylla's friends from school and the nanny academy
The Renaissance Women	Angelina's friends, led by Dolly Miller
Mr and Mrs Shackleton	Toby's parents, who had Nick to stay in school holidays
Adam Deathridge	Nick's father, retired naval architect, now a painter
William Wittersworth	Gus's father who does his best to advise Sibylla
Amanda Bolus & The Harpies	Gus's sisters
Hein	Nick's apprentice master at his engineering works in Basel
Eugenie Bott	Hein's secretary, Nick's first girlfriend
Papi and Mami Bott	Eugenie's parents, Mami likes Nick, Papi has fierce fights with him
The Grati brothers	Gianni and Gino - Sibylla gets engaged to Gianni in an attempt to have a "normal" life but Gino interferes

CHARACTERS

Claire and Tomas	Owners of Tuscan castle where Sibylla goes to get away from the London complications
Dr Tsang	fertility expert (sex guru) based in Hong Kong, Nick's business partner
Conrad and Anna Dumez	Nick's grandparents, now dead
Nathalie Dumez	Nick's mother, also dead
Joey Madigan	whose ghost haunts the story
Maddie Madigan	Joey's very much alive sister

SIBYLLA'S HIERARCHY OF LOVERS

Nick Deathridge	Supplier of medical equipment, father of baby May
Gus Wittersworth	Law student, Sibylla's husband, father of baby Willie
The Grati brothers	Gianni and Gino, wine merchants, probable and possible fathers of baby Augusta
Dr Tsang	Sex guru and gynaecologist from Hong Kong, Nick's business partner
Paul Furzy	student, Gus's friend, Nick's brother-in-law
Toby Shackleton	Nick's friend and solicitor
Also in attendance:	**Adam Deathridge** (Nick's father), **Father William Wittersworth** (Gus's father) and **Luigi Grati** (father of Gianni and Gino)

SOURCES

Books referred to in the text, explicitly or implied

The White Goddess	Robert Graves
Portrait of a Lady	Henry James
Chronicle of a Death Foretold	Gabriel Garcia Marquez
Nicholas Nickleby	Charles Dickens
Dombey & Son	Charles Dickens
The Aleph	Jorge Luis Borges
Poems: para las seis cuerdas (For Six Strings)	Jorge Luis Borges
Ecstasy and the "Praise of Folly"	M.A. Screech
Laughter at the Foot of the Cross	M.A. Screech
The Dead	James Joyce
Finnegans Wake	James Joyce
Death Devoted Heart, Sex and the Sacred Wagner's Tristan and Isolde	Roger Scruton
Alice Through the Looking-Glass	Lewis Carroll
Inferno	Dante
Decameron	Boccaccio
King James's Bible	
Canterbury Tales	Chaucer
The Magic Mountain	Thomas Mann
Memoirs	General Henri Guisan
Between the Alps and a Hard Place	Angelo M Codevilla
The Retreat from Moscow	Captain Bourgoigne

Art referred to in the text, explicitly or implied

The Simplon Monument	Erwin Harold Bauman
Primavera	Sandro Botticelli
Venus and Mars	Sandro Botticelli

The Temptation of Adam	James Barry
St George and the Dragon	Paolo Ucello
Theseus	Canova
The Earl of Bellamont	Joshua Reynolds

Music referred to in the text, explicitly or implied

Die Lorelei, Poem by H Heine	The woman who lures men to destruction on the rocks of desire — what Nick says Sibylla is. However unwittingly, it's what she does.
Jacinto Chiclana Poem by Borges, Music Piazzolla.	The search for the man behind the rumour and speculations.
Rock & Roll Fantasy Bad Company.	Nick and Joey run away from school and are saved by rock and roll.
Rivers of Babylon Sinead O'Connor	Joey's song of homesickness for the Limpopo. It haunts Nick that they never made it there, the nearest he got was a crash landing on the wrong side of the Drakensberg.
Ave Maria, Bach/Gounod , O'Riordan with Pavarotti,	Sibylla's Christmas with her Great-Aunt. Kathleen, mimicked by Nick
Chanson Épique, from Ravel's Don Quichotte suite, José van Dam:	Nick serenades Monsieur Michel with a prayer for chastity.

Tuxedo Junction, Joe Loss	Nick learns to dance with Mrs Shackleton and her wartime 78's.
Finnegans Wake	Christy Moore: Joey's funeral.
20th Century Boy Girlschool	Nick auctions himself off to Swiss Heini's girls.
Pièce en Forme de Habanera, Ravel	As played by James Ehnes. Mr Mug the instrument dealer teaches Nick to play it when trying to seduce his girlfriends into buy him a violin. Here played on a Guarneri de Jesu which Nick buys for himself when no one else will.
Bullfight From Marocana, Homàge a Picasso.	Nick and Paul in Madrid, where Nick talks revolution with the South Americans.
La Copa de la Vida, Paso doble	It's about winning at all costs.
Milonga de Manuel Flores Poem by Borges.	Nick's imaginary death scenario, a firing squad with four bullets.
Tango in the Night, Fleetwood Mac	Paul and Sibylla dance on the lawn
Russian Hymn, The Orthdox baptism	With Nick's Cossack choir.
Nathalie Gilbert Becaud	Nick commemorates his mother with the

SOURCES

à Olympia.

Cossacks in the brothel.

La Cumparsita
Astor Piazzolla

Gianni danced the conventional version, Nick deconstructs it — the way he chooses Ravel to deconstruct Strauss for the wedding waltz.

Shostakovich: Jazz Suite #2

Mozartists Vienna: Sibylla dreams of dancing with Nick.

Send in the Clowns,
Tiger Lilies Circus Songs

To create a distraction when things are going wrong

Montgolfière,
Gianmaria Testa

An image of Gianni's life passing.

Chanson Romanesque

Ravel's Don Quichotte. Nick at the boar hunt saving Sibylla with his blood.

A Don Nicanor Paredes
Poem by Borges,
music Piazzolla

Portrait of a strong man, killed in a quarrel — what will you do in a heaven without horses, wine, gambling?

Manolete,
Manitas de Plata

Death of the bullfighter, bleeding into the sand. The end.

Confiances,
Gotan Project

The meaning of the final chapter, and my reason for writing.